Twenty-Five
Short Stories by

STEPHEN VINCENT BENÉT

Twenty-five Short Stories by
STEPHEN VINCENT BENÉT

THE SUN DIAL PRESS

Garden City, New York

PUBLISHER'S NOTE

In October 1941 William Rose Benét was asked by the editors of *The Saturday Review of Literature* to write about his brother Stephen Vincent—to write about him not as one poet about another, but as one man writing about his brother.

William Rose Benét wrote the article under the title "My Brother Steve." It appeared in *The Saturday Review of Literature* for November 15, 1941, and proved to be one of the most popular articles ever published in the magazine.

When Stephen Vincent Benét died on March 13, 1943, *The Saturday Review of Literature* decided to publish a special memorial issue. To lead off that issue (March 27, 1943) the editors reprinted William Rose Benét's "My Brother Steve," in this slightly abridged form.

The article appears in this book by special arrangement with the author and *The Saturday Review of Literature*.

MY BROTHER STEVE

*A Poet Who Has Never Cared Much About
An Ivory Tower*

THE life of a writer is a constant fight for his integrity, for his best and most honest expression. The more successful one becomes, the more pitfalls present themselves, the more false lures attract. I have watched my brother become a first-rate writing man, support a wife and three children, and at the same time save his own soul. Nor has he ever shirked a real assignment.

Like many a man who has lived to accomplish a great deal (notably the late Theodore Roosevelt) Steve's early constitution was not of the most robust. Consequently, he did not go in very heavily for games, and began to lead an interior life of the mind. At the same time, his taste in books was catholic enough. He easily descended to "Peck's Bad Boy" and an American humorist with the peculiar typographical pseudonym of "M. Quad." He still contends to this day that the incident where Peck's bad boy fed his father white rubber hose for spaghetti revealed a remarkable power of invention on the part of the author. He read Lang, "E. Nesbit," dozens of Henty books (like thousands of other boys), Dumas—and from Howard Pyle's "Men of Iron" and some of William Morris's poetry and prose, he began to gain an idea of how the past could be presented in terms of realistic detail.

At about the age of ten he was sent to the Hitchcock

Military Academy in California, where one boy he remembers was the son of the famous early French flier, Moisant. Neither boy, I think, cared for that school. Like so many writers in youth, Steve was bullied a good deal, schoolboy misery preserved for us in such poems from his second book, "Young Adventure," as "Going Back to School" and the sympathetic poem about Shelley at Eton. Not that my brother was a self-pitier. He took what was coming to him from the Nazi-minded of that day, and licked his wounds in secret. He came to know that life was not exactly that of a knight in the days of chivalry, and began to develop the protective integument we all have to assume.

By the time I was established in New York as a publisher's reader, Steve was down in Augusta, Georgia, with my Father and Mother. To the latter he owed much through his early years not only for devoted care but for lively understanding. Just prior to the change of base, at the age of thirteen, he had won a cash prize from the *Saint Nicholas League* with a poem, "The Regret of Dives." It was apparent from this poem that he did not, however, desire to become rich. He has since told us that he was then under the impression that *Dives* rhymed with *hives,* though fortunately the name occurred only in the poem's title. He got three dollars for it and spent it on the train coming East from California. In another poem of the period he stigmatized "The Proud Man," imagining himself sitting in a tower aloof from the world, till at last a glance from a window showed him how all mankind had passed him by and gone beyond him. The execution of these verses leaves something to be desired, but the point-of-view remained characteristic. My brother has never cared much about an ivory tower.

A rare issue of a book-collector's quarterly of eight years ago contains an essay of Steve's called "The Sixth Man," in which he describes our father's influence upon his formative years, the big house in California, and how he came to realize early in life that poetry "was not a dead thing or an alien thing or a dry game of words. I knew there were rules and that you could break the rules but that you must never break them unintentionally. I knew it was always written by the living, even though the date-line said that the man was dead."

Steve entered Yale. The first World War was just coming over the horizon. In his sophomore year my brother was taken on the *Lit*, of which he later became Chairman. Those happened to be great years for writing among under-graduates in the Eastern universities. Yale had Archibald Mac-Leish, Thornton Wilder, Philip Barry. Harvard could boast Dos Passos, Cummings, and T. S. Eliot. At Princeton were F. Scott Fitzgerald, Edmund Wilson, and John Peale Bishop. It was such a renaissance as has not shone again.

In his junior year Steve wrote the Yale University Prize Poem, "The Drug Shop, or, Endymion in Edmonstoun," a poem about Keats; and in the same year, after enlisting and then being rejected from the Army because of defective eyesight, he entered the State Department as a cipher-clerk, a profession also then adorned by Mr. James Thurber, afterward author of "The Seal in the Bedroom." Later on Steve became a clerk in the Office of the Counselor. At that time he roomed in Washington with John Franklin Carter (later well-known under a pseudonym as a writer on political and international subjects), Thornton Wilder, and Bill Taylor. After the war he returned to college for his B.A.; and his second book of poems, "Young Adventure," was published by the Yale University Press.

Subsequent to graduation, Steve worked the next summer in the office of Charles W. Hoyt, Planned Advertising, the only business office in which, to my knowledge, he has ever labored. He went back to the Yale Graduate School to take his M.A. in one year, a possible thing at that time. He presented, in lieu of a thesis, his third book of poems, "Heavens and Earth," and Ex-Governor Wilbur Cross, then head of the Graduate School, accepted the substitution. In that young and enthusiastic volume you will find in the section, "The Tall Town," a poem of the war called "Colloquy of the Statues," and poems about lunch-time on Broadway, the strike-pickets on lower Fifth Avenue, morning on 32nd Street, and the red and white flashes by night of the Metropolitan Tower, reflections of my brother's thoughts while pursuing for a brief moment the almighty dollar of national advertising!

By this time Steve had definitely decided to throw in his lot with literature. He spent the summer after leaving Yale in writing his first novel, "The Beginning of Wisdom," and went over to Paris with John Carter, to study, presumably, at the Sorbonne. In Paris he got some reading done, and some drinking, and incidentally met the delightful and talented girl he was soon to marry. She was working for the Paris edition of the Chicago *Tribune* and for the London *Daily Mail*. When they returned to the United States separately, to consult their respective parents and prepare for marriage, Steve turned to and, under high pressure, wrote his second novel, "Young People's Pride," which Carl Brandt serialized for him with Henry Blackman Sell of

Harper's Bazaar. The book is dedicated to Rosemary Carr with a special delightful poem, and on the first page occurs the name of one of the characters, Johnny Chipman—part of the name of John Chipman Farrar, who is today head of the publishing house of Farrar & Rinehart and Steve's own publisher.

The serial money enabled my brother and his wife, after their wedding in Chicago, to return to Paris and begin life together in that city of cities that had early won their hearts.

Out at Neuilly, Steve dug in, toted masses of books home from a Paris library, and went to work recreating the American Civil War. Those long armchair discussions with his father, in California and Georgia, must have recurred to him vividly! His utter surprise when the finished book became a best-seller is a story that has often been told. When asked by a ship-news reporter what it felt like, he characteristically remarked that to him it was as though he had given birth to a grand piano. Prior to this, his longest flight into history had been a novel concerning the Minorcan revolt at New Smyrna, Florida, called "Spanish Bayonet." Then our father had been alive. This time the only shadow on Steve's success was the fact that our father was gone, though he had lived to read portions of the manuscript in its early stages.

The success of this book enabled him to proceed with his writing more at his own pace. It also brought him the Pulitzer Prize. His short stories grew better and better. Today one of the most famous is being interpreted on the screen by Walter Huston, Edward Arnold, and others. But at first he was loath to collect them. He brought out, instead, a collection of ballads and poems, work of the past fifteen years.

Here were, among other excellent things, his earlier *Nation* Prize poem, "King David," the famous "Mountain Whip-poorwill," that fine sonnet sequence called "The Golden Corpse," and also a strangely moving earlier poem of untried youth, which he had attempted to revise. But it was now 1930 and the poem had first been written in 1917. So the new last verse reads:

After the thirteenth year, the water runs as before,
The gemmed wave in the water, the starlight on the gem,
All but the crew who sailed there, and they return no more,
But the words are as they were written. I cannot alter them.

That too I find characteristic of Steve; for one of his virtues is loyalty—not blind, not sentimental, but considered, wise, and final. He has something in his character like a rampart. It cannot be moved. Five or six years later, in "Burning City," which contains his great poem against dictators, he gives us several fiery glimpses of what it is to be a real poet.

He had written his new novel, "James Shore's Daughter," and now at last he launched selected "Stories of Several Worlds" in "Thirteen o'Clock." Among them stands "The Devil and Daniel Webster" (now appearing on the screen), "The King of the Cats," and "Daniel Webster and the Sea Serpent." Already his wife and he had collaborated on a gay book in rhyme concerning historic Americans.

By now I have had to regard my younger brother as by way of becoming an American institution! "Stephen Benét Wins O. Henry Story Prize"—"Roosevelt Medal Awarded Stephen Benét"—"Re-elected Vice President of National Institute"—"Member of the American Academy"—and so on *ad infinitum!* One source of pale envy on my part, incidentally, has been the way Steve has always collected prizes. Every time they put one up, they decide to give it to him! He was always lucky with slot-machines, too, I remember. Frank Morley once organized the "Brothers Club," because his brother Christopher was getting altogether too famous. I am a charter member of that organization—just because of Steve!

There are three children now, an older daughter who is, indeed, no longer a child, but a young lady; a son at Exeter; a younger daughter of highly original gifts. There is Rosemary, Steve's wife, who was born to understand just why he has wished to write exactly as he has written. She lends his household infinite charm, collaborates with him on the portraits of other writers that they do for Irita Van Doren's *Books,* translates Colette from the French, and judges children's books with rare ability. And now there is the Whistler House in the old whaling port of Stonington, Connecticut, where Steve and Rosemary hope to spend years that are sure to be anything but "declining"! In town, there is the large old-fashioned house in the East Sixties, with a more secluded air-conditioned study now, on an upper floor, where work upon a pioneer epic, among other projects, goes steadily forward.

If one has been at one time pretty hard hit by arthritis, one does not stand quite as straight as one has in the past, even though one's spirit may be like a lance. But one does not lose, for all that, the persistent twinkle, the drawlingly American sense of humor, the keen appraisal of the follies and crimes of the times. There is a southern tinge to the hospitality too—a courtesy and kindness at once apparent, a consideration that caused a young in-law of mine once to remark, "Why good Lord, he was asking me *my* opinion!"

Steve has developed in a manner I can thoroughly admire. Perhaps it is true, as he avers, that once I was in a position to read to him most of Bryant's translation of the Iliad, or to write a foreword and draw a cover for an early unpublished work then known as "Poems and Battle Songs." I can, indeed, remember the time when I actually used to tell him stories. Today, how utterly preposterous that seems!

Steve has not been spared his full share of the acerbity of contemporary criticism. But he can usually tell exactly what is eating the critics and why. He drawls, "Oh we-ll—!" He does not take himself too seriously. He has enjoyed his work, and the rewards thereof. He could calculate to a nicety just when he knew he was hitting the ball, and when he wasn't. Lately, it has seemed to one admiring relative, he has hit it pretty consistently right upon the nose. "Wait till you come to forty year!" warned Thackeray. But today we know that that is just when life begins. Steve is three years past, and but only coming into his own. What matters is what he himself has written in "Thanks":

> The metal heats, the flesh grows numb again
> And I can still go muttering down the street
> Not seeing the interminable world
> Nor the ape-faces, only the live coal

—which is, after all, the writer's one permanent reward. That and the skill that was fought for and hard-won, that burns in the hand now, and can reveal the vision.

WILLIAM ROSE BENÉT.

THIRTEEN O'CLOCK

Stories of Several Worlds

CONTENTS

I

IV

I

BY THE WATERS OF BABYLON

THE north and the west and the south are good hunting ground, but it is forbidden to go east. It is forbidden to go to any of the Dead Places except to search for metal and then he who touches the metal must be a priest or the son of a priest. Afterwards, both the man and the metal must be purified. These are the rules and the laws; they are well made. It is forbidden to cross the great river and look upon the place that was the Place of the Gods—this is most strictly forbidden. We do not even say its name though we know its name. It is there that spirits live, and demons—it is there that there are the ashes of the Great Burning. These things are forbidden—they have been forbidden since the beginning of time.

My father is a priest; I am the son of a priest. I have been in the Dead Places near us, with my father—at first, I was afraid. When my father went into the house to search for the metal, I stood by the door and my heart felt small and weak. It was a dead man's house, a spirit house. It did not have the smell of man, though there were old bones in a corner. But it is not fitting that a priest's son should show fear. I looked at the bones in the shadow and kept my voice still.

Then my father came out with the metal—a good, strong piece. He looked at me with both eyes but I had not run away. He gave me the metal to hold—I took it and did not die. So he knew that I was truly his son and would be a priest in my time. That was when I was very young—nevertheless, my brothers would not have done it, though they are good hunters. After that, they gave me the good piece of meat and the warm corner by the fire. My father watched over me—he was glad that I should be a priest. But when I boasted or wept without a reason, he punished me more strictly than my brothers. That was right.

After a time, I myself was allowed to go into the dead houses and search for metal. So I learned the ways of those houses—and if I saw bones, I was no longer afraid. The bones are light and old—sometimes they will fall into dust if you touch them. But that is a great sin.

I was taught the chants and the spells—I was taught how to stop the running of blood from a wound and many secrets. A priest must know many secrets—that was what my father said. If the hunters think we do all things by chants and spells, they may believe so—it does not hurt them. I was taught how to read in the old books and how to make the old writings—that was hard and took a long time. My knowledge made me happy—it was like a fire in my heart. Most of all, I liked to hear of the Old Days and the stories of the gods. I asked myself many questions that I could not answer, but it was good to ask them. At night, I would lie awake and listen to the wind—it seemed to me that it was the voice of the gods as they flew through the air.

We are not ignorant like the Forest People—our women spin wool on the wheel, our priests wear a white robe. We do not eat grubs from the tree, we have not forgotten the old writings, although they are hard to understand. Nevertheless, my knowledge and my lack of knowledge burned in me—I wished to know more. When I was a man at last, I came to my father and said, "It is time for me to go on my journey. Give me your leave."

He looked at me for a long time, stroking his beard, then he said at last, "Yes. It is time." That night, in the house of the priesthood, I asked for and received purification. My body hurt but my spirit was a cool stone. It was my father himself who questioned me about my dreams.

He bade me look into the smoke of the fire and see —I saw and told what I saw. It was what I have always seen—a river, and, beyond it, a great Dead Place and in it the gods walking. I have always thought about that. His eyes were stern when I told him—he was no longer my father but a priest. He said, "This is a strong dream."

"It is mine," I said, while the smoke waved and my head felt light. They were singing the Star song in the outer chamber and it was like the buzzing of bees in my head.

He asked me how the gods were dressed and I told him how they were dressed. We know how they were dressed from the book, but I saw them as if they were before me. When I had finished, he threw the sticks three times and studied them as they fell.

"This is a very strong dream," he said. "It may eat you up."

"I am not afraid," I said and looked at him with

both eyes. My voice sounded thin in my ears but that was because of the smoke.

He touched me on the breast and the forehead. He gave me the bow and the three arrows.

"Take them," he said. "It is forbidden to travel east. It is forbidden to cross the river. It is forbidden to go to the Place of the Gods. All these things are forbidden."

"All these things are forbidden," I said, but it was my voice that spoke and not my spirit. He looked at me again.

"My son," he said. "Once I had young dreams. If your dreams do not eat you up, you may be a great priest. If they eat you, you are still my son. Now go on your journey."

I went fasting, as is the law. My body hurt but not my heart. When the dawn came, I was out of sight of the village. I prayed and purified myself, waiting for a sign. The sign was an eagle. It flew east.

Sometimes signs are sent by bad spirits. I waited again on the flat rock, fasting, taking no food. I was very still—I could feel the sky above me and the earth beneath. I waited till the sun was beginning to sink. Then three deer passed in the valley, going east—they did not wind me or see me. There was a white fawn with them—a very great sign.

I followed them, at a distance, waiting for what would happen. My heart was troubled about going east, yet I knew that I must go. My head hummed with my fasting—I did not even see the panther spring upon the white fawn. But, before I knew it, the bow was in my hand. I shouted and the panther lifted his head from the fawn. It is not easy to kill a panther with one arrow but the arrow went through his eye and into his brain. He died as he tried to spring—he rolled over, tearing at the ground. Then I knew I was meant to go east—I knew that was my journey. When the night came, I made my fire and roasted meat.

It is eight suns journey to the east and a man passes by many Dead Places. The Forest People are afraid of them but I am not. Once I made my fire on the edge of a Dead Place at night and, next morning, in the dead house, I found a good knife, little rusted. That was small to what came afterward but it made my heart feel big. Always when I looked for game, it was in front of my arrow, and twice I passed hunting parties of the Forest People without their knowing. So I knew my magic was strong and my journey clean, in spite of the law.

Toward the setting of the eighth sun, I came to the banks of the great river. It was half-a-day's journey after I had left the god-road—we do not use the god-roads now for they are falling apart into great blocks of stone, and the forest is safer going. A long way off, I had seen the water through trees but the trees were thick. At last, I came out upon an open place at the top of a cliff. There was the great river below, like a giant in the sun. It is very long, very wide. It could eat all the streams we know and still be thirsty. Its name is Ou-dis-sun, the Sacred, the Long. No man of my tribe had seen it, not even my father, the priest. It was magic and I prayed.

Then I raised my eyes and looked south. It was there, the Place of the Gods.

How can I tell what it was like—you do not know. It was there, in the red light, and they were too big to be houses. It was there with the red light upon it, mighty and ruined. I knew that in another moment the gods would see me. I covered my eyes with my hands and crept back into the forest.

Surely, that was enough to do, and live. Surely it was enough to spend the night upon the cliff. The Forest People themselves do not come near. Yet, all through the night, I knew that I should have to cross the river and walk in the places of the gods, although the gods ate me up. My magic did not help me at all and yet there was a fire in my bowels, a fire in my mind. When the sun rose, I thought, "My journey has been clean. Now I will go home from my journey." But, even as I thought so, I knew I could not. If I went to the place of the gods, I would surely die, but, if I did not go, I could never be at peace with my spirit again. It is better to lose one's life than one's spirit, if one is a priest and the son of a priest.

Nevertheless, as I made the raft, the tears ran out of my eyes. The Forest People could have killed me without fight, if they had come upon me then, but they did not come. When the raft was made, I said the sayings for the dead and painted myself for death. My heart was cold as a frog and my knees like water, but the burning in my mind would not let me have peace. As I pushed the raft from the shore, I began my death song—I had the right. It was a fine song.

"I am John, son of John," I sang. "My people are the Hill
People. They are the men.

I go into the Dead Places but I am not slain.

I take the metal from the Dead Places but I am not
blasted.

I travel upon the god-roads and am not afraid. E-yah! I
have killed the panther, I have killed the fawn!

E-yah! I have come to the great river. No man has come
there before.

It is forbidden to go east, but I have gone, forbidden to go
on the great river, but I am there.

Open your hearts, you spirits, and hear my song.

Now I go to the place of the gods, I shall not return.

My body is painted for death and my limbs weak, but my
heart is big as I go to the place of the gods!"

All the same, when I came to the Place of the Gods,
I was afraid, afraid. The current of the great river is
very strong—it gripped my raft with its hands. That
was magic, for the river itself is wide and calm. I could
feel evil spirits about me, in the bright morning; I
could feel their breath on my neck as I was swept down
the stream. Never have I been so much alone—I tried
to think of my knowledge, but it was a squirrel's heap
of winter nuts. There was no strength in my knowledge
any more and I felt small and naked as a new-hatched
bird—alone upon the great river, the servant of the
gods.

Yet, after a while, my eyes were opened and I saw.
I saw both banks of the river—I saw that once there
had been god-roads across it, though now they were
broken and fallen like broken vines. Very great they
were, and wonderful and broken—broken in the time

of the Great Burning when the fire fell out of the sky.
And always the current took me nearer to the Place of
the Gods, and the huge ruins rose before my eyes.

I do not know the customs of rivers—we are the
People of the Hills. I tried to guide my raft with the
pole but it spun around. I thought the river meant
to take me past the Place of the Gods and out into
the Bitter Water of the legends. I grew angry then—
my heart felt strong. I said aloud, "I am a priest and
the son of a priest!" The gods heard me—they showed
me how to paddle with the pole on one side of the raft.
The current changed itself—I drew near to the Place
of the Gods.

When I was very near, my raft struck and turned
over. I can swim in our lakes—I swam to the shore.
There was a great spike of rusted metal sticking out
into the river—I hauled myself up upon it and sat
there, panting. I had saved my bow and two arrows and
the knife I found in the Dead Place but that was all.
My raft went whirling downstream toward the Bitter
Water. I looked after it, and thought if it had trod me
under, at least I would be safely dead. Nevertheless,
when I had dried my bow-string and re-strung it, I
walked forward to the Place of the Gods.

It felt like ground underfoot; it did not burn me.
It is not true what some of the tales say, that the
ground there burns forever, for I have been there.
Here and there were the marks and stains of the Great
Burning, on the ruins, that is true. But they were old
marks and old stains. It is not true either, what some
of our priests say, that it is an island covered with fogs
and enchantments. It is not. It is a great Dead Place—

greater than any Dead Place we know. Everywhere in it there are god-roads, though most are cracked and broken. Everywhere there are the ruins of the high towers of the gods.

How shall I tell what I saw? I went carefully, my strung bow in my hand, my skin ready for danger. There should have been the wailings of spirits and the shrieks of demons, but there were not. It was very silent and sunny where I had landed—the wind and the rain and the birds that drop seeds had done their work—the grass grew in the cracks of the broken stone. It is a fair island—no wonder the gods built there. If I had come there, a god, I also would have built.

How shall I tell what I saw? The towers are not all broken—here and there one still stands, like a great tree in a forest, and the birds nest high. But the towers themselves look blind, for the gods are gone. I saw a fish-hawk, catching fish in the river. I saw a little dance of white butterflies over a great heap of broken stones and columns. I went there and looked about me—there was a carved stone with cut-letters, broken in half. I can read letters but I could not understand these. They said UBTREAS. There was also the shattered image of a man or a god. It had been made of white stone and he wore his hair tied back like a woman's. His name was ASHING, as I read on the cracked half of a stone. I thought it wise to pray to ASHING, though I do not know that god.

How shall I tell what I saw? There was no smell of man left, on stone or metal. Nor were there many trees in that wilderness of stone. There are many pigeons, nesting and dropping in the towers—the gods must

have loved them, or, perhaps, they used them for sacri-
fices. There are wild cats that roam the god-roads, green-
eyed, unafraid of man. At night they wail like demons
but they are not demons. The wild dogs are more dangerous, for they hunt in a pack, but them I did not
meet till later. Everywhere there are the carved stones,
carved with magical numbers or words.

I went North—I did not try to hide myself. When a
god or a demon saw me, then I would die, but meanwhile I was no longer afraid. My hunger for knowledge
burned in me—there was so much that I could not understand. After awhile, I knew that my belly was
hungry. I could have hunted for my meat, but I did not
hunt. It is known that the gods did not hunt as we do
—they got their food from enchanted boxes and jars.
Sometimes these are still found in the Dead Places—
once, when I was a child and foolish, I opened such a
jar and tasted it and found the food sweet. But my
father found out and punished me for it strictly, for,
often, that food is death. Now, though, I had long gone
past what was forbidden, and I entered the likeliest
towers, looking for the food of the gods.

I found it at last in the ruins of a great temple in
the mid-city. A mighty temple it must have been, for
the roof was painted like the sky at night with its stars
—that much I could see, though the colors were faint
and dim. It went down into great caves and tunnels—
perhaps they kept their slaves there. But when I started
to climb down, I heard the squeaking of rats, so I did
not go—rats are unclean, and there must have been
many tribes of them, from the squeaking. But near
there, I found food, in the heart of a ruin, behind a

door that still opened. I ate only the fruits from the jars
—they had a very sweet taste. There was drink, too, in
bottles of glass—the drink of the gods was strong and
made my head swim. After I had eaten and drunk, I
slept on the top of a stone, my bow at my side.

When I woke, the sun was low. Looking down from
where I lay, I saw a dog sitting on his haunches. His
tongue was hanging out of his mouth; he looked as if
he were laughing. He was a big dog, with a grey-brown
coat, as big as a wolf. I sprang up and shouted at him
but he did not move—he just sat there as if he were
laughing. I did not like that. When I reached for a
stone to throw, he moved swiftly out of the way of the
stone. He was not afraid of me; he looked at me as if I
were meat. No doubt I could have killed him with an
arrow, but I did not know if there were others. Moreover, night was falling.

I looked about me—not far away there was a great,
broken god-road, leading North. The towers were high
enough, but not so high, and while many of the dead-
houses were wrecked, there were some that stood. I
went toward this god-road, keeping to the heights of
the ruins, while the dog followed. When I had reached
the god-road, I saw that there were others behind him.
If I had slept later, they would have come upon me
asleep and torn out my throat. As it was, they were sure
enough of me; they did not hurry. When I went into
the dead-house, they kept watch at the entrance—doubtless they thought they would have a fine hunt. But
a dog cannot open a door and I knew, from the books,
that the gods did not like to live on the ground but
on high.

I had just found a door I could open when the dogs decided to rush. Ha! They were surprised when I shut the door in their faces—it was a good door, of strong metal. I could hear their foolish baying beyond it but I did not stop to answer them. I was in darkness—I found stairs and climbed. There were many stairs, turning around till my head was dizzy. At the top was another door—I found the knob and opened it. I was in a long small chamber—on one side of it was a bronze door that could not be opened, for it had no handle. Perhaps there was a magic word to open it but I did not have the word. I turned to the door in the opposite side of the wall. The lock of it was broken and I opened it and went in.

Within, there was a place of great riches. The god who lived there must have been a powerful god. The first room was a small ante-room—I waited there for some time, telling the spirits of the place that I came in peace and not as a robber. When it seemed to me that they had had time to hear me, I went on. Ah, what riches! Few, even, of the windows had been broken —it was all as it had been. The great windows that looked over the city had not been broken at all though they were dusty and streaked with many years. There were coverings on the floors, the colors not greatly faded, and the chairs were soft and deep. There were pictures upon the walls, very strange, very wonderful— I remember one of a bunch of flowers in a jar—if you came close to it, you could see nothing but bits of color. but if you stood away from it, the flowers might have been picked yesterday. It made my heart feel strange to look at this picture—and to look at the figure of a bird, in some hard clay, on a table and see it so like our birds. Everywhere there were books and writings, many in tongues that I could not read. The god who lived there must have been a wise god and full of knowledge. I felt I had right there, as I sought knowledge also.

Nevertheless, it was strange. There was a washing-place but no water—perhaps the gods washed in air. There was a cooking-place but no wood, and though there was a machine to cook food, there was no place to put fire in it. Nor were there candles or lamps—there were things that looked like lamps but they had neither oil nor wick. All these things were magic, but I touched them and lived—the magic had gone out of them. Let me tell one thing to show. In the washing-place, a thing said "Hot" but it was not hot to the touch—another thing said "Cold" but it was not cold. This must have been a strong magic but the magic was gone. I do not understand—they had ways—I wish that I knew.

It was close and dry and dusty in their house of the gods. I have said the magic was gone but that is not true—it had gone from the magic things but it had not gone from the place. I felt the spirits about me, weighing upon me. Nor had I ever slept in a Dead Place before—and yet, tonight, I must sleep there. When I thought of it, my tongue felt dry in my throat, in spite of my wish for knowledge. Almost I would have gone down again and faced the dogs, but I did not.

I had not gone through all the rooms when the darkness fell. When it fell, I went back to the big room looking over the city and made fire. There was a place to make fire and a box with wood in it, though I do not think they cooked there. I wrapped myself in a floor-covering and slept in front of the fire—I was very tired.

Now I tell what is very strong magic. I woke in the midst of the night. When I woke, the fire had gone out and I was cold. It seemed to me that all around me there were whisperings and voices. I closed my eyes to shut them out. Some will say that I slept again, but I do not think that I slept. I could feel the spirits drawing my spirit out of my body as a fish is drawn on a line.

Why should I lie about it? I am a priest and the son of a priest. If there are spirits, as they say, in the small Dead Places near us, what spirits must there not be in that great Place of the Gods? And would not they wish to speak? After such long years? I know that I felt myself drawn as a fish is drawn on a line. I had stepped out of my body—I could see my body asleep in front of the cold fire, but it was not I. I was drawn to look out upon the city of the gods.

It should have been dark, for it was night, but it was not dark. Everywhere there were lights—lines of light —circles and blurs of light—ten thousand torches would not have been the same. The sky itself was alight —you could barely see the stars for the glow in the sky. I thought to myself "This is strong magic" and trembled. There was a roaring in my ears like the rushing of rivers. Then my eyes grew used to the light and my ears to the sound. I knew that I was seeing the city as it had been when the gods were alive.

That was a sight indeed—yes, that was a sight: I could not have seen it in the body—my body would have died. Everywhere went the gods, on foot and in chariots—there were gods beyond number and counting and their chariots blocked the streets. They had turned night to day for their pleasure—they did not sleep with the sun. The noise of their coming and going was the noise of many waters. It was magic what they could do—it was magic what they did.

I looked out of another window—the great vines of their bridges were mended and the god-roads went East and West. Restless, restless, were the gods and always in motion! They burrowed tunnels under rivers—they flew in the air. With unbelievable tools they did giant works—no part of the earth was safe from them, for, if they wished for a thing, they summoned it from the other side of the world. And always, as they labored and rested, as they feasted and made love, there was a drum in their ears—the pulse of the giant city, beating and beating like a man's heart.

Were they happy? What is happiness to the gods? They were great, they were mighty, they were wonderful and terrible. As I looked upon them and their magic, I felt like a child—but a little more, it seemed to me, and they would pull down the moon from the sky. I saw them with wisdom beyond wisdom and knowledge beyond knowledge. And yet not all they did was well done—even I could see that—and yet their wisdom could not but grow until all was peace.

Then I saw their fate come upon them and that was terrible past speech. It came upon them as they walked the streets of their city. I have been in the fights with the Forest People—I have seen men die. But this was not like that. When gods war with gods, they use weapons we do not know. It was fire falling out of the

sky and a mist that poisoned. It was the time of the
Great Burning and the Destruction. They ran about
like ants in the streets of their city—poor gods, poor
gods! Then the towers began to fall. A few escaped—
yes, a few. The legends tell it. But, even after the city
had become a Dead Place, for many years the poison
was still in the ground. I saw it happen, I saw the last
of them die. It was darkness over the broken city and
I wept.

All this, I saw. I saw it as I have told it, though not
in the body. When I woke in the morning, I was
hungry, but I did not think first of my hunger for my
heart was perplexed and confused. I knew the reason for
the Dead Places but I did not see why it had happened.
It seemed to me it should not have happened, with all
the magic they had. I went through the house looking
for an answer. There was so much in the house I could
not understand—and yet I am a priest and the son of
a priest. It was like being on one side of the great river,
at night, with no light to show the way.

Then I saw the dead god. He was sitting in his chair,
by the window, in a room I had not entered before
and, for the first moment, I thought that he was alive.
Then I saw the skin on the back of his hand—it was
like dry leather. The room was shut, hot and dry—no
doubt that had kept him as he was. At first I was afraid
to approach him—then the fear left me. He was sitting
looking out over the city—he was dressed in the clothes
of the gods. His age was neither young nor old—I could
not tell his age. But there was wisdom in his face and
great sadness. You could see that he would have not
run away. He had sat at his window, watching his city

die—then he himself had died. But it is better to lose one's life than one's spirit—and you could see from the face that his spirit had not been lost. I knew, that, if I touched him, he would fall into dust—and yet, there was something unconquered in the face.

That is all of my story, for then I knew he was a man —I knew then that they had been men, neither gods nor demons. It is a great knowledge, hard to tell and believe. They were men—they went a dark road, but they were men. I had no fear after that—I had no fear going home, though twice I fought off the dogs and once I was hunted for two days by the Forest People. When I saw my father again, I prayed and was purified. He touched my lips and my breast, he said, "You went away a boy. You come back a man and a priest." I said, "Father, they were men! I have been in the Place of the Gods and seen it! Now slay me, if it is the law—but still I know they were men."

He looked at me out of both eyes. He said, "The law is not always the same shape—you have done what you have done. I could not have done it my time, but you come after me. Tell!"

I told and he listened. After that, I wished to tell all the people but he showed me otherwise. He said, "Truth is a hard deer to hunt. If you eat too much truth at once, you may die of the truth. It was not idly that our fathers forbade the Dead Places." He was right —it is better the truth should come little by little. I have learned that, being a priest. Perhaps, in the old days, they ate knowledge too fast.

Nevertheless, we make a beginning. It is not for the metal alone we go to the Dead Places now—there are the books and the writings. They are hard to learn. And the magic tools are broken—but we can look at them and wonder. At least, we make a beginning. And, when I am chief priest we shall go beyond the great river. We shall go to the Place of the Gods—the place new-york—not one man but a company. We shall look for the images of the gods and find the god ASHING and the others—the gods Licoln and Biltmore and Moses. But they were men who built the city, not gods or demons. They were men. I remember the dead man's face. They were men who were here before us. We must build again.

II

THE BLOOD OF THE MARTYRS

THE man who expected to be shot lay with his eyes open, staring at the upper left-hand corner of his cell. He was fairly well over his last beating, and they might come for him any time now. There was a yellow stain in the cell corner near the ceiling; he had liked it at first, then disliked it; now he was coming back to liking it again.

He could see it more clearly with his glasses on, but he only put on his glasses for special occasions now— the first thing in the morning, and when they brought the food in, and for interviews with the General. The lenses of the glasses had been cracked in a beating some months before, and it strained his eyes to wear them too long. Fortunately, in his present life he had very few occasions demanding clear vision. But, nevertheless, the accident to his glasses worried him, as it worries all near-sighted people. You put your glasses on the first thing in the morning and the world leaps into proportion; if it does not do so, something is wrong with the world.

The man did not believe greatly in symbols, but his chief nightmare, nowadays, was an endless one in which, suddenly and without warning, a large piece of glass would drop out of one of the lenses and he would grope around the cell, trying to find it. He would grope very carefully and gingerly, for hours of darkness, but the end was always the same—the small, unmistakable crunch of irreplaceable glass beneath his heel or his knee. Then he would wake up sweating, with his hands cold. This dream alternated with the one of being shot, but he found no great benefit in the change.

As he lay there, you could see that he had an intellectual head—the head of a thinker or a scholar, old and bald, with the big, domed brow. It was, as a matter of fact, a well-known head; it had often appeared in the columns of newspapers and journals, sometimes when the surrounding text was in a language Professor Malzius could not read. The body, though stooped and worn, was still a strong peasant body and capable of surviving a good deal of ill-treatment, as his captors had found out. He had fewer teeth than when he came to prison, and both the ribs and the knee had been badly set, but these were minor matters. It also occurred to him that his blood count was probably poor. However, if he could ever get out and to a first-class hospital, he was probably good for at least ten years more of work. But, of course, he would not get out. They would shoot him before that, and it would be over.

Sometimes he wished passionately that it would be over—tonight—this moment; at other times he was shaken by the mere blind fear of death. The latter he tried to treat as he would have treated an attack of malaria, knowing that it was an attack, but not always with success. He should have been able to face it better than most—he was Gregor Malzius, the scientist—but that did not always help. The fear of death persisted, even when one had noted and classified it as a purely physical reaction. When he was out of here, he would be able to write a very instructive little paper on the fear of death. He could even do it here, if he had writing materials, but there was no use asking for those. Once they had been given him and he had spent two days quite happily. But they had torn up the work and spat upon it in front of his face. It was a childish thing to do, but it discouraged a man from working.

It seemed odd that he had never seen anybody shot, but he never had. During the war, his reputation and his bad eyesight had exempted him from active service. He had been bombed a couple of times when his reserve battalion was guarding the railway bridge, but that was quite different. You were not tied to a stake, and the airplanes were not trying to kill you as an individual. He knew the place where it was done here, of course. But prisoners did not see the executions, they merely heard, if the wind was from the right quarter.

He had tried again and again to visualize how it would be, but it always kept mixing with an old steel engraving he had seen in boyhood—the execution of William Walker, the American filibuster, in Honduras. William Walker was a small man with a white semi-Napoleonic face. He was standing, very correctly dressed, in front of an open grave, and before him a ragged line of picturesque natives were raising their muskets. When he was shot he would instantly and tidily fall into the grave, like a man dropping through a trap door; as a boy, the extreme neatness of the arrangement had greatly impressed Gregor Malzius. Behind the wall there were palm trees, and, somewhere off to the right, blue and warm, the Caribbean Sea. It would not be like that at all, for his own execution; and yet, whenever he thought of it, he thought of it as being like that.

Well, it was his own fault. He could have accepted the new regime; some respectable people had done that. He could have fled the country; many honorable people had. A scientist should be concerned with the eternal, not with transient political phenomena; and a scientist should be able to live anywhere. But thirty years at the university were thirty years, and, after all, he was Malzius, one of the first biochemists in the world. To the last, he had not believed that they would touch him. Well, he had been wrong about that.

The truth, of course, was the truth. One taught it or one did not teach it. If one did not teach it, it hardly mattered what one did. But he had no quarrel with any established government; he was willing to run up a flag every Tuesday, as long as they let him alone. Most people were fools, and one government was as good as another for them—it had taken them twenty years to accept his theory of cell mutation. Now, if he'd been like his friend Bonnard—a fellow who signed protests, attended meetings for the cause of world peace, and generally played the fool in public—they'd have had some reason to complain. An excellent man in his field, Bonnard—none better—but. outside of it, how deplorably like an actor, with his short gray beard, his pink cheeks and his impulsive enthusiasms! Any government could put a fellow like Bonnard in prison—though it would be an injury to science and, therefore, wrong. For that matter, he thought grimly, Bonnard would enjoy being a martyr. He'd walk gracefully to the execution post

with a begged cigarette in his mouth, and some theatrical last quip. But Bonnard was safe in his own land
—doubtless writing heated and generous articles on
The Case of Professor Malzius—and he, Malzius, was
the man who was going to be shot. He would like a
cigarette, too, on his way to execution; he had not
smoked in five months. But he certainly didn't intend
to ask for one, and they wouldn't think of offering him
any. That was the difference between him and Bonnard.

His mind went back with longing to the stuffy
laboratory and stuffier lecture hall at the university; his
feet yearned for the worn steps he had climbed ten
thousand times, and his eyes for the long steady look
through the truthful lens into worlds too tiny for the
unaided eye. They had called him "The Bear" and
"Old Prickly," but they had fought to work under him,
the best of the young men. They said he would explain
the Last Judgment in terms of cellular phenomena, but
they had crowded to his lectures. It was Williams, the
Englishman, who had made up the legend that he carried a chocolate éclair and a set of improper post cards
in his battered brief case. Quite untrue, of course—
chocolate always made him ill, and he had never looked
at an improper post card in his life. And Williams
would never know that he knew the legend, too; for
Williams had been killed long ago in the war. For a
moment, Professor Malzius felt blind hate at the
thought of an excellent scientific machine like Williams
being smashed in a war. But blind hate was an improper emotion for a scientist, and he put it aside.

He smiled grimly again; they hadn't been able to
break up his classes—lucky he was The Bear! He'd seen

one colleague hooted from his desk by a band of determined young hoodlums—too bad, but if a man couldn't keep order in his own classroom, he'd better get out. They'd wrecked his own laboratory, but not while he was there.

It was so senseless, so silly. "In God's name," he said reasonably, to no one, "what sort of conspirator do you think I would make? A man of my age and habits! I am interested in cellular phenomena!" And yet they were beating him because he would not tell about the boys. As if he had even paid attention to half the nonsense! There were certain passwords and greetings—a bar of music you whistled, entering a restaurant; the address of a firm that specialized, ostensibly, in vacuum cleaners. But they were not his own property. They belonged to the young men who had trusted The Bear. He did not know what half of them meant, and the one time he had gone to a meeting, he had felt like a fool. For they were fools and childish—playing the childish games of conspiracy that people like Bonnard enjoyed. Could they even make a better world than the present? He doubted it extremely. And yet, he could not betray them; they had come to him, looking over their shoulders, with darkness in their eyes.

A horrible, an appalling thing—to be trusted. He had no wish to be a guide and counselor of young men. He wanted to do his work. Suppose they were poor and ragged and oppressed; he had been a peasant himself. he had eaten black bread. It was by his own efforts that he was Professor Malzius. He did not wish the confidences of boys like Gregopolous and the others—for, after all, what was Gregopolous? An excellent and untiring laboratory assistant—and a laboratory assistant he would remain to the end of his days. He had pattered about the laboratory like a fox terrier, with a fox terrier's quick bright eyes. Like a devoted dog, he had made a god of Professor Malzius. "I don't want your problems, man. I don't want to know what you are doing outside the laboratory." But Gregopolous had brought his problems and his terrible trust none the less, humbly and proudly, like a fox terrier with a bone. After that—well, what was a man to do?

He hoped they would get it over with, and quickly. The world should be like a chemical formula, full of reason and logic. Instead, there were all these young men, and their eyes. They conspired, hopelessly and childishly, for what they called freedom against the new regime. They wore no overcoats in winter and were often hunted and killed. Even if they did not conspire, they had miserable little love affairs and ate the wrong food—yes, even before, at the university, they had been the same. Why the devil would they not accept? Then they could do their work. Of course, a great many of them would not be allowed to accept—they had the wrong ideas or the wrong politics—but then they could run away. If Malzius, at twenty, had had to run from his country, he would still have been a scientist. To talk of a free world was a delusion; men were not free in the world. Those who wished got a space of time to get their work done. That was all. And yet, he had not accepted—he did not know why.

Now he heard the sound of steps along the corridor. His body began to quiver and the places where he had been beaten hurt him. He noted it as an interesting reflex. Sometimes they merely flashed the light in the cell and passed by. On the other hand, it might be death. It was a hard question to decide.

The lock creaked, the door opened. "Get up, Malzius!" said the hard, bright voice of the guard. Gregor Malzius got up, a little stiffly, but quickly.

"Put on your glasses, you old fool!" said the guard, with a laugh. "You are going to the General."

Professor Malzius found the stone floors of the corridor uneven, though he knew them well enough. Once or twice the guard struck him, lightly and without malice, as one strikes an old horse with a whip. The blows were familiar and did not register on Professor Malzius' consciousness; he merely felt proud of not stumbling. He was apt to stumble; once he had hurt his knee.

He noticed, it seemed to him, an unusual tenseness and officiousness about his guard. Once, even, in a brightly lighted corridor the guard moved to strike him, but refrained. However, that, too, happened occasionally, with one guard or another, and Professor Malzius merely noted the fact. It was a small fact, but an important one in the economy in which he lived.

But there could be no doubt that something unusual was going on in the castle. There were more guards than usual, many of them strangers. He tried to think, carefully, as he walked, if it could be one of the new national holidays. It was hard to keep track of them all. The General might be in a good humor. Then they would merely have a cat-and-mouse conversation for half an hour and nothing really bad would happen.

Once, even, there had been a cigar. Professor Malzius, the scientist, licked his lips at the thought.

Now he was being turned over to a squad of other guards, with salutings. This was really unusual; Professor Malzius bit his mouth, inconspicuously. He had the poignant distrust of a monk or an old prisoner at any break in routine. Old prisoners are your true conservatives; they only demand that the order around them remains exactly the same.

It alarmed him as well that the new guards did not laugh at him. New guards almost always laughed when they saw him for the first time. He was used to the laughter and missed it—his throat felt dry. He would have liked, just once, to eat at the university restaurant before he died. It was bad food, ill cooked and starchy, food good enough for poor students and professors, but he would have liked to be there, in the big smoky room that smelt of copper boilers and cabbage, with a small cup of bitter coffee before him and a cheap cigarette. He did not ask for his dog or his notebooks, the old photographs in his bedroom, his incomplete experiments or his freedom. Just to lunch once more at the university restaurant and have people point out The Bear. It seemed a small thing to ask, but of course it was quite impossible.

"Halt!" said a voice, and he halted. There were, for the third time, salutings. Then the door of the General's office opened and he was told to go in.

He stood, just inside the door, in the posture of attention, as he had been taught. The crack in the left lens of his glasses made a crack across the room, and his eyes were paining him already, but he paid no attention to that. There was the familiar figure of the General with his air of a well-fed and extremely healthy tomcat, and there was another man, seated at the General's desk. He could not see the other man very well—the crack made him bulge and waver—but he did not like his being there.

"Well, professor," said the General, in an easy, purring voice.

Malzius's entire body jerked. He had made a fearful, an unpardonable omission. He must remedy it at once. "Long live the state," he shouted in a loud thick voice, and saluted. He knew, bitterly, that his salute was ridiculous and that he looked ridiculous, making it. But perhaps the General would laugh—he had done so before. Then everything would be all right, for it was not quite as easy to beat a man after you had laughed at him.

The General did not laugh. He made a half turn instead, toward the man at the desk. The gesture said, "You see, he is well trained." It was the gesture of a man of the world, accustomed to deal with unruly peasants and animals—the gesture of a man fitted to be General.

The man at the desk paid no attention to the General's gesture. He lifted his head, and Malzius saw him more clearly and with complete unbelief. It was not a man but a picture come alive. Professor Malzius had seen the picture a hundred times; they had made him salute and take off his hat in front of it, when he had had a hat. Indeed, the picture had presided over his beatings. The man himself was a little smaller, but the picture was a good picture. There were many dictators in the world, and this was one type. The face was white, beaky and semi-Napoleonic; the lean, military body sat squarely in its chair. The eyes dominated the face, and the mouth was rigid. I remember also a hypnotist, and a woman Charcot showed me, at his clinic in Paris, thought Professor Malzius. But there is also, obviously, an endocrine unbalance. Then his thoughts stopped.

"Tell the man to come closer," said the man at the desk. "Can he hear me? Is he deaf?"

"No, Your Excellency," said the General, with enormous, purring respect. "But he is a little old, though perfectly healthy. . . . Are you not, Professor Malzius?"

"Yes, I am perfectly healthy. I am very well treated here," said Professor Malzius, in his loud thick voice. They were not going to catch him with traps like that, not even by dressing up somebody as the Dictator. He fixed his eyes on the big old-fashioned inkwell on the General's desk—that, at least, was perfectly sane.

"Come closer," said the man at the desk to Professor Malzius, and the latter advanced till he could almost touch the inkwell with his fingers. Then he stopped with a jerk, hoping he had done right. The movement removed the man at the desk from the crack in his lenses, and Professor Malzius knew suddenly that it was true. This was, indeed, the Dictator, this man with the rigid mouth. He began to talk.

"I have been very well treated here and the General has acted with the greatest consideration," he said. "But I am Professor Gregor Malzius—professor of biochemistry. For thirty years I have lectured at the university; I am a fellow of the Royal Society, a corresponding member of the Academy of Sciences at Berlin, at Rome,

at Boston, at Paris and Stockholm. I have received the
Nottingham Medal, the Lamarck Medal, the Order of
St. John of Portugal and the Nobel Prize. I think my
blood count is low, but I have received a great many
degrees and my experiments on the migratory cells are
not finished. I do not wish to complain of my treatment,
but I must continue my experiments."

He stopped, like a clock that has run down, surprised to hear the sound of his own voice. He noted,
in one part of his mind, that the General had made a
move to silence him, but had himself been silenced
by the Dictator.

"Yes, Professor Malzius," said the man at the desk,
in a harsh, toneless voice. "There has been a regrettable
error." The rigid face stared at Professor Malzius. Professor Malzius stared back. He did not say anything.

"In these days," said the Dictator, his voice rising,
"the nation demands the submission of every citizen.
Encircled by jealous foes, our reborn land yet steps
forward toward her magnificent destiny." The words
continued for some time, the voice rose and fell. Professor Malzius listened respectfully; he had heard the
words many times before and they had ceased to have
meaning to him. He was thinking of certain cells of
the body that rebel against the intricate processes of
Nature and set up their own bellicose state. Doubtless
they, too, have a destiny, he thought, but in medicine
it is called cancer.

"Jealous and spiteful tongues in other countries
have declared that it is our purpose to wipe out learning and science," concluded the Dictator. "That is not
our purpose. After the cleansing, the rebirth. We mean

to move forward to the greatest science in the world—
our own science, based on the enduring principles of
our nationhood." He ceased abruptly, his eyes fell into
their dream. Very like the girl Charcot showed me in
my young days, thought Professor Malzius; there was
first the ebullition, then the calm.

"I was part of the cleansing? You did not mean to
hurt me?" he asked timidly.

"Yes, Professor Malzius," said the General, smiling,
"you were part of the cleansing. Now that is over. His
Excellency has spoken."

"I do not understand," said Professor Malzius, gazing at the fixed face of the man behind the desk.

"It is very simple," said the General. He spoke in a
slow careful voice, as one speaks to a deaf man or a
child. "You are a distinguished man of science—you
have received the Nobel Prize. That was a service to the
state. You became, however, infected by the wrong
political ideas. That was treachery to the state. You
had, therefore, as decreed by His Excellency, to pass
through a certain period for probation and rehabilitation. But that, we believe, is finished."

"You do not wish to know the names of the young
men any more?" said Professor Malzius. "You do not
want the addresses?"

"That is no longer of importance," said the General
patiently. "There is no longer opposition. The leaders
were caught and executed three weeks ago."

"There is no longer opposition," repeated Professor
Malzius.

"At the trial, you were not even involved."

"I was not even involved," said Professor Malzius. "Yes."

"Now," said the General, with a look at the Dictator, "we come to the future. I will be frank—the new state is frank with its citizens."

"It is so," said the Dictator, his eyes still sunk in his dream.

"There has been—let us say—a certain agitation in foreign countries regarding Professor Malzius," said the General, his eyes still fixed on the Dictator. "That means nothing, of course. Nevertheless, your acquaintance, Professor Bonnard, and others have meddled in matters that do not concern them."

"They asked after me?" said Professor Malzius, with surprise. "It is true, my experiments were reaching a point that——"

"No foreign influence could turn us from our firm purpose," said the Dictator. "But it is our firm purpose to show our nation first in science and culture as we have already shown her first in manliness and statehood. For that reason, you are here, Professor Malzius." He smiled.

Professor Malzius stared. His cheeks began to tremble.

"I do not understand," said Professor Malzius. "You will give me my laboratory back?"

"Yes," said the Dictator, and the General nodded as one nods to a stupid child.

Professor Malzius passed a hand across his brow.

"My post at the university?" he said. "My experiments?"

"It is the purpose of our regime to offer the fullest

encouragement to our loyal sons of science," said the Dictator.

"First of all," said Professor Malzius, "I must go to a hospital. My blood count is poor. But that will not take long." His voice had become impatient and his eyes glowed. "Then—my notebooks were burned, I suppose. That was silly, but we can start in again. I have a very good memory, an excellent memory. The theories are in my head, you know," and he tapped it. "I must have assistants, of course; little Gregopolous was my best one——"

"The man Gregopolous has been executed," said the General, in a stern voice. "You had best forget him."

"Oh," said Professor Malzius. "Well, then, I must have someone else. You see, these are important experiments. There must be some young men—clever ones—they cannot all be dead. I will know them." He laughed a little, nervously. "The Bear always got the pick of the crop," he said. "They used to call me The Bear, you know." He stopped and looked at them for a moment with ghastly eyes. "You are not fooling me?" he said. He burst into tears.

When he recovered he was alone in the room with the General. The General was looking at him as he himself had looked once at strange forms of life under the microscope, with neither disgust nor attraction, but with great interest.

"His Excellency forgives your unworthy suggestion," he said. "He knows you are overwrought."

"Yes," said Professor Malzius. He sobbed once and dried his glasses.

"Come, come," said the General, with a certain bluff

heartiness. "We mustn't have our new president of the National Academy crying. It would look badly in the photographs."

"President of the Academy?" said Professor Malzius quickly. "Oh, no; I mustn't be that. They make speeches; they have administrative work. But I am a scientist, a teacher."

"I'm afraid you can't very well avoid it," said the General, still heartily, though he looked at Professor Malzius. "Your induction will be quite a ceremony. His Excellency himself will preside. And you will speak on the new glories of our science. It will be a magnificent answer to the petty and jealous criticisms of our neighbors. Oh, you needn't worry about the speech," he added quickly. "It will be prepared; you will only have to read it. His Excellency thinks of everything."

"Very well," said Professor Malzius; "and then may I go back to my work?"

"Oh, don't worry about that," said the General, smiling. "I'm only a simple soldier; I don't know about those things. But you'll have plenty of work."

"The more the better," said Malzius eagerly. "I still have ten good years."

He opened his mouth to smile, and a shade of dismay crossed the General's face.

"Yes," he said, as if to himself. "The teeth must be attended to. At once. And a rest, undoubtedly, before the photographs are taken. Milk. You are feeling sufficiently well, Professor Malzius?"

"I am very happy," said Professor Malzius. "I have been very well treated and I come of peasant stock."

"Good," said the General. He paused for a moment, and spoke in a more official voice.

"Of course, it is understood, Professor Malzius——" he said.

"Yes?" said Professor Malzius. "I beg your pardon. I was thinking of something else."

"It is understood, Professor Malzius," repeated the General, "that your—er—rehabilitation in the service of the state is a permanent matter. Naturally, you will be under observation, but, even so, there must be no mistake."

"I am a scientist," said Professor Malzius impatiently. "What have I to do with politics? If you wish me to take oaths of loyalty, I will take as many as you wish."

"I am glad you take that attitude," said the General, though he looked at Professor Malzius curiously. "I may say that I regret the unpleasant side of our interviews. I trust you bear no ill will."

"Why should I be angry?" said Professor Malzius. "You were told to do one thing. Now you are told to do another. That is all."

"It is not quite so simple as that," said the General rather stiffly. He looked at Professor Malzius for a third time. "And I'd have sworn you were one of the stiff-necked ones," he said. "Well, well, every man has his breaking point, I suppose. In a few moments you will receive the final commands of His Excellency. Tonight you will go to the capitol and speak over the radio. You will have no difficulty there—the speech is written. But it will put a quietus on the activities of our friend Bonnard and the question that has been raised in the

British Parliament. Then a few weeks of rest by the sea and the dental work, and then, my dear president of the National Academy, you will be ready to undertake your new duties. I congratulate you and hope we shall meet often under pleasant auspices." He bowed from the waist to Malzius, the bow of a man of the world, though there was still something feline in his mustaches. Then he stood to attention, and Malzius, too, for the Dictator had come into the room.

"It is settled?" said the Dictator. "Good. Gregor Malzius, I welcome you to the service of the new state. You have cast your errors aside and are part of our destiny."

"Yes," said Professor Malzius, "I will be able to do my work now."

The Dictator frowned a little.

"You will not only be able to continue your invaluable researches," he said, "but you will also be able— and it will be part of your duty—to further our national ideals. Our reborn nation must rule the world for the world's good. There is a fire within us that is not in other stocks. Our civilization must be extended everywhere. The future wills it. It will furnish the subject of your first discourse as president of the Academy."

"But," said Professor Malzius, in a low voice, "I am not a soldier. I am a biochemist. I have no experience in these matters you speak of."

The Dictator nodded. "You are a distinguished man of science," he said. "You will prove that our women must bear soldiers, our men abandon this nonsense of republics and democracies for trust in those born to rule them. You will prove by scientific law that certain races—our race in particular—are destined to rule the world. You will prove they are destined to rule by the virtues of war, and that war is part of our heritage."

"But," said Professor Malzius, "it is not like that. I mean," he said, "one looks and watches in the laboratory. One waits for a long time. It is a long process, very long. And then, if the theory is not proved, one discards the theory. That is the way it is done. I probably do not explain it well. But I am a biochemist; I do not know how to look for the virtues of one race against another, and I can prove nothing about war, except that it kills. If I said anything else, the whole world would laugh at me."

"Not one in this nation would laugh at you," said the Dictator.

"But if they do not laugh at me when I am wrong, there is no science," said Professor Malzius, knotting his brows. He paused. "Do not misunderstand me," he said earnestly. "I have ten years of good work left; I want to get back to my laboratory. But, you see, there are the young men—if I am to teach the young men."

He paused again, seeing their faces before him. There were many. There was Williams, the Englishman, who had died in the war, and little Gregopolous with the fox-terrier eyes. There were all who had passed through his classrooms, from the stupidest to the best. They had shot little Gregopolous for treason, but that did not alter the case. From all over the world they had come—he remembered the Indian student and the Chinese. They wore cheap overcoats, they were hungry for knowledge, they ate the bad, starchy food of the poor restaurants, they had miserable little love affairs and played childish games of politics, instead of doing their work. Nevertheless, a few were promising—all must be given the truth. It did not matter if they died, but they must be given the truth. Otherwise there could be no continuity and no science.

He looked at the Dictator before him—yes, it was a hysteric face. He would know how to deal with it in his classroom—but such faces should not rule countries or young men. One was willing to go through a great many meaningless ceremonies in order to do one's work—wear a uniform or salute or be president of the Academy. That did not matter; it was part of the due to Caesar. But not to tell lies to young men on one's own subject. After all, they had called him The Bear and said he carried improper post cards in his brief case. They had given him their terrible confidence—not for love or kindness, but because they had found him honest. It was too late to change.

The Dictator looked sharply at the General. "I thought this had been explained to Professor Malzius," he said.

"Why, yes," said Professor Malzius. "I will sign any papers. I assure you I am not interested in politics—a man like myself, imagine! One state is as good as another. And I miss my tobacco—I have not smoked in five months. But, you see, one cannot be a scientist and tell lies."

He looked at the two men.

"What happens if I do not?" he said, in a low voice. But, looking at the Dictator, he had his answer. It was a fanatic face.

"Why, we shall resume our conversations, Professor Malzius," said the General, with a simper.

"Then I shall be beaten again," said Professor Malzius. He stated what he knew to be a fact.

"The process of rehabilitation is obviously not quite complete," said the General, "but perhaps, in time——"

"It will not be necessary," said Professor Malzius. "I cannot be beaten again." He stared wearily around the room. His shoulders straightened—it was so he had looked in the classroom when they had called him The Bear. "Call your other officers in," he said in a clear voice. "There are papers for me to sign. I should like them all to witness."

"Why——" said the General. "Why——" He looked doubtfully at the Dictator.

An expression of gratification appeared on the lean, semi-Napoleonic face. A white hand, curiously limp, touched the hand of Professor Malzius.

"You will feel so much better, Gregor," said the hoarse, tense voice. "I am so very glad you have given in."

"Why, of course, I give in," said Gregor Malzius. "Are you not the Dictator? And besides, if I do not, I shall be beaten again. And I cannot—you understand? —I cannot be beaten again."

He paused, breathing a little. But already the room was full of other faces. He knew them well, the hard faces of the new regime. But youthful some of them too.

The Dictator was saying something with regard to

receiving the distinguished scientist, Professor Gregor Malzius, into the service of the state.

"Take the pen," said the General in an undertone. "The inkwell is there, Professor Malzius. Now you may sign."

Professor Malzius stood, his fingers gripping the big, old-fashioned inkwell. It was full of ink—the servants of the Dictator were very efficient. They could shoot small people with the eyes of fox terriers for treason, but their trains arrived on time and their inkwells did not run dry.

"The state," he said, breathing. "Yes. But science does not know about states. And you are a little man— a little, unimportant man."

Then, before the General could stop him, he had picked up the inkwell and thrown it in the Dictator's face. The next moment the General's fist caught him on the side of the head and he fell behind the desk to the floor. But lying there, through his cracked glasses, he could still see the grotesque splashes of ink on the Dictator's face and uniform, and the small cut above his eye where the blood was gathering. They had not fired; he had thought he would be too close to the Dictator for them to fire in time.

"Take that man out and shoot him. At once," said the Dictator in a dry voice. He did not move to wipe the stains from his uniform—and for that Professor Malzius admired him. They rushed then, each anxious to be first. But Professor Malzius made no resistance.

As he was being hustled along the corridors, he fell now and then. On the second fall, his glasses were

broken completely, but that did not matter to him.
They were in a great hurry, he thought, but all the
better—one did not have to think while one could not
see.

Now and then he heard his voice make sounds of
discomfort, but his voice was detached from himself.
There was little Gregopolous—he could see him very
plainly—and Williams, with his fresh English coloring
—and all the men whom he had taught.

He had given them nothing but work and the truth;
they had given him their terrible trust. If he had been
beaten again, he might have betrayed them. But he
had avoided that.

He felt a last weakness—a wish that someone might
know. They would not, of course; he would have died
of typhoid in the castle and there would be regretful
notices in the newspapers. And then he would be forgotten, except for his work, and that was as it should
be. He had never thought much of martyrs—hysterical
people in the main. Though he'd like Bonnard to have
known about the ink; it was in the coarse vein of humor
that Bonnard could not appreciate. But then, he was
a peasant; Bonnard had often told him so.

They were coming out into an open courtyard now;
he felt the fresh air of outdoors. "Gently," he said. "A
little gently. What's the haste?" But already they were
tying him to the post. Someone struck him in the face
and his eyes watered. "A schoolboy covered with ink,"
he muttered through his lost teeth. "A hysterical schoolboy too. But you cannot kill truth."

They were not good last words, and he knew that

they were not. He must try to think of better ones—
not shame Bonnard. But now they had a gag in his
mouth; just as well; it saved him the trouble.

His body ached, bound against the post, but his
sight and his mind were clearer. He could make out the
evening sky, gray with fog, the sky that belonged to no
country, but to all the world.

He could make out the gray high buttress of the
castle. They had made it a jail, but it would not always
be a jail. Perhaps in time it would not even exist. But
if a little bit of truth were gathered, that would always
exist, while there were men to remember and redis-
cover it. It was only the liars and the cruel who always
failed.

Sixty years ago, he had been a little boy, eating black
bread and thin cabbage soup in a poor house. It had
been a bitter life, but he could not complain of it. He
had had some good teachers and they had called him
The Bear.

The gag hurt his mouth—they were getting ready
now. There had been a girl called Anna once; he had
almost forgotten her. And his rooms had smelt a certain way and he had had a dog. It did not matter what
they did with the medals. He raised his head and
looked once more at the gray foggy sky. In a moment
there would be no thought, but, while there was
thought, one must remember and note. His pulse rate
was lower than he would have expected and his breathing oddly even, but those were not the important
things. The important thing was beyond, in the gray
sky that had no country, in the stones of the earth and

the feeble human spirit. The important thing was truth.

"Ready!" called the officer. "Aim! Fire!" But Professor Malzius did not hear the three commands of the officer. He was thinking about the young men.

THE KING OF THE CATS

"BUT, my *dear*," said Mrs. Culverin, with a tiny gasp, "you can't actually mean—a *tail!*"

Mrs. Dingle nodded impressively. "Exactly. I've seen him. Twice. Paris, of course, and then, a command appearance at Rome—we were in the Royal box. He conducted—my dear, you've never heard such effects from an orchestra—and, my dear," she hesitated slightly, "he conducted *with it.*"

"How perfectly, fascinatingly too horrid for words!" said Mrs. Culverin in a dazed but greedy voice. "We *must* have him to dinner as soon as he comes over— he is coming over, isn't he?"

"The twelfth," said Mrs. Dingle with a gleam in her eyes. "The New Symphony people have asked him to be guest-conductor for three special concerts—I do hope you can dine with *us* some night while he's here—he'll be very busy, of course—but he's promised to give us what time he can spare——"

"Oh, thank you, dear," said Mrs. Culverin, abstractedly, her last raid upon Mrs. Dingle's pet British novelist still fresh in her mind. "You're always so delightfully hospitable—but you mustn't wear yourself out— the rest of us must do *our* part—I know Henry and myself would be only too glad to——"

"That's very sweet of you, darling." Mrs. Dingle also

48

remembered the larceny of the British novelist. "But we're just going to give Monsieur Tibault—sweet name, isn't it! They say he's descended from the Tybalt in 'Romeo and Juliet' and that's why he doesn't like Shakespeare—we're just going to give Monsieur Tibault the simplest sort of time—a little reception after his first concert, perhaps. He hates," she looked around the table, "large, mixed parties. And then, of course, his— er—little idiosyncrasy——" she coughed delicately. "It makes him feel a trifle shy with strangers."

"But I don't understand yet, Aunt Emily," said Tommy Brooks, Mrs. Dingle's nephew. "Do you really mean this Tibault bozo has a tail? Like a monkey and everything?"

"Tommy dear," said Mrs. Culverin, crushingly, "in the first place Monsieur Tibault is not a bozo—he is a very distinguished musician—the finest conductor in Europe. And in the second place——"

"He has," Mrs. Dingle was firm. "He has a tail. He conducts with it."

"Oh, but honestly!" said Tommy, his ears pinkening. "I mean—of course, if you say so, Aunt Emily, I'm sure he has—but still, it sounds pretty steep, if you know what I mean! How about it, Professor Tatto?"

Professor Tatto cleared his throat. "Tck," he said, putting his fingertips together cautiously, "I shall be very anxious to see this Monsieur Tibault. For myself, I have never observed a genuine specimen of *homo caudatus,* so I should be inclined to doubt, and yet . . . In the Middle Ages, for instance, the belief in men— er—tailed or with caudal appendages of some sort, was both widespread and, as far as we can gather, well-founded. As late as the Eighteenth Century, a Dutch sea-captain with some character for veracity recounts the discovery of a pair of such creatures in the island of Formosa. They were in a low state of civilization, I believe, but the appendages in question were quite distinct. And in 1860, Dr. Grimbrook, the English surgeon, claims to have treated no less than three African natives with short but evident tails—though his testimony rests upon his unsupported word. After all, the thing is not impossible, though doubtless unusual. Web feet—rudimentary gills—these occur with some frequency. The appendix we have with us always. The chain of our descent from the ape-like form is by no means complete. For that matter," he beamed around the table, "what can we call the last few vertebrae of the normal spine but the beginnings of a concealed and rudimentary tail? Oh, yes—yes—it's possible—quite—that in an extraordinary case—a reversion to type—a survival—though, of course——"

"I told you so," said Mrs. Dingle triumphantly. *"Isn't* it fascinating? Isn't it, Princess?"

The Princess Vivrakanarda's eyes, blue as a field of larkspur, fathomless as the centre of heaven, rested lightly for a moment on Mrs. Dingle's excited countenance.

"Ve-ry fascinating," she said, in a voice like stroked, golden velvet. "I should like—I should like ve-ry much to meet this Monsieur Tibault."

"Well, *I* hope he breaks his neck!" said Tommy Brooks, under his breath—but nobody ever paid much attention to Tommy.

Nevertheless as the time for Mr. Tibault's arrival

in these States drew nearer and nearer, people in general began to wonder whether the Princess had spoken quite truthfully—for there was no doubt of the fact that, up till then, she had been the unique sensation of the season—and you know what social lions and lionesses are

It was, if you remember, a Siamese season, and genuine Siamese were at quite as much of a premium as Russian accents had been in the quaint old days when the Chauve-Souris was a novelty. The Siamese Art Theatre, imported at terrific expense, was playing to packed houses. "Gushuptzgu," an epic novel of Siamese farm life, in nineteen closely-printed volumes, had just been awarded the Nobel prize. Prominent pet-and-newt dealers reported no cessation in the appalling demand for Siamese cats. And upon the crest of this wave of interest in things Siamese, the Princess Vivrakanarda poised with the elegant nonchalance of a Hawaiian water-baby upon its surfboard. She was indispensable. She was incomparable. She was everywhere.

Youthful, enormously wealthy, allied on one hand to the Royal Family of Siam and on the other to the Cabots (and yet with the first eighteen of her twenty-one years shrouded from speculation in a golden zone of mystery) , the mingling of races in her had produced an exotic beauty as distinguished as it was strange. She moved with a feline, effortless grace, and her skin was as if it had been gently powdered with tiny grains of the purest gold—yet the blueness of her eyes, set just a trifle slantingly, was as pure and startling as the sea on the rocks of Maine. Her brown hair fell to her knees—she had been offered extraordinary sums by the

Master Barbers' Protective Association to have it shin-
gled. Straight as a waterfall tumbling over brown rocks,
it had a vague perfume of sandalwood and suave spices
and held tints of rust and the sun. She did not talk
very much—but then she did not have to—her voice
had an odd, small, melodious huskiness that haunted
the mind. She lived alone and was reputed to be very
lazy—at least it was known that she slept during most
of the day—but at night she bloomed like a moon-
flower and a depth came into her eyes.

It was no wonder that Tommy Brooks fell in love
with her. The wonder was that she let him. There
was nothing exotic or distinguished about Tommy—
he was just one of those pleasant, normal young men
who seem created to carry on the bond business by
reading the newspapers in the University Club during most of the day, and can always be relied upon at
night to fill an unexpected hole in a dinner-party. It
is true that the Princess could hardly be said to do more
than tolerate any of her suitors—no one had ever
seen those aloofly arrogant eyes enliven at the entrance
of any male. But she seemed to be able to tolerate
Tommy a little more than the rest—and that young
man's infatuated day-dreams were beginning to be beset
by smart solitaires and imaginary apartments on Park
Avenue, when the famous M. Tibault conducted his
first concert at Carnegie Hall.

Tommy Brooks sat beside the Princess. The eyes he
turned upon her were eyes of longing and love, but
her face was as impassive as a mask, and the only remark she made during the preliminary bustlings was

that there seemed to be a number of people in the audience. But Tommy was relieved, if anything, to find her even a little more aloof than usual, for, ever since Mrs. Culverin's dinner-party, a vague disquiet as to the possible impression which this Tibault creature might make upon her had been growing in his mind. It shows his devotion that he was present at all. To a man whose simple Princetonian nature found in "Just a Little Love, a Little Kiss," the quintessence of musical art, the average symphony was a positive torture, and he looked forward to the evening's programme itself with a grim, brave smile.

"Ssh!" said Mrs. Dingle, breathlessly. "He's coming!" It seemed to the startled Tommy as if he were suddenly back in the trenches under a heavy barrage, as M. Tibault made his entrance to a perfect bombardment of applause.

Then the enthusiastic noise was sliced off in the middle and a gasp took its place—a vast, windy sigh, as if every person in that multitude had suddenly said, "Ah." For the papers had not lied about him. The tail was there.

They called him theatric—but how well he understood the uses of theatricalism! Dressed in unrelieved black from head to foot (the black dress-shirt had been a special token of Mussolini's esteem), he did not walk on, he strolled, leisurely, easily, aloofly, the famous tail curled nonchalantly about one wrist—a suave, black panther lounging through a summer garden with that little mysterious weave of the head that panthers have when they pad behind bars—the glittering darkness of his eyes unmoved by any surprise or elation. He

nodded, twice, in regal acknowledgment, as the clap-
ping reached an apogee of frenzy. To Tommy there was
something dreadfully reminiscent of the Princess in the
way he nodded. Then he turned to his orchestra.

A second and louder gasp went up from the audience at this point, for, as he turned, the tip of that incredible tail twined with dainty carelessness into some
hidden pocket and produced a black baton. But Tommy
did not even notice. He was looking at the Princess
instead.

She had not even bothered to clap, at first, but now
—He had never seen her moved like this, never. She
was not applauding, her hands were clenched in her
lap, but her whole body was rigid, rigid as a steel bar,
and the blue flowers of her eyes were bent upon the
figure of M. Tibault in a terrible concentration. The
pose of her entire figure was so still and intense that
for an instant Tommy had the lunatic idea that any
moment she might leap from her seat beside him as
lightly as a moth, and land, with no sound, at M.
Tibault's side to—yes—to rub her proud head against
his coat in worship. Even Mrs. Dingle would notice in
a moment.

"Princess——" he said, in a horrified whisper,
"Princess——"

Slowly the tenseness of her body relaxed, her eyes
veiled again, she grew calm.

"Yes, Tommy?" she said, in her usual voice, but
there was still something about her . . .

"Nothing, only—oh, hang—he's starting!" said
Tommy, as M. Tibault, his hands loosely clasped before
him, turned and *faced* the audience. His eyes dropped,

his tail switched once impressively, then gave three little preliminary taps with his baton on the floor.

Seldom has Gluck's overture to "Iphigenie in Aulis" received such an ovation. But it was not until the Eighth Symphony that the hysteria of the audience reached its climax. Never before had the New Symphony played so superbly—and certainly never before had it been led with such genius. Three prominent conductors in the audience were sobbing with the despairing admiration of envious children toward the close, and one at least was heard to offer wildly ten thousand dollars to a well-known facial surgeon there present for a shred of evidence that tails of some variety could by any stretch of science be grafted upon a normally decaudate form. There was no doubt about it—no mortal hand and arm, be they ever so dexterous, could combine the delicate elan and powerful grace displayed in every gesture of M. Tibault's tail.

A sable staff, it dominated the brasses like a flicker of black lightning; an ebon, elusive whip, it drew the last exquisite breath of melody from the woodwinds and ruled the stormy strings like a magician's rod. M. Tibault bowed and bowed again—roar after roar of frenzied admiration shook the hall to its foundations— and when he finally staggered, exhausted, from the platform, the president of the Wednesday Sonata Club was only restrained by force from flinging her ninety-thousand-dollar string of pearls after him in an excess of aesthetic appreciation. New York had come and seen—and New York was conquered. Mrs. Dingle was immediately besieged by reporters, and Tommy Brooks

looked forward to the "little party" at which he was to
meet the new hero of the hour with feelings only a
little less lugubrious than those that would have come
to him just before taking his seat in the electric chair.

The meeting between his Princess and M. Tibault
was worse and better than he expected. Better because,
after all, they did not say much to each other—and
worse because it seemed to him, somehow, that some
curious kinship of mind between them made words
unnecessary. They were certainly the most distin-
guished-looking couple in the room, as he bent over
her hand. "So darlingly foreign, both of them, and
yet so different," babbled Mrs. Dingle—but Tommy
couldn't agree.

They were different, yes—the dark, lithe stranger
with the bizarre appendage tucked carelessly in his
pocket, and the blue-eyed, brown-haired girl. But that
difference only accentuated what they had in common
—something in the way they moved, in the suavity of
their gestures, in the set of their eyes. Something deeper,
even, than race. He tried to puzzle it out—then, looking
around at the others, he had a flash of revelation. It
was as if that couple were foreign, indeed—not only
to New York but to all common humanity. As if they
were polite guests from a different star.

Tommy did not have a very happy evening, on the
whole. But his mind worked slowly, and it was not
until much later that the mad suspicion came upon
him in full force.

Perhaps he is not to be blamed for his lack of imme-
diate comprehension. The next few weeks were weeks

of bewildered misery for him. It was not that the Princess's attitude toward him had changed—she was just as tolerant of him as before, but M. Tibault was always there. He had a faculty of appearing as out of thin air —he walked, for all his height, as lightly as a butterfly—and Tommy grew to hate that faintest shuffle on the carpet that announced his presence.

And then, hang it all, the man was so smooth, so infernally, unrufflably smooth! He was never out of temper, never embarrassed. He treated Tommy with the extreme of urbanity, and yet his eyes mocked, deep-down, and Tommy could do nothing. And, gradually, the Princess became more and more drawn to this stranger, in a soundless communion that found little need for speech—and that, too, Tommy saw and hated, and that, too, he could not mend.

He began to be haunted not only by M. Tibault in the flesh, but by M. Tibault in the spirit. He slept badly, and when he slept, he dreamed—of M. Tibault, a man no longer, but a shadow, a spectre, the limber ghost of an animal whose words came purringly between sharp little pointed teeth. There was certainly something odd about the whole shape of the fellow— his fluid ease, the mould of his head, even the cut of his fingernails—but just what it was escaped Tommy's intensest cogitation. And when he did put his finger on it at length, at first he refused to believe.

A pair of petty incidents decided him, finally, against all reason. He had gone to Mrs. Dingle's, one winter afternoon, hoping to find the Princess. She was out with his aunt, but was expected back for tea, and he wandered idly into the library to wait. He was just about to switch on the lights, for the library was always dark even in summer, when he heard a sound of light breathing that seemed to come from the leather couch in the corner. He approached it cautiously and dimly made out the form of M. Tibault, curled up on the couch, peacefully asleep.

The sight annoyed Tommy so that he swore under his breath and was back near the door on his way out, when the feeling we all know and hate, the feeling that eyes we cannot see are watching us, arrested him. He turned back—M. Tibault had not moved a muscle of his body to all appearance—but his eyes were open now. And those eyes were black and human no longer. They were green—Tommy could have sworn it—and he could have sworn that they had no bottom and gleamed like little emeralds in the dark. It only lasted a moment, for Tommy pressed the light-button automatically—and there was M. Tibault, his normal self, yawning a little but urbanely apologetic, but it gave Tommy time to think. Nor did what happened a trifle later increase his peace of mind.

They had lit a fire and were talking in front of it— by now Tommy hated M. Tibault so thoroughly that he felt that odd yearning for his company that often occurs in such cases. M. Tibault was telling some anecdote and Tommy was hating him worse than ever for basking with such obvious enjoyment in the heat of the flames and the ripple of his own voice.

Then they heard the street-door open, and M. Tibault jumped up—and jumping, caught one sock on a sharp corner of the brass fire-rail and tore it open in a jagged flap. Tommy looked down mechanically at the tear—a second's glance, but enough—for M. Tibault, for the first time in Tommy's experience, lost his temper completely. He swore violently in some spitting, foreign tongue—his face distorted suddenly—he clapped his hand over his sock. Then, glaring furiously at Tommy, he fairly sprang from the room, and Tommy could hear him scaling the stairs in long, agile bounds.

Tommy sank into a chair, careless for once of the fact that he heard the Princess's light laugh in the hall. He didn't want to see the Princess. He didn't want to see anybody. There had been something revealed when M. Tibault had torn that hole in his sock—and it was not the skin of a man. Tommy had caught a glimpse of—black plush. Black velvet. And then had come M. Tibault's sudden explosion of fury. Good *Lord*—did the man wear black velvet stockings under his ordinary socks? Or could he—could he—but here Tommy held his fevered head in his hands.

He went to Professor Tatto that evening with a series of hypothetical questions, but as he did not dare confide his real suspicions to the Professor, the hypothetical answers he received served only to confuse him the more. Then he thought of Billy Strange. Billy was a good sort, and his mind had a turn for the bizarre. Billy might be able to help.

He couldn't get hold of Billy for three days and lived through the interval in a fever of impatience. But finally they had dinner together at Billy's apartment, where his queer books were, and Tommy was able to blurt out the whole disordered jumble of his suspicions.

Billy listened without interrupting until Tommy was quite through. Then he pulled at his pipe. "But, my dear *man*——" he said, protestingly.

"Oh, I know—I know——" said Tommy, and waved his hands, "I know I'm crazy—you needn't tell me that —but I tell you, the man's a cat all the same—no, I don't see how he could be, but he is—why, hang it, in the first place, everybody knows he's got a tail!"

"Even so," said Billy, puffing. "Oh, my dear Tommy, I don't doubt you saw, or think you saw, everything you say. But, even so——" He shook his head.

"But what about those other birds, werwolves and things?" said Tommy.

Billy looked dubious. "We-ll," he admitted, "you've got me there, of course. At least—a tailed man *is* possible. And the yarns about werwolves go back far enough, so that—well, I wouldn't say there aren't or haven't been werwolves—but then I'm willing to believe more things than most people. But a wer-cat— or a man that's a cat and a cat that's a man—honestly, Tommy——"

"If I don't get some real advice I'll go clean off my hinge. For Heaven's sake, tell me something to *do!*"

"Lemme think," said Billy. "First, you're pizen-sure this man is——"

"A cat. Yeah," and Tommy nodded violently.

"Check. And second—if it doesn't hurt your feelings, Tommy—you're afraid this girl you're in love with has—er—at least a streak of—felinity—in her— and so she's drawn to him?"

"Oh, Lord, Billy, if I only knew!"

"Well—er—suppose she really is, too, you know—would you still be keen on her?"

"I'd marry her if she turned into a dragon every Wednesday!" said Tommy, fervently.

Billy smiled. "H'm," he said, "then the obvious thing to do is to get rid of this M. Tibault. Lemme think."

He thought about two pipes full, while Tommy sat on pins and needles. Then, finally, he burst out laughing.

"What's so darn funny?" said Tommy, aggrievedly.

"Nothing, Tommy, only I've just thought of a stunt —something so blooming crazy—but if he is—h'm— what you think he is—it *might* work——" And, going to the bookcase, he took down a book.

"If you think you're going to quiet my nerves by reading me a bedtime story——"

"Shut up, Tommy, and listen to this—if you really want to get rid of your feline friend."

"What is it?"

"Book of Agnes Repplier's. About cats. Listen.

" 'There is also a Scandinavian version of the ever famous story which Sir Walter Scott told to Washington Irving, which Monk Lewis told to Shelley and which, in one form or another, we find embodied in the folklore of every land'—now, Tommy, pay attention—'the story of the traveller who saw within a ruined abbey, a procession of cats, lowering into a grave a little coffin with a crown upon it. Filled with horror, he hastened from the spot; but when he had reached his destination, he could not forbear relating to a friend the wonder he had seen. Scarcely had the tale been told

when his friend's cat, who lay curled up tranquilly by
the fire, sprang to its feet, cried out, "Then I am the
King of the Cats!" and disappeared in a flash up the
chimney.'

"Well?" said Billy, shutting the book.

"By gum!" said Tommy, staring. "By gum! Do you
think there's a chance?"

"*I* think we're both in the booby-hatch. But if you
want to try it——"

"Try it! I'll spring it on him the next time I see
him. But—listen—I can't make it a ruined abbey——"

"Oh, use your imagination! Make it Central Park—
anywhere. Tell it as if it happened to you—seeing the
funeral procession and all that. You can lead into it
somehow—let's see—some general line—oh, yes—
'Strange, isn't it, how fact so often copies fiction. Why,
only yesterday——' See?"

"Strange, isn't it, how fact so often copies fiction,"
repeated Tommy dutifully. "Why, only yesterday——"

"I happened to be strolling through Central Park
when I saw something very odd."

"I happened to be strolling through—here, gimme
that book!" said Tommy, "I want to learn the rest of
it by heart!"

Mrs. Dingle's farewell dinner to the famous Monsieur Tibault, on the occasion of his departure for his
Western tour, was looked forward to with the greatest
expectations. Not only would everybody be there, including the Princess Vivrakananda, but Mrs. Dingle, a
hinter if there ever was one, had let it be known that at
this dinner an announcement of very unusual interest

to Society might be made. So everyone, for once, was almost on time, except for Tommy. He was at least fifteen minutes early, for he wanted to have speech with his aunt alone. Unfortunately, however, he had hardly taken off his overcoat when she was whispering some news in his ear so rapidly that he found it difficult to understand a word of it.

"And you mustn't breathe it to a soul!" she ended, beaming. "That is, not before the announcement—I think we'll have *that* with the salad—people never pay very much attention to salad——"

"Breathe what, Aunt Emily?" said Tommy, confused.

"The Princess, darling—the dear Princess and Monsieur Tibault—they just got engaged this afternoon, dear things! Isn't it *fascinating?*"

"Yeah," said Tommy, and started to walk blindly through the nearest door. His aunt restrained him.

"Not there, dear—not in the library. You can congratulate them later. They're just having a sweet little moment alone there now——" And she turned away to harry the butler, leaving Tommy stunned.

But his chin came up after a moment. He wasn't beaten yet.

"Strange, isn't it, how often fact copies fiction?" he repeated to himself in dull mnemonics, and, as he did so, he shook his fist at the library door.

Mrs. Dingle was wrong, as usual. The Princess and M. Tibault were not in the library—they were in the conservatory, as Tommy discovered when he wandered aimlessly past the glass doors.

He didn't mean to look, and after a second he
turned away. But that second was enough.

Tibault was seated in a chair and she was crouched
on a stool at his side, while his hand, softly, smoothly,
stroked her brown hair. Black cat and Siamese kitten.
Her face was hidden from Tommy, but he could see
Tibault's face. And he could hear.

They were not talking, but there was a sound between them. A warm and contented sound like the
murmur of giant bees in a hollow tree—a golden, musical rumble, deep-throated, that came from Tibault's
lips and was answered by hers—a golden purr.

Tommy found himself back in the drawing-room,
shaking hands with Mrs. Culverin, who said, frankly,
that she had seldom seen him look so pale.

The first two courses of the dinner passed Tommy
like dreams, but Mrs. Dingle's cellar was notable, and
by the middle of the meat course, he began to come
to himself. He had only one resolve now.

For the next few moments he tried desperately to
break into the conversation, but Mrs. Dingle was talking, and even Gabriel will have a time interrupting Mrs.
Dingle. At last, though, she paused for breath and
Tommy saw his chance.

"Speaking of that," said Tommy, piercingly, without knowing in the least what he was referring to,
"Speaking of that——"

"As I was saying," said Professor Tatto. But Tommy
would not yield. The plates were being taken away. It
was time for salad.

"Speaking of that," he said again, so loudly and
strangely that Mrs. Culverin jumped and an awkward

hush fell over the table. "Strange, isn't it, how often fact copies fiction?" There, he was started. His voice rose even higher. "Why, only to-day I was strolling through——" and, word for word, he repeated his lesson. He could see Tibault's eyes glowing at him, as he described the funeral. He could see the Princess, tense.

He could not have said what he had expected might happen when he came to the end; but it was not bored silence, everywhere, to be followed by Mrs. Dingle's acrid, "Well, Tommy, is that *quite* all?"

He slumped back in his chair, sick at heart. He was a fool and his last resource had failed. Dimly he heard his aunt's voice, saying, "Well, then——" and realized that she was about to make the fatal announcement.

But just then Monsieur Tibault spoke.

"One moment, Mrs. Dingle," he said, with extreme politeness, and she was silent. He turned to Tommy.

"You are—positive, I suppose, of what you saw this afternoon, Brooks?" he said, in tones of light mockery.

"Absolutely," said Tommy sullenly. "Do you think I'd——"

"Oh, no, no, no," Monsieur Tibault waved the implication aside, "but—such an interesting story—one likes to be sure of the details—and, of course, you *are* sure—*quite* sure—that the kind of crown you describe was on the coffin?"

"Of course," said Tommy, wondering, "but——"

"Then I'm the King of the Cats!" cried Monsieur Tibault in a voice of thunder, and, even as he cried it, the house-lights blinked—there was the soft thud of an explosion that seemed muffled in cotton-wool from the minstrel gallery—and the scene was lit for a second by an obliterating and painful burst of light that vanished in an instant and was succeeded by heavy, blinding clouds of white, pungent smoke.

"Oh, those *horrid* photographers," came Mrs. Dingle's voice in a melodious wail. "I *told* them not to take the flashlight picture till dinner was over, and now they've taken it *just* as I was nibbling lettuce!"

Someone tittered a little nervously. Someone coughed. Then, gradually the veils of smoke dislimned and the green-and-black spots in front of Tommy's eyes died away.

They were blinking at each other like people who have just come out of a cave into brilliant sun. Even yet their eyes stung with the fierceness of that abrupt illumination and Tommy found it hard to make out the faces across the table from him.

Mrs. Dingle took command of the half-blinded company with her accustomed poise. She rose, glass in hand. "And now, dear friends," she said in a clear voice, "I'm sure all of us are very happy to——" Then she stopped, open-mouthed, an expression of incredulous horror on her features. The lifted glass began to spill its contents on the tablecloth in a little stream of amber. As she spoke, she had turned directly to Monsieur Tibault's place at the table—and Monsieur Tibault was no longer there.

Some say there was a bursting flash of fire that disappeared up the chimney—some say it was a giant cat that leaped through the window at a bound, without breaking the glass. Professor Tatto puts it down to a mysterious chemical disturbance operating only over

M. Tibault's chair. The butler, who is pious, believes the devil in person flew away with him, and Mrs. Dingle hesitates between witchcraft and a malicious ectoplasm dematerializing on the wrong cosmic plane. But be that as it may, one thing is certain—in the instant of fictive darkness which followed the glare of the flashlight, Monsieur Tibault, the great conductor, disappeared forever from mortal sight, tail and all.

Mrs. Culverin swears he was an international burglar and that she was just about to unmask him, when he slipped away under cover of the flashlight smoke, but no one else who sat at that historic dinner-table believes her. No, there are no sound explanations, but Tommy thinks he knows, and he will never be able to pass a cat again without wondering.

Mrs. Tommy is quite of her husband's mind regarding cats—she was Gretchen Woolwine, of Chicago—for Tommy told her his whole story, and while she doesn't believe a great deal of it, there is no doubt in her heart that one person concerned in the affair was a *perfect* cat. Doubtless it would have been more romantic to relate how Tommy's daring finally won him his Princess—but, unfortunately, it would not be veracious. For the Princess Vivrakanarda, also, is with us no longer. Her nerves, shattered by the spectacular denouement of Mrs. Dingle's dinner, required a sea-voyage, and from that voyage she has never returned to America.

Of course, there are the usual stories—one hears of her, a nun in a Siamese convent, or a masked dancer at Le Jardin de ma Soeur—one hears that she has been murdered in Patagonia or married in Trebizond—but, as far as can be ascertained, not one of these gaudy fables has the slightest basis of fact. I believe that Tommy, in his heart of hearts, is quite convinced that the sea-voyage was only a pretext, and that by some unheard-of means, she has managed to rejoin the formidable Monsieur Tibault, wherever in the world of the visible or the invisible he may be—in fact, that in some ruined city or subterranean palace they reign together now, King and Queen of all the mysterious Kingdom of Cats. But that, of course, is quite impossible.

A STORY BY ANGELA POE

I WAS a very young man in the publishing business at the time—even younger, I think, than most young men are nowadays, for this was before the war. Diana poised her bow at the sky above a Madison Square Garden that was actually on Madison Square—and some of the older men in our New York office still wore the paper sleeve-protectors and worn alpaca coats of an older day. There are young offices and old ones: brisk, shiny, bumptious new offices that positively buzz with expert inefficiency; and resigned, rather wistful little offices that have come to know they will never do well in the world. But the prevailing atmosphere of Thrushwood, Collins, and Co. was that of substantial tradition and solid worth. The faded carpet in the reception-room had been trodden by any number of famous feet—perhaps by not quite so many as I avouched to the young men of other publishers, but still the legends were there. Legends of Henry James and William Dean Howells and a young man from India named Kipling who was taken for a boy from the printer's and sent off with a flea in his ear. New authors were always greatly impressed by our atmosphere—until they looked over their contracts and discovered that even their Australian rights had, somehow or other, become the inalienable property of Thrushwood, Col-

lins, and Co. But then they had only to see Mr. Thrushwood to be convinced that their most successful works
were being published from a rigid sense of duty at a
distinct financial loss.

I had the desk that was farthest away from both
radiators and window, in the front office, so I broiled
in summer and froze in winter and was perfectly happy.
I was in New York, I was part of the making of books,
I saw celebrities, and every Sunday I wrote home about
it to my family. True, some of the celebrities were not
nearly so impressive in the flesh as in the print; but
that made me feel I was seeing Real Life at last. And
there was always Mr. Thrushwood, with his thin, worn,
cameo face and his white plume of hair, to restore my
faith in mankind. When he put his hand on my shoulder and said, "You're coming along nicely, Robbins,"
I felt an accolade. I did not discover until later that I
was doing three men's work, but, if I had known it,
then, I would not have cared. And when Randall Day,
of Harper's, irreverently alluded to us as "The Holy
Burglars," I flung the insinuation back in his teeth,
with an apt quotation about Philistines. For we talked
about Philistines, then.

As a matter of fact, we had an excellent list, on the
whole—for, though Mr. Thrushwood, like most successful publishers, hardly ever read a book, he had a
remarkable nose for the promising and the solid. On
the other hand, there were names which, as an idealist,
I boggled over—and the first and foremost of these was
Angela Poe. I could tolerate Caspar Breed and his lean-
jawed, stern-muscled cowboys with the hearts of little
children. I could stomach Jeremy Jason, the homespun

philosopher, whose small green ooze-leather booklets, "A Wayfarer's Creed," "A Wayfarer's Vow," "A Wayfarer's Hearthstone," produced much the same sensation in me as running a torn fingernail over heavy plush. Publishers must live, and other publishers had their Breeds and their Jasons. But Angela Poe was not merely an author—she was something like breakfast-food or chewing-gum, an American institution, untidy, inescapable, and vast. I could have forgiven her—and Thrushwood, Collins—if she had sold moderately well. But long ago, the New York Times had ceased to say anything about her except, "Another Angela Poe . . . sure to appeal to her huge audience . . ." before its painstaking resumé of the plot. I often wondered what unhappy reviewer wrote those resumés. For he must have had to read the books, from "Wanda of the Marshes" to "Ashes of Roses," and I did not see how that was possible for any one man.

The settings of the novels ranged from the fjords of Norway to the coasts of Tasmania, and every page betrayed that intimate knowledge of a foreign country which can only be acquired by a thorough study of the chattier sort of guide-books. But though the scene might shift, the puppets remained defiantly the same. Even in Tasmania, the wild roses in the heroine's cheeks remained quite unaffected by the climate and the malign but singularly unintelligent snares of the cynical villain in riding-clothes. The villains almost always wore riding-clothes, as I remember it, and were usually militant atheists, though of high social position. The heroines were petite, unworldly, and given to calling the native flora pet names. And over all, insipid, lingering, and sweet as the taste of a giant marshmallow, there brooded the inimitable style of Angela Poe. Occasionally, this style would goad some fledgling reviewer to fury and he would write the sort of scarifying review that only very young reviewers write. Then the girl at our reception desk would be warned and Mr. Thrushwood would put off all other appointments for the day. For Angela Poe read all her reviews with passion.

It was on such an occasion that I saw her for the first time. I was passing Mr. Thrushwood's private office, when Mr. Collins popped out of it with a worried look on his face. A dumpy little man who haunted the business department, he left all personal contacts with authors to Mr. Thrushwood, as a rule. But this time, Angela Poe had descended in Mr. Thrushwood's absence and caught him unprepared.

"Look here, Robbins," he said, with no more preface than a drowning man, "have we got any really magnificent reviews on the last Poe? You know the kind I mean—all honey and butter. The Washoe Gazette has just called her a purveyor of literary lollipops—and if I could get hold of her clipping-agency, there'd be blood on the moon."

"Why," I said, "I'm afraid I——" and then I remembered. Randall Day had the pestilent habit of sending me all the most fulsome reviews of Angela Poe that he could find—and one had arrived only that morning, with a neat border of hearts and flowers drawn around it.

"As a matter of fact, I have," I said, "but——"

"Thank God!" said Mr. Collins fervently and, taking me by the hand, he fairly ran me into the room.

But at first I could see no reason for the odd, tense look on his face—and on that of Mr. Catherwood, our art director, who was also there. The plump, demure, little old lady with the face of a faded pansy who sat in the big chair opposite them had nothing terrifying about her. She was Angela Poe, of course, though ten years older than her oldest publicity-pictures. And then she began to talk.

It was a sweet, tinkling voice, monotonous and constant. And as it went on, about Mr. Thrushwood and all her kind friends in Thrushwood, Collins, and then— I could not mark the transition—about how her flowers in her wee garden were also her friends, I began to realize the secret of the look on Mr. Collins' face. It was boredom, pure and simple, but boredom raised to a fine art. For when Angela Poe was angry she did not fly into a temper any more. She merely talked in her low, sweet voice—and, as she talked, she bored, relentlessly and persistently, like a drill boring into a shell.

It was no use trying to interrupt her or change the conversation—you cannot change a conversation that has no real subject to change. And yet, as she continued, and each moment seemed longer than the last until the brute flesh could hardly be restrained from breaking into a veritable whimper of tedium, I began to realize that she knew exactly what she was about. For somehow or other, we always came back to Angela Poe and the fact that she was waiting for Mr. Thrushwood. Till I began to feel, myself, that Mr. Thrushwood's

absence was a grave calamity of nature and that, if he
did not come soon, I, too, might burst into tears.

Fortunately, he arrived in time, and saved us, as
only Mr. Thrushwood could. Fortunately or unfortunately, for he came while I was showing her the review
that Day had sent me. It mollified her greatly, though
she said, in a serious voice, that of course she never
read reviews. They broke the wings of the butterfly.
I didn't know what she meant by that, but I must have
made some appropriate response. For Mr. Thrushwood,
with one of his Napoleonic gestures, informed me at
five o'clock that afternoon that henceforth my salary
was raised ten dollars a month.

"And, by the way, Robbins," he said, "I don't want
to put too much on you—but Miss Poe liked your
looks today. Well, Miss Poe is just beginning a new
novel—I think this one is to be about Iceland, or pos-
sibly Finland—not that it matters greatly——" and he
gave me a smile of complicity. "But, as you know, we
always get her reference books for her and send them
out every week-end—and she will have them brought
by some member of the staff. It's on the west shore of
the Hudson—and I'm afraid she calls her house The
Eyrie," he went on, with a chuckle. "But she's really
a very sensible little woman—quite a head for business,
yes, indeed, quite a head," and his face held unwilling
respect. "So, if you wouldn't mind? Then that's all
settled. How jolly of you, Robbins!" he said, with his
boyish laugh.

I had meant to tell him I would do nothing of the
sort, but, while you were with him you were under

his spell. Nevertheless, it was with internal revolt that I got on the ferry that week-end, with my bag of books in my hand. And then, when I got to The Eyrie, I met a nice old lady who reminded me of my aunts. She put me at ease at once, she fed me enormously, she fussed over me with just the right amount of fussiness. The tea was solid and bountiful—I was sent to the station in a carriage and pair. To my despair, in the train going back, I discovered that I had enjoyed myself. And through my mind still ran the small, tinkling monotonous voice of Angela Poe—saying nothing, and yet, remembered. I tried very hard to place her; she was like any dozen ladies I knew in Central City, ladies with little gold watches pinned over their bosoms, who fussily but efficiently presided over strawberry festivals and sales at the Woman's Exchange. And she was not— there was something else about her, some quality I could not place. It had made her Angela Poe—and yet, what was it? Her servants, I had noticed, were perfectly trained and civil and the dog got up from the hearthrug when she told it to get up. And yet, instinctively, you gave her your arm, when she came down a staircase. I could not make it out, but I knew, rather shame-facedly, that I was looking forward to returning to The Eyrie. Young men are apt to be hungry—and the tea was superb.

And then, as I told Randall Day, The Eyrie alone was worth the price of admission. It was one of those big wooden houses with wide verandas that the Eighties built on the cliffs of the Hudson—houses that, somehow or other, remind you of grandiose cuckoo-clocks. There were the lawns and the shrubbery, the big, cupolaed

stable and the graveled drive; the hardwood floors and
the heavily framed oil-paintings. It might all have come
out of an Angela Poe novel—she had done it perfectly
down to the last gas-bracket. And through it all wandered Mr. Everard De Lacey, the man one must never
address as Mr. Angela Poe.

It was my first experience with the husband of a
celebrated authoress, and he still remains unique in
my memory. You do not meet them now as often as
you did—those men with the large, mobile mouths,
the Hamlet eyes, and the skin that has known the
grease-paint of a thousand small-town dressing-rooms.
The new actors are another breed. Mr. De Lacey was
not merely an actor, he was a Thespian—and it makes
a difference. He must have been very handsome in his
youth—handsome in the old barnstorming tradition of
black, flashing eyes and Hyacinthine curls—and his
voice still had the rich, portentous boom of Michael
Strogoff, the Courier of the Czar. When he fixed me
with his Hamlet eyes and quoted—it was The Bard—
I felt ashamed of myself for not being a larger audience.
But he was really very considerate about it, and I liked
the way he treated Miss Poe.

For they were obviously and deeply attached to each
other, those two aging people, and one sensed the bond
the moment one saw them together. They deferred to
each other ceremoniously, with a Victorian civility
that I found rather touching. And Everard was by no
means the harmless, necessary husband such husbands
often are. It was agreed that he was "resting" from a
modern and sin-struck stage unworthy of his talents,

but it was also agreed that, at any moment, he might return to the boards, amid the plaudits of welcoming multitudes. Later on I discovered that he had been "resting" for almost thirty years, or since Angela Poe first started to sell by the carload. But that made no difference to either of them.

"I could never have done what I have done without Mr. De Lacey," she would say in her sweet, tinkling voice and Everard would boom in return, "My dear, it was but given me to water and tend the rose. The flowers are all your own." Such things, if said, are oftener said than meant. But you felt that the Poes, I mean the De Laceys, meant them. Then a look would pass between them, the look of two souls who are linked by a deeper tie than the crass world knows.

I seem to be writing a little like Angela Poe myself in describing them. But it was difficult, in that setting, not to become infected with Poe-ishness. If a beautiful girl in a simple muslin frock had met me accidentally in the garden and flitted away with flushed cheeks and a startled cry, I would have been embarrassed but not in the least surprised. And there were times when I fully expected to meet a little lame boy, his pale, courageous face radiant for once with the sunset glow, at almost any corner of the drive. But the De Laceys had no children, though they were extremely kind to the innumerable offspring of Mr. De Lacey's relatives. And that seemed to me rather a shame.

I had come to scoff, you see. But I remained, if not to pray, well, to be rather fascinated. They fed me well, they treated me with ceremonious politeness, they were sentimental, but generous as well. I had to listen a good deal to the tinkling, incessant flow of Angela Poe's words—but, as time wore on, I even became used to that. It was as Mr. Thrushwood had said; she could be extremely sensible, even pungent, when she wished. And she could take criticism, too, which surprised me. At least she could take it from Everard De Lacey. Now and then he would say, in his rich boom, as she sketched a scene or a character for us, "No, my dear, that will not do."

"But, Everard, how is Zepha to escape from the insane asylum, then?"

"That, my dear, I have to leave to your genius. But this passage will not do. I sense it. I feel it. It is not Angela Poe."

"Very well, my dear," she would say submissively, and turn to me with, "Mr. De Lacey is always right, you know." And he would say, at the same moment, "Young Man, I am not always right. But such poor gifts as I possess are always at Mrs. De Lacey's service——"

"The fruits of a richly stored mind, Everard——"

"Well, my dear, perhaps some slight acquaintance with the classics of our tongue—some trifling practical experience in interpreting The Bard——"

Then each would make the other a little bob, and again I would be irresistibly reminded, not of a cuckoo-clock but of one of those wooden weather-prophets where an old woman comes out for fine weather, an old man for rain. Only, here, the old man and the old woman were coming out at the same time.

I hope I have given the impression that they gave

me—that of two aging people, a trifle quaint, more than a trifle ridiculous, but, beyond all that, essential to each other. For that is an important thing for a young man to see, now and then; it restores his faith in the cosmos, though he may not realize it at the time. The first taste of real life, for the young, has its frightening moments: one suddenly discovers that actual people, not in books, commit suicide in gas-filled bedrooms because they would rather die than live; one discovers that others really enjoy being vicious and make a success of it. Then, instinctively, one clings to the first security at hand, like a swimmer to an overturned boat. I wouldn't have thought it possible when I first met them, but one of the things I clung to was the De Laceys.

And as I became more and more drawn into the endless spider-web of the work of Angela Poe, I began to realize how much she owed to her husband. Oh, he could never have written anything—be sure of that. But he knew the well-worn paths of stock-melodrama in all their spurious vitality, he knew when a thing would "go." I know because, inevitably, I followed one book of Angela Poe's from conception to delivery. It was not any better, speaking from the point of view of letters, for his suggestions; for it was perfectly terrible. But it worked; it was Angela Poe; the sun rose over the cardboard mountains at precisely the right instant. And every one of his criticisms helped it on.

Then one day, when I came to The Eyrie, she had a touch of influenza and was in bed. He was obviously worried about her, but insisted on my staying to tea because I always had. I had my own worries at the moment and was glad for a breath of serenity. All his courtliness came into play and he told me a couple of mild theatrical jokes, but you could feel his eyes wandering, his ears listening for any sound from upstairs. If he had not been worried, I wonder—but worry makes people confidential. I thought it a good chance to congratulate him on his part in her work. He listened abstractedly, but I could see he was pleased.

"Glad you think so, my dear fellow, glad you think so," he said. "Often I have said to myself, 'No! This time, old boy, let genius burn unhampered! Who are you to profane the—um—the sacred flame?' But genius —even genius—must have its trammels to bring it down to the level of us workaday folk. And, as the— er—appreciative trammel, perhaps I have played my part. I hope so," he said, quite simply. "She means a great deal to me."

"I know that, sir," I said, but he wasn't listening.

"Yes," he said, "we mean a great deal to each other. I hope she's taking those drops; you know, she hates drops. Yes, indeed, my dear fellow. Our first meeting was like a flash of lightning." He stared at me solemnly. "I wish that Mr. Wedge, her first husband, could have understood it better. But he was an earth-bound soul. He could not comprehend a marriage of true minds."

"Mrs. De Lacey was married before?" I said, and I could not keep the shrillness of surprise from my voice.

"My dear boy," said Mr. De Lacey, looking surprised in his turn, "I forgot that you did not know. She was Mrs. Marvin Wedge when we first met," he said, reflectively, "and beautiful as a just-unfolding rose."

A thousand unphrasable questions rose to my lips and died there. For Mr. De Lacey continued.

"I used to call her the Rose of Goshen," he said. "Goshen, Indiana, dear boy—I was—er—resting there at the time, after my tour with Barrett. I played both grave-diggers and Charles, the wrestler. Charles, the wrestler, is not a large part, but one can make it tell. It was hard to return to Goshen, after that, but there are financial necessities. But as soon as I met Angela, I knew that I had been led. Wedge was—um—proprietor of our hay-and-feed store—rather older than I am; he used to chase me and call me Slats when I was a boy. But I had not known Angela before. She came from Zook Springs."

He paused and stared at me with his Hamlet eyes. I could see the whole scene so plainly—the dusty streets of the small town and the young, down-at-heels actor, back home discouraged, after his trial flight. I could see Angela Poe, forty years ago, in the simple gingham dress of one of her heroines. It must have all been so innocent and high-minded—innocent and unreal as a stage melodrama, even to the cynical figure of the burly hay-and-feed merchant. I could see him, somehow, in his shirt sleeves, roaring with laughter at the timid respectful speeches of—but the boy could not have been called Everard De Lacey, then. And yet, Romance had triumphed in Goshen. I wondered how.

"So Miss Poe was divorced—divorced Mr. Wedge, I mean," I said.

My companion looked curiously shocked. "Dear boy," he said, with dignity, "never once, in any of her books, has Angela Poe drawn a divorced woman."

"I know," I said feebly, though I didn't. "But in real life—"

"The books of Angela Poe are real life," said Mr. De Lacey, crushingly. Then he relented. "No," he said, "Mr. Wedge is not living. He passed over."

"Passed over?"

"Within a year of my return to Goshen. As a matter of fact, he was murdered," he said, with his Hamlet eyes fixed upon me so sternly that, for an instant, I had the horrific idea that I was about to listen to an incredible confession. But I was not. "By a tramp," he said at last. "In his feed store. For purposes of robbery. It was very upsetting for Angela."

I opened and shut my mouth, but no words came forth.

"Yes, really very upsetting. I was glad I could be with her," he said, naïvely. "Though, naturally, we were not married till later. She was married in a tailored dress, but she held a bouquet of orange-blossoms and lilies-of-the-valley. I insisted upon that," he said, with some pride.

"And the tramp?" I said with youth's delight in horrors. "Was he—"

"Oh, he was never found," boomed Mr. De Lacey abstractedly, as a small sound came from upstairs, "but Angela bore up wonderfully. She is a wonderful woman." He rose. "If you'll just excuse me one moment, my dear fellow—"

"I must catch my train," I said. "But thank you, Mr. De Lacey. And be assured I shall respect your confidence," I said, trying to equal his manner.

He nodded seriously. "Yes, yes," he said. "Perhaps

I should have said nothing—but, well, my dear boy, we have grown to know you and value you, in your visits to The Eyrie. And they must not cease with this book—my dear fellow, no. Only, I would not bring up the matter in talking with Miss Poe. She does not like to dwell upon those days; they were not happy ones for her. Mr. Wedge was really—" Words failed him. "Mr. Wedge was really not a very sensitive man," he said.

I assured him of my entire understanding and took my leave. But, all the way home, certain thoughts kept revolving in my mind. I was not surprised that Providence, in the shape of a burglarious tramp, had seen fit to remove the insensitive Mr. Wedge. That was just the sort of thing that happened to Angela Poes. But why had she ever married him, in the first place, and how, having touched real life in her own person, had she been able to forget it so completely in her books? But those were the sorts of questions one could not ask.

And yet in the end I asked them, with youth's temerity. I asked them because I had come to like her—to like them both. And when you like people, you are apt to be more honest with them—that is the trouble.

We had planned to have a little celebration—the three of us—when the book was actually published. But it was not I who put the first copy in her hands. I brought out the dummy and the jacket. That particular Saturday Mr. De Lacey had made one of his rare excursions to New York. I was glad to find her alone, as a matter of fact, for I thought I had noticed a slight constraint between us since my conversation with him. At least, I was conscious that I knew a secret—and kept

wondering if she knew that I knew. And I meant to
tell her, in all honesty, how much the security and peace
of The Eyrie had meant to me through the year. I was
only waiting a good opening. But, naturally, we started
by talking publishing. Her comments were shrewd and
I enjoyed them—though the influenza had left its mark,
and she looked frailer than before. And then suddenly
she startled me by asking what I really thought of her
work.

Six months before, I would merely have buttered
her, buttered her with a trowel, for the good of Thrushwood, Collins, and let it go at that. But now I had come
to like her—and, after all, one has one's convictions.
It wasn't the best butter, and she knew it. And mo-
notonously, relentlessly, in her small, gracious voice,
she kept pressing the point. That should have warned
me, but it didn't. If authors were not megalomaniacs,
no books would ever get written. But I forgot that first
rule of publishing and floundered on.

"And yet, Mr. Robbins, I can feel that you don't
really believe in me—you don't really believe in Angela
Poe," she would say, gently and maddeningly, till at
last with the rashness of youth I took my courage in
both hands.

"It isn't that, Miss Poe," I stammered, "but if you'd
only once—why don't you? It mightn't please your
audience, but a woman of your experiences—of your
life—"

"My life?" she said, with dignity. "And what do you
know of my life, young man?"

"Oh, nothing," I said, blundering from bad to
worse, "but Mr. De Lacey said you both came from

small towns—well, now, a *real* novel about an American small town—"

"So Everard has been telling tales—naughty boy! I must scold him," said Angela Poe brightly. But the brightness was all in the voice. I suddenly had the impression that she thought me a tedious young fool and wished me away. I began to long for Mr. De Lacey's return. But though I strained my ears I heard no echo of his rich boom from any corner of the house.

"Oh," I said, "please don't. They were *such* delightful stories. He—he told me you were married in a traveling dress."

"Dear Everard!" said Angela Poe. "He remembers everything. A dove-gray silk, with white collar and cuffs. I looked very pretty in it. And you think I might make a story of that, Mr. Robbins?"

"We have always hoped—your memoirs—the readers of Angela Poe—" I said.

She shook her head, decisively. "I shall never write my memoirs," she said. "Authors' memoirs never sell, you know—not really. The publishers think they are going to, but they don't. And then, it would lift the veil. Do you know who I am, young man? Do you know that people write me from all over the country, every day? They write me asking me what to do with their lives. And I tell them," she said, sitting up very straight. "I tell them. Very often they do it, too. Because I'm Angela Poe—and they know my picture and my books. So they can write as they might to Another," and she bowed her head for an instant. "And that is not bad for a woman who writes what you think trash, Mr. Robbins. But I always knew I could do it," she ended, unexpectedly. "I always knew I could do it. But things were put in my way."

I could not leave, for it was not my train-time yet, but I began to feel more and more uncomfortable. There was something odd in the sweet, tinkling voice— the note of a fanatic egoism almost religious in its sincerity. I was used to the egoism of authors, but this was in another key.

She passed a handkerchief across her lips for a moment. "Dear, dear, I forget so many things since my illness," she said. "What were we talking about? Oh, yes, you were suggesting an idea to me—a story about an American small town. Do you know them, Mr. Robbins?"

She asked the question so suddenly and fiercely that I almost said no instead of yes. Then she relaxed.

"But of course," she said, a trifle primly, "you do know them. You know how cramped one's cultural opportunities are. And how one is mocked, perhaps, for striving after them? Or perhaps you do not know that?"

It was a rhetorical question, obviously. So I nodded, hoping against hope for the sound of Mr. De Lacey's footfall in the hall.

"Even so," she said sweetly, "you are not a member of the female sex. And they are more easily wounded than gentlemen think. Even Everard has wounded me now and then—oh, not intentionally and I soon forgave him," she said, with a regal gesture. "Still, he has wounded." She was, evidently, talking more to herself than to me, now, but the fact did not increase my comfort.

"I could have forgiven Marvin everything else," she said, "his drinking, his unbridled passions, his coarse jests. That is woman's mission—to submit and forgive. He made jokes about my housekeeping, too. And it would have cost him only eighty dollars to publish my poems. I had the sweetest wreath of field daisies for the cover. I thought he would be a way to higher things; after all, one has so little opportunity in a small town and the feed store was quite successful, financially. But I was mistaken," and she sighed, gently. I was now past wishing for Mr. De Lacey's appearance; I only wished for my train to roar into the room and bear me away. But such things do not happen, unfortunately.

"But I never thought of divorce," the mild, tinkling voice went on. "Never. It crossed my mind, once or twice, but I firmly put it aside. I have always been glad of that. I don't think he really *cared*," she said, opening her pansy eyes widely. "But he might have hurt Everard badly—he was such a very strong man. Sometimes, in the early days of our marriage, he used to carry me around the room on one arm. It frightened me, rather, but I always submitted and forgave. It was always so dusty in the store, too. It used to make me sneeze and then he would laugh. He laughed when Everard read Shakespeare to me. I sneezed that evening, as I was wiping the handle of the hatchet, but no one heard me."

"As you were what?" I said, and my voice was thin and high.

"I suppose it wasn't necessary," she said thoughtfully. "It would be, now, with the fingerprints, but they were quite stupid people and we knew little of fingerprints then. But it seemed tidier—I'd let it fall on the

floor and the floor was dirty. They never really swept
the store. He was sitting with his back to me, reading
my poems and laughing. I'd hidden the new ones, but
he'd found them and broken open the drawer. The
hatchet was an old one—they used to cut the wire on
the feed bales with it. You know, he didn't say anything
at all. He was still laughing and trying to get out of the
chair. But he wasn't quick enough. I burned the money
in the stove and nobody even asked me about the dress.
They say salts of lemon will take out blood stains *immediately*," she murmured. "But it seemed better not
to try though it was quite a nice dress."

"But weren't you ever—didn't they ever—" I
babbled.

"Why, Mr. Robbins, of course," she said, with perfect placidity, "you have no *idea* of the petty malice and
gossip of a small town. But I was in bed, you know,
when they came to tell me—in bed with a bad cold.
Any emotional strain always gives me a very bad cold—
I had quite a bad one the day Everard and I were
married. And everybody knew he used to sit up in the
feed store till all hours, drinking and reading vile
atheist books like that horrid Colonel Ingersoll's. The
old cats said it was because he was afraid to go home.
Afraid of me!" she said with perfect ingenuousness.
"There's no limit to what people will say. Why, they
even talked about Everard, though everybody knew he
was driving a load of vegetables to market with his
father. I thought of that before I went to the store."

"And yet," I said, "you lived in Goshen—you didn't
marry Mr. De Lacey till a year later—"

"A year and a day," she corrected. "That seemed

more fitting. But I went into half mourning at the end of six months. It's rather soon, I know, but I thought I might. As long as I was to be engaged to Everard," and a faint blush colored her cheeks. "I told him I could discuss nothing of the sort while I was still in full mourning and he appreciated my wishes—Everard has always been so considerate. At first, I thought the time would hang very heavy on my hands. But, as a matter of fact, it passed quite quickly. I was writing my first novel," she said, in a hushed voice.

I do not know yet how I got out of the house—I hope with decency. But I had left The Eyrie behind and was well along on my two-mile tramp to the station before I really came to myself. It was her last words— and the picture they gave me—that sent the cold, authentic shudder down my spine. I kept wondering wildly how many successful authors were murderers or murderesses and why the police did not arrest them all. For I could see the whole story and fill in every detail. It was fatally plausible, even to Angela Poe's primness. I could even believe that if the unfortunate Mr. Wedge had paid a printer eighty dollars, he might have lived. For there are egoisms which it is not safe to mock or dam up—if you do, you are tempting the explosion of primal forces.

And then, when I had almost reached the station, I suddenly began to laugh—the healing laughter of sanity. For the whole thing was ridiculous and Angela Poe had taken an impeccable revenge. I had told her what I thought of her work—and subtly, tinklingly, convincingly, she had made me swallow the most prepos-

terous farrago of nonsense she could think of; swallow
it whole. And, in doing so, she had proved her powers
as a story-teller past cavil. But, once away from the monotonous spell of her voice, it was merely impossible to
think of her as a murderess, and yet more impossible
to think of Everard De Lacey as an accomplice. For
accomplice he must have been—after the fact if not
before it. Or else, she had hidden the truth from him all
these years—and that was impossible, too.

For a second, I even thought of turning back to The
Eyrie and humbly admitting to its mistress my folly and
my defeat. But my train, after all, was due in fifteen
minutes, and I had a dinner engagement in New York.
I would write her a letter instead—she would like a
letter. I walked up and down the station platform, com-
posing orotund phrases in my mind.

The late afternoon train from New York arrived
some six minutes before my own, and I was pleased to
see it disgorge the statuesque form of Everard De Lacey.
He shook hands with me and boomed apologies for
missing my visit. "And how did you leave Miss Poe?"
he said, anxiously. "I have been away since early
morning."

"Oh, she was perfectly splendid—I never saw her
looking better," I said, warmed by a glow of secret
laughter. "We talked for hours—she'll tell you."

"That's good—that's good, my dear fellow—you re-
lieve me greatly," he said, while his eyes roved for the
carriage that had not yet arrived. "Jenks is tardy, today," he said. Then he gave me a quick look. "You
didn't happen to mention what you told me in our little
chat when she was so ill?" he said.

"Mention it?" I said with a broad grin. "Oh, yes, indeed."

He seemed curiously relieved. "I am much indebted," he said. "Then you really do feel—and it means something coming from you—that I am of some genuine help to her? To her books, I mean—her career?"

"I do, indeed," I said, though I was now puzzled.

"Excellent," he boomed. "Excellent." He took me by the lapel with the old actor's gesture. "You see," he said, "oh, it's foolish of me, I know—and we are old now, of course. But every now and then I have the feeling that I may not really be indispensable to her. And it worries me greatly."

For the instant, as he said it, I saw fear look out of his eyes. It was not an ignoble fear, but he must have lived with it a long time.

I did not go back to The Eyrie; indeed, I did not go back to Thrushwood, Collins. To do the latter without doing the former would have required explanations and I did not feel like giving them. Instead, I changed my boarding-house, and went to work as a salesman of aluminum-ware. And, after six months of that, I went back to Central City and the place in my father's cement business that had been waiting for me. For I had come to the decision that I was not made for New York, nor the life of letters; I did not have the self-confidence of Angela Poe.

Once, during the six months, I thought I saw Mr. De Lacey on the street, but he did not see me and I fled him. And, naturally, though I tried to escape them,

I saw advertisements of the last completed novel of
Angela Poe. She died when I had been three months in
Central City, and when I read that she was survived by
her husband, the actor, Everard De Lacey, I felt as if
a weight had been lifted from my breast. But he only
survived her a few months. He missed her too much,
I suppose, and some ties are enduring. I should like to
have asked him one question, only one, and now I shall
never know. He certainly played Shakespearian rôles—
and there must have been quite a period, after they
left Goshen, when he was playing. In fact the obituary
mentions Othello and Hamlet. But there is another
rôle—and I wonder if he ever played it and what he
made of it. I think you know the one I mean.

THE TREASURE OF VASCO GOMEZ

THE brig was already a white-sailed toy on blue waters. Soon enough she would be hull down on the horizon, then nothing at all. No man among her crew would ever set foot again willingly on the island where that crew had marooned its captain. And Vasco Gomez, lost and alone on a pin-point of earth set down among waves that seemed to come from the other end of the world, stretched out his arms and laughed loudly for the first time since they had set him ashore.

He was known as a clever man and a lucky captain in every waterside tavern where the freebooters gathered. But this marooning of himself on a lost and uncharted island was the cleverest and luckiest exploit in a career that had held little mercy and no noteworthy failures.

It had not been an easy task. No, even for Vasco Gomez, it had not been easy. His own name for good fortune had worked against him, as had the quite justifiable fear his reputation inspired in the most hard-bitten of free companions. It had taken untiring craft and skill to bring even a crew of wolves to the point of mutiny against Vasco Gomez. And even greater art to see to it that these wolves, once roused, should maroon a living man where he wished to be, and not merely cast a hacked body overside.

But it had been done, and well done—his luck had held. He was alive—he was here. He had taken the first huge step toward his kingdom. And it was time, for, though he was still as strong in body as any three men of the crew that had deserted him, he knew by certain warnings that he had entered middle age.

Middle age. The drying up of the life in a man, the gradual slowing of the heart. And yet, a man stronger and more cunning than the run of men might still manage to have his cake and eat it too—to get off scot-free and whistling—even to grow old. A man like him, for example.

And more than scot-free—rich—if he knew a secret. Rich. His eyes gleamed as he rolled the word on his tongue. He stared around him, measuring the extent of his riches.

They had left him without fresh water, but not a hundred paces inland were a spring and a stream. They had left him without victual, but he knew this island of old. There was provision for the crew of a frigate on the island; the unceasing provision of nature.

They had left him without tools or weapons, except for the sheath-knife hidden in his boot. But he had flint and steel, and the axes in the second cache should not have rusted by now, for they lay in dry soil. For that matter, if worst came to worst, he could hollow a boat by burning out a tree-bole. It might take time—but what was time to him, now? There was no time in this solitude—the measurements of time had ceased. There was only one long hour, his hour, the hour of his kingdom. He felt the first wave of it wash over him, peacefully, slowly. His heart rose in his body to meet it, his lips drank it in.

"A long time on the way—you've been a long time on the way here, Vasco Gomez," he thought to himself. But it was over now. Pedro's treasure lay buried where it had always lain, not ten feet down, between the rock and the palm. He had not yet seen it with his eyes, but he knew that it was still there. For seven years he had carried the secret, locked under his ribs, closer to him than his heart.

He exhaled a long breath, staring back through the years. He was the only man alive who knew.

There had been others who had an inkling. He had made it his business to find them and see that they got no further. There was a legend still, but a legend that few believed. And for a while, of course, there had been Pedro.

He saw the dark cruelty of that insatiable face swim up at him, in memory, like something seen through a wraith of sea fog. He smiled. Pedro was long since turned into leather at Execution Dock. He had not been able to come back, though he'd tried. But Vasco Gomez had come back. And, from the moment that he had landed on the island this noon, the treasure had been Pedro's no longer, but his treasure—the treasure of Vasco Gomez.

The men who had actually buried the spoil were safe enough. Their bones lay in the second cache with the tools of their labor. They would not disturb him. The one thing that did disturb him was the thought

that the bags and chests that held the treasure might
have rotted. In that case he would have to make new
ones, somehow—one could not put to sea with half a
boat-load of naked gold.

Half a boat-load at the least; there might be more.
It would be interesting to see the full extent of the loot.
He had only caught hasty glimpses of it by the bad light
of the lanterns, on that night that was burned in his
memory. But there would be enough for his wants—
enough at the least to buy fat days and fine feathers—
or even God's pardon, perhaps, weighed out in masses
and candles. Enough to buy love and hate—and age
for Gomez.

And all that remained to be done was so simple. A
week, two, to lift the treasure. Two months, three
months, to make a boat and provision it. Longer, perhaps, for he would not attempt the sea journey in the
stormy season, but what was time, now he had all time
to spend? Then a sixty-mile sail in an open boat to
that other island, a daring exploit enough for landsmen,
but child's play for Vasco Gomez. There were tamed
Indians on that other island; he knew them, he had
been careful to make them his friends. Then a little
policy—a little murder, perhaps—another ship—a little
intrigue with the mainland—he knew the fellow who
had the Governor's ear and how to use him. And after
that, anything: a king's coat to wear, a king's commission to carry—"Our well-beloved Vasco Gomez"—a
decent estate at home, a little respectability, a little repentance, an altar of rose marble in an old cathedral
to hold God strictly to the bargain,—and not only this

world but the next one flung open for the penitent buccaneer.

All for gold—all there to be bought by gold. Nothing existed that could not be bought by gold.

He came out of his muse and stared seaward again, eagerly. The brig was only a speck, now; soon the abrupt night would come down. He must gather wood, make a fire, knock over a crab or two, find water, devise a bed. Tomorrow he would start building a hut for himself. Perhaps he might even finish his boat before he lifted the treasure. The treasure could wait—it would not run away. There was no time on earth that could take him from his treasure now.

It was one morning, when Vasco Gomez was busily at work upon his almost completed boat, that he first felt himself definitely alone.

To him it was a strange sensation. So strange, in fact, that when he received the first impact of it, the knife which he was using dropped from his hand as if something had struck him on the wrist. Then, after a moment, he picked up the knife again. But the feeling persisted.

His life, to say the least of it, had been an active and a crowded one. He had dealt with men and women and they had dealt with him, but never without physical impact. If he were to gaze back through the last score of years, he would hardly be able to find a single waking moment, even in shipwreck, when he had been entirely alone, divided from the world. He was alone now.

He was alone, and with that knowledge came

thought. He was not used to thinking—Vasco Gomez—least of all to thinking about himself.

The work he was doing took up some of his thought but not all of it—not enough. Before, in the pauses of action, there had always been the treasure to think about, to plan for. Now the treasure was here. That space in his mind was suddenly filled by other, unaccustomed thoughts.

"Who is this fellow, Vasco Gomez?" he found himself thinking after a while, beset with a queer fear.

"Vasco Gomez? Why, that's you—that's me—you're here, man—you're making a boat!" He said the words aloud; they comforted him. But after a while he began to think again.

Vasco Gomez—he certainly knew who Vasco Gomez was! He saw him fighting, drinking, kissing a wench's shoulder, climbing a ship's red side with a long knife bitten in his teeth. A big, scarred bull of a man, solid and awe inspiring.

But that wasn't Vasco Gomez any more. Vasco Gomez was here. Vasco Gomez was here—and entirely alone.

He felt himself diminish as he thought the words—diminish as the brig had diminished. The brig, too, had been solid and bulky at first—then smaller—then a puppet—a speck on the sea. So now with him. He saw a little man on a toy island—an ant-size figure set down on a spoonful of land in the midst of blue immensities.

His face dripped with sweat, though he had not been working hard. The rasp of his knife on the wood made an acute and lonely sound. It seemed to him that he could hear that small sound go out and out, through infinities of water and air, and still meet no other sound that could be its fellow—and still—meet—no—other —sound.

His mind righted itself with a jerk. No, he had the clue to his thinking. He had been on the island for very nearly five months, as he reckoned. Well, he knew what happened sometimes to men so marooned, the look they got in their eyes, the voices they thought they heard.

He had not expected this to happen to him; he was too strong, too clever. But if it were so, so be it—he now knew where the danger lay and could guard against it. As soon as he had settled this in his mind, he felt restored. The sky and sea shrank back to their proper proportions.

He had hardly expected to finish the boat in less than ten days, but a fury of work took hold of him. While he toiled, he could not diminish—the sky and sea held their places. He found himself now and then trying over sentences in the jargon the Indians spoke. He caught himself listening thirstily as the sentences fell from his mouth. Only they lacked something—they lacked the note of a voice that was not his own.

In four days the boat was finished and afloat in the cove.

He had been gathering provisions during the last months. He had even made a keg for his water. It took no time at all to put these aboard or to rig his improvised sail. He wondered at himself, while he labored, that he labored so feverishly. Surely it did not matter if he set sail in a week or a month, now the season of storms was past. But, in these last days, time was no longer the one long hour that belonged to him and his treasure. It had become again a sifting of hasty grains through the blue hour-glass of the sky—and each grain that fell seemed to steal a little strength from his heart.

He stood up at last, hot and sweating. Night had fallen. All was ready now, except for the actual lifting of the treasure—and it was not sensible to begin that work at night. But he woke before the dawn.

When he had wakened, he lay there a moment without moving; entirely happy. He had known many women in his life, but today was the day of his true nuptials.

The sun was sinking when he uncovered the final chest. He struck a great blow with his axe at a rusty lock and stared. It was the bridal. The gold seemed to leap up at him, from the ground.

Next moment he was down among it, both fists were full. He felt as if he had been running, his breath came and went in the runner's gasp. How good it was to touch, how thick and heavy and smooth—better than any woman's shoulder—better than bread!

Slowly, luxuriously, he broke open the other chests. It was all there—idol and pyx—blood-ruby and rough cut emerald—the grandee's studded scabbard—the soft masks of virgin gold that the heathen priests had worn. He had dreamed of it as a king's ransom—he smiled at the poverty of his dreams.

The abrupt night came, shut down, but he did not stir. He did not light a fire, he did not go back to his hut. Time had resumed its long hour—time was not. He lay all night in the pit, he was perfectly happy.

The dawn came and he rose, but not as he had

risen twenty-four hours ago. That morning, when he got up, he was still poor and an adventurer; this morning he got up rich, with the cares of riches.

He laughed when he thought of his furious labor of the last few days. Time was his friend, not his enemy, there was no need to fight it. The boat was ready—put the gold aboard—cast off—and everything else would follow, as the ship's wake follows the ship.

The business of the Indians first. They were his friends, but even so they would not do all he wanted without reward. Well, there he could get off cheaply—they hardly knew the uses of the yellow metal. But then there was the Governor's friend and the Governor himself—and he frowned. Everything could be bought with a price, no doubt, but, even for the rich, certain things came high.

He knew, none better, what palms would have to be greased.

If it had but matched with the poverty of his dreams —even then, he saw the difficulty. But this king's ran-som—why even the king himself might want a finger in the pie!

Yesterday, he would gladly have given half the treasure to get off safe with the other half. But now he had seen it and touched it.

A dull anger began to rise in him. What business had all these strangers, meddling with his treasure? They hadn't schemed for it or found it.

Now he saw them, one and all, roosted around the edge of the pit like vultures—the Indians, the Governors, the lawyers and courtiers, the women with thirsty eyes, a bishop even, a red-hatted cardinal. Yes, even the

Church itself, even God Himself exacted a portion of the treasure! They came closer, they stretched out their hands, bit by bit, drop by drop, then bled him of his precious gold. They gave him empty, useless things in return—a kiss—a patent of nobility—an altar of rose-marble—but the bleeding never ceased. At last, an old man crouched over the pitiful remnant of a king's ransom—and even then there were creatures coming to bleed him anew. He waved his arm in the air to drive off the vision.

Decidedly, he would have to revise his plans. He hurriedly tried to think of the least—the very least—he must spend to be safe. He pared his bribes down and down—and yet the total appalled him.

Then the mere passage of time brought with it a certain balm. After all, he did not have to set sail till he wished. He would eat and drink and sleep and play with his treasure—and in time some perfect plan might come to him.

The hours slipped into days, the days into weeks. One evening, notching his calendar-stick, he realized with a start that it was nearly two months since he had first uncovered the treasure. It seemed impossible, but it was true. Well, Vasco Gomez, he thought with an odd lethargy, it is time you were setting off, my friend—tomorrow we will begin.

The morrow came, the sea seemed calm as a mill pond. And yet, far down to the south—was not that the edge of a cloud? He shook himself impatiently—was he losing his mind?—a sailor and afraid of a speck of white? With dragging steps, he turned toward his boat.

Then a rescuing thought came to him—the bags for the treasure. The old bags were rotten—he would have to devise new bags, new chests. He felt at peace again immediately; he spent the morning happily, selecting the wood for his chests.

They were finished at last, but not before the stormy season. Vasco Gomez was no madman—he would not put out with such a cargo till the storms were done.

Meanwhile, with his treasure about him, Vasco Gomez lived many lives. Up till now, his life had left him little time for imagination beyond the needs of the day, but now his imagination flowered like a great poppy—his dreams spread a scarlet cloth for his bare feet to tread.

At first they were the simple visions and Elysiums of any sailor—enough food and drink, the easy girls of the ports—but as time went on they grew more elaborate, more refined, more clearly intense. He feasted delicately; music played while he feasted; the wines, poured for him, were the rarest of their kind. He did not gorge or lie drunken. When he went to take the air, outriders went before him; the king called him cousin and kissed him on the cheek. And when he returned to his palace, it was no girl of the ports whose lips were turned to him, but a king's daughter, a mermaid, a creature of light and foam. Sometimes she was dark as the soft nights, sometimes golden as the first spear of morning. It did not matter—she was whatever he wished, she was all women he had known, yet she was always new.

Then his power broadened, his shadow increased. He made wars and calmed them, raised one nation and put down another, appeased famine, tamed the seas

The king no longer called him cousin,—he threw the king bones from his table and the king was grateful. Men whispered among themselves that only the protected of heaven could cast such a shade. And, indeed, to this man came messengers not wholly of this world.

Gomez, walking one morning when the season of storms had passed, came suddenly upon a boat, beached high and dry, protected by a rude shelter. For a moment he stared at it without recognition. Then he remembered—it was his boat, and he would never find better weather for his journey.

He looked the boat over carefully. The storms had not touched her—she was seaworthy still. He launched her in the cove again. Then he went slowly to the place where his chests were kept, and loaded them aboard. Only one thing remained, to fill the chests with the treasure. He dropped a rose-noble in one chest—it made a queer sound on the wood. Then he started for the rest of the treasure.

Two hours later, he sat in the boat, with his head in his hands. He had built his boat too small for the weight she was to carry.

Well, he must build another boat, that was all. But, as he thought this, he knew that even if he could build a boat big enough to bear that weight of gold, the boat would take more than one man to handle.

He could ferry what he now had aboard to the other island, bury it, come back for more. That meant a thousand risks with every voyage. He had lived with his treasure too long. He could not bear to bury a part of it elsewhere and leave it.

Well then, he would put it back in Pedro's old cache, taking only enough away with him to make a fresh start. Hire a ship—come back—to let other men into his secret—to go shares from the very first in what was his alone.

He thought for a long time, wearily revolving plans in his head. He knew that he could follow none of them. There must be another plan. All things were to be bought, if one had gold enough.

He lay all night in the boat, thinking. Morning came at length, and his riddle was still unsolved, but for a while he had ceased to think of it.

He had gone back, for a moment, to one of his many dreams. It was quite a simple dream and made but a poor show among his more ornate visions, yet he liked to dream it, at times.

He saw a tumbledown wine-shop with a dried bush over the door, on the crest of a hill road in Portugal. There was a girl in the wine-shop, a girl with fresh lips and hair as black as her comb.

She had a soldier for a lover, and a proud heart. Gomez was poor and a thief—it was in the days before he went to sea. They drove him away from the wine-shop often enough, but he came back to it. Once the soldier beat him, he took the beating with shut lips. The girl looked on, smiling. When at last Gomez saw that it was useless, he left the soldier in a mountain gully with a knife in his back and ran away before they caught him. Then his real life began.

In Gomez' dream, however, there was no soldier. There was only the girl, and himself as he had been at that time. But she was no longer scornful and they smiled at each other between the kisses.

The dream seemed very real to him, this time. He leaned over the side of the boat and stared at the water idly.

There was a face, reflected in the water. He observed it as he might the face of a stranger at first.

His own face was the face of the boy in his dream— a young, sharp face, ready for good or evil, but as yet not deeply marked with either—the face of youth. This was the withered face of an old man.

Slowly and wonderingly, he passed his hands over his body, regarded his legs, his arms. He had not looked at himself for a long time. But this scarecrow was he. "You've come a long way, Gomez," he muttered.

A new picture came to him, out of his other dreams. The splendid Vasco Gomez, the lord of the treasure, in his fine bed alone. The breath came faintly from the lips of the dying man. On one side of the bed was seated a priest, on the other a lawyer, but the dying eyes saw neither crucifix nor testament. They were staring ahead into darkness, trying to see something they could not fix upon. Outside the door, a servant kept back a silent throng—the throng of the claimants, the inheritors. A black-gloved personage waited in a corner, without impatience. Every man's end.

If some miracle—some incredible bribing of God— could set him ashore on the mainland, with his treasure! Even so, there were only so many lives in the world to live. And, already, he had lived those lives. If not in the body, yet very completely, very thoroughly. The body could do no more for him, the treasure could do no more. All but the one picture of the girl and the wine-shop—and that no treasure could repurchase, for it belonged to a past year.

Vasco Gómez braced one hand in the other hand till the muscles in his back stood out. He had always been a strong man, a clever and wary fighter. Now he must fight again, without ruth or scruple or weakness, as in the old days. But this time the adversary was invisible.

The next morning found him walking the beach, still fighting. Now and then he looked out to sea. It was very calm and clear. Then he realized that even the sea was a servant of his adversary, and turned his eyes away.

He sat down in the sand at last, arms lax, heart and body worn out. He was very tired but he would not give up the fight while breath was in him.

Everything to be bought with gold, he repeated to himself doggedly. One cannot fail with money—everything with a price in money—men—governors—kings—old age—God Himself, at the last. . . .

The wave came from afar—he could hear it coming. He braced himself to meet it, but it was too late. It was no wave of the sea, the sea was quiet enough. This wave gathered—rose—burst over him. He felt the shock, and trembled. He was beaten now.

Everything to be bought with gold, up to God Himself. Not without exception. You could buy much. You could buy candles and masses. But God, at the last, was not to be bought. That was the truth.

Slowly, without revulsion or outcry, for he was beaten, he lay on the sand and felt the cells of his body drink in this truth. After a long while a little stirring of peace began to move in his breast.

He rose at last. He felt weak when he had risen, and when he moved, his steps were the steps of an old man. But he would have strength enough for the work that remained.

He went back to the little cove where his boat was moored, and stood for a moment gazing at the water. Yes, that was the place. He had swum there often but never yet found bottom. The bottom must be very deep.

He took the piece of his treasure nearest to hand—it was one of the golden masks—and let it fall from his hand into the water. It shimmered as it went down, then that too was lost. He gave a sharp sigh, stooped stiffly and picked up the grandee's sword.

At last only one rose-noble was left. He weighed it in his hand a moment, as curiously as if it had been a sea-shell. It had a man's face on one side—the man had a nose like Pedro's. Strange, to put a man's face on a thing like that! He let it fall—it shone through green glooms and was gone.

Up till now, each piece that he had let fall had seemed to carry a small portion of his soul with it as it sank. But now, when there was no more treasure to drown, he felt otherwise. His soul could be divided no longer. It was either here in his body or down under the water with the treasure—but it did not matter, for, wherever it was, it was not in morsels.

He stared at the water anew with mild curiosity. A fish was swimming where the rose-noble had shimmered.

After a while, he wandered back to the beach and sat looking out toward the sea. For a moment he thought of his lost battle, but not with pain or shame. He had fought well and long. Now the fight was over. He would not fight again. There had been only one battle after all—it had lasted all his life—but he was done with it now.

He could not have eaten food for a long time. A day, perhaps more than a day? He could not remember. But when he thought of food, the thought revolted him. He was hungry now, but he was not hungry for bread.

The night fell and found him still on the beach. He thought of going back to his hut, but did not do so. Instead he moved farther up the beach and ensconced himself in a sort of niche, where one boulder overhung another. The bottom boulder was raised—it was out of the way of the landcrabs—the top one was almost a roof. He sat there, with his back propped by the rear of the niche, his hands on his knees. The night air was cool and pleasant, the stars had come out. He looked out over the sea and felt the cool air on his face. There was a horizon there, hidden away in that gulf of starry darkness, but he was not seeking that horizon.

After some hours, he moved a little and spoke. "You've come a long way, Vasco Gomez," he said anew, with a certain touch of affirmation. Nothing replied to the words.

Some eight months later, H.M.S. *Vixen,* sloop-of-war, blown out of her course by contrary gales, sent a boat ashore to the island in the hope of finding fresh water and fruit for a crew already in danger of scurvy.

The lieutenant in charge of the landing-party proceeded with all due precaution at first. But when the water-casks had been filled, and it was evident that the island was uninhabited, he allowed his men some liberty, and himself strolled down the beach.

It was a pretty beach and seemed to encircle the island completely. He had got this far in his musings when a shout from one of the men farther down the beach made him clap his hand to his cutlass. Then he saw that the man was standing up and waving his arms. He walked hurriedly.

The buzzing group of sailors fell back before him. He found himself abruptly face to face with a stranger. The man was seated in a species of natural niche made by two boulders, his hands on his knees, in an attitude of contemplation, his eyes staring out to sea. Some rags of clothing still clung to him and the crabs had not even touched him, but his whole body was the color and texture of leather. He must have been dead for a number of months—what remained was a mummy that the sun· and the wind had embalmed between them. Yet the features were quite recognizable—there was even an expression upon them—an expression that the lieutenant had seen before. He touched his lips with his handkerchief, remembering the last time he had seen it. No, even the work of sun and wind could not account entirely for that emaciation.

A sailor was at his elbow, pulling a forelock.

"Do you know who that is, sir?" he said, in an eager voice. "It's Gomez, the bloody pirate, sir—I seen him before and so has Tom—and serve him right, the Portugee devil, that's what I say!"

"Yes," said the lieutenant, hardly listening, "it may well be he. We heard he had been marooned and—"

"Marooned is right, sir," said the sailor, "the bloody villain! Even his own crew got sick of him at the last and—" He leaned forward as if to spit upon the leathered image.

"Keep your wits about you, my man!" said the lieutenant, sternly, and the sailor retired. Now he and his fellows were reciting the dead man's crimes, but the lieutenant did not hear them.

He was looking at Vasco Gomez. He must be right— you could not mistake that expression, once you had seen it. And yet he could not understand.

His eye traveled down the beach to the land-crabs scuttling busily—yes, there were turtles, beyond there— fruit inland, fish in the sea. A small island, but provision enough to feed a whole ship's crew.

"And yet I could swear that the man died of hunger," muttered the lieutenant to himself. "It is strange."

III

THE CURFEW TOLLS

"It is not enough to be the possessor of genius—the time and the man must conjoin. An Alexander the Great, born into an age of profound peace, might scarce have troubled the world—a Newton, grown up in a thieves' den, might have devised little but a new and ingenious picklock. . . ."

Diversions of Historical Thought by
John Cleveland Cotton.

(The following extracts have been made from the letters of General Sir Charles William Geoffrey Estcourt, C.B., to his sister Harriet, Countess of Stokely, by permission of the Stokely family. Omissions are indicated by triple dots, thus . . .)

St. Philippe-des-Bains, September 3d, 1788.

MY DEAR SISTER: . . . I could wish that my excellent Paris physician had selected some other spot for my convalescence. But he swears by the waters of St. Philip and I swear by him, so I must resign myself to a couple of yawning months ere my constitution mends. Nevertheless, you will get long letters from me, though I fear they may be dull ones. I cannot bring you the gossip of Baden or Aix—except for its baths, St. Philip is but one of a dozen small white towns on this agreeable coast. It has its good inn and its bad inn, its dusty, little square with its dusty, fleabitten beggar, its posting-station and its promenade of scrubby lindens and palms. From the heights one may see Corsica on a clear day, and the Mediterranean is of an unexampled blue. To tell the truth, it is all agreeable enough, and an old Indian campaigner, like myself, should not complain. I am well treated at the Cheval Blanc—am I not an English milord?—and my excellent Gaston looks after me devotedly. But there is a blue-bottle drowsiness about small watering places out of season, and our gallant enemies, the French, know how to bore themselves more exquisitely in their provinces than any nation on earth. Would you think that the daily arrival of the diligence from Toulon would be an excitement? Yet it is to me, I assure you, and to all St. Philip. I walk, I take the waters, I read Ossian, I play piquet with Gaston, and yet I seem to myself but half-alive. . . .

. . . You will smile and say to me, "Dear brother, you have always plumed yourself on being a student of human nature. Is there no society, no character for you to study, even in St. Philippe-des-Bains?" My dear sister, I bend myself earnestly to that end, yet so far with little result. I have talked to my doctor—a good man but unpolished; I have talked to the curé—a good man but dull. I have even attempted the society of the baths, beginning with Monsieur le Marquis de la Percedragon, who has ninety-six quarterings, soiled wristbands, and a gloomy interest in my liver, and ending with Mrs. Macgregor Jenkins, a worthy and red-faced lady whose conversation positively cannonades with dukes and duchesses. But, frankly, I prefer my chair in the garden and my Ossian to any of them, even at the risk of being considered a bear. A witty scoundrel would be the veriest godsend to me, but do such exist in St. Philip? I trow not. As it is, in my weakened condition, I am positively agog when Gaston comes in every morning with his budget of village scandal. A pretty pass to come to, you will say, for a man who has served with Eyre Coote and but for the mutabilities of fortune, not to speak of a most damnable cabal . . . (A long passage dealing with General Estcourt's East Indian services and his personal and unfavorable opinion of Warren Hastings is here omitted from the manuscript.) . . . But, at fifty, a man is either a fool or a philosopher. Nevertheless, unless Gaston provides me with a character to try my wits on, shortly, I shall begin to believe that they too have deteriorated with Indian suns. . . .

September 21st, 1788.

My Dear Sister: . . . Believe me, there is little soundness in the views of your friend, Lord Martindale. The French monarchy is not to be compared with our own, but King Louis is an excellent and well-beloved prince, and the proposed summoning of the States-General cannot but have the most salutary effect. . . . (Three pages upon French politics and the possibility of cultivating sugar-cane in Southern France are here omitted.) . . . As for news of myself, I continue my yawning course, and feel a decided improvement from the waters. . . . So I shall continue them though the process is slow. . . .

You ask me, I fear a trifle mockingly, how my studies in human nature proceed?

Not so ill, my dear sister—I have, at least, scraped

acquaintance with one odd fish, and that, in St. Philip, is a triumph. For some time, from my chair in the promenade, I have observed a pursy little fellow, of my age or thereabouts, stalking up and down between the lindens. His company seems avoided by such notables of the place as Mrs. Macgregor Jenkins and at first I put him down as a retired actor, for there is something a little theatrical in his dress and walk. He wears a wide-brimmed hat of straw, loose nankeen trousers and a quasi-military coat, and takes his waters with as much ceremony as Monsieur le Marquis, though not quite with the same *ton*. I should put him down as a Meridional, for he has the quick, dark eye, the sallow skin, the corpulence and the rodomontish airs that mark your true son of the Midi, once he has passed his lean and hungry youth.

And yet, there is some sort of unsuccessful oddity about him, which sets him off from your successful bourgeois. I cannot put my finger on it yet, but it interests me.

At any rate, I was sitting in my accustomed chair, reading Ossian, this morning, as he made his solitary rounds of the promenade. Doubtless I was more than usually absorbed in my author, for I must have pronounced some lines aloud as he passed. He gave me a quick glance at the time, but nothing more. But on his next round, as he was about to pass me, he hesitated for a moment, stopped, and then, removing his straw hat, saluted me very civilly.

"Monsieur will pardon me," he said, with a dumpy hauteur, "but surely monsieur is English? And surely the lines that monsieur just repeated are from the great poet, Ossian?"

I admitted both charges, with a smile, and he bowed again.

"Monsieur will excuse the interruption," he said, "but I myself have long admired the poetry of Ossian" —and with that he continued my quotation to the end of the passage, in very fair English, too, though with a strong accent. I complimented him, of course, effusively —after all, it is not every day that one runs across a fellow-admirer of Ossian on the promenade of a small French watering place—and after that, he sat down in the chair beside me and we fell into talk. He seems, astonishingly for a Frenchman, to have an excellent acquaintance with our English poets—perhaps he has been a tutor in some English family. I did not press him with questions on this first encounter, though I noted that he spoke French with a slight accent also, which seems odd.

There is something a little rascally about him, to tell you the truth, though his conversation with me was both forceful and elevated. An ill man, too, and a disappointed one, or I miss my mark, yet his eyes, when he talks, are strangely animating. I fancy I would not care to meet him in a *guet-apens*, and yet, he may be the most harmless of broken pedagogues. We took a glass of waters together, to the great disgust of Mrs. Macgregor Jenkins, who ostentatiously drew her skirts aside. She let me know, afterward, in so many words, that my acquaintance was a noted bandit, though, when pressed, she could give no better reason than that he lives a little removed from the town, that "nobody knows

where he comes from" and that his wife is "no better
than she should be," whatever that portentous phrase
entails. Well, one would hardly call him a gentleman,
even by Mrs. Macgregor's somewhat easy standards, but
he has given me better conversation than I have had in
a month—and if he is a bandit, we might discuss thug-
gee together. But I hope for nothing so stimulating,
though I must question Gaston about him. . . .

October 11th.

. . . But Gaston could tell me little, except that my
acquaintance comes from Sardinia or some such island
originally, has served in the French army and is popu-
larly supposed to possess the evil eye. About Madame
he hinted that he could tell me a great deal, but I did
not labor the point. After all, if my friend has been
c-ck-ld-d—do not blush, my dear sister!—that, too, is
the portion of a philosopher, and I find his wide range
of conversation much more palatable than Mrs. Macgregor Jenkins' rewarmed London gossip. Nor has he
tried to borrow money from me yet, something which,
I am frank to say, I expected and was prepared to refuse. . . .

November 20th.

. . . Triumph! My character is found—and a character of the first water, I assure you! I have dined with
him in his house, and a very bad dinner it was. Madame
is not a good housekeeper, whatever else she may be.
And what she has been, one can see at a glance—she
has all the little faded coquetries of the garrison co-
quette. Good-tempered, of course, as such women often
are, and must have been pretty in her best days, though

with shocking bad teeth. I suspect her of a touch of the tarbrush, though there I may be wrong. No doubt she caught my friend young—I have seen the same thing happen in India often enough—the experienced woman and the youngster fresh from England. Well, 'tis an old story—an old one with him, too—and no doubt Madame has her charms, though she is obviously one reason why he has not risen.

After dinner, Madame departed, not very willingly, and he took me into his study for a chat. He had even procured a bottle of port, saying he knew the Englishman's taste for it, and while it was hardly the right Cockburn, I felt touched by the attention. The man is desperately lonely—one reads that in his big eyes. He is also desperately proud, with the quick, touchy sensitiveness of the failure, and I quite exerted myself to draw him out.

And indeed, the effort repaid me. His own story is simple enough. He is neither bandit nor pedagogue, but, like myself, a broken soldier—a major of the French Royal Artillery, retired on half pay for some years. I think it creditable of him to have reached so respectable a rank, for he is of foreign birth—Sardinian, I think I told you—and the French service is by no means as partial to foreigners as they were in the days of the first Irish Brigade. Moreover, one simply does not rise in that service, unless one is a gentleman of quarterings, and that he could hardly claim. But the passion of his life has been India, and that is what interests me. And, 'pon my honor, he was rather astonishing about it.

As soon as, by a lucky chance, I hit upon the subject, his eyes lit up and his sickness dropped away.

Pretty soon he began to take maps from a cabinet in the wall and ply me with questions about my own small experiences. And very soon indeed, I am abashed to state, I found myself stumbling in my answers. It was all book knowledge on his part, of course, but where the devil he could have got some of it, I do not know. Indeed, he would even correct me, now and then, as cool as you please. "Eight twelve pounders, I think, on the north wall of the old fortifications of Madras——" and the deuce of it is, he would be right. Finally, I could contain myself no longer.

"But, major, this is incredible," I said. "I have served twenty years with John Company and thought that I had some knowledge. But one would say you had fought over every inch of Bengal!"

He gave me a quick look, almost of anger, and began to roll up his maps.

"So I have, in my mind," he said, shortly, "but, as my superiors have often informed me, my hobby is a tedious one."

"It is not tedious to me," I said boldly. "Indeed, I have often marveled at your government's neglect of their opportunities in India. True, the issue is settled now——"

"It is by no means settled," he said, interrupting me rudely. I stared at him.

"It was settled, I believe, by Baron Clive, at a spot named Plassey," I said frigidly. "And afterward, by my own old general, Eyre Coote, at another spot named Wandewash."

"Oh, yes—yes—yes," he said impatiently, "I grant you Clive—Clive was a genius and met the fate of

geniuses. He steals an empire for you, and your virtuous
English Parliament holds up its hands in horror be·
cause he steals a few lakhs of rupees for himself as well.
So he blows out his brains in disgrace—you inexplicable English!—and you lose your genius. A great pity.
I would not have treated Clive so. But then, if I had
been Milord Clive, I would not have blown out my
brains."

"And what would you have done, had you been
Clive?" I said, for the man's calm, staring conceit
amused me.

His eyes were dangerous for a moment and I saw
why the worthy Mrs. Macgregor Jenkins had called him
a bandit.

"Oh," he said coolly, "I would have sent a file of
grenadiers to your English Parliament and told it to
hold its tongue. As Cromwell did. Now there was a
man. But your Clive—faugh!—he had the ball at his
feet and he refused to kick it. I withdraw the word
genius. He was a nincompoop. At the least, he might
have made himself a rajah."

This was a little too much, as you may imagine.
"General Clive had his faults," I said icily, "but he
was a true Briton and a patriot."

"He was a fool," said my puffy little major, flatly,
his lower lip stuck out. "As big a fool as Dupleix, and
that is saying much. Oh, some military skill, some talent
for organization, yes. But a genius would have brushed
him into the sea! It was possible to hold Arcot, it was
possible to win Plassey—look!" and, with that, he
ripped another map from his cabinet and began to expound to me eagerly exactly what he would have done

in command of the French forces in India, in 1757, when he must have been but a lad in his twenties. He thumped the paper, he strewed corks along the table for his troops—corks taken from a supply in a tin box, so it must be an old game with him. And, as I listened, my irritation faded, for the man's monomania was obvious. Nor was it, to tell the truth, an ill-designed plan of campaign, for corks on a map. Of course these things are different, in the field.

I could say, with honesty, that his plan had features of novelty, and he gulped the words down hungrily— he has a great appetite for flattery.

"Yes, yes," he said. "That is how it should be done— the thickest skull can see it. And, ill as I am, with a fleet and ten thousand picked men——" He dreamed, obviously, the sweat of his exertions on his waxy face— it was absurd and yet touching to see him dream.

"You would find a certain amount of opposition." I said, in an amused voice.

"Oh, yes, yes," he said quickly, "I do not underrate the English. Excellent horse, solid foot. But no true knowledge of cannon, and I am a gunner——"

I hated to bring him down to earth and yet I felt that I must.

"Of course, major," I said, "you have had great experience in the field."

He looked at me for a moment, his arrogance quite unshaken.

"I have had very little," he said, quietly, "but one knows how the thing should be done or one does not know. And that is enough."

He stared at me for an instant with his big eyes. A

little mad, of course. And yet I found myself saying, "But surely, major—what happened?"

"Why," he said, still quietly, "what happens to folk who have naught but their brains to sell? I staked my all on India when I was young—I thought that my star shone over it. I ate dirty puddings—*corpo di Baccho!*— to get there—I was no De Rohan or Soubise to win the king's favor! And I reached there indeed, in my youth, just in time to be included in the surrender of Pondicherry." He laughed, rather terribly, and sipped at his glass.

"You English were very courteous captors," he said. "But I was not released till the Seven Years War had ended—that was in '63. Who asks for the special exchange of an unknown artillery lieutenant? And then ten years odd of garrison duty at Mauritius. It was there that I met Madame—she is a Creole. A pleasant spot, Mauritius. We used to fire the cannon at the sea birds when we had enough ammunition for target practice," and he chuckled drearily. "By then I was thirty-seven. They had to make me a captain—they even brought me back to France. To garrison duty. I have been on garrison duty, at Toulon, at Brest, at——" He ticked off the names on his fingers but I did not like his voice.

"But surely," I said, "the American war, though a small affair—there were opportunities——"

"And who did they send?" he said quickly. "Lafayette—Rochambeau—De Grasse—the sprigs of the nobility. Oh, at Lafayette's age, I would have volunteered like Lafayette. But one should be successful in youth—after that, the spring is broken. And when one is over forty, one has responsibilities. I have a large

family, you see, though not of my own begetting," and
he chuckled as if at a secret joke. "Oh, I wrote the
Continental Congress," he said reflectively, "but they
preferred a dolt like Von Steuben. A good dolt, an
honest dolt, but there you have it. I also wrote your
British War Office," he said in an even voice. "I must
show you that plan of campaign—sometime—they
could have crushed General Washington with it in
three weeks."

I stared at him, a little appalled.

"For an officer who has taken his king's shilling to
send to an enemy nation a plan for crushing his own
country's ally," I said, stiffly—"well, in England, we
would call that treason."

"And what is treason?" he said lightly. "If we call
it unsuccessful ambition we shall be nearer the truth."
He looked at me, keenly. "You are shocked, General
Estcourt," he said. "I am sorry for that. But have you
never known the curse"—and his voice vibrated—"the
curse of not being employed when you should be employed? The curse of being a hammer with no nail to
drive? The curse—the curse of sitting in a dusty garrison town with dreams that would split the brain of a
Caesar, and no room on earth for those dreams?"

"Yes," I said, unwillingly, for there was something
in him that demanded the truth, "I have known that."

"Then you know hells undreamed of by the Christian," he said, with a sigh, "and if I committed treason
—well, I have been punished for it. I might have been
a brigadier, otherwise—I had Choiseul's ear for a few
weeks, after great labor. As it is, I am here on half pay,
and there will not be another war in my time. More-

over, M. de Ségur has proclaimed that all officers now must show sixteen quarterings. Well, I wish them joy of those officers, in the next conflict. Meanwhile, I have my corks, my maps and my family ailment." He smiled and tapped his side. "It killed my father at thirty-nine —it has not treated me quite so ill, but it will come for me soon enough."

And indeed, when I looked at him, I could well believe it, for the light had gone from his eyes and his cheeks were flabby. We chatted a little on indifferent subjects after that, then I left him, wondering whether to pursue the acquaintance. He is indubitably a character, but some of his speeches leave a taste in my mouth. Yet he can be greatly attractive—even now, with his mountainous failure like a cloak upon him. And yet why should I call it mountainous? His conceit is mountainous enough, but what else could he have expected of his career? Yet I wish I could forget his eyes. . . . To tell the truth, he puzzles me and I mean to get to the bottom of him. . . .

February 12th, 1789.

. . . I have another sidelight on the character of my friend, the major. As I told you, I was half of a mind to break off the acquaintance entirely, but he came up to me so civilly, the following day, that I could find no excuse. And since then, he has made me no embarrassingly treasonable confidences, though whenever we discuss the art of war, his arrogance is unbelievable. He even informed me, the other day, that while Frederick of Prussia was a fair general, his tactics might have been improved upon. I merely laughed and turned the question. Now and then I play a war

game with him, with his corks and maps, and when I
let him win, he is as pleased as a child. . . . His illness
increases visibly, despite the waters, and he shows an
eagerness for my company which I cannot but find
touching. . . . After all, he is a man of intelligence, and
the company he has had to keep must have galled him
at times. . . .

Now and then I amuse myself by speculating what
might have happened to him, had he chosen some other
profession than that of arms. He has, as I have told you,
certain gifts of the actor, yet his stature and figure must
have debarred him from tragic parts, while he certainly does not possess the humors of the comedian.
Perhaps his best choice would have been the Romish
church, for there, the veriest fisherman may hope, at
least, to succeed to the keys of St. Peter. . . . And yet,
Heaven knows, he would have made a very bad
priest! . . .

But, to my tale. I had missed him from our accustomed walks for some days and went to his house—
St. Helen's it is called; we live in a pother of saints'
names hereabouts—one evening to inquire. I did not
hear the quarreling voices till the tousle-haired servant
had admitted me and then it was too late to retreat.
Then my friend bounced down the corridor, his sallow
face bored and angry.

"Ah, General Estcourt!" he said, with a complete
change of expression as soon as he saw me. "What fortune! I was hoping you would pay us a call—I wish to
introduce you to my family!"

He had told me previously of his pair of stepchil-
dren by Madame's first marriage, and I must confess

I felt curious to see them. But it was not of them he spoke, as I soon gathered.

"Yes," he said. "My brothers and sisters, or most of them, are here for a family council. You come in the nick of time!" He pinched my arm and his face glowed with the malicious naïveté of a child. "They do not believe that I really know an English general—it will be a great blow to them!" he whispered as we passed down the corridor. "Ah, if you had only worn your uniform and your Garters! But one cannot have everything in life!"

Well, my dear sister, what a group, when we entered the salon! It is a small room, tawdrily furnished in the worst French taste, with a jumble of Madame's femininities and souvenirs from the Island of Mauritius, and they were all sitting about in the French after-dinner fashion, drinking tisane and quarreling. And, indeed, had the room been as long as the nave of St. Peter's, it would yet have seemed too small for such a crew! An old mother, straight as a ramrod and as forbidding, with the burning eyes and the bitter dignity one sees on the faces of certain Italian peasants—you could see that they were all a little afraid of her except my friend, and he, I must say, treated her with a filial courtesy that was greatly to his credit. Two sisters, one fattish, swarthy and spiteful, the other with the wreck of great beauty and the evident marks of a certain profession on her shabby-fine *toilette* and her pinkened cheeks. An innkeeper brother-in-law called Buras or Durat, with a jowlish, heavily handsome face and the manners of a cavalry sergeant—he is married to the spiteful sis-

ter. And two brothers, one sheep-like, one fox-like, yet
both bearing a certain resemblance to my friend.

The sheep-like brother is at least respectable, I gathered—a provincial lawyer in a small way of business
whose great pride is that he has actually appeared before the Court of Appeals at Marseilles. The other, the
fox-like one, makes his living more dubiously—he seems
the sort of fellow who orates windily in taprooms about
the Rights of Man, and other nonsense of M. Rous-
seau's. I would certainly not trust him with my watch,
though he is trying to get himself elected to the States-
General. And, as regards family concord, it was obvious at first glance that not one of them trusted the
others. And yet, that is not all of the tribe. There are,
if you will believe me, two other brothers living, and
this family council was called to deal with the affairs
of the next-to-youngest, who seems, even in this mé-
lange, to be a black sheep.

I can assure you, my head swam, and when my
friend introduced me, proudly, as a Knight of the Garters, I did not even bother to contradict him. For they
admitted me to their intimate circle at once—there
was no doubt about that. Only the old lady remained
aloof, saying little and sipping her camomile tea as if
it were the blood of her enemies. But, one by one, the
others related to me, with an unasked-for frankness, the
most intimate and scandalous details of their brothers'
and sisters' lives. They seemed united only on two
points, jealousy of my friend, the major, because he is
his mother's favorite, and dislike of Madame Josephine
because she gives herself airs. Except for the haggard
beauty—I must say, that, while her remarks anent her

sister-in-law were not such as I would care to repeat, she seemed genuinely fond of her brother, the major, and expounded his virtues to me through an overpowering cloud of scent.

It was like being in a nest of Italian smugglers, or a den of quarrelsome foxes, for they all talked, or rather barked at once, even the brother-in-law, and only Madame Mère could bring silence among them. And yet, my friend enjoyed it. It was obvious he showed them off before me as he might have displayed the tricks of a set of performing animals. And yet with a certain fondness, too—that is the inexplicable part of it. I do not know which sentiment was upmost in my mind— respect for this family feeling or pity for his being burdened with such a clan.

For though not the eldest, he is the strongest among them, and they know it. They rebel, but he rules their family conclaves like a petty despot. I could have laughed at the farce of it, and yet, it was nearer tears. For here, at least, my friend was a personage.

I got away as soon as I could, despite some pressing looks from the haggard beauty. My friend accompanied me to the door.

"Well, well," he said, chuckling and rubbing his hands, "I am infinitely obliged to you, general. They will not forget this in a hurry. Before you entered, Joseph"—Joseph is the sheep-like one—"was boasting about his acquaintance with a *sous-intendant,* but an English general, bah! Joseph will have green eyes for a fortnight!" And he rubbed his hands again in a perfect paroxysm of delight.

It was too childlike to make me angry. "I am glad, of course, to have been of any service," I said.

"Oh, you have been a great service," he said. "They will not plague my poor Josie for at least half an hour. Ah, this is a bad business of Louis'—a bad business!"— Louis is the black sheep—"but we will patch it up somehow. Hortense is worth three of him—he must go back to Hortense!"

"You have a numerous family, major," I said, for want of something better to say.

"Oh, yes," he said, cheerfully. "Pretty numerous— I am sorry you could not meet the others. Though Louis is a fool—I pampered him in his youth. Well! He was a baby—and Jerome a mule. Still, we haven't done so badly for ourselves; not badly. Joseph makes a go of his law practice—there are fools enough in the world to be impressed by Joseph—and if Lucien gets to the States-General, you may trust Lucien to feather his nest! And there are the grandchildren, and a little money—not much," he said, quickly. "They mustn't expect that from me. But it's a step up from where we started—if papa had lived, he wouldn't have been so ill-pleased. Poor Elisa's gone, but the rest of us have stuck together, and, while we may seem a little rough, to strangers, our hearts are in the right place. When I was a boy," and he chuckled again, "I had other ambitions for them. I thought, with luck on my side, I could make them all kings and queens. Funny, isn't it, to think of a numskull like Joseph as a king! Well, that was the boy of it. But, even so, they'd all be eating chestnuts back on the island without me, and that's something."

He said it rather defiantly, and I did not know which to marvel at most—his preposterous pride in the group or his cool contempt of them. So I said nothing but shook his hand instead. I could not help doing the latter. For surely, if anyone started in life with a mill-stone about his neck . . . and yet they are none of them ordinary people. . . .

> March 13th, 1789.

. . . My friend's complaint has taken a turn for the worse and it is I who pay him visits now. It is the act of a Christian to do so and, to tell the truth, I have become oddly attached to him, though I can give no just reason for the attachment. He makes a bad patient, by the way, and is often abominably rude to both myself and Madame, who nurses him devotedly though unskillfully. I told him yesterday that I could have no more of it and he looked at me with his strangely luminous eyes. "So," he said, "even the English desert the dying." . . . Well, I stayed; after that, what else might a gentleman do? . . . Yet I cannot feel that he bears me any real affection—he exerts himself to charm, on occasion, but one feels he is playing a game . . . yes, even upon his deathbed, he plays a game . . . a complex character. . . .

> April 28th, 1789.

. . . My friend the major's malady approaches its term—the last few days find him fearfully enfeebled. He knows that the end draws nigh; indeed he speaks of it often, with remarkable calmness. I had thought it might turn his mind toward religion, but while he has accepted the ministrations of his Church, I fear it is without the sincere repentance of a Christian. When the priest had left him, yesterday, he summoned me, remarking, "Well, all that is over with," rather more in the tone of a man who has just reserved a place in a coach than one who will shortly stand before his Maker.

"It does no harm," he said, reflectively. "And, after all, it might be true. Why not?" and he chuckled in a way that repelled me. Then he asked me to read to him—not the Bible, as I had expected, but some verses of the poet Gray. He listened attentively, and when I came to the passage, "Hands, that the rod of empire might have swayed," and its successor, "Some mute inglorious Milton here may rest," he asked me to repeat them. When I had done so, he said, "Yes, yes. That is true, very true. I did not think so in boyhood—I thought genius must force its own way. But your poet is right about it."

I found this painful, for I had hoped that his illness had brought him to a juster, if less arrogant, estimate of his own abilities.

"Come, major," I said, soothingly, "we cannot all be great men, you know. And you have no need to repine. After all, as you say, you have risen in the world——"

"Risen?" he said, and his eyes flashed. "Risen? Oh, God, that I should die alone with my one companion an Englishman with a soul of suet! Fool, if I had had Alexander's chance, I would have bettered Alexander! And it will come, too, that is the worst of it. Already Europe is shaking with a new birth. If I had been born under the Sun-King, I would be a Marshal of France;

if I had been born twenty years ago, I would mold a new Europe with my fists in the next half-dozen years. Why did they put my soul in my body at this infernal time? Do you not understand, imbecile? Is there no one who understands?"

I called Madame at this, as he was obviously delirious, and, after some trouble, we got him quieted.

May 8th, 1789.

... My poor friend is gone, and peacefully enough at the last. His death, oddly enough, coincided with the date of the opening of the States-General at Versailles. The last moments of life are always painful for the observer, but his end was as relatively serene as might be hoped for, considering his character. I was watching at one side of the bed and a thunderstorm was raging at the time. No doubt, to his expiring consciousness, the cracks of the thunder sounded like artillery, for, while we were waiting the death-struggle, he suddenly raised himself in the bed and listened intently. His eyes glowed, a beatific expression passed over his features. "The army! Head of the army!" he whispered ecstatically, and, when we caught him, he was lifeless ... I must say that, while it may not be very Christian, I am glad that death brought him what life could not, and that, in the very article of it, he saw himself at the head of victorious troops. Ah, Fame—delusive spectre ... (A page of disquisition by General Estcourt on the vanities of human ambition is here omitted.) ... The face, after death, was composed, with a certain majesty, even ... one could see that he might have been handsome as a youth. ...

May 26th, 1789.

. . . I shall return to Paris by easy stages and reach
Stokely sometime in June. My health is quite restored
and all that has kept me here this long has been the
difficulty I have met with in attempting to settle my
poor friend, the major's affairs. For one thing, he appears to have been originally a native of Corsica, not of
Sardinia as I had thought, and while that explains
much in his character, it has also given occupation to
the lawyers. I have met his rapacious family, individu-
ally and in conclave, and, if there are further gray hairs
on my head, you may put it down to them. . . . However, I have finally assured the major's relict of her
legitimate rights in his estate, and that is something—
my one ray of comfort in the matter being the behavior
of her son by the former marriage, who seems an excellent and virtuous young man. . . .

. . . You will think me a very soft fellow, no doubt,
for wasting so much time upon a chance acquaintance
who was neither, in our English sense, a gentleman nor
a man whose Christian virtues counterbalanced his lack
of true breeding. Yet there was a tragedy about him
beyond his station, and that verse of Gray's rings in my
head. I wish I could forget the expression on his face
when he spoke of it. Suppose a genius born in circumstances that made the development of that genius impossible—well, all this is the merest moonshine. . . .

. . . To revert to more practical matters, I discover
that the major has left me his military memoirs, papers
and commentaries, including his maps. Heaven knows
what I shall do with them! I cannot, in courtesy, burn
them *sur-le-champ,* and yet they fill two huge packing

cases and the cost of transporting them to Stokely will be considerable. Perhaps I will take them to Paris and quietly dispose of them there to some waste-paper merchant. . . In return for this unsought legacy, Madame has consulted me in regard to a stone and epitaph for her late husband, and, knowing that otherwise the family would squabble over the affair for weeks, I have drawn up a design which I hope meets with their approval. It appears that he particularly desired that the epitaph should be writ in English, saying that France had had enough of him, living—a freak of dying vanity for which one must pardon him. However, I have produced the following, which I hope will answer.

Here lies
NAPOLEONE BUONAPARTE
Major of the Royal Artillery
of France.
Born August 15th, 1737
at Ajaccio, Corsica.
Died May 5th, 1789
at St. Philippe-des-Bains

"Rest, perturbed spirit . . ."

. . . I had thought, for some hours, of excerpting the lines of Gray's—the ones that still ring in my head. But, on reflection, though they suit well enough, they yet seem too cruel to the dust.

•

THE SOBBIN' WOMEN

THEY came over the Pass one day in one big wagon
—all ten of them—man and woman and hired
girl and seven big boy children, from the nine-year-old
who walked by the team to the baby in arms. Or so the
story runs—it was in the early days of settlement and
the town had never heard of the Sobbin' Women then.
But it opened its eyes one day, and there were the
Pontipees.

They were there but they didn't stay long—just
time enough to buy meal and get a new shoe for the
lead horse. You couldn't call them unsociable, exactly—
they seemed to be sociable enough among themselves.
But you could tell, somehow, from the look of them,
that they weren't going to settle on ground other people had cleared. They were all high-colored and dark-
haired—handsome with a wilderness handsomeness—
and when you got them all together, they looked more
like a tribe or a nation than an ordinary family. I don't
know how they gave folks that feeling, but they did.
Yes, even the baby, when the town women tried to
handle him. He was a fine, healthy baby, but they said
it was like trying to pet a young raccoon.

Well, that was all there was to it, at the start. They
paid for what they bought in good money and drove
on up into Sobbin' Women Valley—only it wasn't

called Sobbin' Women Valley then. And pretty soon, there was smoke from a chimney there that hadn't been there before. But you know what town gossip is when it gets started. The Pontipees were willing enough tc let other folks alone—in fact, that was what they wanted. But, because it was what they wanted, the town couldn't see why they wanted it. Towns get that way, sometimes.

So, it was mostly cross questions and crooked answers when the Pontipees came into town, to trade off their pelts and such and buy at the store. There wasn't much actual trouble—not after two loafers at the tavern made fun of Pa Pontipee's fur cap and Pa Pontipee stretched them both before you could say "Jack Robinson." But there wasn't a neighborly feeling—yes, you could say that. The women would tell their children about the terrible Pontipees and the men would wag their heads. And when they came in to church—which they did once a year—there'd be a sort of rustle in the congregation, though they always took a back pew and listened perfectly respectful. But the minister never seemed to be able to preach as good a sermon as usual that Sunday—and naturally, he blamed the Pontipees for that. Till, finally, they got to be a sort of legend in the community—the wild folks who lived up the valley like bears in the woods—and, indeed, some said they turned into bears in the winter time, which just shows you what people will say. And, though the boys were well set up, they might as well have been deaf-mutes for all the notice the town-girls took of them—except to squeak and run to the other side of the road when the Pontipees came marching along.

While, as for the Pontipees—nobody knew what they made of it all, for they weren't much on talking. If one of them said "It's a fine day" and another admitted it was, that was conversation that would last them a long while. Besides, they had work enough and to spare, in their own valley, to keep them busy; and, if Ma Pontipee would have liked more society, she never let on. She did her duty by the boys and tried to give them some manners, in spite of their backwoods raising; and that was enough for any woman to do.

But things never stand still in this world, and soon enough, the boys weren't boys any more, they were men. And when the fall of a tree took Pa Pontipee, his wife didn't linger long after him. There was a terrible fuss about the funerals too—for the Pontipee boys got the minister, but they wouldn't let the burials take place in town. They said Pa and Ma wouldn't feel comfortable, all crowded up among strangers in the churchyard, so they laid them to rest in the Valley where they'd lived, and the town found that queerer than ever. But there's worse places to lie than looking out over the fields you've cleared.

After that, though, the town thought some of the boys, at least, would move in from the Valley and get more sociable. They figured they'd have to—they figured with their Pa and Ma gone, the boys would fight amongst themselves—they figured a dozen things. But none of the things they figured happened at all. The Pontipee boys stayed out in the Valley, and when they came to the town, they walked through it as proud as Lucifer, and when they came to the church, they put just the same money in the collection-plate they had when Ma and Pa Pontipee were alive. Some thought it was because they were stupid to count, but I don't think it was that.

They went on just the same, as I say, but things didn't go quite the same for them. For one thing, the hired girl couldn't keep the place the way Ma Pontipee kept it. And besides, she was getting old herself. Well, pretty soon, she up and died. They gave her as good a funeral as they knew how—she'd always been part of the family. But, after that, though the farm went ahead as well as ever, things in the house began to go from bad to worse.

Menlike, they didn't notice what was wrong at first, except there was a lot of dust around and things didn't get put away. But, after each one of them had tried a week of cooking for the others and all the others had cursed out the one who was cooking something proper, they decided something had to be done about it. It took them a long time to decide that—they were slow thinkers as well as slow talkers, the Pontipees. But, when they decided about a thing, it got done.

"The flapjacks are greasy again," said Harry Pontipee, one evening—Harry was the oldest. "You know what we've got to get, brothers? We've got to get a woman to take care of this place. I can lay a tree within two inches of where I want it to fall. I can shoot the eye out of a grey squirrel in a treetop. I can do all a man should do. But I can't cook and make it taste human."

"You're right, brother," said Hob Pontipee—Hob was the youngest. "I can tan deerskin better than an Injun squaw. I can wrastle underholt and overholt and throw any man in this county. I can play on a boxwood fiddle—but I can't sweep dust so it stays swept. It takes a woman to do that, for there seems to be a trick about it. We've got to get a woman."

Then they all joined in saying what they could do—and it was plenty—but they couldn't cook and they couldn't dust and they couldn't make a house comfortable because that was woman's business, and there seemed to be a trick about it. So they had to get a woman to keep house for them. But where were they going to get her?

"We could get a hired girl, maybe," said Hosea Pontipee—the middle one—but, even as he spoke, there wasn't much hope in his voice.

"That hired girl we had was the last one left in the East," said Harry Pontipee. "Some may have growed up, since her time, but I don't want to go back across the Pass on the chance of an out-and-out miracle."

"Well then," said Hob Pontipee, practical, "there's just one thing to do. One of us has to get married. And I think it ought to be Harry—he's the eldest."

Well, that remark nearly caused a break-up in the family. Harry kicked like a cow in fly-time at the bare idea of getting married, and tried to put it on to Halbert, who was next in line. And Halbert passed it on to Harvey, but Harvey said women was snares and delusions, or so he'd heard, and he wouldn't have a strange woman around him for a brand-new plow.

So it went on down to Hob and he wouldn't hear of it—and it wasn't till a couple of chairs had been broken and Hob had a black eye that the ruckus quieted at all. But, gradually, they came to see that one of 'em would have to get married, as a matter of family duty, or they'd all be eating spoiled flapjacks for the rest of their lives. Only then the question came up as to who it was to be, and that started a bigger disturbance than ever.

Finally, they agreed that the only fair way was drawing straws. So Hob held the straws and they drew—and, sure enough, Harry got the long one. Sick enough he looked about it—but there it was. The others started congratulating him and making jokes—especially Hob.

"You'll have to slick up, tomorrow," said Hob, glad it wasn't him. "You'll have to cut your hair and brush your clothes and act pretty, if you're going to be a bridegroom!"

Next morning they got him down and cut his hair and put bear's grease on it and dressed him up in the best clothes they had and sent him into town to look for a wife.

It was all right when he started out from the Valley. He even took a look at himself in a spring and was kind of surprised at the young man who looked back at him. But the nearer he got to town, the queerer and tremblier he felt, and the less able to go about doing what he'd promised.

He tried to remember how it had been when his Pa and Ma had been courting. But, naturally, as he hadn't been born then, he didn't know. Then he tried to think of various girls in the village, but the more he thought of them, the more they mixed in his mind—till, finally, all he could think of was a high, wild bank of rhododendron flowers that mixed and shimmered and laughed at you the closer you came to it.

"Oh, Lordy! It's a heavy responsibility to lay on a man!" he said and mopped his forehead with his sleeve.

Finally, however, he made up his mind. "I'll ask the first woman I see, pretty or ugly!" he said to himself, with the perspiration fairly rolling down his face, though it was a cold March day. And he gave his horse a lick.

But, when he got into town, the first woman he saw was the storekeeper's wife. The second he saw was a little girl in a pinafore—and the third was the minister's daughter. He was all set up to speak to her—but she squeaked and ran to the other side of the street as soon as she saw him and left him standing there with his hat in his hand. That sort of took the courage out of him.

"By the whiskers of Moses!" he said to himself, "this marryin' job is a harder job than I bargained for. I guess I'll go over to the tavern and get me a drink—maybe that will put some ideas in my head."

It was there he saw her—feeding the chickens out in the poultry-yard. Her name was Milly and she was a bound girl, as they had in those days. Next door to a slave she was, for all she'd come of good stock and had some education. She was young and thin, with a sharp little thoughtful face and ragged clothes, but she walked as straight as an Indian as she went about the yard. Harry Pontipee couldn't have said if she were pretty or plain, but, as he watched her through the window, feeding the chickens, something seemed to tell him that he might have better luck with her than he'd had with the others.

Well, he drank his drink and went out.

"Hello, girl," he said, in one of those big voices men use when they're pretending not to be embarrassed.

She looked up at him straight. "Hello, backwoodsman!" she said, friendly enough. She didn't look a bit scared of him and that put him off.

"It's a nice morning," said Harry, louder, trying to lead up to his point.

"It is for some," said the girl, perfectly polite but going on feeding the chickens.

Harry swallowed hard at that. "It'd be a nice morning to get married, thev tell me," he said, with the perspiration breaking out all over him again. He'd meant to say something else, but when it came to the point, he couldn't.

Well, she didn't say anything to that so he had to start all over again.

"My name's Harry Pontipee," he said. "I've got a good farm up the Valley."

"Have you?" said the girl.

"Yes," he said. "It's a right good farm. And some folks seem to think I'd make a good husband."

"Do they?" said the girl. I guess she was smiling by now but Harry couldn't see it—she had her head turned.

"Yes they do," said Harry, kind of desperate, his voice getting louder and louder. "What do you think about it?"

"I couldn't tell on such short acquaintance," said the girl.

"Will you marry me and find out?" said Harry, in a perfect bellow, shaking all over.

"Yes, I will, if you don't ask me quite so loud," she

said, very prim—and even Harry could see she was smiling now.

Well, they made a queer pair when they went up to the minister—the girl still in her chicken-feed clothes, for she didn't have any others, and Harry in his backwoods finery. He'd had to buy out her time from the innkeeper for twelve beaver pelts and a hunting knife.

But when the wedding service was over, "Well, we're married," said Harry, with great relief. "And now we'll be going home."

"Oh, no we won't," said she. "We're going to the store first and buy me some cloth for a decent dress— for landless I may be and dowryless I may be, but I'm a married woman now, and what's fit for a chicken-girl isn't fit for a married woman."

In a sort of daze, he saw her lay out the price of twelve more beaver pelts in cloth and woman's fixings, and beat down the storekeeper on the price, too.

He only asked her a question about one thing—a little pair of slippers she bought. They were fancy slippers, with embroidery on them. "I thought you had a pair of shoes," he said. She turned to him, with a cocky sort of look on her face. "Silly," she said. "How could anyone tell your wife had pretty feet in the shoes I had?"

Well, he thought that over, and, after a while, something in the way she said it and the cocky look on her face made him feel pleased, and he began to laugh. He wasn't used to laughing in front of a girl, but he could see it might have its points.

Then they rode back to the Valley, her riding pillion, with her bundles in the saddlebags. And all the

way back, she was trying him and testing him and trying to find out, by one little remark or another, just
what kind of a man he was. She was a spunky little
girl, and she had more education than she let on. And
long ago, she'd made up her mind to get out of being
a bound girl the first way that offered. But, all the
same, marrying Harry Pontipee was a leap in the dark.

But the more she tried and tested Harry, the better
bargain she seemed to think she'd made. And that took
courage to admit—for the way was a wild one and a
lonesome, and, naturally, she'd heard stories of Pontipee
Valley. She couldn't quite believe they lived with bears,
up there, but she didn't know.

And finally, they came to the house, and there were
dark things moving outside it. "Bears!" thought Milly,
kind of hopeless, and her heart went into her throat,
but she didn't let on.

"W-what's that, Harry dear?" she said, holding on
tight.

"Oh, that's just my brothers," said Harry, kind of
careless, and with that those six hungry six-footers
moved into the light.

"Oh!" said Milly, "you didn't tell me you had six
brothers." But her voice wasn't reproachful, just sort
of soft and quiet.

"I guess it was the wedding kind of knocked it out
of my mind," said Harry. "But, there—you'll see enough
of 'em anyhow, because we all live together."

"Oh," said Milly again, kind of soft. "I see." And
the brothers came up, one by one, and shook hands.
They'd intended to cut quite a few jokes on Harry if

he did come home with a wife, but, somehow, when they looked at Milly, they forgot about that.

Well, they brought her into the house. It was a handsome house, for the times, with genuine window-glass. But Milly rubbed her finger along a window sill and saw it come off black and then she wrote her name in the dust on the mantelpiece.

"What a lovely big house!" she said, coughing a little with the dust she'd raised.

"It's mebbe a little dusty now," said Harry. "But now you're here——"

"Yes," said Milly and passed on to the kitchen. Well, the kitchen was certainly a sight. But Milly didn't seem to notice.

Presently, "What a great big jar of flapjack batter!" she said. "And what a big tub of salt pork!"

"That's for tonight," said Harry. "Me and my brothers is hearty eaters. We haven't been eating so well since we had to cook for ourselves, but now you're here——"

"Yes," said Milly and passed on to the laundry. The laundry was half full of huckaback shirts and such that needed washing—piles and piles of them.

"What a lot of wash!" said Milly.

"That's so," said Harry, kind of pleased. "Me and my brothers is kind of hard on our clothes—all seven of us—so there's lots of washing and mending, but now you're here——"

"Yes," said Milly, swallowing a little. "And now all you men clear out of my kitchen while I get supper. Clear out!" she said, smiling at them, though she didn't feel much like smiling.

I don't know what she said to herself when they'd left her alone. I know what a man would have said and I guess she said that, too. I know she thought at least once of the money in her stocking and how far it was back to town. And then her eye happened to fall on that great big jar of flapjack batter—and, all of a sudden the whole thing struck her as funny, and she laughed till she cried.

But then she found a clean handkerchief and blew her nose and straightened her hair and set about her work.

Those boys hadn't had a supper like that in months and they treated it respectful. And Milly didn't say a word to them about manners then, though, later on, she said plenty. She just sat and watched them, with a curious light in her eyes.

When it was over finally, and they were stuffed, "Mrs. Harry," said Howard. "You're a wonder, Mrs. Harry!" and "You're sure a wonder, Mrs. Harry!" chorused all the rest of them, down to Hob. She could see they meant it, too.

"Thanks," she said, very polite and gracious. "Thank you, Howard, and you, Hosea, and all my brothers."

At the end of three months, there wasn't one of those boys that wouldn't have laid down his life for Milly, and, as for Harry, he just worshipped the ground she walked on. With all that work to do, naturally, she got thinner and thinner and peakeder and peakeder, but she didn't complain. She knew what she wanted and how she was going to get it—and she waited her chance.

Finally Harry noticed how thin she was getting and he spoke to her about it.

"Can't you ever sit down and rest, Milly?" he said one day, watching her fly around the kitchen, doing six things at once.

But she just laughed at him and said, "I'm cooking for you and your six brothers, and that makes work, you know."

Well, he thought that over, inside him, but he didn't say anything, then. But he came up to her in the laundry another time, and when she was dusting the house another time—she was looking peakeder each day—and asked her if she couldn't rest a spell. The last time, he brought his fist down on the table with a bang.

"This has got to stop!" he said. "Me and my six brothers is wearing you to skin and bone with our victuals and our shirts and the dust we track in the house, and I won't have it no more! It's got to stop!"

"Well, Harry," she said, sort of quiet, "if it's got to stop, it's got to—and pretty soon, Harry. Because, I'm expecting, and a woman that's expecting can't work like a woman in her usual health."

Well, after he got his sense back, after hearing that, he called the whole family into consultation that evening and put it to them plain. They'd do anything for Milly by then.

She led the conversation where she wanted it to go, though she didn't seem to, and finally they decided it was up to Halbert, the second oldest, to get married, so his wife could take some of the work off Milly's hands. So next day, Halbert spruced up and went to town to look for a wife. But when he came home, he was alone and all dejected.

"They won't have me," he said, very mournful. "They won't none of 'em have me—and I asked fourteen of 'em."

"Why, what's the matter?" said Milly.

"Well," said Halbert, "it seems they've heard about the seven of us and the lot of victuals we eat and the wash and all—and they say only a fool would marry into a family like that and they don't see how you stand it, Milly."

"Oh, that's what they say, is it?" said Milly, with her eyes as bright as candles. "Well, your turn next, Harvey."

So Harvey tried it and Hosea tried it and all of them tried it. But none of them had any luck. And then, finally, Milly let loose at them, good and proper.

"You great big lumps of men!" she said, with the cocky look on her face. "There's more ways of killing a cat than choking it with cream. If they won't marry you after you've asked 'em—why don't you marry 'em first and ask 'em afterwards?"

"But how can we do that?" said Harvey, who was the stupidest.

"Well," said Milly—and here's where her education came in that I've made such a point of—"I read in a history book once about a bunch of people called Romans who were just in your fix." And she went on to tell them about the Romans—how they were settled in a country that was unfriendly to them, just like the Pontipees, and how they all needed wives, just like the Pontipees, and how, when they couldn't get them in the ordinary way from the other people of the country who were called the Sobbin's or the Sabbin's or some such name, they raided the Sobbin' town one night and carried off a lot of the Sobbin' women and married them.

"And, if you can't do as well for yourselves as a lot of old dead Romans," she ended, "you're no brothers of mine and you can cook your own suppers the rest of your lives."

They all sat around dumbfounded for a while. Finally Hob spoke up.

"That sounds all right, in history," he said, "but this is different. Supposing these women just cry and pine away when we've carried them off—supposing that?"

"Listen to me," said Milly. "I know what I'm talking about. Every one of those girls is crazy to get married—and there's not half enough men in town to go round. They think a lot of you boys, too, for I've heard them talk about you; but they're scared of your being backwoodsmen, and scared of the work, and each one is scared of being the first to leave the others. I'll answer for them, once you've married them. Is there anybody around here who can marry people, except the regular minister?"

"There's a sort of hedge-parson just come to town," said Hob. "I reckon he can tie a knot as tight as any preacher in the county."

"All right," said Milly. "That settles it."

It was the evening of the big sociable that it happened. They held it once a year, around Thanksgiving time, and those who had rifles and weapons left them at the door. The Pontipee boys had never attended before—so there was a good deal of stir when they marched in, all seven of them, with Milly in the middle. The brothers were shaved and clean and dressed up spick and span and Milly never looked better, in a dress she'd made out of store cloth and her embroidered slippers.

There was quite a bit of giggling from the town girls, as the Pontipees entered, and a buzz around the hall, but then the fiddler struck up and people began to dance and play games and enjoy themselves, and pretty soon they forgot the Pontipees were there at all, except that the Pontipee boys acted very polite to everybody—Milly'd taught 'em that—and, I guess, before the evening was over, some of the town girls were wondering why they'd turned down boys like that just because they lived in the backwoods.

But they didn't get much chance to think about it, at that. Because, just as they were all going to sit down to supper—"Ready, boys?" called Milly, in a voice that cut through all the talk and commotion. Everybody turned to look at her. And then there was a gasp and a cry, for "Ready!" chorused the six bachelor Pontipees; and suddenly, each one had one hand on a rifle and the other holding a girl, while Harry and Milly trained a couple more rifles on the rest of the community to keep them quiet. It happened so sudden, half the folks didn't even know it was happening—till the Pontipee boys had their girls outside in the street, and the big doors locked and bolted behind them.

Then there was Cain to raise for fair in the meeting-hall and people started to beat and kick at the doors—out they built solid, in those days. There wasn't any use in trying to shoot the locks off, because the Pontipee boys had tied up the guard over the weapons and dumped him and them outside in a shed.

It wasn't till pretty near dawn that the doors gave way—and when they did, the townspeople took one look outside and groaned. For it was snowing, lickety split, till you couldn't see your hand before your face—and when it snows, in our part of the country, it certainly snows. The blizzard didn't let up for four days, either, and by that time, the pass through the hills to Pontipee Valley was blocked solid, and nothing to do but wait for Spring and the thaw.

And, meanwhile, Milly had her work cut out for her. It wasn't an easy job, convoying three sleigh-loads full of hysterics all that long, cold ride. But she let them hysteric away, and, by the time they got to the Pontipee house, the stolen brides were so tuckered out that they'd quieted down a good deal.

Still, at first, they swore they wouldn't take bite or sup till they were restored to their grieving families. But Milly had some tea ready for them, in a jiffy—and a woman will usually take tea, no matter how mad she is. Well, Milly let them get warm and a little cozy, and then, when they were on their second cups, she made her little speech.

"Ladies," she said, "this affair makes me mighty sad—to see fine girls like you stole away by a lot of uncouth backwoodsmen. And I'd never have lent a hand to it if I'd known the truth of the matter. But, you and me, we'll turn the tables on them yet. You can't get back to your families till the blizzard lets up, but, while you've got to stay here, I'll see you're treated respectful. And just to prove that"—and she took a bunch of keys from her pocket—"I'll lock this house up tight, with us inside it; and, as for those backwoods Pontipees, they can sleep and eat in the stable with the livestock. That'll teach them they can't fool us!"

Well, that little speech—and the tea—cheered the girls up quite a bit. And by the time Milly showed them to their rooms—nice-looking rooms, too—and let them bolt themselves in, they were pretty well convinced that Milly was their friend.

So a week or so went by like that—the girls keeping house for themselves and never seeing hide nor hair of a Pontipee.

At first, it was a regular picnic for the girls. They allowed as how they'd always wanted to live without any men around, and, now they were, it was even better than they'd thought. And Milly agreed with them as hard as she could agree. She made them little speeches about the worthlessness of men in general and husbands in particular that would have raised the hair off any man's head. And, at first, the other girls listened to her and chimed in, and then they listened, but you could see they were being polite. And, by the end of the week, it was awful hard for her to get a real audience.

So, when she began to catch them looking out of windows when they should have been dusting, and peeking from behind curtains to try and get a sight of the terrible Pontipees, she knew it was time for the next step. For things got duller and duller in the house and little spats and quarrels began to break out among the girls. So, one afternoon, she suggested, tactfully, just to break the monotony, that they all go up and rummage in the garret.

They rummaged around and had quite a bit of fun, until finally the minister's daughter opened a long box and gave a little squeal of joy.

"What a lovely wedding-dress—whose was it?" she said, and pulled out the long white veil and the dress itself, while the rest stood round and admired.

"Oh, shucks, that's just an old wedding-dress those backwoodsmen made me make when they thought you were going to marry 'em," said Milly, in a very disgusted voice. "Put it back!" But the girls weren't paying attention.

"Will it fit me, I wonder?" said the minister's daughter.

"It's bad luck, trying on wedding-dresses, if you're not going to have a wedding!" said Milly. "Let's go downstairs and have tea." But the minister's daughter was stepping out of her regular clothes already. The other girls helped fix her up—and then they oh-ed and ah-ed, for, I must say, she made a handsome-looking bride.

"That Pontipee boy named Hob's got curly hair," said the minister's daughter, trailing out her veil. "I always did have a liking for curly hair."

"Hob's not nearly as good-looking as Halbert," said the lawyer's niece, quite violent, and another one said, "Handsome is as handsome does—the one they call Harvey isn't so handsome, maybe, but he certainly has nice eyes."

"There's something about a man around the house

that brisks things up remarkable," said a fourth one. "Not that I want to get married, but Howard's a nice name, even if Pontipee is hitched to it and——"

"Girls, girls—are you crazy, girls?" said Milly, shocked and horrified. But the minute she started to reprove them, they all turned on her, most ungratefully, and there was a regular revolt. So, at last, she had to give in and admit that there were five more wedding-dresses in the garret—and that if anybody was thinking of getting married, there just happened to be a hedge-parson, spending the winter with the Pontipees. But one thing she was firm about.

"Get married if you like," she said. "I can't stop you. But I'm responsible for you to your families—and, after the ceremony's ended, your husbands go back to the stable and stay there, till I know your families approve of them." She looked very fierce about it, and she made them promise. The hedge-parson married them all—all six in their wedding dresses—and then the boys went back to the stable. And, at dinner that night, the minister's daughter burst out crying.

"I hate men just as much as ever!" she wailed. "But it's terrible to be lawful married to a man you can't even see, except now and then out of a window!"

So Milly saw she had to make some new rules and she did. Three afternoons a week, the boys were allowed to call on their new wives, and once in a while, for a great treat, they could stay to supper. But, always with Milly to chaperon.

Well, at first, the husbands and wives were mighty stiff and formal with each other, but, gradually, they got better and better acquainted. Till, pretty soon, the

minister's daughter was letting Hob hold her hand,
when she thought Milly wasn't looking, and the lawyer's
niece was asking permission to sew a button on Halbert's coat--and there was a general atmosphere of
courting around the Pontipee place that'd make an old
bachelor sick.

Milly took it all in but she never stopped chaperon-
ing.

Well, finally, it was one day along in January. Milly
woke up in the morning—and she knew she was near
her time. But, first thing in the morning, as always,
she reached underneath her pillow for her keys—and
then she smiled. For somebody must have stolen them
while she was sleeping—and when she got up, and
went to the window in her wrapper, the door of the
house was wide open. And there was Hob and his wife,
helping each other shovel snow from the doorstep,
and Halbert and his wife were throwing snowballs at
Harvey and his, and Howard was kissing the doctor's eldest behind the kitchen door. "Praise be!" said
Milly. "I can have my baby in peace"—and she went
down to congratulate them all.

Only then, there were the families and the relatives
still to fix. But Milly had a plan for that—she had plans
for everything. When they stole the girls away, they
left a letter she drew up, signed by all the boys and
expressing all the honorable intentions you could put
a name to. But she was afraid that wouldn't cool down
the townspeople much, even when they thought it over,
and it didn't.

One day when the first thaws had come and Milly's

baby was about six weeks old, Hob came running in from his lookout post.

"They're coming, Milly!" he said. "The whole dum town! They've got rifles and scythes and ropes and they look mighty wild and bloodthirsty! What'll we do?"

"Do?" said Milly, perfectly calm. "You get the boys together and keep out of sight—and tell the girls to come here. For it's women's work, now, that'll save us, if anything will."

When she got the girls together, she gave them their orders. I guess they were a bit white-faced, but they obeyed. Then she looked out of the window—and there was the town, marching up the road, slow and steady. She'd have liked it better if they'd shouted or cried, but they didn't shout nor cry. The minister was in the lead, with his lips shut, and a six foot rifle in his hand, and his face like an iron mask.

She saw them come up to the gate of the Pontipee place. The gate was wide open and nobody there to hinder. She could see them take that in—and the little waver in the crowd. Because that made them feel queer.

Then they caught themselves and came tramping along toward the house, the minister still in the lead. Milly caught her breath, for they still looked awful mad. She knew what they'd expect when they got near the house—every window barred and every door bolted and red-hot bullets spitting through the loop-holes in the walls.

But the windows were open—you could see white curtains in them; there were plants on some of the sills. The door of the house stood ajar and Milly's cat was asleep on the doorstone, there in the sun.

They stood outside that door for quite a little bit, just milling around and staring. It was very quiet; they could hear their own breath breathe and their own hearts knock. Finally the minister brushed his face, as if he were brushing a cobweb away from it, and he gripped his gun and went up on the porch and knocked at the open door. He'd intended to stomp up those steps like a charge of cavalry, but he walked soft, instead. He couldn't have told you why.

He knocked once and he knocked again—and then Milly was standing in the door, with her baby in her arms.

Somebody at the back of the crowd dropped the scythe he was carrying, and another one coughed in his hand.

"You're just in time to christen my child, your reverence," said Milly. "Have you brought that rifle to help you christen my child?"

The minister's eyes dropped, after a minute, and he lowered his rifle but he still held it in the crook of his arm.

"Your child?" he said, and his voice was as low as Milly's, but there was a fierceness in it. "What about my child?"

"Listen!" said Milly, raising her hand, and the whole crowd fell dead still. Then from somewhere in the house came the hum of a spinning-wheel, low and steady, and a woman's voice, humming with the wheel.

"That's your child you hear, your reverence," said Milly. "Does she sound hurt, your reverence, or does she sound content?"

The minister hesitated for a moment and the crowd

fell dead still again. Then they all heard the hum of the wheel and the hum of the woman's voice, humming back and forth to each other, as they did their work in the world.

"She sounds content—heaven help me!" said the minister, and a twist went over his face. But then there was a sudden outburst of cries and questions from the others. "My child, what about my child?" "Where's Mary?" "Is Susy safe?"

"Listen!" said Milly again, and they all fell silent once more. And, from somewhere, there came the splash of a churn and the voice of a woman talking to the butter to make it come; and the rattling of pans in a kitchen and a woman singing at her work; and the slap of clothes on a laundry board and the little clatter a woman makes setting table.

"There's your children," said Milly. "Hear 'em? Don't they sound all right? And—dinner will be ready in about half an hour—and you're all staying, I hope."

Then the daughters came out and their folks rushed to them; and, after all the crying and conniptions were over, Milly introduced the parents to their sons-in-law.

THE DEVIL AND DANIEL WEBSTER

IT'S a story they tell in the border country, where Massachusetts joins Vermont and New Hampshire. Yes, Dan'l Webster's dead—or, at least, they buried him. But every time there's a thunderstorm around Marshfield, they say you can hear his rolling voice in the hollows of the sky. And they say that if you go to his grave and speak loud and clear, "Dan'l Webster— Dan'l Webster!" the ground'll begin to shiver and the trees begin to shake. And after a while you'll hear a deep voice saying, "Neighbor, how stands the Union?" Then you better answer the Union stands as she stood, rock-bottomed and copper-sheathed, one and indivisible, or he's liable to rear right out of the ground. At least, that's what I was told when I was a youngster.

You see, for a while, he was the biggest man in the country. He never got to be President, but he was the biggest man. There were thousands that trusted in him right next to God Almighty, and they told stories about him that were like the stories of patriarchs and such. They said, when he stood up to speak, stars and stripes came right out in the sky, and once he spoke against a river and made it sink into the ground. They said, when he walked the woods with his fishing rod, Killall, the trout would jump out of the streams right into his pockets, for they knew it was no use putting up a fight against him; and, when he argued a case, he could turn on the harps of the blessed and the shaking of the earth underground. That was the kind of man he was, and his big farm up at Marshfield was suitable to him. The chickens he raised were all white meat down through the drumsticks, the cows were tended like children, and the big ram he called Goliath had horns with a curl like a morning-glory vine and could butt through an iron door. But Dan'l wasn't one of your gentlemen farmers; he knew all the ways of the land, and he'd be up by candlelight to see that the chores got done. A man with a mouth like a mastiff, a brow like a mountain and eyes like burning anthracite—that was Dan'l Webster in his prime. And the biggest case he argued never got written down in the books, for he argued it against the devil, nip and tuck and no holds barred. And this is the way I used to hear it told.

There was a man named Jabez Stone, lived at Cross Corners, New Hampshire. He wasn't a bad man to start with, but he was an unlucky man. If he planted corn, he got borers; if he planted potatoes, he got blight. He had good-enough land, but it didn't prosper him; he had a decent wife and children, but the more children he had, the less there was to feed them. If stones cropped up in his neighbor's field, boulders boiled up in his; if he had a horse with the spavins, he'd trade it for one with the staggers and give something extra. There's some folks bound to be like that, apparently. But one day Jabez Stone got sick of the whole business.

He'd been plowing that morning and he'd just

broke the plowshare on a rock that he could have sworn hadn't been there yesterday. And, as he stood looking at the plowshare, the off horse began to cough —that ropy kind of cough that means sickness and horse doctors. There were two children down with the measles, his wife was ailing, and he had a whitlow on his thumb. It was about the last straw for Jabez Stone. "I vow," he said, and he looked around him kind of desperate—"I vow it's enough to make a man want to sell his soul to the devil! And I would, too, for two cents!"

Then he felt a kind of queerness come over him at having said what he'd said; though, naturally, being a New Hampshireman, he wouldn't take it back. But, all the same, when it got to be evening and, as far as he could see, no notice had been taken, he felt relieved in his mind, for he was a religious man. But notice is always taken, sooner or later, just like the Good Book says. And, sure enough, next day, about suppertime, a soft-spoken, dark-dressed stranger drove up in a handsome buggy and asked for Jabez Stone.

Well, Jabez told his family it was a lawyer, come to see him about a legacy. But he knew who it was. He didn't like the looks of the stranger, nor the way he smiled with his teeth. They were white teeth, and plentiful—some say they were filed to a point, but I wouldn't vouch for that. And he didn't like it when the dog took one look at the stranger and ran away howling, with his tail between his legs. But having passed his word, more or less, he stuck to it, and they went out behind the barn and made their bargain. Jabez Stone had to prick his finger to sign, and the stranger lent him a silver pin. The wound healed clean, but it left a little white scar.

After that, all of a sudden, things began to pick up and prosper for Jabez Stone. His cows got fat and his horses sleek, his crops were the envy of the neighborhood, and lightning might strike all over the valley, but it wouldn't strike his barn. Pretty soon, he was one of the prosperous people of the county; they asked him to stand for selectman, and he stood for it; there began to be talk of running him for state senate. All in all, you might say the Stone family was as happy and contented as cats in a dairy. And so they were, except for Jabez Stone.

He'd been contented enough, the first few years. It's a great thing when bad luck turns; it drives most other things out of your head. True, every now and then, especially in rainy weather, the little white scar on his finger would give him a twinge. And once a year, punctual as clockwork, the stranger with the handsome buggy would come driving by. But the sixth year, the stranger lighted, and, after that, his peace was over for Jabez Stone.

The stranger came up through the lower field, switching his boots with a cane—they were handsome black boots, but Jabez Stone never liked the look of them, particularly the toes. And, after he'd passed the time of day, he said, "Well, Mr. Stone, you're a hummer! It's a very pretty property you've got here, Mr. Stone."

"Well, some might favor it and others might not," said Jabez Stone, for he was a New Hampshireman.

"Oh, no need to decry your industry!" said the

stranger, very easy, showing his teeth in a smile. "After all, we know what's been done, and it's been according to contract and specifications. So when—ahem—the mortgage falls due next year, you shouldn't have any regrets."

"Speaking of that mortgage, mister," said Jabez Stone, and he looked around for help to the earth and the sky, "I'm beginning to have one or two doubts about it."

"Doubts?" said the stranger, not quite so pleasantly.

"Why, yes," said Jabez Stone. "This being the U.S.A. and me always having been a religious man." He cleared his throat and got bolder. "Yes, sir," he said, "I'm beginning to have considerable doubts as to that mortgage holding in court."

"There's courts and courts," said the stranger, clicking his teeth. "Still, we might as well have a look at the original document." And he hauled out a big black pocketbook, full of papers. "Sherwin, Slater, Stevens, Stone," he muttered. "I, Jabez Stone, for a term of seven years—— Oh, it's quite in order, I think."

But Jabez Stone wasn't listening, for he saw something else flutter out of the black pocketbook. It was something that looked like a moth, but it wasn't a moth. And as Jabez Stone stared at it, it seemed to speak to him in a small sort of piping voice, terrible small and thin, but terrible human. "Neighbor Stone!" it squeaked. "Neighbor Stone! Help me! For God's sake, help me!"

But before Jabez Stone could stir hand or foot, the stranger whipped out a big bandanna handkerchief, caught the creature in it, just like a butterfly, and started tying up the ends of the bandanna.

"Sorry for the interruption," he said. "As I was saying——"

But Jabez Stone was shaking all over like a scared horse.

"That's Miser Stevens' voice!" he said, in a croak. "And you've got him in your handkerchief!"

The stranger looked a little embarrassed.

"Yes, I really should have transferred him to the collecting box," he said with a simper, "but there were some rather unusual specimens there and I didn't want them crowded. Well, well, these little contretemps will occur."

"I don't know what you mean by contertan," said Jabez Stone, "but that was Miser Stevens' voice! And he ain't dead! You can't tell me he is! He was just as spry and mean as a woodchuck, Tuesday!"

"In the midst of life——" said the stranger, kind of pious. "Listen!" Then a bell began to toll in the valley and Jabez Stone listened, with the sweat running down his face. For he knew it was tolled for Miser Stevens and that he was dead.

"These long-standing accounts," said the stranger with a sigh; "one really hates to close them. But business is business."

He still had the bandanna in his hand, and Jabez Stone felt sick as he saw the cloth struggle and flutter.

"Are they all as small as that?" he asked hoarsely.

"Small?" said the stranger. "Oh, I see what you mean. Why, they vary." He measured Jabez Stone with his eyes, and his teeth showed. "Don't worry, Mr.

Stone," he said. "You'll go with a very good grade. I
wouldn't trust you outside the collecting box. Now, a
man like Dan'l Webster, of course—well, we'd have to
build a special box for him, and even at that, I imagine
the wing spread would astonish you. But, in your case,
as I was saying——

"Put that handkerchief away!" said Jabez Stone, and
he began to beg and to pray. But the best he could get
at the end was a three years' extension, with conditions.

But till you make a bargain like that, you've got no
idea of how fast four years can run. By the last months
of those years, Jabez Stone's known all over the state
and there's talk of running him for governor—and it's
dust and ashes in his mouth. For every day, when he
gets up, he thinks, "There's one more night gone," and
every night when he lies down, he thinks of the black
pocketbook and the soul of Miser Stevens, and it makes
him sick at heart. Till, finally, he can't bear it any
longer, and, in the last days of the last year, he hitches
up his horse and drives off to seek Dan'l Webster. For
Dan'l was born in New Hampshire, only a few miles
from Cross Corners, and it's well known that he has a
particular soft spot for old neighbors.

It was early in the morning when he got to Marshfield, but Dan'l was up already, talking Latin to the
farm hands and wrestling with the ram, Goliath, and
trying out a new trotter and working up speeches to
make against John C. Calhoun. But when he heard a
New Hampshireman had come to see him, he dropped
everything else he was doing, for that was Dan'l's way.
He gave Jabez Stone a breakfast that five men couldn't
eat, went into the living history of every man and

woman in Cross Corners, and finally asked him how he could serve him.

Jabez Stone allowed that it was a kind of mortgage case.

"Well, I haven't pleaded a mortgage case in a long time, and I don't generally plead now, except before the Supreme Court," said Dan'l, "but if I can, I'll help you."

"Then I've got hope for the first time in ten years," said Jabez Stone, and told him the details.

Dan'l walked up and down as he listened, hands behind his back, now and then asking a question, now and then plunging his eyes at the floor, as if they'd bore through it like gimlets. When Jabez Stone had finished, Dan'l puffed out his cheeks and blew. Then he turned to Jabez Stone and a smile broke over his face like the sunrise over Monadnock.

"You've certainly given yourself the devil's own row to hoe, Neighbor Stone," he said, "but I'll take your case."

"You'll take it?" said Jabez Stone, hardly daring to believe.

"Yes," said Dan'l Webster. "I've got about seventy-five other things to do and the Missouri Compromise to straighten out, but I'll take your case. For if two New Hampshiremen aren't a match for the devil, we might as well give the country back to the Indians."

Then he shook Jabez Stone by the hand and said, "Did you come down here in a hurry?"

"Well, I admit I made time," said Jabez Stone.

"You'll go back faster," said Dan'l Webster, and he told 'em to hitch up Constitution and Constellation to the carriage. They were matched grays with one white forefoot, and they stepped like greased lightning.

Well, I won't describe how excited and pleased the whole Stone family was to have the great Dan'l Webster for a guest, when they finally got there. Jabez Stone had lost his hat on the way, blown off when they overtook a wind, but he didn't take much account of that. But after supper he sent the family off to bed, for he had most particular business with Mr. Webster. Mrs. Stone wanted them to sit in the front parlor, but Dan'l Webster knew front parlors and said he preferred the kitchen. So it was there they sat, waiting for the stranger, with a jug on the table between them and a bright fire on the hearth—the stranger being scheduled to show up on the stroke of midnight, according to specifications.

Well, most men wouldn't have asked for better company than Dan'l Webster and a jug. But with every tick of the clock Jabez Stone got sadder and sadder. His eyes roved round, and though he sampled the jug you could see he couldn't taste it. Finally, on the stroke of 11:30 he reached over and grabbed Dan'l Webster by the arm.

"Mr. Webster, Mr. Webster!" he said, and his voice was shaking with fear and a desperate courage. "For God's sake, Mr. Webster, harness your horses and get away from this place while you can!"

"You've brought me a long way, neighbor, to tell me you don't like my company," said Dan'l Webster, quite peaceable, pulling at the jug.

"Miserable wretch that I am!" groaned Jabez Stone. "I've brought you a devilish way, and now I see my folly. Let him take me if he wills. I don't hanker after it, I must say, but I can stand it. But you're the Union's stay and New Hampshire's pride! He mustn't get you, Mr. Webster! He mustn't get you!"

Dan'l Webster looked at the distracted man, all gray and shaking in the firelight, and laid a hand on his shoulder.

"I'm obliged to you, Neighbor Stone," he said gently. "It's kindly thought of. But there's a jug on the table and a case in hand. And I never left a jug or a case half finished in my life."

And just at that moment there was a sharp rap on the door.

"Ah," said Dan'l Webster, very coolly, "I thought your clock was a trifle slow, Neighbor Stone." He stepped to the door and opened it. "Come in!" he said.

The stranger came in—very dark and tall he looked in the firelight. He was carrying a box under his arm— a black, japanned box with little air holes in the lid. At the sight of the box, Jabez Stone gave a low cry and shrank into a corner of the room.

"Mr. Webster, I presume," said the stranger, very polite, but with his eyes glowing like a fox's deep in the woods.

"Attorney of record for Jabez Stone," said Dan'l Webster, but his eyes were glowing too. "Might I ask your name?"

"I've gone by a good many," said the stranger carelessly. "Perhaps Scratch will do for the evening. I'm often called that in these regions."

Then he sat down at the table and poured himself a

drink from the jug. The liquor was cold in the jug, but it came steaming into the glass.

"And now," said the stranger, smiling and showing his teeth, "I shall call upon you, as a law-abiding citizen, to assist me in taking possession of my property."

Well, with that the argument began—and it went hot and heavy. At first, Jabez Stone had a flicker of hope, but when he saw Dan'l Webster being forced back at point after point, he just scrunched in his corner, with his eyes on that japanned box. For there wasn't any doubt as to the deed or the signature—that was the worst of it. Dan'l Webster twisted and turned and thumped his fist on the table, but he couldn't get away from that. He offered to compromise the case; the stranger wouldn't hear of it. He pointed out the property had increased in value, and state senators ought to be worth more; the stranger stuck to the letter of the law. He was a great lawyer, Dan'l Webster, but we know who's the King of Lawyers, as the Good Book tells us, and it seemed as if, for the first time, Dan'l Webster had met his match.

Finally, the stranger yawned a little. "Your spirited efforts on behalf of your client do you credit, Mr. Webster," he said, "but if you have no more arguments to adduce, I'm rather pressed for time"—and Jabez Stone shuddered.

Dan'l Webster's brow looked dark as a thundercloud.

"Pressed or not, you shall not have this man!" he thundered. "Mr. Stone is an American citizen, and no American citizen may be forced into the service of a foreign prince. We fought England for that in '12 and we'll fight all hell for it again!"

"Foreign?" said the stranger. "And who calls me a foreigner?"

"Well, I never yet heard of the dev—of your claiming American citizenship," said Dan'l Webster with surprise.

"And who with better right?" said the stranger, with one of his terrible smiles. "When the first wrong was done to the first Indian, I was there. When the first slaver put out for the Congo, I stood on her deck. Am I not in your books and stories and beliefs, from the first settlements on? Am I not spoken of, still, in every church in New England? 'Tis true the North claims me for a Southerner and the South for a Northerner, but I am neither. I am merely an honest American like yourself—and of the best descent—for, to tell the truth, Mr. Webster, though I don't like to boast of it, my name is older in this country than yours."

"Aha!" said Dan'l Webster, with the veins standing out in his forehead. "Then I stand on the Constitution! I demand a trial for my client!"

"The case is hardly one for an ordinary court," said the stranger, his eyes flickering. "And, indeed, the lateness of the hour——"

"Let it be any court you choose, so it is an American judge and an American jury!" said Dan'l Webster in his pride. "Let it be the quick or the dead; I'll abide the issue!"

"You have said it," said the stranger, and pointed his finger at the door. And with that, and all of a sudden, there was a rushing of wind outside and a noise of footsteps. They came, clear and distinct, through the night. And yet, they were not like the footsteps of living men.

"In God's name, who comes by so late?" cried Jabez Stone, in an ague of fear.

"The jury Mr. Webster demands," said the stranger, sipping at his boiling glass. "You must pardon the rough appearance of one or two; they will have come a long way."

And with that the fire burned blue and the door blew open and twelve men entered, one by one.

If Jabez Stone had been sick with terror before, he was blind with terror now. For there was Walter Butler, the loyalist, who spread fire and horror through the Mohawk Valley in the times of the Revolution; and there was Simon Girty, the renegade, who saw white men burned at the stake and whooped with the Indians to see them burn. His eyes were green, like a catamount's, and the stains on his hunting shirt did not come from the blood of the deer. King Philip was there, wild and proud as he had been in life, with the great gash in his head that gave him his death wound, and cruel Governor Dale, who broke men on the wheel. There was Morton of Merry Mount, who so vexed the Plymouth Colony, with his flushed, loose, handsome face and his hate of the godly. There was Teach, the bloody pirate, with his black beard curling on his breast. The Reverend John Smeet, with his strangler's hands and his Geneva gown, walked as daintily as he had to the gallows. The red print of the rope was still around his neck, but he carried a perfumed handkerchief in one hand. One and all, they came into the room with the fires of hell still upon them, and the stranger named their names and their deeds as they came, till the tale of twelve was told. Yet the stranger had told the truth—they had all played a part in America.

"Are you satisfied with the jury, Mr. Webster?" said the stranger mockingly, when they had taken their places.

The sweat stood upon Dan'l Webster's brow, but his voice was clear.

"Quite satisfied," he said. "Though I miss General Arnold from the company."

"Benedict Arnold is engaged upon other business," said the stranger, with a glower. "Ah, you asked for a justice, I believe."

He pointed his finger once more, and a tall man, soberly clad in Puritan garb, with the burning gaze of the fanatic, stalked into the room and took his judge's place.

"Justice Hathorne is a jurist of experience," said the stranger. "He presided at certain witch trials once held in Salem. There were others who repented of the business later, but not he."

"Repent of such notable wonders and undertakings?" said the stern old justice. "Nay, hang them—hang them all!" And he muttered to himself in a way that struck ice into the soul of Jabez Stone.

Then the trial began, and, as you might expect, it didn't look anyways good for the defense. And Jabez Stone didn't make much of a witness in his own behalf. He took one look at Simon Girty and screeched, and they had to put him back in his corner in a kind of swoon.

It didn't halt the trial, though; the trial went on, as trials do. Dan'l Webster had faced some hard juries and hanging judges in his time, but this was the hardest he'd ever faced, and he knew it. They sat there with a kind of glitter in their eyes, and the stranger's smooth voice went on and on. Every time he'd raise an objection, it'd be "Objection sustained," but whenever Dan'l objected, it'd be "Objection denied." Well, you couldn't expect fair play from a fellow like this Mr. Scratch.

It got to Dan'l in the end, and he began to heat, like iron in the forge. When he got up to speak he was going to flay that stranger with every trick known to the law, and the judge and jury too. He didn't care if it was contempt of court or what would happen to him for it. He didn't care any more what happened to Jabez Stone. He just got madder and madder, thinking of what he'd say. And yet, curiously enough, the more he thought about it, the less he was able to arrange his speech in his mind.

Till, finally, it was time for him to get up on his feet, and he did so, all ready to bust out with lightnings and denunciations. But before he started he looked over the judge and jury for a moment, such being his custom. And he noticed the glitter in their eyes was twice as strong as before, and they all leaned forward. Like hounds just before they get the fox, they looked, and the blue mist of evil in the room thickened as he watched them. Then he saw what he'd been about to do, and he wiped his forehead, as a man might who's just escaped falling into a pit in the dark.

For it was him they'd come for, not only Jabez Stone. He read it in the glitter of their eyes and in the way the stranger hid his mouth with one hand. And if he fought them with their own weapons, he'd fall into their power; he knew that, though he couldn't have told you how. It was his own anger and horror that burned in their eyes; and he'd have to wipe that out or the case was lost. He stood there for a moment, his black eyes burning like anthracite. And then he began to speak.

He started off in a low voice, though you could hear every word. They say he could call on the harps of the blessed when he chose. And this was just as simple and easy as a man could talk. But he didn't start out by condemning or reviling. He was talking about the things that make a country a country, and a man a man.

And he began with the simple things that everybody's known and felt—the freshness of a fine morning when you're young, and the taste of food when you're hungry, and the new day that's every day when you're a child. He took them up and he turned them in his hands. They were good things for any man. But without freedom, they sickened. And when he talked of those enslaved, and the sorrows of slavery, his voice got like a big bell. He talked of the early days of America and the men who had made those days. It wasn't a spread-eagle speech, but he made you see it. He admitted all the wrong that had ever been done. But he showed how, out of the wrong and the right, the suffering and the starvations, something new had come. And everybody had played a part in it, even the traitors.

Then he turned to Jabez Stone and showed him as he was—an ordinary man who'd had hard luck and

wanted to change it. And, because he'd wanted to
change it, now he was going to be punished for all
eternity. And yet there was good in Jabez Stone, and
he showed that good. He was hard and mean, in some
ways, but he was a man. There was sadness in being a
man, but it was a proud thing too. And he showed what
the pride of it was till you couldn't help feeling it.
Yes, even in hell, if a man was a man, you'd know it.
And he wasn't pleading for any one person any more,
though his voice rang like an organ. He was telling
the story and the failures and the endless journey of
mankind. They got tricked and trapped and bamboozled, but it was a great journey. And no demon that
was ever foaled could know the inwardness of it—it
took a man to do that.

The fire began to die on the hearth and the wind
before morning to blow. The light was getting gray in
the room when Dan'l Webster finished. And his words
came back at the end to New Hampshire ground, and
the one spot of land that each man loves and clings to.
He painted a picture of that, and to each one of that
jury he spoke of things long forgotten. For his voice
could search the heart, and that was his gift and his
strength. And to one, his voice was like the forest and
its secrecy, and to another like the sea and the storms
of the sea; and one heard the cry of his lost nation in
it, and another saw a little harmless scene he hadn't
remembered for years. But each saw something. And
when Dan'l Webster finished he didn't know whether or
not he'd saved Jabez Stone. But he knew he'd done a
miracle. For the glitter was gone from the eyes of judge

and jury, and, for the moment, they were men again, and knew they were men.

"The defense rests," said Dan'l Webster, and stood there like a mountain. His ears were still ringing with his speech, and he didn't hear anything else till he heard Judge Hathorne say, "The jury will retire to consider its verdict."

Walter Butler rose in his place and his face had a dark, gay pride on it.

"The jury has considered its verdict," he said, and looked the stranger full in the eye. "We find for the defendant, Jabez Stone."

With that, the smile left the stranger's face, but Walter Butler did not flinch.

"Perhaps 'tis not strictly in accordance with the evidence," he said, "but even the damned may salute the eloquence of Mr. Webster."

With that, the long crow of a rooster split the gray morning sky, and judge and jury were gone from the room like a puff of smoke and as if they had never been there. The stranger turned to Dan'l Webster, smiling wryly.

"Major Butler was always a bold man," he said. "I had not thought him quite so bold. Nevertheless, my congratulations, as between two gentlemen."

"I'll have that paper first, if you please," said Dan'l Webster, and he took it and tore it into four pieces. It was queerly warm to the touch. "And now," he said, "I'll have you!" and his hand came down like a bear trap on the stranger's arm. For he knew that once you bested anybody like Mr. Scratch in fair fight, his power

on you was gone. And he could see that Mr. Scratch
knew it too.

The stranger twisted and wriggled, but he couldn't
get out of that grip. "Come, come, Mr. Webster," he
said, smiling palely. "This sort of thing is ridic—ouch!
—is ridiculous. If you're worried about the costs of
the case, naturally, I'd be glad to pay——"

"And so you shall!" said Dan'l Webster, shaking him
till his teeth rattled. "For you'll sit right down at that
table and draw up a document, promising never to
bother Jabez Stone nor his heirs or assigns nor any
other New Hampshireman till doomsday! For any hades
we want to raise in this state, we can raise ourselves,
without assistance from strangers."

"Ouch!" said the stranger. "Ouch! Well, they never
did run very big to the barrel, but—ouch!—I agree!"

So he sat down and drew up the document. But
Dan'l Webster kept his hand on his coat collar all the
time.

"And, now, may I go?" said the stranger, quite
humble, when Dan'l'd seen the document was in proper
and legal form.

"Go?" said Dan'l, giving him another shake. "I'm
still trying to figure out what I'll do with you. For
you've settled the costs of the case, but you haven't
settled with me. I think I'll take you back to Marshfield," he said, kind of reflective. "I've got a ram there
named Goliath that can butt through an iron door. I'd
kind of like to turn you loose in his field and see what
he'd do."

Well, with that the stranger began to beg and to
plead. And he begged and he pled so humble that

finally Dan'l, who was naturally kindhearted, agreed to let him go. The stranger seemed terrible grateful for that and said, just to show they were friends, he'd tell Dan'l's fortune before leaving. So Dan'l agreed to that, though he didn't take much stock in fortune-tellers ordinarily. But, naturally, the stranger was a little different.

Well, he pried and he peered at the lines in Dan'l's hands. And he told him one thing and another that was quite remarkable. But they were all in the past.

"Yes, all that's true, and it happened," said Dan'l Webster. "But what's to come in the future?"

The stranger grinned, kind of happily, and shook his head.

"The future's not as you think it," he said. "It's dark. You have a great ambition, Mr. Webster."

"I have," said Dan'l firmly, for everybody knew he wanted to be President.

"It seems almost within your grasp," said the stranger, "but you will not attain it. Lesser men will be made President and you will be passed over."

"And, if I am, I'll still be Daniel Webster," said Dan'l. "Say on."

"You have two strong sons," said the stranger, shaking his head. "You look to found a line. But each will die in war and neither reach greatness."

"Live or die, they are still my sons," said Dan'l Webster. "Say on."

"You have made great speeches," said the stranger. "You will make more."

"Ah," said Dan'l Webster.

"But the last great speech you make will turn many of your own against you," said the stranger. "They will call you Ichabod; they will call you by other names. Even in New England, some will say you have turned your coat and sold your country, and their voices will be loud against you till you die."

"So it is an honest speech, it does not matter what men say," said Dan'l Webster. Then he looked at the stranger and their glances locked.

"One question," he said. "I have fought for the Union all my life. Will I see that fight won against those who would tear it apart?"

"Not while you live," said the stranger, grimly, "but it will be won. And after you are dead, there are thousands who will fight for your cause, because of words that you spoke."

"Why, then, you long-barreled, slab-sided, lantern-jawed, fortune-telling note shaver!" said Dan'l Webster, with a great roar of laughter, "be off with you to your own place before I put my mark on you! For, by the thirteen original colonies, I'd go to the Pit itself to save the Union!"

And with that he drew back his foot for a kick that would have stunned a horse. It was only the tip of his shoe that caught the stranger, but he went flying out of the door with his collecting box under his arm.

"And now," said Dan'l Webster, seeing Jabez Stone beginning to rouse from his swoon, "let's see what's left in the jug, for it's dry work talking all night. I hope there's pie for breakfast, Neighbor Stone."

But they say that whenever the devil comes near

Marshfield, even now, he gives it a wide berth. And he hasn't been seen in the state of New Hampshire from that day to this. I'm not talking about Massachusetts or Vermont.

DANIEL WEBSTER AND THE
SEA SERPENT

IT happened, one summer's day, that Dan'l Webster and some of his friends were out fishing. That was in the high days of his power and his fame, when the question wasn't if he was going to be President but when he was going to be President, and everybody at Kingston depot stood up when Dan'l Webster arrived to take the cars. But in spite of being Secretary of State and the biggest man in New England, he was just the same Dan'l Webster. He bought his Jamaica personal and in the jug at Colonel Sever's store in Kingston, right under a sign saying ENGLISH AND WEST INDIA GOODS, and he never was too busy to do a hand's turn for a friend. And, as for his big farm at Marshfield, that was just the apple of his eye. He buried his favorite horses with their shoes on, standing up, in a private graveyard, and wrote Latin epitaphs for them, and he often was heard to say that his big Hungarian bull, Saint Stephen, had more sense in his rear off hoof than most politicians. But, if there was one thing he loved better than Marshfield itself, it was the sea and the waters around it, for he was a fisherman born.

This time, he was salt-water fishing in the Comet, well out of sight of land. It was a good day for fishing, not too hazy, but not too clear, and Dan'l Webster en-

joyed it, as he enjoyed everything in life, except maybe
listening to the speeches of Henry Clay. He'd stolen a
half-dozen days to come up to Marshfield, and well he
needed the rest, for we'd nearly gone to war with England the year before, and now he was trying to fix up
a real copper-riveted treaty that would iron out all the
old differences that still kept the two countries unfriendly. And that was a job, even for Dan'l Webster.
But as soon as he stepped aboard the Comet, he was
carefree and heartwhole. He had his real friends around
him and he wouldn't allow a word of politics talked on
the boat—though that rule got broken this time, and
for a good reason, as you'll see. And when he struck his
first cod, and felt the fish take the hook, a kind of big
slow smile went over his features, and he said, "Gentlemen, this is solid comfort." That was the kind of man
he was.

I don't know how many there were of them aboard
—half a dozen or so—just enough for good company.
We'll say there were George Blake and Rufus Choate
and young Peter Harvey and a boy named Jim Billings.
And, of course, there was Seth Peterson, Dan'l's boat
captain, in his red flannel shirt, New England as cod
and beach plums, and Dan'l Webster's fast friend. Dan'l
happened to be Secretary of State, and Seth Peterson
happened to be a boat captain, but that didn't make any
difference between them. And, once the Comet left
dock, Seth Peterson ran the show, as it's right that a
captain should.

Well, they'd fished all morning and knocked off for
a bite of lunch, and some had had segars and snoozes
afterward, and some hadn't, but in any case, it was

around midafternoon, and everybody was kind of comfortable and contented. They still fished, and they fished
well, but they knew in an hour or so they'd be heading
back for home with a fine catch on board. So maybe
there was more conversation than Seth Peterson would
have approved of earlier, and maybe some jokes were
passed and some stories told. I don't know, but you
know how it is when men get together at the end of
a good day. All the same, they were still paying attention to their business—and I guess it was George Blake
that noticed it first.

"Dan'l," he said, breathing hard, "I've got something on my line that pulls like a Morgan horse."

"Well, yank him in!" sang out Dan'l, and then his
face changed as his own line began to stiffen and twang.
"George," he said, "I beat you! I got something on my
line that pulls like a pair of steers!"

"Give 'em more line, Mr. Webster!" yells Seth
Peterson, and Dan'l did. But at that, the line ran out
so fast it smoked when it hit the water, and any hands
but Dan'l Webster's would have been cut to the bone.
Nor you couldn't see where it went to, except Something deep in the waters must be pulling it out as a
cat pulls yarn from a ball. The veins in Dan'l Webster's
arm stood out like cords. He played the fish and played
the fish; he fought it with every trick he knew. And
still the little waves danced and the other men gaped
at the fight—and still he couldn't bring the Something
to time.

"By the big elm at Marshfield!" he said at last, with
his dark face glowing and a fisherman's pride in his
eyes. "Have I hooked on to a frigate with all sails set?

I've payed out a mile of my own particular line, and she still pulls like ten wild horses. Gentlemen, what's this?"

And even as he said it, the tough line broke in two with a crack like a musket-shot, and out of the deep of ocean, a mile away, the creature rose, majestic. Neighbors, that was a sight! Shaking the hook from its jaw, it rose, the sea serpent of the Scriptures, exact and to specifications as laid down in the Good Book, with its hairy face and its furlong on furlong of body, wallowing and thrashing in the troubled sea. As it rose, it gave a long low melancholy hoot, like a kind of forsaken steamboat; and when it gave out that hoot, young Jim Billings, the boy, fainted dead away on the deck. But nobody even noticed him—they were all staring at the sea serpent with bulging eyes.

Even Dan'l Webster was shaken. He passed his hand for a moment across his brow and gave a sort of inquiring look at the jug of Jamaica by the hatch.

"Gentlemen," he said in a low voice, "the evidence —the ocular evidence would seem to be conclusive. And yet, speaking as a lawyer——"

"Thar she blows! I never thought to see her again!" yells Seth Peterson, half driven out of his mind by the sight, as the sea serpent roiled the waters. "Thar she blows, by the Book of Genesis! Oh, why ain't I got a harpoon?"

"Quiet, Seth," said Dan'l Webster. "Let us rather give thanks for being permitted to witness this glorious and unbelievable sight." And then you could see the real majesty of the man, for no sooner were the words out of his mouth than the sea serpent started swimming straight toward the Comet. She came like a railway train and her wake boiled out behind her for an acre. And yet, there was something kind of skittish about her, too—you might say that she came kind of shaking her skirts and bridling. I don't know what there was about her that made you sure she was a female, but they were all sure.

She came, direct as a bullet, till you could count the white teeth shining in her jaws. I don't know what the rest of them did—though doubtless some prayers were put up in a hasty way—but Dan'l Webster stood there and faced her, with his brow dark and his eyes like a sleepy lion's, giving her glance for glance. Yes, there was a minute, there, when she lifted her head high out of water and they looked at each other eye to eye. They say hers were reddish but handsome. And then, just as it seemed she'd crash plumb through the Comet, she made a wide wheel and turned. Three times she circled the boat, hooting lonesomely, while the Comet danced up and down like a cork on the waves. But Dan'l Webster kept his footing, one hand gripping the mast, and whenever he got a chance, he fixed her with his eye. Till finally, on the third circuit, she gave one last long hoot—like twenty foghorns at once, it was, and nearly deafened them all—and plunged back whence she'd come, to the bottomless depths of the sea.

But even after the waters were calm again, they didn't say anything for quite a while. Till, finally, Seth Peterson spoke.

"Well, Mr. Webster," he said, "that one got away" —and he grinned a dry grin.

"Leviathan of the Scriptures! Give me paper and

pen," said Dan'l Webster. "We must write this down and attest it." And then they all began to talk.

Well, he wrote an account of just what they'd seen, very plain and honest. And everybody there signed his name to it. Then he read it over to them again aloud. And then there was another silence, while they looked at one another.

Finally, Seth Peterson shook his head, slow and thoughtful.

"It won't do, Dan'l," he said, in a deep voice.

"Won't do?" said Dan'l Webster, with his eyes blazing. "What do you mean, Seth?"

"I mean it just won't do, Dan'l," said Seth Peterson, perfectly respectful, but perfectly firm. "I put it up to you, gentlemen," he said, turning to the others. "I can go home and say I've seen the sea serpent. And everybody'll say, 'Oh, that's just that old liar, Seth Peterson.' But if it's Dan'l Webster says so—can't you see the difference?"

He paused for a minute, but nobody said a word.

"Well, I can," he said. He drawled out the words very slow. "Dan'l Webster—Secretary of State—sees and talks to a sea serpent—off Plymouth Bay. Why, it would plumb ruin him! And I don't mind being ruint, but it's different with Dan'l Webster. Would you vote for a man for President who claimed he'd saw the sea serpent? Well, would you? Would anybody?"

There was another little silence, and then George Blake spoke.

"He's right, Dan'l," he said, while the others nodded. "Give me that paper." He took it from Dan'l Webster's hand and threw it in the sea.

"And now," he said in a firm voice, "I saw cod. Nothing but cod. Except maybe a couple of halibut. Did any gentleman here see anything else?"

Well, at that, it turned out, of course, that nobody aboard had seen anything but cod all day. And with that, they put back for shore. All the same, they all looked over their shoulders a good deal till they got back to harbor.

And yet Dan'l Webster wasn't too contented that evening, in spite of his fine catch. For, after all, he had seen the sea serpent, and not only seen her but played her on the line for twenty-seven minutes by his gold repeater, and, being a fisherman, he'd like to have said so. And yet, if he did—Seth was right—folks would think him crazy or worse. It took his mind off Lord Ashburton and the treaty with England—till, finally, he pushed aside the papers on his desk.

"Oh, a plague on the beast!" he said, kind of crossly. "I'll leave it alone and hope it leaves me alone." So he took his candle and went up to bed. But just as he was dropping off to sleep, he thought he heard a long low hoot from the mouth of Green Harbor River, two miles away.

The next night the hooting continued, and the third day there was a piece in the Kingston paper about the new Government foghorn at Rocky Ledge. Well, the thing began to get on Dan'l Webster's nerves, and when his temper was roused he wasn't a patient man. Moreover, the noises seemed to disturb the stock—at least his overseer said so—and the third night his favorite gray kicked half the door out of her stall. "That sea serpent's getting to be an infernal nuisance," thought

Dan'l Webster. "I've got to protect my property." So, the fourth night he put on his old duck-shooting clothes and took his favorite shotgun, Learned Selden, and went down to a blind at the mouth of Green Harbor River, to see what he could see. He didn't tell anybody else about his intentions, because he still felt kind of sensitive about the whole affair.

Well, there was a fine moon that night, and sure enough, about eleven o'clock, the sea serpent showed up, steaming in from ocean, all one continuous wave length, like a giant garden hose. She was quite a handsome sight, all speckled with the moonlight, but Dan'l Webster couldn't rightly appreciate it. And just as she came to the blind, she lifted her head and looked sorrowfully in the direction of Marshfield and let out a long low soulful hoot like a homesick train.

Dan'l Webster hated to do it. But he couldn't have a sea serpent living in Green Harbor River and scaring the stock—not to speak of the universal consternation and panic there'd be in the countryside when such a thing was known. So he lifted Learned Selden and gave her both barrels for a starter, just a trifle over her head. And as soon as the gun exploded, the sea serpent let out a screech you could hear a mile and headed back for open sea. If she'd traveled fast before, she traveled like lightning now, and it wasn't any time before she was just a black streak on the waters.

Dan'l Webster stepped out of the blind and wiped his brow. He felt sorry, but he felt relieved. He didn't think she'd be back, after that sort of scare, and he wanted to leave everything shipshape before he went down to Washington, next morning. But next day, when he told Seth Peterson what he'd done, he didn't feel so chipper. For, "You shouldn't have done that, Mr. Webster," said Seth Peterson, shaking his head, and that was all he would say except a kind of mutter that sounded like "Samanthy was always particular set in her likes." But Dan'l didn't pay any attention to that, though he remembered it later, and he was quite short with Seth for the first time in their long relationship. So Seth shut up like a quahog, and Dan'l took the cars for Washington.

When he got there he was busy enough, for the British treaty was on the boil, and within twenty-four hours he'd forgot all about the sea serpent. Or thought he had. But three days later, as he was walking home to his house on Lafayette Square, with a senator friend of his, in the cool of the evening, they heard a curious noise. It seemed to come from the direction of the Potomac River.

"Must have got a new whistle for the Baltimore night boat," said the senator. "Noisy too."

"Oh, that's just the bullfrogs on the banks," said Dan'l Webster steadily. But he knew what it was, just the same, and his heart sank within him. But nobody ever called Dan'l Webster a coward. So, as soon as he'd got rid of the senator, he went down to the banks of the Potomac. Well, it was the sea serpent, all right.

She looked a little tired, as well she might, having swum from Plymouth Bay. But as soon as she saw Dan'l Webster, she stretched out her neck and gave a long low loving hoot. Then Dan'l knew what the trouble was and, for once in his life, he didn't know what to do. But he'd brought along a couple of roe herring, in a paper, just in case; so he fed them to her and she hooted, affectionate and grateful. Then he walked back to his house with his head bowed. And that very night he sent a special express letter to Seth Peterson at Marshfield, for, it seemed to him, Seth must know more about the business than he let on.

Well, Seth got to Washington as fast as the cars would bring him, and the very evening he arrived Dan'l sent him over to interview the serpent. But when Seth came back, Dan'l could see by his face that he hadn't made much progress.

"Could you talk to her, Seth?" he said, and his voice was eager. "Can she understand United States?"

"Oh, she can understand it all right," said Seth. "She's even picking up a few words. They was always a smart family, those Rock Ledge serpents, and she's the old maid of the lot, and the best educated. The only trouble with 'em is, they're so terrible sot in their ways."

"You might have warned me, Seth," said Dan'l Webster, kind of reproachful, and Seth looked uncomfortable.

"Well, to tell you the truth," he said, "I thought all of 'em was dead. Nor I never thought she'd act up like this—her father was as respectable a serpent as you'd see in a long summer's day. Her father——"

"Bother her father!" said Dan'l Webster and set his jaw. "Tell me what she says."

"Well, Mr. Webster," said Seth, and stared at his boots, "she says you're quite a handsome man. She says she never did see anybody quite like you," he went on. "I hate to tell you this, Mr. Webster, and I feel kind of responsible, but I think you ought to know. And I told you that you oughtn't to have shot at her—she's pretty proud of that. She says she knows just how you meant it. Well, I'm no great hand at being embarrassed, Mr. Webster, but, I tell you, she embarrassed me. You see, she's been an old maid for about a hundred and fifty years, I guess, and that's the worst of it. And being the last of her folks in those particular waters, there's just no way to restrain her—her father and mother was as sensible, hard-working serpents as ever gave a feller a tow through a fog, but you know how it is with those old families. Well, she says wherever you go, she'll follow you, and she claims she wants to hear you speak before the Supreme Court——"

"Did you tell her I'm a married man?" said Dan'l. "Did you tell her that?"

"Yes, I told her," said Seth, and you could see the perspiration on his forehead. "But she says that doesn't signify—her being a serpent and different—and she's fixing to move right in. She says Washington's got a lovely climate and she's heard all about the balls and the diplomatic receptions. I don't know how she's heard about them, but she has." He swallowed. "I got her to promise she'd kind of lie low for two weeks and not come up the Potomac by daylight—she was fixing to do that because she wants to meet the President. Well, I got her to promise that much. But she says, even so, if you don't come to see her once an evening, she'll hoot till you do, and she told me to tell you that you haven't heard hooting yet. And as soon as the fish market's open, I better run down and buy a barrel of flaked cod, Mr. Webster—she's partial to flaked cod and she usually takes it in the barrel. Well, I don't want to worry you, Mr. Webster, but I'm afraid that we're in a fix."

"A fix!" said Dan'l Webster. "It's the biggest fix I ever was in in my life!"

"Well, it's kind of complimentary, in a way, I guess," said Seth Peterson, "but——"

"Does she say anything else?" said Dan'l Webster, drawing a long breath.

"Yes, Mr. Webster," said Seth Peterson, his eyes on his boots. "She says you're a little shy. But she says she likes that in a man."

Dan'l Webster went to bed that night, but he didn't sleep. He worked and worked those great brains of his till he nearly wore out the wheels, but he still couldn't think of a way to get rid of the sea serpent. And just about the time dawn broke, he heard one long low hoot, faithful and reminiscent, from the direction of the Potomac.

Well, the next two weeks were certainly bad ones for him. For, as the days wore on, the sea serpent got more and more restive. She wanted him to call her Samanthy, which he wouldn't, and she kept asking him when he was going to introduce her into society, till he had to feed her Italian sardines in olive oil to keep her quiet. And that ran up a bill at the fish market that he hated to think of—besides, her continually threatening to come up the Potomac by day. Moreover, and to put the cap on things, the great Webster-Ashburton treaty that was to make his name as Secretary of State had struck a snag and England didn't seem at all partial to admitting the American claims. Oh, it was a weary fortnight and a troublesome one!

The last afternoon of the fortnight, he sat in his office and he didn't know where to turn. For Lord Ashburton was coming to see him for a secret conference that night at nine, and he had to see the sea serpent at ten, and how to satisfy either of them he didn't know. His eyes stared wearily at the papers on his desk. He rang the bell for his secretary.

"The corvette Benjamin Franklin reports——" he said. "This should have gone to the Navy Department, Mr. Jones." Then he glanced at the naval report again and his eyes began to glow like furnaces. "By the bones of Leviathan! I've got it!" he said, with a shout. "Where's my hat, Mr. Jones. I must see the President at once!"

There was a different feeling about the house on Lafayette Square that evening, for Dan'l Webster was himself again. He cracked a joke with Seth Peterson and took a glass of Madeira and turned it to the light. And when Lord Ashburton was announced—a nice, white-haired old gentleman, though a little stiff in his joints—he received him with all the courtesy of a king.

"I am glad to see you so much restored, Mr. Webster," said Lord Ashburton, when the greetings had been exchanged. "And yet I fear I bring you bad news. Concerning clauses six and seven of the proposed treaty between Her Majesty's Government and the United States of America, it is my duty to state——"

"My lord, let us drop the clauses for a moment and take the wider view," said Dan'l Webster, smiling. "This is a matter concerning the future welfare and peace of two great nations. Your government claims the right to search our ships; that right we deny. And our attitude seems to you preposterous. Is that not so?"

"I would hesitate to use the word 'preposterous,' " said Lord Ashburton cautiously. "Yet——"

"And yet," said Dan'l Webster, leaning forward, "there are things which may seem preposterous, and yet are not. Let me put a case. Let us say that Great Britain has the strongest navy afloat."

"Britannia rules the waves," said Lord Ashburton, with a noble smile.

"There were a couple she didn't rule in 1812," said Dan'l Webster, "but let that pass. Let me ask you, Lord Ashburton, and let me ask you solemnly, what could even the power and might of Britain's navy avail against Leviathan?"

"Leviathan?" said Lord Ashburton, rather coldly. "Naturally, I understand the Biblical allusion. Yet——"

"The sea serpent," said Dan'l Webster, kind of impatient. "What could all Britain's navy do against the sea serpent out of the Scriptures?"

Lord Ashburton stared at him as if he had gone mad. "God bless my soul, Mr. Secretary!" he said. "But I fail to see the point of your question. The sea serpent doesn't exist!"

"Doesn't he—I mean she?" said Dan'l Webster, calmly. "And suppose I should prove to you that it does exist?"

"Well, 'pon my word! God bless my soul!" said Lord Ashburton, kind of taken aback. "Naturally—in that case—however—but even so——"

Dan'l Webster touched a bell on his desk. "Lord

Ashburton," he said, kind of solemn, "I am putting my life, and what is dearer to me, my honor and reputation, in your hands. Nevertheless, I feel it necessary, for a better understanding between our two countries."

Seth Peterson came into the room and Dan'l nodded at him.

"Seth," he said, "Lord Ashburton is coming with us to see Samanthy."

"It's all right if you say so, Mr. Webster," said Seth Peterson, "but he'll have to help carry the sardines."

"Well, 'pon my word! Bless my soul! A very strange proceeding!" said Lord Ashburton, but he followed along.

Well, they got to the banks of the Potomac, the three of them, and when they were there, Seth whistled. Samanthy was lying mostly under water, behind a little brushy island, but when she heard the whistle, she began to heave up and uncoil, all shining in the moonlight. It was what you might call a kind of impressive sight. Dan'l Webster looked at Lord Ashburton, but Lord Ashburton's words seemed sort of stuck in his throat.

Finally he got them out. "Bless my soul!" he said. "You Americans are very extraordinary! Is it alive?"

But then all he could do was goggle, for Samanthy had lifted her head, and giving a low friendly hoot, she commenced to swim around the island.

"Now, is that a sea serpent or isn't it?" said Dan'l Webster, with a kind of quiet pride.

"Indubitably," said Lord Ashburton, staring through his eyeglass. "Indubitably," and he kind of cleared his throat. "It is, indeed and in fact, a serpent of the sea. And I am asleep and in bed, in my room at the British Embassy." He pinched himself. "Ouch!" he said. "No, I am not."

"Would you call it sizable, for a sea serpent?" persisted Dan'l Webster.

Lord Ashburton stared again through his eyeglass. "Quite," he said. "Oh, yes, quite, quite!"

"And powerful?" asked Dan'l.

"I should judge so," said Lord Ashburton, faintly, as the sea serpent swam around and around the island and the waves of its wake broke crashing on the bank. "Yes, indeed, a very powerful engine of destruction. May I ask what it feeds upon?"

"Italian sardines, for preference," said Dan'l. "But that's beside the point." He drew a long breath. "Well, my lord," he said, "we're intending to commission that sea serpent as a regular and acknowledged war vessel in the United States Navy. And then, where's your wooden walls?"

Lord Ashburton, he was a diplomat, and his face didn't change expression as he stared first at the sea serpent and then at the face of Dan'l Webster. But after a while, he nodded. "You need not labor the point, Mr. Secretary," he said. "My government, I am sure, will be glad to reconsider its position on the last two clauses and on the right of search."

"Then I'm sure we can reach an agreement," said Dan'l Webster, and wiped the sweat from his brow. "And now, let's feed Samanthy."

He whistled to her himself, a long musical whistle, and she came bounding and looping in toward shore. It took all three of them to heave her the barrel of

sardines, and she swallowed it down in one gulp. After
that, she gave a hoot of thanks and gratitude, and Lord
Ashburton sat down on the bank for a minute and took
snuff. He said that he needed something to clear his
mind.

"Naturally," he said, after a while, "Her Majesty's
Government must have adequate assurances as to the
good conduct of this—this lady." He'd meant to say
"creature" at first, but Samanthy rolled her eye at him
just then, and he changed the word.

"You shall have them," said Dan'l Webster, and
whistled Samanthy even closer. She came in kind of
skittish, flirting her coils, and Lord Ashburton closed
his eyes for a minute. But when Dan'l Webster spoke,
it was in the voice that hushed the Senate whenever
he rose.

"Samanthy," he said, "I speak to you now as Secretary of State of the United States of America." It was the
great voice that had rung in the Supreme Court and replied to Hayne, and even a sea serpent had to listen
respectful. For the voice was mellow and deep, and he
pictured Samanthy's early years as a carefree young serpent, playing with her fellows, and then her hard life of
toil and struggle when she was left lone and lorn, till
even Seth Peterson and Lord Ashburton realized the
sorrow and tragedy of her lonely lot. And then, in the
gentlest and kindest way you could ask, he showed her
where her duty lay.

"For, if you keep on hooting in the Potomac, Samanthy," he said, "you'll become a public menace to
navigation and get sat upon by the Senate Committee
for Rivers and Harbors. They'll drag you up on land,

Samanthy, and put you in the Smithsonian Institution; they'll stick you in a stagnant little pool and children will come to throw you peanuts on Sundays, and their nurses will poke you with umbrellas if you don't act lively enough. The U. S. Navy will shoot at you for target practice, Samanthy, and the scientists will examine you, and the ladies of the Pure Conduct League will knit you a bathing suit, and you'll be bothered every minute by congressmen and professors and visitors and foreign celebrities till you won't be able to call your scales your own. Oh, yes, it'll be fame, Samanthy, but it won't be good enough. Believe me, I know something about fame and it's begging letters from strangers and calls from people you don't know and don't want to know, and the burden and wear and tear of being a public character till it's enough to break your heart. It isn't good enough, Samanthy; it won't give you back your free waters and your sporting in the deep. Yes, Samanthy, it'd be a remarkable thing to have you here in Washington, but it isn't the life you were meant for and I can't take advantage of your trust. And now," he said to Seth Peterson, "just what does she say?"

Seth Peterson listened, attentive, to the hootings.

"She says the Washington climate isn't what she thought it was," he said. "And the Potomac River's too warm; it's bad for her sciatica. And she's plumb tired of sardines."

"Does she say anything about me?" asked Dan'l Webster, anxiously.

"Well," said Seth Peterson, listening, "she says—if you'll excuse me, Mr. Webster—that you may be a great man, but you wouldn't make much of a sea

serpent. She says you haven't got enough coils. She says
—well, she says no hard feelings, but she guesses it was
a mistake on both sides."

He listened again. "But she says one thing," he said.
"She says she's got to have recognition and a husband,
if she has to take this Lord Ashburton. She says he
doesn't look like much, but he might get her introduced at Court."

A great light broke over Dan'l's face and his voice
rang out like thunder. "She shall have them both," he
said. "Come here, Samanthy. By virtue of the authority
vested in me as Secretary of State, and by special order
of the President of the United States and the Secretary
of the Navy, as witness the attached commission in
blank which I now fill in with your name, I hereby at-
tach you to the United States Navy, to rank as a forty-
four-gun frigate on special duty, rating a rear admiral's
flag and a salute of the appropriate number of guns,
wherever encountered in American waters. And, by
virtue of the following special order, I hereby order
you to the South Seas, there to cruise until further
orders for the purpose of seeking a suitable and proper
husband, with all the rights, privileges, duties and ap-
purtenances pertaining to said search and said American citizenship, as aforesaid and Hail Columbia. Signed
John Tyler, President. With which is subjoined a pass-
port signed by Daniel Webster, Secretary of State, bid-
ding all foreign nations let pass without hindrance the
American citizen, Samanthy Doe, on her lawful jour-
neys and errands." He dropped his voice for a moment
and added reflectively, "The American corvette, Benjamin Franklin, reports sighting a handsome young male

sea serpent on February third of the present year, just off the coast of the Sandwich Islands. Said serpent had forty-two coils by actual count, and when last sighted was swimming SSW at full speed."

But hardly had he spoken when Samanthy, for the last time, lifted her head and gave out a last long hoot. She looked upon Dan'l Webster as she did so, and there was regret in her eye. But the regret was tinctured with eagerness and hope.

Then she beat the water to a froth, and, before they really saw her go, she was gone, leaving only her wake on the moonlit Potomac.

"Well," said Dan'l Webster, yawning a little, "there we are. And now, Lord Ashburton, if you'll come home with me, we can draw up that treaty."

"Gladly," said Lord Ashburton, brushing his coat with his handkerchief. "Is it really gone? 'Pon my soul! You know, for a moment, I imagined that I actually saw a sea serpent. You have a very vivid way of putting things, Mr. Webster. But I think I understand the American attitude now, from the—er—analogy you were pleased to draw between such a—er—fabulous animal and the young strength of your growing country."

"I was confident that you would appreciate it, once it was brought to your attention," said Dan'l Webster. But he winked one eye at Seth Peterson, and Seth Peterson winked back.

And I'll say this for Dan'l Webster, too—he kept his promises. All through the time he was Secretary of State, he saw to it that the forty-four-gun frigate, Samanthy Doe, was carried on a special account on the books of the Navy. In fact, there's some people say that she's still so carried, and that it was her give Ericsson the idea for building the Monitor in the Civil War— if she wasn't the Monitor herself. And when the White Fleet went around the world in Teddy Roosevelt's time —well, there was a lookout in the crow's-nest of the flag-ship, one still calm night, as they passed by the palmy isles of the South Seas. And all of a sudden, the water boiled, tremendous and phosphorescent, and there was a pair of sea serpents and seven young ones, circling, calm and majestic, three times around the fleet. He rubbed his eyes and he stared, but there they were. Well, he was the only one that saw it, and they put him in the brig for it next morning. But he swore, till the day he died, they were flying the Stars and Stripes.

IV

GLAMOUR

I USED to read quite a lot of books when I was younger, but now they just make me sore. Marian keeps on bringing them back from the lending library and, occasionally, I'll pick one up and read a few chapters, but sooner or later you're bound to strike something that makes you sick. I don't mean dirt or anything —just foolishness, and people acting the way they never act. Of course, the books she reads are mostly love stories. I suppose they're the worst kind.

But what I understand least is the money angle. It takes money to get drunk and it takes money to go around with a girl—at least that's been my experience. But the people in those books seem to have invented a special kind of money—it only gets spent on a party or a trip. The rest of the time they might as well be paying their bills with wampum, as far as you can figure it out.

Of course, often enough, the people in books are poor. But then they're so darn poor, it's crazy. And, often enough, just when everything's at its worst, some handy little legacy comes along and the new life opens out before them right away, like a great big tulip. Well, I only had one legacy in my life and I know what I did with that. It darn near ruined me.

Uncle Bannard died up in Vermont in 1924, and

when his estate was settled, it came to $1237.62 apiece for Lou and me. Lou's husband put her share in Greater Los Angeles real estate—they live out on the Coast—and I guess they've done pretty well. But I took mine and quit the firm I was with, Rosenberg and Jenkins, mechanical toys and novelties, and went to Brooklyn to write a novel.

It sounds crazy, looking back on it. But I was a bug about reading and writing in those days, and I'd done some advertising copy for the firm that pulled. And that was the time when everybody was getting steamed up about "the new American writers," and it looked like a game without much overhead. I'd just missed the war—I was seventeen when it finished—and I'd missed college because of father's death. In fact, I hadn't **done** much of anything I really wanted since I had to **quit** high school—though the novelty business was all right as businesses go. So when I got a chance to cut loose, I cut.

I figured I could easily live a year on the twelve hundred, and, at first, I thought of France. But there'd be the nuisance of learning frog-talk and the passage there and back. Besides, I wanted to be near a big library. My novel was going to be about the American Revolution, if you can picture it. I'd read "Henry Esmond" over and over and I wanted to write a book like that.

I guess it must have been a bunch of my New England ancestors that picked Brooklyn for me. They were pioneers, all right—but, gosh, how they hated to take any chance but a big one! And I'm like that myself. I like to feel tidy in my mind when I'm taking a chance.

I figured I could be as solitary in Brooklyn as I could in Pisa, and a lot more comfortable. I knew how many words it took to make a novel—I'd counted some of them—so I bought enough paper and a second-hand typewriter and pencils and erasers. That about cleaned out my ready cash. I swore I wouldn't touch the legacy till I was really at work. But I felt like a million dollars —I swear I felt as if I were looking for treasure—when I got into the subway that shiny autumn day, and started across the river to look for a room.

It may have been my ancestors that sent me to Brooklyn, but I don't know what landed me at Mrs. Forge's. Old Wrestling Southgate, the one who was bothered with witches, would probably have called it a flowered snare of the fiend. And I'm not so sure, looking back, that he'd have been wrong.

Mrs. Forge opened the door herself—Serena was out. They'd talked about putting an ad in the paper but they'd just never got around to it; and, naturally, they wouldn't have put up a card. If it hadn't looked like the sort of house I'd wanted, I'd never have rung the bell. As it was, when she came to the door, I thought that I had made a mistake. So the first thing I did was beg her pardon.

She had on her black silk dress—the one with the white ruffles—just as if she were going out calling in the barouche. The minute she started to speak, I knew she was Southern. They all had that voice. I won't try to describe it. There's nothing worse than a whiny one —it beats the New England twang. But theirs didn't whine. They made you think of the sun and long afternoons and slow rivers—and time, time, time, just sliding along like a current, not going anywhere particular, but gay.

I think she liked my begging her pardon, for she took me in and gave me a slice of fruit cake and some lemonade. And I listened to her talk and felt, somehow, as if I'd been frozen for a long time and was just beginning to get warm. There was always a pitcher of lemonade in the ice-box, though the girls drank "coke," mostly. I've seen them come in from the snow, in the dead of winter, and drink it. They didn't think much of the cold, anyway, so they more or less pretended it didn't exist. They were that way.

The room was exactly what I wanted—big and sunny, with an outlook over a little backyard where there was the wreck of a forsythia bush and some spindly grass. I've forgotten to say the house was in one of those old-fashioned side-streets, not far from Prospect Park. But it doesn't matter where it was. It must be gone, now.

You know, it took all my nerve to ask Mrs. Forge the price. She was very polite, but she made me feel like a guest. I don't know if you can understand that. And then she couldn't tell me.

"Well, now, Mr. Southgate," she said, in that soft, gentle, helpless voice that ran on as inexorably as water, "I wish my daughter Eva had been here to receive you. My daughter Eva has accepted a business position since we came here for my daughter Melissa's art training. And I said, only this morning, 'Eva, honey, suppose Serena's away and some young person comes here, askin' for tnat room. I'll be bound to say somethin' to them, sugar, and I'll feel right embarrassed.' But just then some little boys started shoutin' down the street and I never did rightly hear what she answered. So if you're in a hurry, Mr. Southgate, I don't just know what we can do."

"I could leave a deposit," I said. I'd noticed, by this time, that the black silk had a tear in it and that she was wearing a pair of run-down ball-slippers—incredibly small they were. But, all the same, she looked like a duchess.

"Why, I suppose you could, Mr. Southgate," she said, with an obvious lack of interest. "I suppose that would be businesslike. You gentlemen in the North are always so interested in business. I recollect Mr. Forge sayin' before he died, 'Call them d—— Yankees if you like, Milly, but we've all got to live in the same country and I've met some without horns.' Mr. Forge was always so humorous. So, you see, we're quite accustomed to Northerners. You don't happen to be kin to the Mobile Southgates, do you, Mr. Southgate? You'll excuse an old lady's askin'—but you seem to favor them a little, now your face is in the light."

I'm not trying to put down just the way she talked —she didn't say "ah" and "nah"—it was something lighter and suaver. But her talk went on like that. They all did it. It wasn't nervousness or trying to impress you. They found it as easy and restful to talk as most of us do to keep still; and, if the talk never got any where, they'd never expected it would. It was like a drug—it made life into a dream. And, of course, it isn't that.

Finally, I simply went for my stuff and moved in. I didn't know how much I was paying or what meals would be included in it, but I somehow felt that these things would be shown unto me when the time was ripe. That's what an hour and a half with Mrs. Forge did to me. But I did resolve to have a clear understanding with "my daughter, Eva," who seemed to be the business head of the family.

Serena let me in when I came back. I gave her fifty cents to get in her good graces and she took an instant dislike to me which never wavered. She was small and black and withered, with bright little sparks of eyes. I don't know how long she'd been with them, but I thought of her growing on the family, like mistletoe, from immemorial time.

Whenever I heard her singing in the kitchen, I felt as if she were putting a private curse on me. "Honeybird—" she'd croon—"honey-bird, no one gwine tuh fly away wid mah honey-bird. Ole buzzard, he try his wings—he flap and he flap—man wid a gun he see him —hi, hi, hi—shoot ole buzzard wid a buckshot and never tetch mah honey-bird."

I knew who the old buzzard was, all right. And it may sound funny—but it wasn't. It was spooky. Eva wouldn't see it; they'd all treat Serena like a combination of unavoidable nuisance and troublesome child. I don't understand how they can treat servants that way. I mean friendly and grand at the same time. It isn't natural.

It sounds as if I were trying to keep from telling about Eva. I don't know why I'm doing that.

I got unpacked and pretty well settled. My room was on the third floor, back, but I could hear the girls coming home. There'd be the door and steps and a voice saying, "Honey, I'm so tired—I'm just plumb dragged out," and Mrs. Forge saying, "Now, honey, you rest yourself." There were three of those. I kind of wondered why they were all so tired. Later on, I found that was just something they said.

But then Mrs. Forge would begin to talk and they wouldn't be tired any more. They'd be quite excited and there'd be a good deal of laughter. I began to feel very uncomfortable. And then I got stubborn. After all, I'd rented the room.

So, when Eva finally knocked at the door, I just grunted, "Come in!" the way you would to a chamber-maid. She opened the door and stood in the doorway, hesitant. I imagine Melissa had bet her she wouldn't have the nerve.

"Mr. Southgate, I believe?" she said, quite vaguely, as if I might be anything from a cloud to a chest of drawers.

"Dr. Livingstone, I presume?" I said. There was an old picture on the wall—the two Englishmen meeting formally in the middle of a paper jungle. But I'll hand her something—she saw I wasn't trying to be fresh.

"I reckon we have been making a lot of racket," she said. "But that's mostly Melissa. She never was rightly raised. Won't you give us the favor of your company downstairs, Mr. Southgate? We-all don't act crazy. We just sound like it."

She was dark, you know, and yet she had that white skin. There's a kind of flower called freesia—when the petals are very white, they have the color of her skin. And there's a strong sweetness to it—strong and ghostly at the same time. It smells like spring with the ghosts

in it, between afternoon and dusk. And there's a word
they call glamour. It was there.

She had small white teeth and red lips. There was
one little freckle in the hollow of her throat—I don't
know how she happened to have only one. Louisa was
the beauty and Melissa the artist. They'd settled it that
way. I couldn't have fallen in love with Louisa or
Melissa. And yet, I liked to see them all together—the
three sisters—I'd liked to have lived in a big, cool house
by a river and spent my life seeing them all together.
What fool thoughts you get, when you're young. I'd
be the Northern cousin who managed the place. I used
to send myself to sleep with it, every night, for months.

Mrs. Forge wasn't in it, or Serena. It was a big place
—it went on for miles and miles. Most of the land
wasn't good for much and the Negroes were bone-lazy,
but I made them work. I'd get up in the first mist of
morning and be in the saddle all day, overseeing and
planning. But, always, I'd be coming back, on a tired
horse, up that flowery avenue and they'd be waiting for
me on the porch, the three white dresses bunched like
a bouquet.

They'd be nice to me, because I was weary, and
I'd go upstairs to the room looking over the river and
change out of my hot clothes and wash. Then Eva
would send me up a long drink with mint in it and I'd
take it slowly. After supper, when I wasn't doing accounts, they'd sing or we'd all play some foolish sort
of round game with ivory counters. I guess I got most
of it out of books, but it was very real to me. That's
one trouble with books—you get things out of them.

Often we got old, but it never seemed to change

us much. Once in a while the other girls were married and, sometimes, I married Eva. But we never had any children and none of us ever moved away. I kept on working like a dog and they accepted it and I was content. We had quite a few neighbors, at first, but I got tired of that. So I made it a river island you could only reach by boat, and that was more satisfactory.

It wasn't a dream, you know, or anything sappy like that. I just made it up in my head. Toward the end of the year, I'd lie awake for hours, making it up, but it never seemed to tire me. I never really told Eva about it at all, not even when we were engaged. Maybe it would have made a difference, but I don't think so.

She wasn't the kind of person you'd tell any dreams to. She was in the dream. I don't mean she was noble or fatal or like a ghost. I've had her in my arms and she was warm and alive and you could have had children by her, because things are that way. But that wasn't the point—that wasn't the point at all.

She didn't even have much imagination. None of them had. They just lived, like trees. They didn't plan or foresee. I've spent hours trying to explain to Mrs. Forge that, if you had ten dollars, it wasn't just ten dollars, it was something you could put in a savings bank. She'd listen, very politely. But ten dollars, to her, was just something that went away. They thought it was fine if you had money, but they thought it was equally fine if you had a good-looking nose. Money was rather like rain to them—it fell or it didn't—and, they knew there wasn't any way to make it rain.

I'm sure they'd never have come North at all, if it hadn't been for some obscure family dispute. They often seemed to wonder about it themselves. And I heard the dispute talked about dozens of times but I never really got the gist of it, except that it was connected with two things, the new spur-track to the turpentine plant, and Cousin Belle. "Cousin Belle, she just acted so mean—she gave up her manners," Mrs. Forge would say, placidly. "She left us no reco'se, Bannard—no reco'se at all." And then the girls would chime in. I suppose they got the money to come North from selling land to the turpentine plant, but even of that I am not sure.

Anyhow, they had golden visions, as they would have. Louisa was going to be a great actress and Melissa a great artist—and Eva—I don't know exactly what Eva expected, even now. But it was something. And it was all going to happen without any real work, it was going to fall from a cloud. Oh, yes, Melissa and Louisa went to classes and Eva had a job, but those, you felt, were stop-gaps. They were passing the time till the cloud opened and the manna fell.

I'll say this for them—it didn't seem to hurt them to have their visions fail. The only person it really hurt was me.

Because I believed them, at first. How could I help it? The dream I had wasn't so wrong. They were living on an island—an island in the middle of Brooklyn—a piece of where they came from. People came to the house—art students and such—there were always plenty of young men. But, once inside the house, they submitted to the house. Serena would pass the cold ham, at supper, and you'd look out of the window and be surprised to find it snowing, for the window should

have been open and the warm night coming through
I don't know what roomers they'd ever had before
but in my time there was only myself and Mr. Budd.
He was a fat little clerk of fifty, very respectable, and
he stayed because of the food, for Serena was a magnificent, wasteful cook.

Yes, I believed it, I believed in it all. It was like an
enchantment. It was glamour. I believed in all they said
and I saw them all going back to Chantry—the three
famous sisters with their three distinguished husbands
—like people in a fairy-tale.

We'd all have breakfast together, but the only person who talked much then was Mr. Budd. The Forges
never were properly alive till later in the day. At breakfast, you saw them through a veil. Sometimes I'd feel
my heart beat, staring at Eva, because she looked like
one of those shut flowers in greenhouses—something
shut and mysterious so you fairly held your breath,
waiting for it to open. I suppose it was just because she
took a long time to wake up.

Then Mr. Budd and the girls would go away, and,
when my bed was made, I'd go up and work. I'm not
saying much about the novel, but I worked hard on it.
I'd made a little chart on cardboard with 365 squares
and each day I'd ink one in.

I'd go out for lunch and take a walk afterwards.
A man has to have regular exercise, and that's free.
Then I'd work some more, until they started to come
home. I couldn't work after that—not after the first
months. But I'd make myself not listen for Eva's step.

The first time I kissed Eva was the New Year's party.
One of Louisa's beaus had brought some red wine and

we were singing and fooling around. Serena was off for
the evening and Eva and I were out in the kitchen,
looking for clean glasses. We were both feeling gay
and it just seemed natural. I didn't even think of it
again till the next afternoon, when we'd all gone to
the movies. And then I suddenly began to shake all
over, as if I had a chill, remembering, and she said,
"What is it, honey?" and her hand slipped into my
hand.

That was how it began. And that night I started
inventing the river plantation. And I'm not a fool and
I've been around. But I held hands with that girl
through January, February, and most of March before
I really kissed her again. I can't explain it at all. She
wasn't being coy or mean or trying to fight me. It was
as if we were floating downstream in a boat together,
and it was so pleasant to look at her and be near her,
you didn't need any more. The pain hadn't started,
then.

And yet, all through that time, something in me was
fighting, fighting, to get out of the boat, to get away
from the river. It wasn't my river at all, you know.
It never was. And part of me knew it. But, when you're
in love, you haven't got common sense.

By the end of March, the novel was more than half
finished. I'd allowed two months for revision and making contacts, which seemed sensible. And, one evening,
it was cold, and Eva and I took a walk in the park. And
when we came in, Mrs. Forge made us some hot cocoa
—the other girls had gone to bed early, for once—and,
while we were drinking it, Mrs. Forge fell asleep in
her chair. And we put down our cups, as if it were a

signal, and kissed—and the house was very quiet and we could hear her breathing, like sleep itself, through the long kiss.

Next morning, I woke up and the air felt warm and, when I looked out in the yard, there were leaves on the forsythia bush. Eva was just the same at breakfast, shut and mysterious, and I was just the same. But, when I went up to work, I shook my fist at old Wrestling Southgate, the fellow that was bothered with witches. Because I was going to marry Eva, and he could go to grass.

I tell you, they didn't plan or foresee. I told Mrs. Forge very straight just how I stood—finances and everything—and they treated it like a party. They were all as kind and excited as they could be, except Serena. She just refused to believe it and sang a lot more about buzzards. And, somehow or other, that made me feel queerer than ever. Because I knew Serena hated me but I knew she was a real person. I could understand her, she was close to the ground. And I loved the others but I didn't understand them, and sometimes I wouldn't be sure they were quite real. It was that way with Eva, even though we were in love.

I could kiss her but I couldn't be sure that she was always there when I kissed her. It wasn't coldness, it was merely another climate. I could talk for hours about what we were going to do when we were married and every time I stopped she'd say, "Go on, honey, it makes me feel so nice to hear you talk." But she'd have been as pleased if I'd sung it instead. God knows I didn't expect her to understand the novelty business, or even writing. But, sometimes, I'd honestly feel as if we didn't speak the same language. Which was foolish, because she wasn't foreign.

I remember getting angry with her one evening because I found out she was still writing to this boy friend, down South, and hadn't even told him about us. She opened her eyes very wide.

"Why, honey," she said, in the most reasonable of voices, "I couldn't stop writing Furfew right off like that. I've just always been sort of engaged to Furfew."

"Well, now you're engaged to me," I said.

"I know," she said. "That's why I can't stop writing him, honey. It would hurt Furfew something dreadful if he knew I had to stop writing him because I was engaged to you."

"Look here," I said, wondering which of us was crazy, "are we going to be married?"

"Of co'se, honey."

"Then what," I said, "has this Furfew got to with it? Are you engaged to him or me?"

"Of co'se I'm engaged to you, honey, and we're going to get married. But Furfew, he's kind of like kin, and we been engaged a long time. It seems right mean and uncivil to break off with him short like that."

"I don't believe it," I said, "I don't believe there are any Furfews. It sounds like something you grow under glass. What's he like?"

She thought for a long time.

"He's right cute," she said finally. "But he's got a little doin's of a black moustache."

I managed to find out, however, that he owned the turpentine plant and was considered quite the John D. Rockefeller of Chantry. I was so used to no one in

Chantry ever having any money that was worth anything, that this came as an unpleasing surprise. After that, Furfew used to try to come to the river plantation in a very shiny motor-launch with a red-and-white awning and I would warn him off with a shotgun.

But then the money business began. You like to give a girl presents when you're in love—you like to do things right. Well, Lord knows, Eva was no gold-digger—she was as likely to be pleased with a soda as a pair of imported gloves. On the other hand, she was as likely to be pleased with the gloves.

I kept on schedule with the work, but I couldn't with the money. Each week, I'd be just a little over the line. I tell you, the people in books don't know about money. The people who write them can tell what it's like to be broke. But they don't tell what it's like to go around with clothes enough to cover you and food enough to satisfy you, and still have your heart's desire depend on money you haven't got.

Sure, I could have gone back in the novelty business and Eva could have kept on working. That would have been right for nine people out of ten. But it wouldn't have been right for the way I felt about Eva. It can be like that.

I wanted to come to her—oh, like a rescuer, I suppose. Like a prince, like the Northern cousin that saved the plantation. I didn't want to make the best of things —I wanted it all. You can't compromise with glamour. Or that's the way I feel.

Besides, I'd put in eight months' work on that novel and it didn't seem sensible to throw it all away. It might be a ladder to climb out on. It might have been.

Eva never complained, but she never understood. She'd just say we could all go back and live in Chantry. Well, I'm not that kind of man. If it had only been the river plantation! But, by now, I knew Chantry as well as if I'd been born there, and there wasn't a thing for me to do. Except maybe a job in Furfew's turpentine plant. And wouldn't that have been pretty?

Then, gradually, I got to know that the Forges, too, were almost at the end of their string. I had to get it casually—they never talked about those things directly. But when you keep on spending what you've got, there comes a time when you don't have it any more. Only, it always surprised them. I wish I was built that way.

It was the middle of July by this time, and one Saturday afternoon Eva came home and said she'd been let off at her office. They were cutting down the staff. I'd just been going over my accounts, and when she told me that, I started laughing as if I couldn't stop.

She looked rather surprised at first, but then she laughed, too.

"Why, honey," she said, "you're the killin'est. You always take things so serious. And then, sometimes, you don't take them serious a bit."

"It's an old Northern custom," I said. "They call it 'Laugh, clown, laugh.' For God's sake, Eva, what are we going to do?"

"Why, honey," she said, "I suppose I could get me another position." She never told me it was up to me. She never would have. "But I just sort of despise those mean old offices. Do you think I ought to get me another position, honey?"

"Oh, darling, it doesn't matter," I said, still laughing. "Nothing matters but us."

"That's mighty sweet of you, honey," she said and she looked relieved. "That's just the way I feel. And, when we get married, we'll fix things up right nice for Melissa and Louisa, won't we? And mother, of co'se, because she just can't stand Cousin Belle."

"Sure," I said. "Sure. When we're married, we'll fix up everything." And we went out in the back yard to look at the forsythia bush. But that night, Furfew brought his launch inshore and landed on the lower end of the island. He pitched camp there, and I could see his fire at night, through a glass.

I can't describe the next two months very well. They were all mixed up, the reality and the dream. Melissa and Louisa had to give up their classes, so we were all home, and lots of people came to the house. Some of them were callers and some of them were bill-collectors but, whoever they were, they generally stayed to a meal. Serena never minded that, she liked company. I remember paying a grocery bill, with almost the last of my legacy, toward the end. There were eight hams on the bill and ten cases of "coke." It hadn't been paid for a long time.

Often, we'd all pile into an old Ford that belonged to one of the art students and go down to a public beach for the day. Eva didn't care so much about swimming but she loved to lie in the sand. And I'd lie beside her, painfully happy, and we'd hardly say anything at all. My God, but she was beautiful against those beach colors—the clear greens of the water and the hot white and tan of the sand. But then, she was just as beautiful.

sitting in the plush rocker in the front parlor, under that green lamp.

They say the time between the Ordinance of Secession and the firing on Sumter was one of the gayest seasons Charleston ever had. I can understand that. They'd come to the brink of something, and fate was out of their hands. I got to feel that way.

Everything mixed, I tell you, everything mixed. I'd be sitting on the beach with Eva and, at the same time, I'd be riding around the river plantation, getting reports from my foreman and planning years ahead. I got to love that place. Even toward the end, it was safe, it didn't change. Of course, we kept having more and more trouble with Furfew; he kept extending his lines from the lower end of the island, but it never came to actual warfare—just fights between our men.

Meanwhile, I finished the novel and started revising it. And sometimes Eva would say why didn't we get married, anyway, and I knew we couldn't. You can't get married without some future ahead of you. So we started having arguments, and that was bad.

Why didn't I just seduce her like the big, brave heroes in books? Well, there were times when I thought it might be the answer for both of us. But it never happened. It wasn't shame or good principles. It just isn't so awfully easy to seduce a dream.

I knew they were writing letters but I didn't want to know any more. I knew the legacy was gone and my savings account was going, but I didn't care. I just wanted things to go on.

Finally, I heard that Furfew was coming North. I was going around like a sleepwalker most of the time, then, so it didn't hit me, at first. And then it did hit me.

Eva and I were out in the back yard. We'd fixed up an old swing seat there and it was dusky. Serena was humming in the kitchen. "Ole buzzard he fly away now —buzzard he fly away." I can't sing, but I can remember the way she sang it. It's funny how things stick in your head.

Eva had her head on my shoulder and my arms were around her. But we were as far away as Brooklyn and New York with the bridges down. Somebody was making love, but it wasn't us.

"When's he coming?" I said, finally.

"He's drivin' up in his car," she said. "He started yesterday."

"Young Lochinvar complete with windshield," I said. "He ought to be careful of those roads. Has he got a good car?"

"Yes," she said. "He's got a right pretty car."

"Oh, Eva, Eva," I said. "Doesn't it break your heart?"

"Why, honey," she said. "Come here to me."

We held each other a long time. She was very gentle. I'll remember that.

I stayed up most of that night, finishing revision on the novel. And, before I went to sleep, Furfew came to the house on the river plantation and walked in. I was standing in the hall and I couldn't lift a hand to him. So then I knew how it was going to be.

He came in the flesh, next afternoon. Yes, it was a good car. But he didn't look like Benedict Arnold. He was tall and black-haired and soft-voiced and he had on the sort of clothes they wear. He wasn't so old, either, not much older than I was. But the minute I saw him beside Eva, I knew it was all up. You only had to look at them. They were the same kind.

Oh, sure, he was a good business man. I got that in a minute. But, underneath all the externals, they were the same kind. It hadn't anything to do with the faithfulness or meanness. They were just the same breed of cats. If you're a dog and you fall in love with a cat, that's just your hard luck.

He'd brought up some corn with him and he and I sat up late, drinking it. We were awfully polite and noble in our conversation but we got things settled just the same. The funny thing is, I liked him. He was Young Lochinvar, he was little Mr. Fix-it, he was death and destruction to me, but I couldn't help liking him. He could have come to the island when Eva and I were married. He'd have been a great help. I'd have built him a house by the cove. And that's queer.

Next day, they all went out in the car for a picnic, and I stayed home, reading my novel. I read it all through—and there was nothing there. I'd tried to make the heroine like Eva, but even that hadn't worked. Sometimes you get a novelty like that—it looks like a world-beater till you get it into production. And then, you know you've just got to cut your losses. Well, this was the same proposition.

So I took it down to the furnace and watched it burn. It takes quite a while to burn four hundred sheets of paper in a cold furnace. You'd be surprised.

On my way back, I passed through the kitchen where Serena was. We looked at each other and she put her hand on the bread-knife.

"I'll like to see you burning in hell, Serena," I said. I'd always wanted to say that. Then I went upstairs, feeling her eyes on my back like the point of the bread-knife.

When I lay down on the bed, I knew that something was finished. It wasn't only Eva or the novel. I guess it was what you call youth. Well, we've all got to lose it, but generally it just fades out.

I lay there a long time, not sleeping, not thinking. And I heard them coming back and, after a while, the door opened gently and I knew it was Eva. But my eyes were shut and I didn't make a move. So, after another while, she went away.

There isn't much else to tell. Furfew settled everything up—don't tell me Southerners can't move fast when they want to—and the packers came and four days later they all started back for Chantry in the car. I guess he wasn't taking any chances, but he needn't have worried. I knew it was up. Even hearing Cousin Belle had "come around" didn't excite me. I was past that.

Eva kissed me goodbye—they all did, for that matter—the mother and the three sisters. They were sort of gay and excited, thinking of the motor-trip and getting back. To look at them, you wouldn't have said they'd ever seen a bill-collector. Well, that was the way they were.

"Don't write," I said to Eva. "Don't write, Mrs. Lochinvar."

She puckered her brows as she did when she was really puzzled.

"Why, honey, of co'se I'll write," she said. "Why wouldn't I write you, honey?"

I am sure she did, too. I can see the shape of the letters. But I never got them because I never left an address.

The person who was utterly dumbfounded was Mr. Budd. We camped in the house for a week, getting our own meals and sleeping under overcoats—the lease wasn't up till the first and Furfew had made an arrangement with the owner. And Mr. Budd couldn't get over it.

"I always knew they were crazy," he said. "But I'll never get such cooking again." I could see him looking into a future of boarding-houses. "You're young," he said. "You can eat anything. But when a man gets my age——"

He was wrong, though. I wasn't young. If I had been, I wouldn't have spent that week figuring out three novelties. Two of them were duds, but the third was Jiggety Jane. You've seen her—the little dancing doll that went all over the country when people were doing the Charleston. I made the face like Serena's at first, but it looked too lifelike, so we changed the face. The other people made most of the money, but I didn't care. I never liked the darn thing anyway. And it gave me a chance to start on my own.

They couldn't stop me after that. You're harder to stop, once you get rid of your youth. No, I don't think it was ironic or any of those things. You don't, outside of a book. There wasn't any connection between the two matters.

That fall I met Marian and we got married a year

later. She's got a lot of sense, that girl, and it's wor[k]
out fine. Maybe we did have the children a little quick,
but she'd always wanted children. When you've got
children and a home, you've got something to keep
you steady. And, if she gets a kick out of reading love
stories, let her. So I don't have to.

In a book, I'd have run across Eva, or seen Furfew's
name in a paper. But that's never happened and I suppose it never will. I imagine they're all still in Chantry,
and Chantry's one of those places that never gets in the
news. The only thing I can't imagine is any of them
being dead.

I wouldn't mind seeing Furfew again, for that matter. As I say, I liked the man. The only thing I hold
against him is his moving them back, that way, before
the lease was up. It was all right and he had his reasons.
But they had two weeks left—two weeks till the first.
And that would just have finished the year.

And when I get to sleep nowadays, Marian's there
in the next bed, so that's all right, too. I've only tried
to go back to the river plantation once, after a conven-
tion in Chicago when I was pretty well lit. And then,
I couldn't do it. I was standing on the other side of
the river and I could see the house across the water.
Just the way it always was, but it didn't look lived in.
At least nobody came to the window—nobody came
out.

YBODY WAS VERY NICE

YES, I guess I have put on weight since you last
saw me—not that you're any piker yourself,
Spike. But I suppose you medicos have to keep in shape
—probably do better than we downtown. I try to play
golf in the week-ends, and I do a bit of sailing. But
four innings of the baseball game at reunion was
enough for me. I dropped out, after that, and let Art
Corliss pitch.

You really should have been up there. After all, the
Twentieth is quite a milestone—and the class is pretty
proud of its famous man. What was it that magazine
article said: "most brilliant young psychiatrist in the
country"? I may not know psychiatry from marbles, but
I showed it to Lisa, remarking that it was old Spike
Garrett, and for once she was impressed. She thinks
brokers are pretty dumb eggs. I wish you could stay
for dinner—I'd like to show you the apartment and
the twins. No, they're Lisa's and mine. Boys, if you'll
believe it. Yes, the others are with Sally—young Barbara's pretty grown up, now.

Well, I can't complain. I may not be famous like
you, Spike, but I manage to get along, in spite of the
brain trusters, and having to keep up the place on Long
Island. I wish you got East oftener—there's a pretty
view from the guest house, right across the Sound—

and if you wanted to write a book or anything, we'd know enough to leave you alone. Well, they started calling me a partner two years ago, so I guess that's what I am. Still fooling them, you know. But, seriously, we've got a pretty fine organization. We run a conservative business, but we're not all stuffed shirts, in spite of what the radicals say. As a matter of fact, you ought to see what the boys ran about us in the last Bawl Street Journal. Remind me to show it to you.

But it's your work I want to hear about—remember those bull-sessions we used to have in Old Main? Old Spike Garrett, the Medical Marvel! Why, I've even read a couple of your books, you old horse thief, believe it or not! You got me pretty tangled up on all that business about the id and the ego, too. But what I say is, there must be something in it if a fellow like Spike Garrett believes it. And there is, isn't there? Oh, I know you couldn't give me an answer in five minutes. But as long as there's a system—and the medicos know what they're doing.

I'm not asking for myself, of course—remember how you used to call me the 99 per-cent normal man? Well, I guess I haven't changed. It's just that I've gotten to thinking recently, and Lisa says I go around like a bear with a sore head. Well, it isn't that. I'm just thinking. A man has to think once in a while. And then, going back to reunion brought it all up again.

What I mean is this—the thing seemed pretty clear when we were in college. Of course, that was back in '15, but I can remember the way most of us thought. You fell in love with a girl and married her and settled down and had children and that was that. I'm not being simple-minded about it—you knew people get divorced, just as you knew people died, but it didn't seem something that was likely to happen to you. Especially if you came from a small Western city, as I did. Great Scott, I can remember when I was just a kid and the Prentisses got divorced. They were pretty prominent people and it shook the whole town.

That's why I want to figure things out for my own satisfaction. Because I never expected to be any Lothario—I'm not the type. And yet Sally and I got divorced and we're both remarried, and even so, to tell you the truth, things aren't going too well. I'm not saying a word against Lisa. But that's the way things are. And it isn't as if I were the only one. You can look around anywhere and see it, and it starts you wondering.

I'm not going to bore you about myself and Sally. Good Lord, you ushered at the wedding, and she always liked you. Remember when you used to come out to the house? Well, she hasn't changed—she's still got that little smile—though, of course, we're all older. Her husband's a doctor, too—that's funny, isn't it?—and they live out in Montclair. They've got a nice place there and he's very well thought of. We used to live in Meadowfield, remember?

I remember the first time I saw her after she married McConaghey—oh, we're perfectly friendly, you know. She had on red nail polish and her hair was different, a different bob. And she had one of those handbags with her new initials on it. It's funny, the first time, seeing your wife in clothes you don't know. Though Lisa and I have been married eight years, for that matter, and Sally and I were divorced in '28.

Of course, we have the children for part of the summer. We'll have Barbara this summer—Bud'll be in camp. It's a little difficult sometimes, but we all co-operate. You have to. And there's plenty to do on Long Island in the summer, that's one thing. But they and Lisa get along very well—Sally's brought them up nicely that way. For that matter, Doctor McConaghey's very nice when I see him. He gave me a darn good prescription for a cold and I get it filled every winter. And Jim Blake—he's Lisa's first husband—is really pretty interesting, now we've got to seeing him again. In fact, we're all awfully nice—just as nice and polite as we can be. And sometimes I get to wondering if it mightn't be a good idea if somebody started throwing fits and shooting rockets, instead. Of course I don't really mean that.

You were out for a week end with us in Meadow-field—maybe you don't remember it—but Bud was about six months old then and Barbara was just running around. It wasn't a bad house, if you remember the house. Dutch Colonial, and the faucet in the pantry leaked. The landlord was always fixing it, but he never quite fixed it right. And you had to cut hard to the left to back into the garage. But Sally liked the Japanese cherry tree and it wasn't a bad house. We were going to build on Rose Hill Road eventually. We had the lot picked out, if we didn't have the money, and we made plans about it. Sally never could remember to put in the doors in the plan, and we laughed about that.

It wasn't anything extraordinary, just an evening. After supper, we sat around the lawn in deck chairs and drank Sally's beer—it was long before Repeal

We'd repainted the deck chairs ourselves the Sunday before and we felt pretty proud of them. The light stayed late, but there was a breeze after dark, and once Bud started yipping and Sally went up to him. She had on a white dress, I think—she used to wear white a lot in the summers—it went with her blue eyes and her yellow hair. Well, it wasn't anything extraordinary— we didn't even stay up late. But we were all there. And if you'd told me that within three years we'd both be married to other people, I'd have thought you were raving.

Then you went West, remember, and we saw you off on the train. So you didn't see what happened, and, as a matter of fact, it's hard to remember when we first started meeting the Blakes. They'd moved to Meadowfield then, but we hadn't met them.

Jim Blake was one of those pleasant, ugly-faced people with steel glasses who get right ahead in the law and never look young or old. And Lisa was Lisa. She's dark, you know, and she takes a beautiful burn. She was the first girl there to wear real beach things or drink a special kind of tomato juice when everybody else was drinking cocktails. She was very pretty and very good fun to be with—she's got lots of ideas. They entertained a good deal because Lisa likes that—she had her own income, of course. And she and Jim used to bicker a good deal in public in an amusing way —it was sort of an act or seemed like it. They had one little girl, Sylvia, that Jim was crazy about. I mean it sounds normal, doesn't it, even to their having the kind of Airedale you had then? Well, it all seemed normal enough to us, and they soon got to be part of the crowd. You know, the young married crowd in every suburb.

Of course, that was '28 and the boom was booming and everybody was feeling pretty high. I suppose that was part of it—the money—and the feeling you had that everything was going faster and faster and wouldn't stop. Why, it was Sally herself who said that we owed ourselves a whirl and mustn't get stodgy and settled while we were still young. Well, we had stuck pretty close to the grindstone for the past few years, with the children and everything. And it was fun to feel young and sprightly again and buy a new car and take in the club gala without having to worry about how you'd pay your house account. But I don't see any harm in that.

And then, of course, we talked and kidded a lot about freedom and what have you. Oh, you know the kind of talk—everybody was talking it then. About not being Victorians and living your own life. And there was the older generation and the younger generation. I've forgotten a lot of it now, but I remember there was one piece about love not being just a form of words mumbled by a minister, but something pretty special. As a matter of fact, the minister who married us was old Doctor Snell and he had the kind of voice you could hear in the next county. But I used to talk about that mumbling minister myself. I mean, we were enlightened, for a suburb, if you get my point. Yes, and pretty proud of it, too. When they banned a book in Boston, the lending library ordered six extra copies. And I still remember the big discussion we had about perfect freedom in marriage when even the straight Republicans voted the radical ticket. All except Chick

Bewleigh, and he was a queer sort of bird, who didn't even believe that stocks had reached a permanently high plateau.

But, meanwhile, most of us were getting the 8:15 and our wives were going down to the chain store and asking if that was a really nice head of lettuce. At least that's the way we seemed. And, if the crowd started kidding me about Mary Sennett, or Mac Church kissed Sally on the ear at a club revel, why, we were young, we were modern, and we could handle that. I wasn't going to take a shotgun to Mac, and Sally wasn't going to put on the jealous act. Oh, we had it all down to a science. We certainly did.

Good Lord, we had the Blakes to dinner, and they had us. They'd drop over for drinks or we'd drop over there. It was all perfectly normal and part of the crowd. For that matter, Sally played with Jim Blake in the mixed handicap and they got to the semifinals. No, I didn't play with Lisa—she doesn't like golf. I mean that's the way it was.

And I can remember the minute it started, and it wasn't anything, just a party at the Bewleighs'. They've got a big, rambling house and people drift around. Lisa and I had wandered out to the kitchen to get some drinks for the people on the porch. She had on a black dress, that night, with a big sort of orange flower on it. It wouldn't have suited everybody, but it suited her.

We were talking along like anybody and suddenly we stopped talking and looked at each other. And I felt, for a minute, well, just the way I felt when I was first in love with Sally. Only this time, it wasn't Sally. It happened so suddenly that all I could think of was,

"Watch your step!" Just as if you'd gone into a room in the dark and hit your elbow. I guess that makes it genuine, doesn't it?

We picked it up right away and went back to the party. All she said was, "Did anybody ever tell you that you're really quite a menace, Dan?" and she said that in the way we all said those things. But, all the same, it had happened. I could hear her voice all the way back in the car. And yet, I was as fond of Sally as ever. I don't suppose you'll believe that, but it's true.

And next morning, I tried to kid myself that it didn't have any importance. Because Sally wasn't jealous, and we were all modern and advanced and knew about life. But the next time I saw Lisa, I knew it had.

I want to say this. If you think it was all romance and rosebuds, you're wrong. A lot of it was merry hell. And yet, everybody whooped us on. That's what I don't understand. They didn't really want the Painters and the Blakes to get divorced, and yet they were pretty interested. Now, why do people do that? Some of them would carefully put Lisa and me next to each other at table and some of them would just as carefully not. But it all added up to the same thing in the end—a circus was going on and we were part of the circus. It's interesting to watch the people on the high wires at the circus and you hope they don't fall. But, if they did, that would be interesting too. Of course, there were a couple of people who tried, as they say, to warn us. But they were older people and just made us mad.

Everybody was so nice and considerate and understanding. Everybody was so nice and intelligent and fine. Don't misunderstand me. It was wonderful, being with Lisa. It was new and exciting. And it seemed to be wonderful for her, and she'd been unhappy with Jim. So, anyway, that made me feel less of a heel, though I felt enough of a heel, from time to time. And then, when we were together, it would seem so fine.

A couple of times we really tried to break it, too—at least twice. But we all belonged to the same crowd, and what could you do but run away? And, somehow, that meant more than running away—it meant giving in to the Victorians and that mumbling preacher and all the things we'd said we didn't believe in. Or I suppose Sally might have done like old Mrs. Pierce, back home. She horsewhipped the dressmaker on the station platform and then threw herself crying into Major Pierce's arms and he took her to Atlantic City instead. It's one of the town's great stories and I always wondered what they talked about on the train. Of course, they moved to Des Moines after that—I remember reading about their golden wedding anniversary when I was in college. Only nobody could do that nowadays, and, besides, Lisa wasn't a dressmaker.

So, finally, one day, I came home, and there was Sally, perfectly cold, and, we talked pretty nearly all night. We'd been awfully polite to each other for quite a while before—the way you are. And we kept polite, we kept a good grip on ourselves. After all, we'd said to each other before we were married that if either of us ever——and there it was. And it was Sally who brought that up, not me. I think we'd have felt better if we'd fought. But we didn't fight.

Of course, she was bound to say some things about Lisa, and I was bound to answer. But that didn't last long and we got our grip right back again. It was funny, being strangers and talking so politely, but we did it. I think it gave us a queer kind of pride to do it. I think it gave us a queer kind of pride for her to ask me politely for a drink at the end, as if she were in somebody else's house, and for me to mix it for her, as if she were a guest.

Everything was talked out by then and the house felt very dry and empty, as if nobody lived in it at all. We'd never been up quite so late in the house, except after a New Year's party or when Buddy was sick, that time. I mixed her drink very carefully, the way she liked it, with plain water, and she took it and said "Thanks." Then she sat for a while without saying anything. It was so quiet you could hear the little drip of the leaky faucet in the pantry, in spite of the door being closed. She heard it and said, "It's dripping again. You better call up Mr. Vye in the morning—I forgot. And I think Barbara's getting a cold—I meant to tell you." Then her face twisted and I thought she was going to cry, but she didn't.

She put the glass down—she'd only drunk half her drink—and said, quite quietly, "Oh, damn you, and damn Lisa Blake, and damn everything in the world!" Then she ran upstairs before I could stop her and she still wasn't crying.

I could have run upstairs after her, but I didn't. I stood looking at the glass on the table and I couldn't think. Then, after a while, I heard a key turn in a lock. So I picked up my hat and went out for a walk—I hadn't been out walking that early in a long time. Finally, I found an all-night diner and got some coffee.

Then I came back and read a book till the maid got down—it wasn't a very interesting book. When she came down, I pretended I'd gotten up early and had to go into town by the first train, but I guess she knew.

I'm not going to talk about the details. If you've been through them, you've been through them; and if you haven't, you don't know. My family was fond of Sally, and Sally's had always liked me. Well, that made it tough. And the children. They don't say the things you expect them to. I'm not going to talk about that.

Oh, we put on a good act, we put on a great show! There weren't any fists flying or accusations. Everybody said how well we did it, everybody in town. And Lisa and Sally saw each other, and Jim Blake and I talked to each other perfectly calmly. We said all the usual things. He talked just as if it were a case. I admired him for it. Lisa did her best to make it emotional, but we wouldn't let her. And I finally made her see that, court or no court, he'd simply have to have Sylvia. He was crazy about her, and while Lisa's a very good mother, there wasn't any question as to which of them the kid liked best. It happens that way, sometimes.

For that matter, I saw Sally off on the train to Reno. She wanted it that way. Lisa was going to get a Mexican divorce—they'd just come in, you know. And nobody could have told, from the way we talked in the station. It's funny, you get a queer bond, through a time like that. After I'd seen her off—and she looked small in the train—the first person I wanted to see wasn't Lisa, but Jim Blake. You see, other people are fine, but un-less you've been through things yourself, you don't quite understand them. But Jim Blake was still in Meadowfield, so I went back to the club.

I hadn't ever really lived in the club before, except for three days one summer. They treat you very well, but, of course, being a college club, it's more for the youngsters and the few old boys who hang around the bar. I got awfully tired of the summer chintz in the dining room and the Greek waiter I had who breathed on my neck. And you can't work all the time, though I used to stay late at the office. I guess it was then I first thought of getting out of Spencer Wilde and making a new connection. You think about a lot of things at a time like that.

Of course, there were lots of people I could have seen, but I didn't much want to—somehow, you don't. Though I did strike up quite a friendship with one of the old boys. He was about fifty-five and he'd been divorced four times and was living permanently at the club. We used to sit up in his little room—he'd had his own furniture moved in and the walls were covered with pictures—drinking Tom Collinses and talking about life. He had lots of ideas about life, and about matrimony, too, and I got quite interested, listening to him. But then he'd go into the dinners he used to give at Delmonico's, and while that was interesting, too, it wasn't much help, except to take your mind off the summer chintz.

He had some sort of small job, downtown, but I guess he had an income from his family too. He must have. But when I'd ask him what he did, he'd always say, "I'm retired, my boy, very much retired, and how about a touch more beverage to keep out the sun?"

He always called it beverage, but they knew what he meant at the bar. He turned up at the wedding, when Lisa and I were married, all dressed up in a cutaway, and insisted on making us a little speech—very nice it was too. Then we had him to dinner a couple of times, after we'd got back, and somehow or other, I haven't seen him since. I suppose he's still at the club— I've got out of the habit of going there, since I joined the other ones, though I still keep my membership.

Of course, all that time, I was crazy about Lisa and writing her letters and waiting till we could be married. Of course I was. But, now and then, even that would get shoved into the background. Because there was so much to do and arrangements to make and people like lawyers to see. I don't like lawyers very much, even yet, though the people we had were very good. But there was all the telephoning and the conferences. Somehow, it was like a machine—a big machine—and you had to learn a sort of new etiquette for everything you did. Till, finally, it got so that about all you wanted was to have the fuss over and not talk about it any more.

I remember running into Chick Bewleigh in the club, three days before Sally got her decree. You'd like Chick—he's the intellectual type, but a darn good fellow too. And Nan, his wife, is a peach—one of those big, rangy girls with a crazy sense of humor. It was nice to talk to him because he was natural and didn't make any cracks about grass-bachelors or get that look in his eye. You know the look they get. We talked about Meadowfield—just the usual news—the Bakers were splitting up and Don Sikes had a new job and the Wilsons were having a baby. But it seemed good to hear it.

"For that matter," he said, drawing on his pipe, "we're adding to the population again ourselves. In the fall. How we'll ever manage four of them! I keep telling Nan she's cockeyed, but she says they're more fun than a swimming pool and cost less to keep up, so what can you do!"

He shook his head and I remembered that Sally always used to say she wanted six. Only now it would be Lisa, so I mustn't think about that.

"So that's your recipe for a happy marriage," I said. "Well, I always wondered."

I was kidding, of course, but he looked quite serious.

"Kinder, Küche und Kirche?" he said. "Nope, that doesn't work any more, what with pre-schools, automats and the movies. Four children or no four children, Nan could still raise hell if she felt like raising hell. And so could I, for that matter. Add blessings of civilization," and his eyes twinkled.

"Well then," I said, "what is it?" I really wanted to know.

"Oh, just bull luck, I suppose. And happening to like what you've got," he answered, in a sort of embarrassed way.

"You can do that," I said. "And yet——"

He looked away from me.

"Oh, it was a lot simpler in the old days," he said. "Everything was for marriage—church, laws, society. And when people got married, they expected to stay that way. And it made a lot of people as unhappy as hell. Now the expectation's rather the other way, at least in this great and beautiful nation and among people like us. If you get a divorce, it's rather like going to the dentist—unpleasant sometimes, but lots of people have been there before. Well, that's a handsome system, too, but it's got its own casualty list. So there you are. You takes your money and you makes your choice. And some of us like freedom better than the institution and some of us like the institution better, but what most of us would like is to be Don Juan on Thursdays and Benedick, the married man, on Fridays, Saturdays and the rest of the week. Only that's a bit hard to work out, somehow," and he grinned.

"All the same," I said, "you and Nan——"

"Well," he said. "I suppose we're exceptions. You see, my parents weren't married till I was seven. So I'm a conservative. It might have worked out the other way."

"Oh," I said.

"Yes," he said. "My mother was English, and you may have heard of English divorce laws. She ran away with my father and she was perfectly right—her husband was a very extensive brute. All the same, I was brought up on the other side of the fence, and I know something about what it's like. And Nan was a minister's daughter who thought she ought to be free. Well, we argued about things a good deal. And, finally, I told her that I'd be very highly complimented to live with her on any terms at all, but if she wanted to get married, she'd have to expect a marriage, not a trip to Coney Island. And I made my point rather clear by blacking her eye, in a taxi, when she told me she was thinking seriously of spending a week end with my deadly rival, just to see which one of us she really

loved. You can't spend a romantic week end with somebody when you've got a black eye. But you can get
married with one and we did. She had raw beefsteak
on it till two hours before the wedding, and it was the
prettiest sight I ever saw. Well, that's our simple story."

"Not all of it," I said.

"No," he said, "not all of it. But at least we didn't
start in with any of this bunk about if you meet a
handsomer fellow it's all off. We knew we were getting
into something. Bewleigh's Easy Guide to Marriage in
three installments—you are now listening to the Voice
of Experience, and who cares? Of course, if we hadn't—
ahem—liked each other, I could have blacked her eye
till doomsday and got nothing out of it but a suit for
assault and battery. But nothing's much good unless it's
worth fighting for. And she doesn't look exactly like a
downtrodden wife."

"Nope," I said, "but all the same——"

He stared at me very hard—almost the way he used
to when people were explaining that stocks had reached
a permanently high plateau.

"Exactly," he said. "And there comes a time, no
matter what the intention, when a new face heaves into
view and a spark lights. I'm no Adonis, God knows, but
it's happened to me once or twice. And I know what I
do then. I run. I run like a rabbit. It isn't courageous
or adventurous or fine. It isn't even particularly moral,
as I think about morals. But I run. Because, when all's
said and done, it takes two people to make a love affair
and you can't have it when one of them's not there.
And, dammit, Nan knows it, that's the trouble. She'd
ask Helen of Troy to dinner just to see me run. Well,

goodbye, old man, and our best to Lisa, of course——"

After he was gone, I went and had dinner in the grill. I did a lot of thinking at dinner, but it didn't get me anywhere. When I was back in the room, I took the receiver off the telephone. I was going to call long distance. But your voice sounds different on the phone, and, anyway, the decree would be granted in three days. So when the girl answered, I told her it was a mistake.

Next week Lisa came back and she and I were married. We went to Bermuda on our wedding trip. It's a very pretty place. Do you know, they won't allow an automobile on the island?

The queer thing was that at first I didn't feel married to Lisa at all. I mean, on the boat, and even at the hotel. She said, "But how exciting, darling!" and I suppose it was.

Now, of course, we've been married eight years, and that's always different. The twins will be seven in May —two years older than Sally's Jerry. I had an idea for a while that Sally might marry Jim Blake—he always admired her. But I'm glad she didn't—it would have made things a little too complicated. And I like McConaghey—I like him fine. We gave them an old Chinese jar for a wedding present. Lisa picked it out. She has very good taste and Sally wrote us a fine letter.

I'd like to have you meet Lisa sometime—she's interested in intelligent people. They're always coming to the apartment—artists and writers and people like that.

Of course, they don't always turn out the way she expects. But she's quite a hostess and she knows how to handle things. There was one youngster that used to rather get in my hair. He'd call me the Man of Wal

Street and ask me what I thought about Picabia or one of those birds, in a way that sort of said, "Now watch this guy stumble!" But as soon as Lisa noticed it, she got rid of him. That shows she's considerate.

Of course, it's different, being married to a person. And I'm pretty busy these days and so is she. Sometimes, if I get home and there's going to be a party, I'll just say good night to the twins and fade out after dinner. But Lisa understands about that, and I've got my own quarters. She had one of her decorator friends do the private study and it really looks very nice.

I had Jim Blake in there one night. Well, I had to take him somewhere. He was getting pretty noisy and Lisa gave me the high sign. He's doing very well, but he looks pretty hard these days and I'm afraid he's drinking a good deal, though he doesn't often show it. I don't think he ever quite got over Sylvia's dying. Four years ago. They had scarlet fever at the school. It was a great shock to Lisa, too, of course, but she had the twins and Jim never married again. But he comes to see us, every once in a while. Once, when he was tight, he said it was to convince himself about remaining a bachelor, but I don't think he meant that.

Now, when I brought him into the study, he looked around and said, "Shades of Buck Rogers! What one of Lisa's little dears produced this imitation Wellsian nightmare?"

"Oh, I don't remember," I said. "I think his name was Slivovitz."

"It looks as if it had been designed by a man named Slivovitz," he said. "All dental steel and black glass.

I recognize the Lisa touch. You're lucky she didn't put
murals of cogwheels on the walls."

"Well, there was a question of that," I said.

"I bet there was," he said. "Well, here's how, old
man! Here's to two great big wonderful institutions
marriage and divorce!"

I didn't like that very much and told him so. But
he just wagged his head at me.

"I like you, Painter," he said. "I always did. Some
times I think you're goofy, but I like you. You can't
insult me—I won't let you. And it isn't your fault."

"What isn't my fault?" I said.

"The setup," he said. "Because, in your simple little
heart, you're an honest monogamous man, Painter—
monogamous as most. And if you'd stayed married to
Sally, you'd have led an honest monogamous life. But
they loaded the dice against you, out at Meadowfield,
and now Lord knows where you'll end up. After all, I
was married to Lisa myself for six years or so. Tell me,
isn't it hell?"

"You're drunk," I said.

"*In vino veritas,*" said he. "No, it isn't hell—I take
that back. Lisa's got her damn-fool side, but she's an
attractive and interesting woman—or could be, if she'd
work at it. But she was brought up on the idea of
Romance with a big R, and she's too bone-lazy and
bone-selfish to work at it very long. There's always
something else, just over the horizon. Well, I got tired
of fighting that, after a while. And so will you. She
doesn't want husbands—she wants clients and followers.
Or maybe you're tired already."

"I think you'd better go home, Jim," I said. "I don't want to have to ask you."

"Sorry," he said. "*In vino veritas.* But it's a funny setup, isn't it? What Lisa wanted was a romantic escapade—and she got twins. And what you wanted was marriage—and you got Lisa. As for me," and for a minute his face didn't look drunk any more, "what I principally wanted was Sylvia and I've lost that. I could have married again, but I didn't think that'd be good for her. Now, I'll probably marry some client I've helped with her decree—we don't touch divorce, as a rule, just a very, very special line of business for a few important patrons. I know those—I've had them in the office. And won't that be fun for us all! What a setup it is!" and he slumped down in his chair and went to sleep. I let him sleep for a while and then had Briggs take him down in the other elevator. He called up next day and apologized—said he knew he must have been noisy, though he couldn't remember anything he said.

The other time I had somebody in the study was when Sally came back there once, two years ago. We'd met to talk about college for Barbara and I'd forgotten some papers I wanted to show her. We generally meet downtown. But she didn't mind coming back—Lisa was out, as it happened. It made me feel queer, taking her up in the elevator and letting her in at the door. She wasn't like Jim—she thought the study was nice.

Well, we talked over our business and I kept looking at her. You can see she's older, but her eyes are still that very bright blue, and she bites her thumb when she's interested. It's a queer feeling. Of course, I was used to seeing her, but we usually met downtown. You know, I wouldn't have been a bit surprised if she'd pushed the bell and said, "Tea, Briggs. I'm home." She didn't, naturally.

I asked her, once, if she wouldn't take off her hat and she looked at me in a queer way and said, "So you can show me your etchings? Dan, Dan, you're a dangerous man!" and for a moment we both laughed like fools.

"Oh, dear," she said, drying her eyes, "that's very funny. And now I must be going home."

"Look here, Sally," I said, "I've always told you— but, honestly, if you need anything—if there's anything——"

"Of course, Dan," she said. "And we're awfully good friends, aren't we?" But she was still smiling.

I didn't care. "Friends!" I said. "You know how I think about you. I always have. And I don't want you to think——"

She patted my shoulder—I'd forgotten the way she used to do that.

"There," she said. "Mother knows all about it. And we really are friends, Dan. So——"

"I was a fool."

She looked at me very steadily out of those eyes.

"We were all fools," she said. "Even Lisa. I used to hate her for a while. I used to hope things would happen to her. Oh, not very bad things. Just her finding out that you never see a crooked picture without straightening it, and hearing you say: 'A bird can't fly on one wing,' for the dozenth time. The little things everybody has to find out and put up with. But I don't even do that any more."

"If you'd ever learned to put a cork back in a bottle," I said. "I mean the right cork in the right bottle. But——"

"I do so! No, I suppose I never will." And she laughed. She took my hands. "Funny, funny, funny," she said. "And funny to have it all gone and be friends."

"Is it all gone?" I said.

"Why, no, of course not," she said. "I don't suppose it ever is, quite. Like the boys who took you to dances. And there's the children, and you can't help remembering. But it's gone. We had it and lost it. I should have fought for it more, I suppose, but I didn't. And then I was terribly hurt and terribly mad. But I got over that. And now I'm married to Jerry. And I wouldn't give him up, or Jerry Junior, for anything in the world. The only thing that worries me is sometimes when I think it isn't quite a fair deal for him. After all, he could have married—well, somebody else. And yet he knows I love him."

"He ought to," I said rather stiffly. "He's a darn lucky guy, if you ask me."

"No, Dan. I'm the lucky girl. I'm hoping this minute that Mrs. Potter's X-rays turn out all right. He did a beautiful job on her. But he always worries."

I dropped her hands.

"Well, give him my best," I said.

"I will, Dan. He likes you, you know. Really he does. By the way, have you had any more of that bursitis? There's a new treatment—he wanted me to ask you——"

"Thanks," I said, "but that all cleared up."

"I'm glad. And now I must fly. There's always shopping when you come in from the suburbs. Give my best to Lisa and tell her I was sorry not to see her. She's out, I suppose."

"Yes," I said. "She'll be sorry to miss you—you wouldn't stay for a cocktail? She's usually in around then."

"It sounds very dashing, but I mustn't. Jerry Junior lost one of his turtles and I've got to get him another. Do you know a good pet shop? Well, Bloomingdale's, I suppose—after all, I've got other things to get."

"There's a good one two blocks down on Lexington," I said. "But if you're going to Bloomingdale's—— Well, goodbye, Sally, and good luck."

"Goodbye, Dan. And good luck to you. And no regrets."

"No regrets," I said, and we shook hands.

There wasn't any point in going down to the street with her, and besides I had to phone the office. But before I did, I looked out, and she was just getting into a cab. A person looks different, somehow, when they don't know you're seeing them. I could see the way she looked to other people—not young any more, not the Sally I'd married, not even the Sally I'd talked with, all night in that cold house. She was a nice married woman who lived in Montclair and whose husband was a doctor; a nice woman, in shopping for the day, with a new spring hat and a fifty-trip ticket in her handbag. She'd had trouble in her life, but she'd worked it out. And, before she got on the train, she'd have a black-and-white soda, sitting on a stool at the station, or maybe she didn't do that any more. There'd be lots of things in her handbag, but I wouldn't know about any of them nor what locks the keys fitted. And, if she were dying, they'd send for me, because that would be etiquette. And the same if I were dying. But we'd had something and lost it—the way she said—and that was all that was left.

Now she was that nice Mrs. McConaghey. But she'd never be quite that to me. And yet, there was no way to go back. You couldn't even go back to the house in Meadowfield—they'd torn it down and put up an apartment instead.

So that's why I wanted to talk to you. I'm not complaining and I'm not the kind of fellow that gets nerves. But I just want to know—I just want to figure it out. And sometimes it keeps going round and round in your head. You'd like to be able to tell your children something, especially when they're growing up. Well, I know what we'll tell them. But I wonder if it's enough.

Not that we don't get along well when Bud and Barbara come to see us. Especially Barbara—she's very tactful and she's crazy about the twins. And now they're growing up, it's easier. Only, once in a while, something happens that makes you think. I took Barbara out sailing last summer. She's sixteen and a very sweet kid, if I say it myself. A lot of kids that age seem pretty hard, but she isn't.

Well, we were just talking along, and, naturally, you like to know what your children's plans are. Bud thinks he wants to be a doctor like McConaghey and I've no objection. I asked Barbara if she wanted a career, but she said she didn't think so.

"Oh, I'd like to go to college," she said, "and maybe

work for a while, afterwards, the way mother did, you know. But I haven't any particular talents, dad. I could kid myself, but I haven't. I guess it's just woman's function and home and babies for me."

"Well, that sounds all right to me," I said, feeling very paternal.

"Yes," she said, "I like babies. In fact, I think I'll get married pretty young, just for the experience. The first time probably won't work, but it ought to teach you some things. And then, eventually, you might find somebody to tie to."

"So that's the way it is with the modern young woman?" I said.

"Why, of course," she said. "That's what practically all the girls say—we've talked it all over at school. Of course, sometimes it takes you quite a while. Like Helen Hastings' mother. She just got married for the fourth time last year, but he really is a sweet! He took us all to the matinee when I was visiting Helen and we nearly died. He's a count, of course, and he's got the darlingest accent. I don't know whether I'd like a count, though it must be fun to have little crowns on your handkerchiefs like Helen's mother. What's the matter, daddy? Are you shocked?"

"Don't flatter yourself, young lady—I've been shocked by experts," I said. "No, I was just thinking. Suppose we—well, suppose your mother and I had stayed together? How would you have felt about it then?"

"But you didn't, did you?" she said, and her voice wasn't hurt or anything, just natural. "I mean, almost nobody does any more. Don't worry, daddy. Bud and I understand all about it—good gracious, we're grown up! Of course, if you and mother had," she said, rather dutifully, "I suppose it would have been very nice. But then we'd have missed Mac, and he really is a sweet, and you'd have missed Lisa and the twins. Anyhow, it's all worked out now. Oh, of course, I'd rather hope it would turn out all right the first time, if it wasn't too stodgy or sinister. But you've got to face facts, you know."

"Face facts!" I said. "Dammit, Barbara!"

Then I stopped, because what did I have to say?

Well, that's the works, and if you've got any dope on it, I wish you'd tell me. There are so few people you can talk to—that's the trouble. I mean everybody's very nice, but that's not the same thing. And, if you start thinking too much, the highballs catch up on you. And you can't afford that—I've never been much of a drinking man.

The only thing is, where does it stop, if it does? That's the thing I'm really afraid of.

It may sound silly to you. But I've seen other people—well, take this Mrs. Hastings, Barbara talked about. Or my old friend at the club. I wonder if he started in, wanting to get married four times. I know I didn't—I'm not the type and you know it.

And yet, suppose, well, you do meet somebody who treats you like a human being. I mean somebody who doesn't think you're a little goofy because you know more about American Can than who painted what. Supposing, even, they're quite a lot younger. That shouldn't make all the difference. After all, I'm no Lothario. And Lisa and I aren't thinking of divorce or anything like that. But, naturally, we lead our own lives, and you ought to be able to talk to somebody. Of course, if it could have been Sally. That was my fault. But it isn't as if Maureen were just in the floor show. She's got her own specialty number. And, really, when you get to know her, she's a darned intelligent kid.

A DEATH IN THE COUNTRY

AFTER the years, Tom Carroll was going back to Waynesville—to stand by a kinswoman's grave, in the country of his youth. The names of the small, familiar stations were knots on a thread that led back into the darkness of childhood. He was glad Claire had not come. She hated death and memories. She hated cramped, local trains that smelled of green plush and cinders. Most of all she would hate Waynesville, even in mid-September and the grave light of afternoon.

Well, he wasn't looking forward to a pleasant time. He felt fagged and on edge already. There was work for the active partner of Norman, Buckstone, and Carroll in his brief-case, but he could not get down to the work. Instead he remembered, from childhood, the smell of dyed cloth and poignant, oppressive flowers, the black wisp tied on the knocker, the people coming to the door. The house was full of a menace—full of a secret—there were incomprehensible phrases, said in a murmur, and a man in black gloves who came, and a strangeness behind a shut door. Run out and play, run out and play; but there was no right way to play any more—even out in the yard you could smell the sweet, overpowering flowers—even out in the street you could see the people coming and coming, making that little pause as they saw the black wisp. Beautiful, they said, she looks beautiful; but the glimpse of the face was not mother, only somebody coldly asleep. Our sister has gone to dear Jesus . . . we shall meet on that beautiful shore . . . but the man spoke words, and the harsh box sank into the hole, and from it nothing arose, not even a white thing, not even silver vapor; the clay at the sides of the hole was too yellow and thick and cold. He's too young to realize, said a great many voices— but for months nothing was right. The world had stopped being solid, and people's smiles were different, and mother was Jesus's sister, and they gave her clothes away. Then, after a long time, the place was green again and looked just like the other graves, and the knife in your pocket was a comfort, going out there Sundays in the street car.

Barbarous. And to-morrow would be barbarous, as well. The family met only at funerals and weddings, now; and there had been more funerals than weddings for the past ten years. The big Christmas tree was gone from the house on Hessian Street—the majestic tree whose five-pointed, sparkling star had scratched against the ceiling of heaven in the back parlor, spreading wide its green boughs to shelter all generations and tribes of the Pyes and Merritts and Chipmans, their wives and their children, their menservants and their maidservants, their Noah's arks and cigar-cases and bottles of *eau-de-cologne*. The huge tablecloth of Thanksgiving lay folded away at the bottom of a chest—the tables now were too small. There would never be another turkey, with a breast like a mountainside, to fall into endless slices under the shining magic of Uncle Melrose's knife. Aunt Louise and Aunt Emmy had been the last of Hessian Street and, after to-morrow, there would only be Aunt Emmy and the ghosts.

The faces around the table had been masterful and full of life. They had been grown-up and permanent—one could not imagine them young or growing old. Together, they made a nation; they were the earth. If one took the trains of the morning, even as far as Bradensburg, lo, Uncle Melrose was there, at his desk with the little brass postage-scale on top of it, as it had been from the first. If one walked out to Mount Pleasant through the buckeye fall, at the end there was the white gate of Cousin Edna and the iron nigger boy with the rainstreaked face, holding out his black hand stiffly for the buckboards that drove no more. There were princes and dominations and thrones and powers; but what were these beside Aunt Emmy and Cousin Millie, beside the everlasting forms of Mrs. Bache and Mr. Beaver, of the ladies at the Women's Exchange and the man who lighted the gas street-lamps with a long brass spike? Then, suddenly, the earth had begun to crumble. A wind blew, a bell sounded, and they were dispersed. There were shrunken old people, timorous and pettish, and a small, heart-stifling town. These and the grown-up children, more strange than strangers. But Hessian Street was over—the great tree was down.

"And Uncle Melrose was a pompous old windbag," thought Tom Carroll. "And yet, if he were alive, I'd be calling him 'Sir.' Oh, Claire's right—the jungle's the jungle—she's saner than I am, always."

It was one of the many maxims Claire found in books. The family was the jungle that you grew up in and, if you did not, somehow, break through to light

and air of your own when you were young, you died,
quickly or slowly but surely, stifled out, choked down
by the overpowering closeness of your own kin. Tom
Carroll knew this much—that New York, after Waynesville, had been like passing from the large, squabbling,
overheated room of Christmas afternoon into the
anonymous peace of a bare and windy street. He had
been lonely, often—he had missed Hessian Street and
them all. But, oh the endless, intricate, unimportant
diplomacy—the feuds and the makings-up—the inflexi-
ble machine of the Family, crushing all independence.
Not again, not ever again! And yet, here he was, on
the train.

Well, nobody could say that he shirked it. He would
have to take charge when he got there, like it or not.
It wouldn't be easy, straightening everything out—he'd
rather handle the Corliss case any day—but he'd done it
in other emergencies and he supposed he could do it
again. After all, who else was there? Jerry Pye? His
mouth narrowed, thinking of Jerry.

The conductor bawled the names of familiar stations, the long, autumnal twilight began beyond the
window. If only things could go smoothly just this once!
But something always cropped up—something always
had to be smoothed over and explained. *Morton Center, Morton Center!* If Aunt Louise had left no will—
and she very probably hadn't—there'd be the dickens
of a time, securing the estate to Aunt Emmy. But it
must be done—he'd ride roughshod over Jerry Pye if
necessary. *Brandy Hill! Brandy Hill!* . . If only
nobody would tell him to be sure and notice Mrs.
Bache! He could easily fix a pension for Aunt Emmy,

but how to do it best? She'd have to leave Hessian Street, of course. Even cutting the old house into apartments hadn't really solved the problem. She could get a small, comfortable, modern flat over in the new section. The silver candlesticks were the only things Claire would have liked, but they would go to Jerry because Jerry had always failed.

Waynesville, next stop! The flowers had been wired from New York. *Waynesville!* We're coming in. There's an A. & P. on Main Street, and Ellerman's Bazaar is gone. *Waynesville!* . . . And God bless Uncle Melrose and Aunt Louise and Aunt Emmy and all my dear relations and friends and Spot and make me a good boy and not afraid of the dark. *Waynesville!*

Right down the middle of Main Street the train clanged till it stopped in front of the bald, new station. Tom Carroll sighed. It was as he had prophesied. Jerry Pye was there to meet him.

He got off the train, and the cousins shook hands. "Have a good trip, Tom?"

"Not bad. Real fall weather, isn't it?"

"Yes, it's a real fall. You took the limited as far as Bradensburg, I suppose?"

"Yes, that seemed the quickest thing for me to do."

"They say she's quite a train," said Jerry Pye. "I was on her once—three years ago, you know. Well, I thought, here's where the old man blows himself for once. Minnie would hardly believe me when I told her. 'Jerry Pye!' she said, 'I don't know what's come over you. You never take me on any limiteds!' 'Well,' I said, 'maybe it is extra-fare, but I just decided the old man could blow himself for once!' Well, you should have

seen her expression! Though I guess it wouldn't mean
much to you, at that. I guess extra-fare trains don't
mean much in people's lives when they come from
New York."

"I could have taken a slower train," said Tom Carroll, carefully, "but it wouldn't have saved any time."

This remark seemed to amuse Jerry Pye intensely.
His thin, sallow face—the face of a dyspeptic fox—
gloated with mirth for an instant. Then he sobered
himself, abruptly and pointedly.

"You always were a case, Tom," he said, "always.
But this is a sad occasion."

"I didn't mean to be funny," said Tom Carroll.
"Had I better get a taxi or is that your car?"

"Oh, we've got the family mistake—a dollar down
and a dollar whenever they catch you!" Jerry Pye
grinned and sobered himself again with the automatism
of a mechanical figure. "I drove up in her night before
last," he said, pointedly, as they got in. "Evans is a good
man and all that, but he's apt to figure a little close on
the cars; and as long as ours is dark blue, it'll look perfectly dignified."

"I telegraphed Aunt Emmy," said Tom Carroll and
stopped. There was no possible use in trying to explain
oneself to Jerry Pye.

"Yes, indeed," said Jerry, instantly. "Aunt Emmy
appreciated it very much. Very much indeed. 'Tom's
always very busy,' I told her. 'But don't you worry,
Aunt Emmy. Tom may be a big man now, but his
heart's in the right place. He'll be here.'"

"I told her," said Tom Carroll, distinctly and in

spite of himself, "that in case anything of the sort came up, she had only to—"

"Oh," said Jerry, brightly, "we all knew that. We all knew you couldn't be expected to send one of your big cars all the way from New York to Waynesville. How's Claire?"

"Claire was very sorry indeed not to be able to come," said Tom, his hands gripping his knees. "We have one car," he said.

"That's just what I said," said Jerry Pye triumphantly. "I told Aunt Emmy—'you couldn't expect Tom to take the car away from Claire—she'll need it when he's away, shopping and seeing her friends—and naturally she hardly knew Aunt Louise. You wait and see. She'll send handsome flowers,' I said."

"Oh, God, make me a good boy!" prayed Tom Carroll, internally. "It can't last more than ten minutes. Ten minutes isn't really long." He braced himself. "How is Aunt Emmy?" he said.

Their speed instantly dropped to a respectful twenty miles an hour.

"She's wonderful," said Jerry Pye. "Simply wonderful. Of course, Minnie's been a great help to her and then, the end was very peaceful. Just seemed to breathe away." His voice had an obvious relish. "One minute she was there—as bright as a button, considering everything—and the next minute—" He shook his head.

"I'm glad," said Tom Carroll. "I mean——"

"Oh, we wouldn't have wanted her to suffer," said Jerry Pye in a shocked voice, as if he were denying some uncouth suggestion of Tom's. "No, sir, we wouldn't have wanted that. Now when Minnie's mother passed

over—I don't know whether I ever told you the whole
story, Tom—but from the Friday before—"

He continued, but had only come to the personal
idiosyncrasies of the first night nurse when they turned
into Hessian Street.

They got out of the car. Jerry Pye was mopping his
forehead, though the day was chill. Yes, there was the
black wisp on the knocker. But there was a row of bell-
pushes where the old name-plate had been. The bricks
in the sidewalk were rose-red and old and worn—the
long block of quiet houses kept its faded dignity, in
spite of a sign, "Pappas' Smoke Shop," a sign, "The
Hessian Sergeant—Tea and Antiques." The linden
trees had not perished, though their shade was thin.

"If this were a city," thought Tom Carroll, "people
would have found out by now that it was quaint and
painted the doors green and had studio-parties. Well,
anyhow, that hasn't happened."

"Everyone's been very respectful," said Jerry Pye,
nodding at the black wisp. "I mean, some people might
be touchy when everybody has to use the same front-
door. But Mr. Rodman came to me himself—they're
the second-floor back. Just leave your bag in the car,
Tom. It won't be in the way. I think Minnie's seen us
—we figured out if you came to-day this ought to be
the train."

Tom Carroll did not repeat that he had telegraphed
or that there was only one afternoon train to Waynesville. He kissed his cousin-in-law's flustered cheek and
was kissed by her in return. Minnie was always flustered; she had been a plump, flustered robin of a girl at
her wedding; she was unaltered now save for the dust

of gray in her abundant, unbecoming hair; they had never exchanged three words, except on family matters; and yet, they always kissed. He wondered if Minnie, too, ever found this circumstance strange. He should not wonder, of course, especially now.

"How's Aunt Emmy?" said Jerry Pye, in the anxious tones of one just returned from a long absence. "There isn't any change?"

"No, dear," said Minnie, solemnly, "she's just the same. She's wonderful. Mrs. Robinson and Mrs. Bache are with her, now. Remember—we must all be very nice to Mrs. Bache, Cousin Tom."

"I did put a tick-tack on her window, once," said Tom Carroll, reflectively. "But I haven't done that for a long time. Not for thirty years."

Minnie, the robin, was shocked for a moment, but brightened.

"That's right," she said. "We must all keep up for Aunt Emmy. Now, if you'll just go in—" She stood aside.

The spare, small, hawk-nosed figure rose from the stiff-backed chair as Tom Carroll entered. "Good evening, Thomas. I am glad you are here," said the unfaltering voice. "I think you know my good neighbors, Mrs. Bache and Mrs. Robinson."

Tom Carroll took the thin, dry, forceful hands. By God, she is wonderful, he thought, in spite of their saying it—it's taken me years to unlearn what she taught me, but she's remarkable. Why don't they let her alone? *Aunt Emmy, Aunt Emmy, you have grown so small! You rapped on my chapped knuckles with a steel thimble when I was cold; you ran me through and*

through like the emery-bag in your workbox with your
sharp and piercing eyes; you let me see that you thought
my father a rascal; you made me lie and cheat because
of the terror of your name—and now you have grown
small and fragile and an old woman, and there is not
even injustice left in Hessian Street.

The moment passed. Tom Carroll found himself
mechanically answering Mrs. Bache's questions while
his eyes roved about the room. The conch-shell was still
on the mantelpiece, but one of the blue vases was gone.
This was the front-parlor—the room of reward and
punishment, of visitors and chill, the grandest room in
the world—this room with the shabby carpet and the
huge forbidding pieces of black walnut that never could
have come in through a mortal door. What could you
do with it all, what could you do? What could be done
with a conch-shell and an iron oak-leaf and a set of
yellowed pictures for a broken stereopticon? It was incredible that civilized people should ever have cher-
ished such things. It was incredible that he had ever
put the conch-shell to his ear and held his breath with
wonder, hearing the sea.

"It was just like another home to the Major and
myself. Always," said Mrs. Bache. "I can hear your dear
grandmother now, before the Major was taken, when
he had his trouble. 'Alice, my child, you're young,' she
said. 'But, young or old, we all have to bear our cross.
The Major is a good man—he'll always be welcome in
Hessian Street.' The Major never forgot it. He was very
badly treated but he never forgot a kindness. And now,
Emmy and I are the last—Emmy and I are the last."

She fumbled for her handkerchief in her vast lap.

"There, there, Mrs. Bache," said Tom Carroll, inadequately, "Grandmother must have been a wonderful woman."

"You never even saw her," said Mrs. Bache, viciously, "Tom Carroll saw to that. Oh, why couldn't it have been me, instead of Louise?" she said. "I've been ready to go so long!"

Tom Carroll's face felt stiff, but he found the handkerchief. After a moment Mrs. Bache arose, enormously yet with a curious dignity.

"Come, Sarah," she said to the dim figure in black that was Mrs. Robinson, "It's time for us to go. I've been making a fool of myself. Good-by, Emma. Frank will take us to the church to-morrow. Try to get some rest."

Minnie was whispering to him that Mrs. Bache was very much broken and that Cousin Tom must not mind. Tom Carroll whispered back at appropriate intervals. He did not mind Mrs. Bache. But there was always so much whispering, and it hurt one's head.

Now they were all standing in the narrow hall, and the others were looking at him.

"We can just slip in for a minute before anyone else comes," whispered Minnie, "I know Cousin Tom would rather—"

"Of course," said Tom Carroll. "Thank you, Cousin Minnie." He must have been working too hard, he thought—perhaps he and Claire could go off for a trip together when he got back. Because, after all, it was Aunt Louise who was dead. He knew that perfectly well. And yet, until Minnie had spoken, he hadn't been thinking about her at all.

The statue lay on the walnut bed in the partitioned room that had once been part of the back parlor. Over the head of the bed was a cross of dry, brittle palm-leaves tied with a purple ribbon, and a church-calendar. Against the opposite wall was the highboy that he remembered, with the small china slipper upon it, and above it the ageless engraving of the great Newfoundland dog, head lifted, lying upon the stone blocks of an English quay. "A Member of the Royal Humane Society." There were brown spots on the margin of the engraving now, Tom Carroll noticed. The window was a little open, but everywhere were the massed, triumphant flowers.

A white, transparent veil lay on the face of the statue. The features showed dimly through it, as if Aunt Louise lay in a block of ice. Tom Carroll felt cold. Now Aunt Emmy, putting Minnie aside, went slowly to lift the veil.

Tom Carroll, waking at three o'clock in the morning in his room at the Penniquit House, knew instantly what was in store for him. He might lie on the hillocks of his bed as long as he liked but he would not be allowed to sleep any more.

"You're acting like somebody on the edge of a first-class nervous breakdown," he told himself sternly. "And yet, you haven't been working so hard."

The last year hadn't been easy, but no year was. When times were good, you worked hard to take advantage of them. And when they were bad, you naturally had to work. That was how you got to be somebody, in a city. It was something Waynesville could never understand.

He thought of their life in the city—his and Claire's —for solace. It was cool and glittering and civilized as a cube of bright steel and glass. He thought of the light, pleasant furniture in the apartment, the clean, bright colors, the crisp sunlight on stone and metal, the bright, clean, modern, expensive school where a doctor looked down the boys' throats every morning and they had special blocks of wood to hammer nails in, since apartments were hardly the places to hammer nails. He thought of his office and the things on his desk and the crowded elevators of morning and night. He thought of the crammed red moving vans of October and the spring that bloomed before April in the flower-shops and the clever men, putting in the new telephones. He thought of night beside Claire, hearing the dim roar of the city till at last the uneasy lights of the sky were quieted in the breathing-space before dawn.

It was she who had really held their life to its pattern. She had not let them be trapped; she had kept them free as air from the first day. There had been times when he had weakened—he admitted it—but she had kept her level head and never given in.

It had been that way about the old farmhouse in Connecticut and the cooperative apartment in town. He had wanted to buy them both, at different times. It was the Waynesville coming out in him, he supposed. But she had demurred.

"Oh, Tom, let's not tie ourselves up yet!" she had said. "Yes, I know it does seem silly just going on paying rent and having nothing to show for it but a leak in the washstand. But the minute you buy places to live in, they start to own you. You aren't free. You aren't young. You're always worrying. Don't talk to me about just playing with a few acres, not really farming. That was the way Grandfather started. Oh, Tom, don't you see—we're so *right* the way we are! Now, let's go over it sensibly, figures and all."

And she had been right. The old farmhouse, with its lilac hedge, now stood twenty feet away from a four-lane road; the cooperative apartment had failed and crippled its owner-tenants. She had been precisely right. She almost always was.

She had been entirely and unsentimentally right about her mother's coming to live with them for six months out of the year, when that had seemed unescapable.

"It's darling of you, Tom, but, dear old man, it never would work in the world. We've got to be modern and intelligent about the important things. Mother had me, and I'm devoted to her; but, when we're together for more than a week we get on each other's nerves like the very devil. It'll actually be a help to Hattie to have her for the winters—Hattie's always having a fearful time with the children. And we can have her for a long visit in the summer, and in between she can take the trips she's always wanted to take with that terrible Mrs. Tweed. Of course, I don't mean we ought to leave the whole financial end to Hattie and Joe. I'll insist on our doing our share. But I do think people ought to have *some* independence even when they are old and not just be shipped around from one relative to another like parcels, the way they did with

Aunt Vi! It's more than sweet of you, Tom, darling. But you see how it is."

Tom Carroll had seen, with some relief, that they were not likely to have Mrs. Fanshawe as a permanent addition to their household, and he had acquiesced. Not that he disliked Mrs. Fanshawe. He got on very well with the rather nervous little lady—which was strange, considering how unlike she was to Claire. It struck him at times that Mrs. Fanshawe, from what he knew of her, had never been a remarkably independent person, and that to begin one's complete independence at the age of sixty-seven might be something of a task. But Claire must know her mother better than he did.

She did get on Claire's nerves and she did spoil the children—he could see that plainly enough. But, then, her visits were seldom very long. Claire would hardly have time to decline three or four invitations because mother was with them for a quiet little time before something would happen to call Mrs. Fanshawe away. And yet she seemed to like his calling her Mother May and pretending he was jealous of Hattie and Joe for stealing away his best girl. She'd laugh her brisk, nervous laugh and say he'd better look out or sometime she'd take him at his word and stay forever. And Claire would be saying, patiently, "Now, mother, are you sure that you have your ticket? And Tom will get you some magazines to read on the train." Afterwards Claire would say, "Oh, Tom, how can you? But she adores it!" and he would mumble something and feel rather pleased. Then Claire would kiss him and go to the telephone.

Only one of the visits had been in the least unfortunate. Claire had been tired that evening, and it was a pity that the conversation had happened to run on the future of the children. "But, of course, you and Tom are planning to make a real home for them sometime?" Mrs. Fanshawe had said. Well, naturally, she could hardly be expected to understand the way he and Claire happened to feel about "homes" in the Waynesville sense. And it had all come right the following morning —had not Mrs. Fanshawe nervously stayed an extra two days in proof? But the evening had carried him back to the hurt feelings of Hessian Street. Tom Carroll was glad there had been another visit before Mrs. Fanshawe died.

She had died in the waiting room of the Auburndale Station, on her way back to Hattie's, after a pleasant month with her old friend, Mrs. Tweed. Even so, she had been considerate; for the station agent knew her and got hold of the Morrises at once—there had been some mix-up about her telegram. Later, they had found out that she had known about her heart trouble for some time.

He had expected to take Claire on to the funeral, but Claire had been adamant. "I will not have you do it, Tom. It'll be bad enough by myself. But I will not have you mixed up in it—it isn't fair. We can have bad memories separately, but I won't have us have them together." She had grown almost hysterical about it— Claire! And so she had gone alone.

He had been very much worried till she returned, with a white changed face that refused to give any details of those three days. "Don't ask me, Tom. I've told you everything I can—oh, yes, everybody was kind and they had her hymns . . . but, oh Tom, it's so terrible. Terrible. The most barbarous, the most humiliating custom I know! I'll tell you this right now, I'm not going to wear mourning. I don't believe in it and I won't submit to it. All the black dresses—mother didn't really like black. Oh, Tom, Tom, when I die don't dare wear mourning for me!"

He had got her to bed and quieted at last. But she had not been herself—the true Claire—for months afterward, though, as soon as she could, she had taken up the strands of their life again and woven the pattern even more deftly and swiftly, as if each new thread were precious and each second not to be recalled.

Naturally, then, it was only right for him to come to this death in his own country alone. Any other course would have been a monstrous selfishness. And yet he wished that he could go to sleep.

Perhaps, if he thought once more of that shining cube of steel and glass that was their planned security, sleep would come. Even death in New York was different and impersonal. Except for the very mighty, it was an anonymous affair. The man in 10B died and, the next fall, they redecorated the apartment for other tenants. In a month or so even the doorman had forgotten; the newsdealer wrote another name on the morning papers. A name dropped out of the 'phone book . . . you had moved again, with October . . . moved to another city—the city at the sprawling edge of town where lie the streets and avenues of the numberless, quickly buried dead. There, too, you would be part of the crowd, and your neighbors would be strangers, as it had been in life. Your dwelling would be well kept-up, for that was written in the contract. No ghosts could ever arise from that suburban earth. For this, John Merritt and Samuel Pye had built a house in the wilderness to be a shelter and a refuge for them and their seed to the generations of generations. It was just.

Something cracked in the shining cube of glass and steel. The girders crunched on one another, wrenching apart; the glass tumbled into nothingness, falling a long way. There was nothing left but the perplexed, forgotten spirit, roused out of long sleep at last to strive, unprepared, against its immortal adversary.

Claire was all right, but she was afraid of death. He was all right, but he was afraid of death. The clever people they knew were entirely right, but most of them were deadly afraid of death.

If the life they led was rich—if it was the good life —why were they so afraid? It was not because they so joyed in all things under the sun that it was bitter to leave them. That was mortal and understandable, that had always been. But this was a blinder fear.

It had not been in sorrow or remorse that Claire had grieved for her mother. She had grieved the most because she had been afraid. And that made Claire a monster, which she was not. But there was something in it, all the same. He could admit it in her because he could admit it in himself. He lay sleepless, dreading the morrow. And yet he was not a coward so far as he knew.

They had won, but where was the victory? They had escaped from Waynesville and Hessian Street, from Fanshawe and Pye and Merritt, but where was the escape? If they were afraid in these years, how were they to deal with the years to come? Tom Carroll heard the clock in the courthouse strike five strokes. And then, when it seemed to him he could never sleep again, he fell asleep.

They drove at the slow pace down Hessian Street into Main, through the bright, morning sunlight. Tom Carroll felt ashamed of the dreams and waking of the night. He had never felt more solid and confident and assured than he did now, sitting beside Aunt Emmy, his tact and his shoulder ready for her the moment the inevitable breakdown came. Thank God! Jerry Pye was driving his own car. Jerry muddled things so. As for what was to come, that would merely be pathetic—the few old people painfully come together to mourn not only one of their own but a glory that had departed, the Waynesville of their youth. He hoped Aunt Emmy would not notice how few they were. But she, too, was old; and the old lived in the past. She could people the empty pews with the faces that once had been there. It was better so. The lords of Hessian and Bounty Streets had ruled the town with a high hand, even as they sank into poverty, but that was ended. You had only to look along Main to see the new names on the shop-fronts. They knew not Hessian Street, these Caprellos and Szukalskis, but they thrived and inherited the land. Even Waynesville was growing up—there was little charm left in it, but it was alive. And here was the old brick church of the memories.

He helped Aunt Emmy expertly from the car, but she would not take his arm. Well, he respected her courage. He stood tactfully to shield her from the sight of the coffin, just being lifted down from that other, windowless car. But before he knew it Jerry Pye was beside them.

"Aunt Emmy," said Jerry Pye incredibly, "did Aunt Louise really want old Zenas to be one of the coffin-bearers? Because he's there now, and it'll be too late unless somebody tells him . . ."

He actually made a gesture with his hand. Tom Carroll would have been glad to strangle his cousin. But miraculously Aunt Emmy did not break.

She even walked past Tom Carroll to look deliberately at the six black-suited negroes who now had their burden ready to carry into the church. Tom Carroll looked as well. They were none of them under forty, and their faces were grave and sober, but there was something ceremonial in their attitude that struck Tom Carroll strangely. They were sad but they were not constrained—they were doing something they felt to be right and they did it naturally and with ceremony. They would remember the ceremony always when the sadness had passed.

"Zenas, Joram, Joseph, William, Henry, Devout," said Aunt Emmy, in a half-whisper. "Yes, that's right. That's right. Zenas should be there. Louise would have missed Zenas. No, Tommy, we will let them pass, please."

When the coffin had passed, to the sway of the easy shoulders, they followed it in. It was the beginning of Tom Carroll's astonishment. The astonishment did not lessen when he found the church half full, and not only with the old.

He had always thought of Aunt Louise as Aunt Emmy's shadow—in his boyhood as someone always hurried but vaguely sweet whose peppermint-drops took away the taste of Aunt Emmy's wrath; in his manhood as a responsibility at the back of his mind. But the minister was a young man, and neither Pye nor Merritt, and he spoke of the Louise Pye, whose singlehanded effort had turned the ramshackle old School For The Instruction Of Freed Negroes into an institution model for its time, in terms that assumed his hearers knew and appreciated the difficulties of that task.

Phrases came to Tom Carroll's ears. They were the conventional phrases of oratory, yet the speaker meant them. "Unsparing of time or labor." "The rare gift of personality." "The quiet achievement of many years." "We can say to-day, in all truth, a light has gone from among us. . . ." But this was Aunt Louise!

And after the service, and on the way to the grave, and after the service there, the astonishment continued. He was by Aunt Emmy's side, and the people spoke to him. Nearly everyone who spoke to him knew his name. They did not find it odd or kind or a favor that he should be there—he was Julia Merritt's son, who was working in New York. You didn't hear as much about him as you did about Jerry Pye, but it was natural that he should return. Not only Mrs. Bache was under the impression that he had come principally to hear the reading of Aunt Louise's will. They did not think ill of him for it, merely prudent. He could explain nothing, even if he had wished to. There was nothing to explain.

He could not count the number of times he was

told that the cross of yellow roses was beautiful—did they know by telepathy that it was from him and Claire? He had thought it garish and out of place beside the other flowers, the late asters and first chrysanthemums, the zinnias and snapdragons, the bronzes and reds and golds of the country fall. But that he could not say.

The negroes who had borne the coffin knew him. They spoke to him gravely in their rich voices when all was done. Aunt Emmy had a curious phrase for each of them. "Thank you, Devout. Thank you, Joram. Miss Louise will be pleased." It would seem macabre, telling it to Claire. It was not; it was only simple. But that she would not believe.

He remembered, as if in a dream, his plans for succor and comfort when Aunt Emmy should collapse. But it was he who felt physically exhausted when they got back to the house.

This, too, was the moment that he had dreaded the most. Last night he had been able to have dinner at the hotel, but this time there was no escaping the cold meal laid in the basement dining room, the haunted and undue fragrance of flowers that had filled the house for a while. But, when the food was in front of him he was hungry and ate. They all ate, even Aunt Emmy. Minnie did what waiting was necessary and did it, for once, without fluster. Jerry Pye seemed tired and subdued. Once Tom Carroll caught himself feeling sorry for him, once he tried to help him out in a story that was meant to be cheerful and fell flat.

"You know," said Minnie, in a flat voice, pouring coffee, "it seems as if Aunt Louise hadn't gone away so far as before it happened."

Tom Carroll knew what she meant. He felt it too —that presence of the dead, but not grimly nor as a ghost. The presence was as real as the October sky, and as removed from flesh. It did not have to mean that all tired souls were immortal—it had its own peace.

After the meal was over, Tom Carroll walked in the back yard and smoked with Jerry Pye. Now and then he remembered from childhood the fear that had walked there with him, with the scent of the overpowering flowers. But, search as he would, he could not find that fear. The few flowers left in the beds were bronze and scentless; there was no fear where they bloomed.

It was time to go in for the reading of Aunt Louise's will. Tom Carroll listened obediently. He did not even mention the names of Norman, Buckstone, and Carroll. Once, when Mr. Dabney, the lawyer, looked at him and said, "You are a member of the New York Bar, I believe, Mr. Carroll?" he felt surprised at being able to say "yes."

It was a long and personal will made up of many small bequests. He could see Aunt Louise going through her innumerable boxes, trying hard to be fair.

"To my nephew, Thomas Carroll, and his wife, Claire Fanshawe Carroll, the pair of silver candlesticks belonging to my dear Father."

Tom Carroll felt the slow red creeping into his face.

They shook hands with Mr. Dabney. They spoke of what was to be done. Tom Carroll did not proffer assistance. There was no need.

Jerry Pye was offering him a lift as far as Bradensburg—Minnie would be staying with Aunt Emmy for the next week or so, but he must get back to work.

But Tom Carroll thought he had better wait till the morning.

"Well, I guess you'll be more comfortable here at that," said Jerry Pye. "I'll have to hit her up if I want to get home before 3 G.M. So long, Tom. You see Minnie doesn't step out with a handsomer fellow now the old man's away. And take care of the Pye candlesticks—at that, I guess they'll look better in your place than they would in ours. Our kids might use 'em for baseball bats. Say, give my best to Claire."

He was gone. "Now, Tommy," said Aunt Emmy in her tired, indomitable voice, "you go back to the hotel and get a rest—you look tuckered out. Nelly Jervis is coming in here to get the supper. Half-past six."

They were sitting in the front parlor again that evening, he and she. It wasn't late, but Minnie had been sent to bed, unwilling. She wouldn't close an eye, she said; but they knew she was already asleep.

"It's queer what a good nurse Minnie is," said Aunt Emmy reflectively. "Seems as if it was the only thing that ever got her shut of her fussiness—taking care of sick people. You'd think she'd drop crumbs in the bed, but she never does. I don't know what we'd have done without her. Well, she's a right to be tired."

"How about you, Aunt Emmy?"

"Oh," said Aunt Emmy, "they used to say there'd be some people the Fool Killer would still be looking for on Judgment Day. I guess I'm one of them. Of course I'm tired, Tommy. When I'm tired enough, I'll tell you and go to bed."

"Look here, Aunt Emmy," said Tom Carroll, "if there's anything I can do——"

"And what could you do, Tommy?"

"Well, wouldn't you like a car?" he said, awkwardly, "or somebody to stay with you—or another place. They say those apartments over by the——"

"I was born here," said Aunt Emmy, with a snap of her lips, "and now Louise has gone, I've got just enough money to die here. It isn't the same, but I'm suited. And, of all the horrors of age, deliver me from a paid companion. If I need anything like that I'll get Susan Bache to move in here. She's a fool and she's a tattler," said Aunt Emmy, clearly, "but I'm used to her. And Minnie'll come up, every now and then. Don't worry about me, Tom Carroll. We've all of us been on your back long enough."

"On my back?" said Tom Carroll, astounded.

"Well, I'd like to know where else it was," said Aunt Emmy. "You got Louise's money back from that rascal that bamboozled her, and I know twice you pulled Jerry Pye out of the mudhole, and then there was Cousin Edna all those years. Not to speak of what you did for Melrose. Melrose was my own brother, but he ought to have been ashamed of himself, the way he hindered you. Oh, don't you worry about Waynesville, Tommy—you've no call. You did right to get out when you did and as you did, and Waynesville knows it, too. Not that Waynesville would ever admit George Washington was any great shakes, once he'd moved away. But you wait till you die, Tom Carroll"—and she actually chuckled—"and you see what the *Waynesville Blade* says about her distinguished son. They told Louise for twenty years she was crazy, teaching negroes to read and write. But they've got two columns about her this evening and an editorial. I've cut it out and I'm going to paste it under her picture. Louise was always the loving one, and I never grudged her that. But I did grudge her forgiving where I didn't see cause to forgive. But that's all done." She rustled the paper in her lap.

"How are your boys, Tommy?" she said. "They look smart enough in their pictures."

"We think they are," said Tom Carroll. "I hope you're right."

"They ought to be," said Aunt Emmy. "The Fanshawes never lacked smartness, whatever else they lacked, and your father was a bright man. Well, I've seen Jeremiah's and Minnie's. Boy and girl. Don't laugh at me, because it doesn't seem possible, but Jeremiah makes a good father. I never could get on with children —you ought to know that if anyone does—but I think they'll amount to something. Well, it's time the family was getting some sense again."

"Aunt Emmy!" said Tom Carroll, protestingly.

"Was this a happy house?" said Aunt Emmy, fiercely. "For me it was—yes—because I grew up in it. And I always had Louise and I don't regret anything. But was it happy for your mother and you? You know it wasn't, and a good thing your father took her out of it, adventurer or no adventurer, and a bad thing she had to come back. Well, we did our duty according to our lights. But that wasn't enough. There's no real reason, you know, why families have to get that way, except they seem to. But they will get to thinking they're God Almighty, and, after a while, that gets taken notice of. I'll say this—it wasn't the money with us. We held up our heads with it or without it. But maybe we held them too stiff."

She sank into a brooding silence. Behind her in the corner the vague shadows of innumerable Pyes and Merritts seemed to gather and mingle and wait. After a while she roused herself.

"Where are you going to live, Tommy?" she said.

"I've been thinking about a place in the country sometime," said Tom Carroll. "If Waynesville were a little different——"

Aunt Emmy shook her head.

"You couldn't come back here, Tommy," she said. "It's finished here. And that's just as well. But, if you're going to build your own house, you'd better do it soon. You won't be happy without it—you've got too much Merritt in you. The Merritts made their own places. It was the Pyes that sat on the eggs till finally they tried to hatch chickens out of a doorknob, because it was easier than looking for a new roost. But you haven't much Pye. All the same, you won't be contented till you've got some roots put down. The Fanshawes, they could live in a wagon and like it, but the Bouverins were like the Merritts—when they'd rambled enough, they cleared ground. And Claire looks a lot more Bouverin than Fanshawe to me, whether she likes it or not."

"I didn't know you knew Claire's family," said Tom Carroll.

"She probably wouldn't tell you," said Aunt Emmy. "Well, that's natural enough. Good Goshen! I remember Claire Fanshawe, a peaked little slip of a child, at Anna Bouverin's funeral, just before they left Bradensburg. The coffin was still open, and some ignoramus

or other thought it would be fitting for all the grandchildren to come and kiss their grandma good-by. Mind
you, after they'd said good-by to her once already,
before she died. I could have told them better, little
as I know children. Well, it didn't make much difference to Hattie; she always had the nerves of an ox.
But Claire was just over typhoid and after they made
her do it she had what *I'd* call a shaking chill, in a
grown person. And *yet,* they made her get up and recite
the Twenty-Third Psalm in front of everybody—just
because she was smart for her age, and a little child
shall lead them. Her mother didn't stop them—too
proud of her knowing it, I guess. But that was the Fanshawe of it—they had to play-act whatever happened."

Tom Carroll had his head in his hands.

"She never told me," he said. "She never told me
at all."

"No?" said Aunt Emmy, looking at him sharply.
"Well, she was young and maybe she forgot it. I imagine Hattie did."

"Claire never has," said Tom Carroll.

"Well," said Aunt Emmy, "I'll tell you something,
Tommy. When you get to my age you've seen life and
death. And there's just one thing about death, once
you start running away from the thought of it, it runs
after you. Till finally you're scared even to talk about
it and, even if your best friend dies, you'll forget him
as quick as you can because the thought's always waiting. But once you can make yourself turn around and
look at it—it's different. Oh, you can't help the grief.
But you can get a child so it isn't afraid of the dark
—though if you scared it first it'll take a longer while."

"Tell me," said Tom Carroll in a low voice, "were there—very sweet flowers—when my mother died?"

"It was just before Easter," said Aunt Emmy softly. "You could smell the flowers all through the house. But we didn't have any play-acting," she added, quickly. "Not with you. Melrose had that bee in his bonnet, but Louise put her foot down. But it's hard to explain to a child."

"It's hard to explain anyway," said Tom Carroll.

"That's true," said Aunt Emmy. "It's a queer thing," she said. "I never smell lilac without thinking of Lucy Marshall. She was a friend of mine, and then we fell out, and when we were young we used to play by a lilac bush in her yard. It used to trouble me for a long time before I put the two things together. But the pain went out of it then."

"Yes. The pain goes out when you know," said Tom Carroll. "It's not knowing that makes you afraid."

"If Hattie was closer to her, she could do it," said Aunt Emmy. "But the way things are——"

"It'll have to be me," said Tom Carroll. "And I don't know how."

"Well, you're fond of her," said Aunt Emmy. "They say that helps." She rose. "I'll give you the candlesticks in the morning, Tom."

"Can't I leave them with you, Aunt Emmy?"

"What's the use?" said Aunt Emmy practically. "To tell you the truth, Tommy, I'd got right tired of shining them. Besides, they'll look well in your house, when you get your house."

BLOSSOM AND FRUIT

WHEN the spring was in its mid-term and the apple trees entirely white they would walk down by the river, talking as they went, their voices hardly distinguishable from the voices of birds or waters. Their love had begun with the winter; they were both in their first youth. Those who watched them made various prophecies—none of which was fulfilled —laughed, criticized, or were sentimental according to the turn of their minds. But these two were ignorant of the watching and, if they had heard the prophecies, they would hardly have understood them.

Between them and the world was a wall of glass— between them and time was a wall of glass—they were not conscious of being either young or old. The weather passed over them as over a field or a stream—it was there but they took no account of it. There was love and being alive, there was the beating of the heart, apart or together. This had been, this would be, this was—it was impossible to conceive of a world created otherwise. He knew the shape of her face, in dreams and out of them; she could shut her eyes, alone, and feel his hands on her shoulders. So it went, so they spoke and answered, so they walked by the river. Later on, once or twice, they tried to remember what they had said—a great deal of nonsense?—but the words were already gone. They could hear the river running; he could remember a skein of hair; she, a blue shirt open at the throat and an eager face. Then, after a while, these two were not often remembered.

All this had been a number of years ago. But now that the old man had returned at last to the place where he had been born, he would often go down to the river-field. Sometimes a servant or a grandchild would carry the light camp chair and the old brown traveling-rug; more often he would go alone. He was still strong— he liked to do for himself; there was no use telling him he'd catch his death walking through the wet grass, it only set him in his ways.

When at last he had reached his goal—a certain ancient apple tree whose limbs were entirely crooked with bearing—he would set the chair under it, sit down, wrap his legs in the rug, and remain there till he was summoned to come in. He was alone but not lonely; if anyone passed by he would talk; if no one passed he was content to be silent. There was almost always a book in his lap, but he very seldom read it; his own life, after all, was the book that suited him best, it did not grow dull with rereading. There is little to add, he thought, little to add; but he was not sorry. The text remained; it was a long text, and many things that had seemed insignificant and obscure in the living took on sudden clarities and significances, now he remembered.

Yes, he thought, that is how most people live their actual lives—skimming it through, in a hurry to get to the end and find out who got married and who got rich. Well, that's something that can't be helped. But

when you know the end you can turn back and try to
find out the story. Only most people don't want to,
he thought, and smiled. Looks too queer to suit them
—reading your own book backwards. But it's a great
pleasure to me. He relaxed, let his hands lie idle in his
lap, let the pictures drift before his eyes.

The picture of the boy and girl by the river. He
could stand off from it now and regard it, without sorrow or longing; no ghost cried in his flesh because of it,
though it was a part of that flesh and with that flesh
would die. And yet, for a moment, he had almost been
in the old mood again, recovered the old ecstasy. Whatever love was, he had been in love at that time. But
what was love?

They met by stealth because of reasons no longer
important; it lasted through all of one long dry summer in the small town that later became a city. Outside, the street baked, the white dust blew up and
down, but it was fresh and pleasant in the house.

She was a dark-haired woman, a widow, some years
older than he—he was a young man in a tall collar, his
face not yet lined or marked but his body set in the
pattern which it would keep. Her name was Stella.
She had a cool voice, sang sometimes; they talked a
great deal. They made a number of plans which were
not accomplished—they were hotly in love.

He remembered being with her one evening toward
the end of summer, in the trivial room. On the table
was a bowl of winesaps—he had been teasing her about
them—she said she liked the unripened color best.

They talked a little more, then she grew silent; her face, turned toward his, was white in the dusk.

That autumn an accident took him away from the town. When he came back, a year later, she had moved to another state. Later he heard that she had married again, and the name of the man. A great while later he read of her death.

The old man's rug had slipped from his knees; he gathered it up again and tucked it around him. He could not quite get back into the man who had loved and been loved by Stella, but he could not escape him, either. He saw that youth and the boy who had walked by the river. Each had a woman by his side, each stared at the other hostilely, each, pointing to his own companion, said, "This is love." He smiled a trifle dubiously at their frowning faces—both were so certain—and yet he included them both. Which was right, which wrong? He puzzled over the question but could come to no decision. And if neither were right—or both—why then, what was love?

You certainly strike some queer things when you read the book backwards, he thought. I guess I'd better call it a day and quit. But, even as he thought so, another picture arose.

They had been married for a little more than two years, their first child was eight months old. He was a man in his thirties, doing well, already a leader in the affairs of the growing town. She was five years younger, tall for a woman; she had high color in those days. They had known comparatively little of each other before their marriage—indeed, had not been very deeply in love; but living together had changed them.

He came back to the house on Pine Street, told the news of his day, heard about the neighbors, the errands, the child. After dinner they sat in the living room, he smoked and read the newspaper, she had sewing in her lap. They talked to each other in snatches; when their eyes met, something went, something came. At ten o'clock she went upstairs to feed the child; he followed some time later. The child was back in its crib again; they both looked at her a moment—sleep already lay upon her like a visible weight —how deeply, how swiftly she sank towards sleep! They went out, shut the door very softly, stood for a moment in the hallway, and embraced. Then the woman released herself.

"I'm going to bed now, Will," she said. "Be sure and turn out the lights when you come up."

"I won't be long," he said. "It's been a long day."

He stretched his arms, looking at her. She smiled deeply, turned away. The door of their room shut behind her.

When he had extinguished the lights and locked the doors he went up to the long garret that stretched the whole length of the house. They had had the house only two years, but the garret had already accumulated its collection of odds and ends; there were various discarded or crippled objects that would never be used again, that would stay here till the family moved, till someone died. But what he had come to see was a line of apples mellowing on a long shelf, in the dusty darkness. They had been sent in from the farm—you could smell their faint, unmistakable fragrance from the doorway. He took one up, turned it over in his hand, felt its weight and texture, firm and smooth and cool. You couldn't get a better eating apple than that, and this was the right place for them to mellow.

Mary's face came before him, looking at him in the hallway; the thought of it was like the deep stroke of a knife that left, as it struck, no pain. Yes, he thought, I'm alive—we're pretty fond of each other. Some impulse made him put down the apple and push up the little skylight of the garret to let the air blow in on his face. It was a clean cold—it was autumn; it made the blood run in him to feel it. He stood there for several minutes, drinking in cold autumn, thinking about his wife. Then at last he shut the skylight and went downstairs to their room.

A third couple had joined the others under the tree, a third image asserted itself, by every settled line in its body, the possessor not only of a woman but of a particular and unmistakable knowledge. The old man observed one and all, without envy but curiously. If they could only get to talking with one another, he thought, why then, maybe, we'd know something. But they could not do it—it was not in the cards. All each could do was to make an affirmation, "This is love."

The figures vanished, he was awake again. When you were old you slept lightly but more often, and these dreams came. Mary had been dead ten years; their children were men and women. He had always expected Mary to outlive him, but things had not happened so. She would have been a great comfort. Yet when he thought of her dead, though his grief was real, it came to him from a distance. He and she were nearer together than he and grief. And yet if he met her again it would be strange.

The flower came out on the branch, the fruit budded and grew. At last it fell or was picked, and the thing started over again. You could figure out every process of growth and decline, but that did not get you any nearer the secret. Only, he'd like to know.

He turned his eyes toward the house—somebody coming for him. His eyes were still better for far-away things than near, and he made out the figure quite plainly. It was the girl who had married his grand-nephew, Robert. She called him "Father Hancock" or "Gramp" like the rest of them, but still, she was different from the rest.

For a moment her name escaped him. Then he had it. Jenny. A dark-haired girl, pleasant spoken, with a good free walk to her—girls stepped out freer, on the whole, than they had in his day. As for cutting their hair and the rest of it—well, why shouldn't they? It was only the kind of people who wrote to newspapers who made a fuss about such things. And they always had to make a fuss about something. He chuckled deeply, wondering what a newspaper would make of it if a highly respected old citizen wrote and asked them what was love. "Crazy old fool—ought to be in an asylum." Well, maybe at that, they'd be right.

He watched the girl coming on as he would have watched a rabbit run through the grass or a cloud march along the sky. There was something in her walk that matched both rabbit and cloud—something light and free and unbroken. But there was something else in her walk as well.

"Lunch, Father Hancock!" she called while she was still some yards away. "Snapper beans and black-cherry pie!"

"Well, I'm hungry," said the old man. "You know me, Jenny—never lost appetite yet. But you can have my slice of the pie; you've got younger teeth than mine."

"Stop playing you're a centenarian, Father Hancock," said the girl. "I've seen you with Aunt Maria's pies before."

"I might take a smidgin', at that," said the old man reflectively, "just to taste. But you can have all I don't eat, Jenny—and that's a fair offer."

"It's too fair," said the girl. "I'd eat you out of house and home to-day." She stretched her arms toward the sky. "Gee, I feel hungry!" she said.

"It's right you should," said the old man, placidly. "And don't be ashamed of your dinner either. Eat solid and keep your strength up."

"Do I look as if I needed to keep my strength up?" she said with a laugh.

"No. But it's early to tell," said the old man, gradually disentangling himself from his coverings. He stood up, declining her offered hand. "Thank you, my dear," he said. "I never expected to see my own great-grandnephew. But don't be thinking of that. It'll be your baby, boy or girl, and that's what's important."

The girl's hand went slowly to her throat while color rose in her face. Then she laughed.

"Father Hancock!" she said. "You—you darned old

wizard! Why Robert doesn't know about it yet and———"

"He wouldn't," said the old man briefly. "Kind of inexperienced at that age. But you can't fool me, my dear. I've seen too much and too many."

She looked at him with trouble in her eyes.

"Well, as long as you know . . ." she said. "But you won't let on to the rest of them . . . of course I'll tell Robert soon, but———"

"I know," said the old man. "They carry on. Never could see so much sense in all that carrying on, but relations do. And being the first great-grandchild. No, I won't tell 'em. And I'll be as surprised as Punch when they finally tell me."

"You're a good egg," said the girl gratefully. "Thanks ever so much. I don't mind your knowing."

They stood for a moment in silence, his hand on her shoulder. The girl shivered suddenly.

"Tell me, Father Hancock," she said suddenly, in a muffled voice, not looking at him, "is it going to be pretty bad?"

"No, child, it won't be so bad." She said nothing, but he could feel the tenseness in her body relax.

"It'll be for around November, I expect?" he said, and went on without waiting for her reply. "Well, that's a good time, Jenny. You take our old cat, Marcella— she generally has her second lot of kittens around in October or November. And those kittens, they do right well."

"Father Hancock! You're a positive disgrace!" So she said, but he knew from the tone of her voice that she was not angry with him and once more, as they went together towards the house, he felt the stroke of youth upon him, watching her walk so well.

About the middle of summer, when the green of the fields had turned to yellow and brown, Will Hancock's old friend John Sturgis drove over one day to visit him.

A son and a granddaughter accompanied John Sturgis, as well as two other vaguer female relatives whom the young people called indiscriminately "Cousin" and "Aunt"; and for a while the big porch of the Hancock house knew the bustle of tribal ceremony. Everyone was a little anxious, everyone was a little voluble; this was neither a funeral nor a wedding but, as an occasion, it ranked with those occasions, and in the heart of every Hancock and Sturgis present was a small individual grain of gratitude and pride at being there to witness the actual meeting of two such perishable old men.

The relatives possessed the old men and displayed them. The old men sat quietly, their tanned hands resting on their knees. They knew they were being possessed, but they too felt pride and pleasure. It was, after all, remarkable that they should be here. The young people didn't know how remarkable it was.

Finally, however, Will Hancock rose.

"Come along down-cellar, John," he said gruffly. "Got something to show you."

It was the familiar opening of an immemorial gambit. And it brought the expected reply.

"Now, father," said Will Hancock's eldest daughter,

"if you'll only wait a minute, Maria will be out with the lemonade, and I had her bake some brownies."

"Lemonade!" said Will Hancock and sniffed. "Hold your tongue, Mary," he said gently. "I'm going to give John Sturgis something good for what ails him."

As he led the way down-cellar he smiled to himself. They would be still protesting, back on the porch. They would be saying that cellars were damp and old men delicate, that cider turned into acid, and that at their age you'd think they'd have more sense. But there would be no real heart in the protestations. And if the ceremonial visit to the cellar had been omitted there would have been disappointment. Because then their old men would not have been quite so remarkable, after all.

They passed through the dairy-cellar, with its big tin milk-pans, and into the cider-cellar. It was cool there but with a sweet-smelling coolness; there was no scent of damp or mold. Three barrels stood in a row against the wall; on the floor was a yellow patch of light. Will Hancock took a tin cup from a shelf and silently tapped the farthest barrel. The liquid ran in the cup. It was old cider, yellow as wheat-straw, and when he raised it toward his nostrils the soul of the bruised apple came to him.

"Take a seat, John," he said, passing over the full cup. His friend thanked him and sank into the one disreputable armchair. Will Hancock filled another cup and sat down upon the middle barrel.

"Well, here's to crime, John!" he said. It was the time-honored phrase.

"Mud in your eye!" said John Sturgis fiercely. He sipped the cider.

"Ah!" he said, "tastes better every year, Will."

"She ought to, John. She's goin' along with us."

They both sat silent for a time, sipping appreciatively, their worn eyes staring at each other, taking each other in. Each time they met again now was a mutual triumph for both; they looked forward to each time and back upon it, but they had known each other so long that speech had become only a minor necessity between them.

"Well," said John Sturgis at last, when the cups had been refilled, "I hear you got some more expectations in your family, Will. That's fine."

"That's what they tell me," said Will Hancock. "She's a nice girl, Jenny."

"Yes, she's a nice girl," said John Sturgis indifferently. "It'll be some news for Molly when I get home. She'll be right interested. She was hopin' we might beat you to it, with young Jack and his wife. But no signs yet."

He shook his head and a shadow passed over his face.

"Well, I don't know that you set so much store by it," said Will Hancock consolingly, "though it's interesting."

"Oh, they'll have a piece in the paper," said John Sturgis with a trace of bitterness. "Four generations. Even if it isn't a great-grandchild, so to speak. I know 'em." He took a larger sip of cider.

"That won't do me a speck of good when I get home," he confided. "And Molly, she'll think I was crazy. But what's the use of livin' if you've got to live so tetchy all the time?"

"I never saw you looking better, John," said Will Hancock, heartily. "Never did."

"I'm spry enough most days," admitted John Sturgis. "And as for you, you look like a four-year-old. But it's the winter——"

He left the sentence uncompleted, and both fell silent for a moment, thinking of the coming winter. Winter, the foe of old men.

At last John Sturgis leaned forward. His cheeks had a ghost of color in them now, his eyes an unexpected brightness.

"Tell me, Will," he said, eagerly, "you and me—we've seen a good deal in our time. Well, tell me this —just how do you figure it all out?"

Will Hancock could not pretend to misunderstand the question. Nor could he deny his friend the courtesy of a reply.

"I haven't a notion," he said at last, slowly and gravely. "I've thought about it, Lord knows—but I haven't a notion, John."

The other sank back into his chair, disappointedly.

"Well now, that's too bad," he grumbled, "for I've been thinkin' about it. Seems to me as if I didn't do much else *but* think most of the time. But you're the educated one; and if you haven't a notion—well——"

His eyes stared into space, without fear or anger, but soberly. Will Hancock tried to think of some way to help his friend.

He saw again before him those three figures under the apple tree, each a part of himself, each with a woman beside it, each saying, "This is love." Now, as he fell into reverie, a fourth couple joined them—an old man, still erect, and a girl who still walked with a light step though her body was heavy now.

He stared at these last visitors, incredulously at first, and then with a little smile. Nearly every day of the summer Jenny had come to call him when he sat under his tree. He could see her looking across the gulf that separated them—and finding things not so bad as she had thought they might be. Why, I might have been an old tree myself, he thought. Or an old rock you went out to when you wanted to be alone.

There had been her relatives and his. There had been all the women. But it was to him that she had come. To the others he was and would be "Father Hancock" and their own remarkable old man. But Jenny was not really one of his own; and because of that she had from him a certain calming wisdom that he did not know he possessed.

He heard an insect cry in the deep grass and smelled the smell of the hay, the smell of summer days. Love? It was not love, of course, nor could be, by any stretch of language. To her it had been summer and an old tree; and to him, he knew what it had been. He was fond of her, naturally, but that was not the answer. It was not she who had moved him. But for an instant, on the cords of the defeated flesh, he had heard a note struck clearly, the vibration of a single and silver wire. As he thought of this, the wire vibrated anew, the imperishable accent rang. Then it was mute—it would not be struck again.

"I tried to figure it out the other day," he said to John Sturgis, "what love was, first. But——"

Then he stopped. It was useless. John Sturgis was his old friend, but there was no way to tell John Sturgis the thoughts in his mind.

"It's funny your sayin' that," said John Sturgis reflectively. "You know I came back to the house the other day, and there was Molly asleep in the chair. I was scared for a minute but then I saw she was sleeping. Only she didn't wake up right away—I guess I came in light. Well, I stood there looking at her. You came to our golden wedding, Will; but her cheeks were pink and she looked so pretty in her sleep. I just went over and kissed her, like an old fool. Now what makes a man act like that?"

He paused for a moment.

"It's so blame' hard to figure out," he said. "When you're young you've got the strength but you haven t got the time. And when you're old you've got time enough, but I'm always goin' to sleep."

He drained the last drop in his cup and rose.

"Well, Sam'll be lookin' for me," he said. "It was good cider."

As they passed through the dairy a black, whiskered face appeared at the small barred window and vanished guiltily at the sound of Will Hancock's voice.

"That old cat's always trying to get in to the milk," he said. "She ought to take shame on her, all the kittens she's had. But I guess this'll be her last litter, this fall. She's getting on."

The tribal ceremonies of departure were drawing toward a close. Will Hancock shook John Sturgis' hand.

"Come over again, John, and bring along Molly next time," he said. "There's always a drop in the barrel."

"And it's a prize drop," said John Sturgis. "Thank you, Will. But I don't figure on gettin' over again this summer. Next spring, maybe."

"Sure," said Will. But between them both, as they knew, lay the shadow of the cold months, the shadow to be lived through. Will Hancock watched his friend being helped into the car, watched the car drive away. "John's beginning to go," he thought with acceptance. "And that's probably just what John's telling Sam about me."

He turned back toward his family. He was tired, but he could not give in. The family clustered about him, talking and questioning. John's visit had made him, for the moment, an even more remarkable old man than ever; and he must play his role for the rest of them, worthily, now John had gone. So he played it, and they saw no difference. But he kept wondering what day the winter would set in.

The first gales of autumn had come and passed; when Will Hancock got up in the morning he saw white rime on the ground. It had melted away by eleven, but next morning it was back again. At last, when he walked down to his apple tree he walked under bare boughs.

That night he went early to his room, but before he got in bed he stood for a while at the window, looking at the sky. It was a winter sky, the stars were hard in it. Yet the day had been mild enough. Jenny wanted her child born in the Indian Summer. Perhaps she would still have her wish.

He slept more lightly than ever these nights—the first thing roused him. So when the noises began in the house he was awake at once. But he lay there for some time, dreamily, not even looking at his watch. The footsteps went up and down stairs, and he listened to them; a voice said something sharply and was hushed; somebody was trying to telephone. He knew them all, those sounds of whispering haste that wake up a house at night.

Yes, he thought, all the same it's hard on the women. Or the men too, for that matter. But sooner or later, the doctor would come and take from his small black bag the miraculous doll wrapped up in the single cabbage leaf. He himself had once been such a doll, though he couldn't remember it. Now they would not want him out there, but he would go all the same.

He rose, put on his dressing-gown, and tiptoed down the long corridor. He heard a shrill whisper in his ear, *"Father!* Are you *crazy?* Go back to *bed!"* But he shook his head at the whisper and went on. At the head of the stairs he met his grandnephew, Robert. There was sweat on the boy's face and he breathed as if he had been running. They looked at each other a moment, with sympathy but without understanding.

"How is she?" said Will Hancock.

"All right, thanks, Gramp," said the boy in a grateful voice as he kept fumbling in his dressing-gown pocket for a cigarette that was not there. "The doctor's coming over but we—we don't think it's the real thing yet "

Someone called to the boy, and he disappeared again. The corridor abruptly seemed very full of Will Hancock's family. They were clustering around him, buzzing reassuringly, but he paid little attention.

Suddenly, from behind a closed door, he heard Jenny's voice, clear and amused. "Why how perfectly sweet of Father Hancock, Bob! But I'm sorry they woke him—and all for a false alarm."

The reassuring buzzes around him recommenced. He shook them off impatiently and walked back toward his room. But when he was hidden from the others he gave a single guilty look behind him and made for the back stairs. They won't follow me, he thought; got too much to talk about.

He switched on the light in the cider-cellar, drawing his dressing-gown closer about him. It was cold in the cellar now and it would be colder still. But cider was always cider, and he felt thirsty.

He drank the yellow liquid reflectively, swinging his heels against the side of the barrel. Upstairs they would still be whispering and consulting. And maybe the doctor would come with his black bag after all, and to-morrow there would be a piece in the paper to make John Sturgis jealous. But there wasn't anything he could do about it.

No, even for Jenny, there was nothing more he could do. She had taken his wisdom, such as it was, and used it. And he was glad of that. But now he knew from the light tone of her voice that she was beyond such wisdom as he had. The wire had ceased its vibration, the leaves of the tree were shed, like dry wisdom on the ground. Well, she was a nice girl, and Robert a

decent boy. They would have other children doubtless,
and those children children in their turn.

He heard a low sound from the other corner of the
cellar and went over to see what had made it. Then
he whistled. "Well, old lady," he said, "you certainly
don't waste your time." It was the old black house-cat
who had stared through the dairy window at himself
and John Sturgis. Already she was licking the third of
her new kittens while the two first-born nuzzled at her,
squeaking from time to time.

He bent over and stroked her head. She looked at
him troubledly. "It's all right," he said reassuringly.
"They've forgotten about us both—and no wonder. But
I'll stick around."

He refilled his cup and sat down upon the barrel,
swinging his heels. There was nothing here that he
could do, either—cats were wiser than humans in such
matters. But, nevertheless, he would stay.

As the cider sank in the cup and he grew colder
he fell into a waking dream. Now and then he went
over to stroke the cat, but he did it automatically. He
was here, in a bare old cellar, drinking cider which
would doubtless disagree with him, and in all prob-
ability catching his death of cold. And upstairs, perhaps, were life and death and the doctor—new life fighting to come into the world and death waiting a chance
to seize it as it came, as death always did. Moreover,
these lives and deaths were his lives and deaths, after a
fashion, for he was part of their chain. But, for the
moment, he was disconnected from them. He was beyond life and death.

He saw again, in front of him, the three couples of

his first dream—and himself and Jenny—himself giving Jenny, unconsciously, the wisdom he did not know. "This is love—this is love—this is love—" and so it was, each phase of it, for each man there spoke the truth of his own heart. Then he looked at the apple tree and saw that it was in flower, but fruit hung on it as well, green fruit and ripe, and even as he looked a wind was blowing the last leaves from the bare bough.

He shivered a little, he was very cold. He put his cup back on the shelf and went over for a last look at the old cat. The travail was over—she lay on her side, beset by the new-born. There was green, inexplicable light in her eyes as he stooped over her, and when he patted her head she stretched one paw out over her kittens like an arm.

He rose stiffly and left her, turning out the light. As he went up the stairs, "Adorable life," he thought, "I know you. I know you were given only to be given away."

The house was silent again, as he tiptoed back to his room. His vigil had been unsuspected, his watch quite useless; and yet he had kept a vigil and a watch. To-morrow might have been too late for it—even now he trembled with cold. Yet, when he stood before the window, he looked long at the winter sky. The stars were still hard points of light, and he would not see them soft again, but earth would continue to turn round, in spite of all these things.

TALES BEFORE MIDNIGHT

CONTENTS

I

I

INTO EGYPT

IT had finally been decided to let them go and now, for three days, they had been passing. The dust on the road to the frontier had not settled for three days or nights. But the strictest orders had been given and there were very few incidents. There could easily have been more.

Even the concentration camps had been swept clean, for this thing was to be final. After it, the State could say "How fearless we are — we let even known conspirators depart." It is true that, in the case of those in the concentration camps, there had been a preliminary rectification — a weeding, so to speak. But the news of that would not be officially published for some time and the numbers could always be disputed. If you kill a few people, they remain persons with names and identities, but, if you kill in the hundreds, there is simply a number for most of those who read the newspapers. And, once you start arguing about numbers, you begin to wonder if the thing ever happened at all. This too had been foreseen.

In fact, everything had been foreseen — and with great acuteness. There had been the usual diplomatic tension, solved, finally, by the usual firm stand. At the last moment, the other Powers had decided to co-operate. They had done so unwillingly, grudgingly, and

3

with many representations, but they had done so. It was another great victory. And everywhere the trains rolled and the dust rose on the roads, for, at last and at length, the Accursed People were going. Every one of them, man, woman and child, to the third and the fourth generation — every one of them with a drop of that blood in his veins. And this was the end of it all and, by sunset on the third day, the land would know them no more. It was another great victory — perhaps the greatest. There would be a week of celebration after it, with appropriate ceremonies and speeches, and the date would be marked in the new calendar, with the date of the founding of the State and other dates.

Nevertheless, and even with the noteworthy efficiency of which the State was so proud, any mass evacuation is bound to be a complicated and fatiguing affair. The lieutenant stationed at the crossroads found it so — he was young and in the best of health but the strain was beginning to tell on him, though he would never have admitted it. He had been a little nervous at first — a little nervous and exceedingly anxious that everything should go according to plan. After all, it was an important post, the last crossroads before the frontier. A minor road, of course — they'd be busier on the main highways and at the ports of embarkation — but a last crossroads, nevertheless. He couldn't flatter himself it was worth a decoration — the bigwigs would get those. But, all the same, he was expected to evacuate so many thousands — he knew the figures by heart. Easy enough to sav one had only to follow the plan! That might do for civilians — an officer was an officer. Would he show

himself enough of an officer, would he make a fool of
himself in front of his men? Would he even, perhaps,
by some horrible, unforeseen mischance, get his road
clogged with fleeing humanity till they had to send
somebody over from Staff to straighten the tangle out?
The thought was appalling.

He could see it happening in his mind — as a boy,
he had been imaginative. He could hear the staff
officer's words while he stood at attention, eyes front.
One's first real command and a black mark on one's
record! Yes, even if it was only police work — that
didn't matter — a citizen of the State, a member of the
Party must be held to an unflinching standard. If one
failed to meet that standard there was nothing left in
life. His throat had been dry and his movements a little
jerky as he made his last dispositions and saw the first
black specks begin to straggle toward the crossroads.

He could afford to laugh at that now, if he had had
time. He could even afford to remember old Franz, his
orderly, trying to put the brandy in his coffee, that first
morning. "It's a chilly morning, Lieutenant," but there
had been a question in Franz's eyes. He'd refused the
brandy, of course, and told Franz off properly, too.
The new State did not depend on Dutch courage but
on the racial valor of its citizens. And the telling-off had
helped — it had made his own voice firmer and given
a little fillip of anger to his pulse. But Franz was an old
soldier and imperturbable. What was it he had said,
later? "The lieutenant must not worry. Civilians are
always sheep — it is merely a matter of herding them."
An improper remark, of course, to one's lieutenant,

but it had helped settle his mind and make it cooler.
Yes, an orderly like Franz was worth something, once
one learned the knack of keeping him in his place.

Then they had begun to come, slowly, stragglingly,
not like soldiers. He couldn't remember who had been
the first. It was strange but he could not — he had been
sure that he would remember. Perhaps a plodding
family, with the scared children looking at him — perhaps one of the old men with long beards and burning
eyes. But, after three days, they all mixed, the individual
faces. As Franz had said, they became civilian sheep —
sheep that one must herd and keep moving, keep moving always through day and night, moving on to the
frontier. As they went, they wailed. When the wailing
grew too loud, one took measures; but, sooner or later it
always began again. It would break out down the road,
die down as it came toward the post. It seemed to
come out of their mouths without their knowledge —
the sound of broken wood, of wheat ground between
stones. He had tried to stop it completely at first, now
he no longer bothered. And yet there were many — a
great many — who did not wail.

At first, it had been interesting to see how many
different types there were. He had not thought to find
such variety among the Accursed People — one had
one's own mental picture, reinforced by the pictures in
the newspapers. But, seeing them was different. They
were not all like the picture. They were tall and short,
plump and lean, black-haired, yellow-haired, red-haired.
It was obvious, even under the film of dust, that some
had been rich, others poor, some thoughtful, others

active. Indeed, it was often hard to tell them, by the looks. But that was not his affair — his affair was to keep them moving. All the same, it gave you a shock, sometimes, at first.

Perhaps the queerest thing was that they all looked so ordinary, so much a part of everyday. That was because one had been used to seeing them — it could be no more than that. But, under the film of dust and heat, one would look at a face. And then one think, unconsciously, "Why, what is that fellow doing, so far from where he lives? Why, for heaven's sake, is he straggling along this road? He doesn't look happy." Then the mind would resume control and one would remember. But the thought would come, now and then, without orders from the mind.

He had seen very few that he knew. That was natural — he came from the South. He had seen Willi Schneider, to be sure — that had been the second day and it was very dusty. When he was a little boy, very young, he had played in Willi's garden with Willi, in the summers, and, as they had played, there had come to them, through the open window, the ripple of a piano and the clear, rippling flow of Willi's mother's voice. It was not a great voice — not a Brunhild voice — but beautiful in *lieder* and beautifully sure. She had sung at their own house; that was odd to remember. Of course, her husband had not been one of them — a councilor, in fact. Needless to say, that had been long before the discovery that even the faintest trace of that blood tainted. As for Willi and himself, they had been friends — yes, even through the first year or so at school.

Both of them had meant to run away and be cowboys, and they had had a secret password. Naturally, things had changed, later on.

For a horrible moment, he had thought that Willi would speak to him — recall the warm air of summer and the smell of linden and those young, unmanly days. But Willi did not. Their eyes met, for an instant, then both had looked away. Willi was helping an old woman along, an old woman who muttered fretfully as she walked, like a cat with sore paws. They were both of them covered with dust and the old woman went slowly. Willi's mother had walked with a quick step and her voice had not been cracked or fretful. After play, she had given them both cream buns, laughing and moving her hands, in a bright green dress. It was not permitted to think further of Willi Schneider.

That was the only real acquaintance but there were other, recognizable faces. There was the woman who had kept the newsstand, the brisk little waiter at the summer hotel, the taxi chauffeur with the squint and the heart specialist. Then there was the former scientist — one could still tell him from his pictures — and the actor one had often seen. That was all that one knew and not all on the same day. That was enough. He had not imagined the taxi chauffeur with a wife and children and that the youngest child should be lame. That had surprised him — surprised him almost as much as seeing the heart specialist walking along the road like any man. It had surprised him, also, to see the scientist led along between two others and to recognize the fact that he was mad.

But that also mixed with the dust — the endless, stifling cloud of the dust, the endless, moving current. The dust got in one's throat and one's eyes — it was hard to cut, even with brandy, from one's throat. It lay on the endless bundles people carried; queer bundles, bulging out at the ends, with here a ticking clock, and there a green bunch of carrots. It lay on the handcarts a few of them pushed — the handcarts bearing the sort of goods that one would snatch, haphazard, from a burning house. It rose and whirled and penetrated — it was never still. At night, slashed by the efficient searchlights that made the night bright as day, it was still a mist above the road. As for sleep — well, one slept when one could, for a couple of hours after midnight, when they too slept, ungracefully, in heaps and clumps by the road. But, except for the first night, he could not even remember Franz pulling his boots off.

His men had been excellent, admirable, indefatigable. That was, of course, due to the Leader and the State, but still, he would put it in his report. They had kept the stream moving, always. The attitude had been the newly prescribed one — not that of punishment, richly as that was deserved, but of complete aloofness, as if the Accursed People did not even exist. Naturally, now and then, the men had had their fun. One could not blame them for that — some of the incidents had been extremely comic. There had been the old woman with the hen — a comedy character. Of course, she had not been permitted to keep the hen. They should have taken it away from her at the inspection point. But she had looked very funny, holding on to the squawking chicken by the tail feathers, with the tears running down her face.

Yes, the attitude of the men would certainly go in his report. He would devote a special paragraph to the musicians also — they had been indefatigable. They had played the prescribed tunes continually, in spite of the dust and the heat. One would hope that those tunes would sink into the hearts of the Accursed People, to be forever a warning and a memory. Particularly if they happened to know the words. But one could never be sure about people like that.

Staff cars had come four times, the first morning, and once there had been a general. He had felt nervous, when they came, but there had been no complaint. After that, they had let him alone, except for an occasional visit — that must mean they thought him up to his work. Once, even, the road had been almost clear, for a few minutes — he was moving them along faster than they did at the inspection point. The thought had gone to his head for an instant, but he kept cool — and, soon enough, the road had been crowded again.

As regarded casualties — he could not keep the exact figure in his head, but it was a minor one. A couple of heart attacks — one the man who had been a judge, or so the others said. Unpleasant but valuable to see the life drain out of a face like that. He had made himself watch it — one must harden oneself. They had wanted to remove the body — of course, that had not been allowed. The women taken in childbirth had been adequately dealt with — one could do nothing to assist. But he had insisted, for decency's sake, on a screen, and

Franz had been very clever at rigging one up. Only two of those had died, the rest had gone on — they showed a remarkable tenacity. Then there were the five executions, including the man suddenly gone crazy, who had roared and foamed. A nasty moment, that — for a second the whole current had stopped flowing. But his men had jumped in at once — he himself had acted quickly. The others were merely incorrigible stragglers and of no account.

And now, it was almost over and soon the homeland would be free. Free as it never had been — for, without the Accursed People, it would be unlike any other country on earth. They were gone, with their books and their music, their false, delusive science and their quick way of thinking. They were gone, all the people like Willi Schneider and his mother, who had spent so much time in talking and being friendly. They were gone, the willful people, who clung close together and yet so willfully supported the new and the untried. The men who haggled over pennies, and the others who gave — the sweater, the mimic, the philosopher, the discoverer — all were gone. Yes, and with them went their slaves' religion, the religion of the weak and the humble, the religion that fought so bitterly and yet exalted the prophet above the armed man.

One could be a whole man, with them gone, without their doubts and their mockery and their bitter, self-accusing laughter, their melancholy, deep as a well, and their endless aspiration for something that could not be touched with the hand. One could be solid and virile and untroubled, virile and huge as the old,

thunderous gods. It was so that the Leader had spoken,
so it must be true. And the countries who weakly received them would be themselves corrupted into warm
unmanliness and mockery, into a desire for peace and
a search for things not tangible. But the homeland
would stand still and listen to the beat of its own heart
— not even listen, but stand like a proud fierce animal,
a perfect, living machine. To get children, to conquer
others, to die gloriously in battle — that was the end
of man. It had been a long time forgotten, but the
Leader had remembered it. And, naturally, one could
not do that completely with them in the land, for they
had other ideas.

He thought of these things dutifully because it was
right to think of them. They had been repeated and
repeated in his ears till they had occupied his mind.
But, meanwhile, he was very tired and the dust still
rose. They were coming by clumps and groups, now —
the last stragglers — they were no longer a solid, flowing
current. The afternoon had turned hot — unseasonably
hot. He didn't want any more brandy — the thought of
it sickened his stomach. He wanted a glass of beer — iced
beer, cold and dark, with foam on it — and a chance
to unbutton his collar. He wanted to have the thing
done and sit down and have Franz pull off his boots.
If it were only a little cooler, a little quieter — if even
these last would not wail so, now and then — if only
the dust would not rise! He found himself humming,
for comfort, a Christmas hymn — it brought a little
frail coolness to his mind.

"Silent night, holy night,
All is calm, all is bright. . . ."

The old gods were virile and thunderous, but, down
in the South, they would still deck the tree, in kindli-
ness. Call it a custom — call it anything you like — it
still came out of the heart. And it was a custom of the
homeland — it could not be wrong. Oh, the beautiful,
crisp snow of Christmas Day, the greetings between
friends, the bright, lighted tree! Well, there'd be a
Christmas to come. Perhaps he'd be married, by then
— he had thought of it, often. If he were, they would
have a tree — young couples were sentimental, in the
South. A tree and a small manger beneath it, with the
animals and the child. They carved the figures out of
wood, in his country, with loving care — the thought of
them was very peaceful and cool. In the old days, he
had always given Willi Schneider part of his almond
cake — one knew it was not Willi's festival but one
was friendly, for all that. And that must be forgotten.
He had had no right to give Willi part of his almond
cake — it was the tree that mattered, the tree and the
tiny candles, the smell of the fresh pine and the clear,
frosty sweetness of the day. They would keep that, he
and his wife, keep it with rejoicing, and Willi would
not look in through the window, with his old face or his
new face. He would not look in at all, ever any more.
For now the homeland was released, after many years.

Now the dust was beginning to settle — the current
in the road had dwindled to a straggling trickle. He
was able to think, for the first time, of the land to which

that trickle was going — a hungry land, the papers said, in spite of its boastful ways. The road led blankly into it, beyond the rise of ground — hard to tell what it was like. But they would be dispersed, not only here, but over many lands. Of course, the situation was not comparable — all the same, it must be a queer feeling. A queer feeling, yes, to start out anew, with nothing but the clothes on your back and what you could push in a handcart, if you had a handcart. For an instant the thought came, unbidden, "It must be a great people that can bear such things." But they were the Accursed People — the thought should not have come.

He sighed and turned back to his duty. It was really wonderful — even on the third day there was such order, such precision. It was something to be proud of — something to remember long. The Leader would speak of it, undoubtedly. The ones who came now were the very last stragglers, the weakest, but they were being moved along as promptly as if they were strong. The dust actually no longer rose in a cloud — it was settling, slowly but surely.

He did not quite remember when he had last eaten. It did not matter, for the sun was sinking fast, in a red warm glow. In a moment, in an hour, it would be done — he could rest and undo his collar, have some beer. There was nobody on the road now — nobody at all. He stood rigidly at his post — the picture of an officer, though somewhat dusty — but he knew that his eyes were closing. Nobody on the road — nobody for a whole five minutes . . . for eight . . . for ten.

He was roused by Franz's voice in his ear — he must have gone to sleep, standing up. He had heard of that happening to soldiers on the march — he felt rather proud that, now, it had happened to him. But there seemed to be a little trouble on the road — he walked forward to it, stiffly, trying to clear his throat.

It was a commonplace grouping — he had seen dozens like it in the course of the three days — an older man, a young woman, and, of course, the child that she held. No doubt about them, either — the man's features were strongly marked, the woman had the liquid eyes. As for the child, that was merely a wrapped bundle. They should have started before — stupid people — the man looked strong enough. Their belongings were done up like all poor people's belongings.

He stood in front of them, now, erect and a soldier. "Well," he said. "Don't you know the orders? No live-stock to be taken. Didn't they examine you, down the road?" ("And a pretty fool I'll look like, reporting one confiscated donkey to Headquarters," he thought, with irritation. "We've been able to manage, with the chickens, but this is really too much! What can they be thinking of at the inspection point? Oh, well, they're tired too, I suppose, but it's my responsibility.")

He put a rasp in his voice — he had to, they looked at him so stupidly. "Well?" he said. "Answer me! Don't you know an officer when you see one?"

"We have come a long way," said the man, in a low voice. "We heard there was danger to the child. So we are going. May we pass?" The voice was civil enough, but the eyes were dark and large, the face tired and worn. He was resting one hand on his staff, in a peasant gesture. The woman said nothing at all and one felt that she would say nothing. She sat on the back of the gray donkey and the child in her arms, too, was silent, though it moved.

The lieutenant tried to think rapidly. After all, these were the last. But the thoughts buzzed around his head and would not come out of his mouth. That was fatigue. It should be easy enough for a lieutenant to give an order.

He found himself saying, conversationally, "There are just the three of you?"

"That is all," said the man and looked at him with great simplicity. "But we heard there was danger to the child. So we could not stay any more. We could not stay at all."

"Indeed," said the lieutenant and then said again, "indeed."

"Yes," said the man. "But we shall do well enough — we have been in exile before." He spoke patiently and yet with a certain authority. When the lieutenant did not answer, he laid his other hand on the rein of the gray donkey. It moved forward a step and with it, also, the child stirred and moved. The lieutenant, turning, saw the child's face now, and its hands, as it turned and moved its small hands to the glow of the sunset.

"If the lieutenant pleases — " said an eager voice, the voice of the Northern corporal.

"The lieutenant does not please," said the lieutenant. He nodded at the man. "You may proceed."

"But Lieutenant — " said the eager voice.

"Swine and dog," said the lieutenant, feeling something snap in his mind, "are we to hinder the Leader's plans because of one gray donkey? The order says — all out of the country by sunset. Let them go. You will report to me, Corporal, in the morning."

He turned on his heel and walked a straight line to the field hut, not looking back. When Franz, the orderly, came in a little later, he found him sitting in a chair.

"If the lieutenant would take some brandy — " he said, respectfully.

"The lieutenant has had enough brandy," said the lieutenant, in a hoarse, dusty voice. "Have my orders been obeyed?"

"Yes, Lieutenant."

"They are gone — the very last of them?"

"Yes, Lieutenant."

"They did not look back?"

"No, Lieutenant."

The lieutenant said nothing, for a while, and Franz busied himself with boots. After some time, he spoke.

"The lieutenant should try to sleep," he said. "We have carried out our orders. And now, they are gone."

"Yes," said the lieutenant, and, suddenly, he saw them again, the whole multitude, dispersed among every country — the ones who had walked his road, the ones at the points of embarkation. There were a great many of them, and that he had expected. But they were not dispersed as he had thought. They were not dispersed as he had thought, for, with each one went shame, like a visible burden. And the shame was not theirs, though they carried it — the shame belonged to the land that had driven them forth — his own land. He could see it growing and spreading like a black blot — the shame of his country spread over the whole earth.

"The lieutenant will have some brandy," he said. "Quickly, Franz."

When the brandy was brought, he stared at it for a moment, in the cup.

"Tell me, Franz," he said. "Did you know them well? Any of them? Before?"

"Oh yes, Lieutenant," said Franz, in his smooth, orderly's voice. "In the last war, I was billeted — well, the name of the town does not matter, but the woman was one of them. Of course that was before we knew about them," he said, respectfully. "That was more than twenty years ago. But she was very kind to me — I used to make toys for her children. I have often wondered what happened to her — she was very considerate and kind. Doubtless I was wrong, Lieutenant? But that was in another country."

"Yes, Franz," said the lieutenant. "There were children, you say?"

"Yes, Lieutenant."

"You saw the child today? The last one?"

"Yes, Lieutenant."

"Its hands had been hurt," said the lieutenant. "In the middle. Right through. I saw them. I wish I had not seen that. I wish I had not seen its hands."

II

JOHNNY PYE AND THE FOOL-KILLER

YOU don't hear so much about the Fool-Killer these days, but when Johnny Pye was a boy there was a good deal of talk about him. Some said he was one kind of person, and some said another, but most people agreed that he came around fairly regular. Or, it seemed so to Johnny Pye. But then, Johnny was an adopted child, which is, maybe, why he took it so hard.

The miller and his wife had offered to raise him, after his own folks died, and that was a good deed on their part. But, as soon as he lost his baby teeth and started acting the way most boys act, they began to come down on him like thunder, which wasn't so good. They were good people, according to their lights, but their lights were terribly strict ones, and they believed that the harder you were on a youngster, the better and brighter he got. Well, that may work with some children, but it didn't with Johnny Pye.

He was sharp enough and willing enough — as sharp and willing as most boys in Martinsville. But, somehow or other, he never seemed to be able to do the right things or say the right words — at least when he was home. Treat a boy like a fool and he'll act like a fool, I say, but there's some folks need convincing. The miller and his wife thought the way to smarten Johnny was to treat him like a fool, and finally they got so he pretty much believed it himself.

And that was hard on him, for he had a boy's imagination, and maybe a little more than most. He could stand the beatings and he did. But what he couldn't stand was the way things went at the mill. I don't suppose the miller intended to do it. But, as long as Johnny Pye could remember, whenever he heard of the death of somebody he didn't like, he'd say, "Well, the Fool-Killer's come for so-and-so," and sort of smack his lips. It was, as you might say, a family joke, but the miller was a big man with a big red face, and it made a strong impression on Johnny Pye. Till, finally, he got a picture of the Fool-Killer, himself. He was a big man, too, in a checked shirt and corduroy trousers, and he went walking the ways of the world, with a hickory club that had a lump of lead in the end of it. I don't know how Johnny Pye got that picture so clear, but, to him, it was just as plain as the face of any human being in Martinsville. And, now and then, just to test it, he'd ask a grown-up person, kind of timidly, if that was the way the Fool-Killer looked. And, of course, they'd generally laugh and tell him it was. Then Johnny would wake up at night, in his room over the mill, and listen for the Fool-Killer's step on the road and wonder when he was coming. But he was brave enough not to tell anybody that.

Finally, though, things got a little more than he could bear. He'd done some boy's trick or other — let the stones grind a little fine, maybe, when the miller wanted the meal ground coarse — just carelessness, you know. But he'd gotten two whippings for it, one from the miller and one from his wife, and, at the end of it, the miller had said, "Well, Johnny Pye, the Fool-Killer ought to be along for you most any day now. For I never did see a boy that was such a fool." Johnny looked to the miller's wife to see if she believed it, too, but she just shook her head and looked serious. So he went to bed that night, but he couldn't sleep, for every time a bough rustled or the mill wheel creaked, it seemed to him it must be the Fool-Killer. And, early next morning, before anybody was up, he packed such duds as he had in a bandanna handkerchief and ran away.

He didn't really expect to get away from the Fool-Killer very long — as far as he knew, the Fool-Killer got you wherever you went. But he thought he'd give him a run for his money, at least. And when he got on the road, it was a bright spring morning, and the first peace and quiet he'd had in some time. So his spirits rose, and he chunked a stone at a bullfrog as he went along, just to show he was Johnny Pye and still doing business.

He hadn't gone more than three or four miles out of Martinsville, when he heard a buggy coming up the road behind him. He knew the Fool-Killer didn't need a buggy to catch you, so he wasn't afraid of it, but he stepped to the side of the road to let it pass. But it stopped, instead, and a black-whiskered man with a stovepipe hat looked out of it.

"Hello, bub," he said. "Is this the road for East Liberty?"

"My name's John Pye and I'm eleven years old,"

said Johnny, polite but firm, "and you take the next left fork for East Liberty. They say it's a pretty town — I've never been there myself." And he sighed a little, because he thought he'd like to see the world before the Fool-Killer caught up with him.

"H'm," said the man. "Stranger here, too, eh? And what brings a smart boy like you on the road so early in the morning?"

"Oh," said Johnny Pye, quite honestly, "I'm running away from the Fool-Killer. For the miller says I'm a fool and his wife says I'm a fool and almost everybody in Martinsville says I'm a fool except little Susie Marsh. And the miller says the Fool-Killer's after me — so I thought I'd run away before he came."

The black-whiskered man sat in his buggy and wheezed for a while. When he got his breath back, "Well, jump in, bub," he said. "The miller may say you're a fool, but I think you're a right smart boy to be running away from the Fool-Killer all by yourself. And I don't hold with small-town prejudices and I need a right smart boy, so I'll give you a lift on the road."

"But, will I be safe from the Fool-Killer, if I'm with you?" said Johnny. "For, otherwise, it don't signify."

"Safe?" said the black-whiskered man, and wheezed again. "Oh, you'll be safe as houses. You see, I'm a herb doctor — and some folks think, a little in the Fool-Killer's line of business, myself. And I'll teach you a trade worth two of milling. So jump in, bub."

"Sounds all right the way you say it," said Johnny, "but my name's John Pye," and he jumped into the buggy. And they went rattling along toward East Liberty with the herb doctor talking and cutting jokes till Johnny thought he'd never met a pleasanter man. About half a mile from East Liberty, the doctor stopped at a spring.

"What are we stopping here for?" said Johnny Pye.

"Wait and see," said the doctor, and gave him a wink. Then he got a haircloth trunk full of empty bottles out of the back of the buggy and made Johnny fill them with spring water and label them. Then he added a pinch of pink powder to each bottle and shook them up and corked them and stowed them away.

"What's that?" said Johnny, very interested.

"That's Old Doctor Waldo's Unparalleled Universal Remedy," said the doctor, reading from the label.

"Made from the purest snake oil and secret Indian herbs, it cures rheumatism, blind staggers, headache, malaria, five kinds of fits, and spots in front of the eyes. It will also remove oil or grease stains, clean knives and silver, polish brass, and is strongly recommended as a general tonic and blood purifier. Small size, one dollar — family bottle, two dollars and a half."

"But I don't see any snake oil in it," said Johnny, puzzled, "or any secret Indian herbs."

"That's because you're not a fool," said the doctor, with another wink. "The Fool-Killer wouldn't, either. But most folks will."

And, that very same night, Johnny saw. For the doctor made his pitch in East Liberty and he did it handsome. He took a couple of flaring oil torches and stuck them on the sides of the buggy; he put on a diamond stickpin and did card tricks and told funny stories till he had the crowd goggle-eyed. As for Johnny, he let him play on the tambourine. Then he started talking about Doctor Waldo's Universal Remedy, and, with Johnny to help him, the bottles went like hot cakes. Johnny helped the doctor count the money afterward, and it was a pile.

"Well," said Johnny, "I never saw money made easier. You've got a fine trade, Doctor."

"It's cleverness does it," said the doctor, and slapped him on the back.

"Now a fool's content to stay in one place and do one thing, but the Fool-Killer never caught up with a good pitchman yet."

"Well, it's certainly lucky I met up with you," said Johnny, "and, if it's cleverness does it, I'll learn the trade or bust."

So he stayed with the doctor quite a while — in fact, till he could make up the remedy and do the card tricks almost as good as the doctor. And the doctor liked Johnny, for Johnny was a biddable boy. But one night they came into a town where things didn't go as they usually did. The crowd gathered as usual, and the doctor did his tricks. But, all the time, Johnny could see a sharp-faced little fellow going through the crowd and whispering to one man and another. Till, at last, right in the middle of the doctor's spiel, the sharp-faced fellow gave a shout of "That's him all right! I'd know them whiskers anywhere!" and, with that, the crowd growled once and began to tear slats out of the nearest fence. Well, the next thing Johnny knew, he and the doctor were being ridden out of town on a rail, with the doctor's long coattails flying at every jounce.

They didn't hurt Johnny particular — him only being a boy. But they warned 'em both never to show their faces in that town again, and then they heaved the doctor into a thistle patch and went their ways.

"Owoo!" said the doctor, "ouch!" as Johnny was helping him out of the thistle patch. "Go easy with those thistles! And why didn't you give me the office, you blame little fool?"

"Office?" said Johnny. "What office?"

"When that sharp-nosed man started snooping around," said the doctor. "I thought that infernal main street looked familiar — I was through there two years ago, selling solid gold watches for a dollar apiece."

"But the works to a solid gold watch would be worth more than that," said Johnny.

"There weren't any works," said the doctor, with a groan, "but there was a nice lively beetle inside each case and it made the prettiest tick you ever heard."

"Well, that certainly was a clever idea," said Johnny. "I'd never have thought of that."

"Clever?" said the doctor. "Ouch — it was ruination! But who'd have thought the fools would bear a grudge for two years? And now we've lost the horse and buggy, too — not to speak of the bottles and the money. Well, there's lots more tricks to be played and we'll start again."

But, though he liked the doctor, Johnny began to feel dubious. For it occurred to him that, if all the doctor's cleverness got him was being ridden out of town on a rail, he couldn't be so far away from the Fool-Killer as he thought. And, sure enough, as he was going to sleep that night, he seemed to hear the Fool-Killer's footsteps coming after him — step, step, step. He pulled his jacket up over his ears, but he couldn't shut it out. So, when the doctor had got in the way of starting business over again, he and Johnny parted company. The doctor didn't bear any grudge; he shook hands with Johnny and told him to remember that cleverness was power. And Johnny went on with his running away.

He got to a town, and there was a store with a sign in the window, BOY WANTED, so he went in. There, sure enough, was the merchant, sitting at his desk, and a fine, important man he looked, in his black broadcloth suit.

Johnny tried to tell him about the Fool-Killer, but the merchant wasn't interested in that. He just looked Johnny over and saw that he looked biddable and strong for his age. "But, remember, no fooling around, boy!" said the merchant sternly, after he'd hired him.

"No fooling around?" said Johnny, with the light of hope in his eyes.

"No," said the merchant, meaningly. "We've no room for fools in this business, I can tell you! You work hard, and you'll rise. But, if you've got any foolish notions, just knock them on the head and forget them."

Well, Johnny was glad enough to promise that, and he stayed with the merchant a year and a half. He swept out the store, and he put the shutters up and took them down; he ran errands and wrapped up packages and learned to keep busy twelve hours a day. And, being a biddable boy and an honest one, he rose, just like the merchant had said. The merchant raised his wages and let him begin to wait on customers and learn accounts. And then, one night, Johnny woke up in the middle of the night. And it seemed to him he heard, far away but getting nearer, the steps of the Fool-Killer after him — tramping, tramping.

He went to the merchant next day and said, "Sir, I'm sorry to tell you this, but I'll have to be moving on."

"Well, I'm sorry to hear that, Johnny," said the merchant, "for you've been a good boy. And, if it's a question of salary —"

"It isn't that," said Johnny, "but tell me one thing, sir, if you don't mind my asking. Supposing I did stay with you — where would I end?"

The merchant smiled. "That's a hard question to answer," he said, "and I'm not much given to compliments. But I started, myself, as a boy, sweeping out the store. And you're a bright youngster with lots of go-ahead. I don't see why, if you stuck to it, you shouldn't make the same kind of success that I have."

"And what's that?" said Johnny.

The merchant began to look irritated, but he kept his smile.

"Well," he said, "I'm not a boastful man, but I'll tell you this. Ten years ago I was the richest man in town. Five years ago, I was the richest man in the county. And five years from now — well, I aim to be the richest man in the state."

His eyes kind of glittered as he said it, but Johnny

was looking at his face. It was sallow-skinned and pouchy, with the jaw as hard as a rock. And it came upon Johnny that moment that, though he'd known the merchant a year and a half, he'd never really seen him enjoy himself except when he was driving a bargain.

"Sorry, sir," he said, "but, if it's like that, I'll certainly have to go. Because, you see, I'm running away from the Fool-Killer, and if I stayed here and got to be like you, he'd certainly catch up with me in no —"

"Why, you impertinent young cub!" roared the merchant, with his face gone red all of a sudden. "Get your money from the cashier!" and Johnny was on the road again before you could say "Jack Robinson." But, this time, he was used to it, and walked off whistling.

Well, after that, he hired out to quite a few different people, but I won't go into all of his adventures. He worked for an inventor for a while, and they split up because Johnny happened to ask him what would be the good of his patent, self-winding, perpetual-motion machine, once he did get it invented. And, while the inventor talked big about improving the human race and the beauties of science, it was plain he didn't know. So that night, Johnny heard the steps of the Fool-Killer, far off but coming closer, and, next morning, he went away. Then he stayed with a minister for a while, and he certainly hated to leave him, for the minister was a good man. But they got talking one evening and, as it chanced, Johnny asked him what happened to people who didn't believe in his particular religion. Well, the minister was broad-minded, but there's only one answer to that. He admitted they might be good folks — he even admitted they mightn't exactly go to hell — but he couldn't let them into heaven, no, not the best and the wisest of them, for there were the specifications laid down by creed and church, and, if you didn't fulfill them, you didn't.

So Johnny had to leave him, and, after that, he went with an old drunken fiddler for a while. He wasn't a good man, I guess, but he could play till the tears ran down your cheeks. And, when he was playing his best, it seemed to Johnny that the Fool-Killer was very far away. For, in spite of his faults and his weaknesses, while he played, there was might in the man. But he died drunk in a ditch, one night, with Johnny to hold his head, and, while he left Johnny his fiddle, it didn't do Johnny much good. For, while Johnny could play a tune, he couldn't play like the fiddler — it wasn't in his fingers.

Then it chanced that Johnny took up with a company of soldiers. He was still too young to enlist, but they made a kind of pet of him, and everything went swimmingly for a while. For the captain was the bravest man Johnny had ever seen, and he had an answer for everything, out of regulations and the Articles of War. But then they went West to fight Indians and the same old trouble cropped up again. For one night the captain said to him, "Johnny, we're going to fight the enemy tomorrow, but you'll stay in camp."

"Oh, I don't want to do that," said Johnny; "I want to be in on the fighting."

"It's an order," said the captain, grimly. Then he

gave Johnny certain instructions and a letter to take to his wife.

"For the colonel's a copper-plated fool," he said, "and we're walking straight into an ambush."

"Why don't you tell him that?" said Johnny.

"I have," said the captain, "but he's the colonel."

"Colonel or no colonel," said Johnny, "if he's a fool, somebody ought to stop him."

"You can't do that, in an army," said the captain. "Orders are orders." But it turned out the captain was wrong about it, for, next day, before they could get moving, the Indians attacked and got badly licked. When it was all over, "Well, it was a good fight," said the captain, professionally. "All the same, if they'd waited and laid an ambush, they'd have had our hair. But, as it was, they didn't stand a chance."

"But why didn't they lay an ambush?" said Johnny.

"Well," said the captain, "I guess they had their orders too. And now, how would you like to be a soldier?"

"Well, it's a nice outdoors life, but I'd like to think it over," said Johnny. For he knew the captain was brave and he knew the Indians had been brave — you couldn't find two braver sets of people. But, all the same, when he thought the whole thing over, he seemed to hear steps in the sky. So he soldiered to the end of the campaign and then he left the army, though the captain told him he was making a mistake.

By now, of course, he wasn't a boy any longer; he was getting to be a young man with a young man's thoughts and feelings. And, half the time, nowadays, he'd forget about the Fool-Killer except as a dream he'd had when he was a boy. He could even laugh at it now and then, and think what a fool he'd been to believe there was such a man.

But, all the same, the desire in him wasn't satisfied, and something kept driving him on. He'd have called it ambitiousness, now, but it came to the same thing. And with every new trade he tried, sooner or later would come the dream — the dream of the big man in the checked shirt and corduroy pants, walking the ways of the world with his hickory stick in one hand. It made him angry to have that dream, now, but it had a singular power over him. Till, finally, when he was turned twenty or so, he got scared.

"Fool-Killer or no Fool-Killer," he said to himself. "I've got to ravel this matter out. For there must be some one thing a man could tie to, and be sure he wasn't a fool. I've tried cleverness and money and half a dozen other things, and they don't seem to be the answer. So now I'll try book learning and see what comes of that."

So he read all the books he could find, and whenever he'd seem to hear the steps of the Fool-Killer coming for the authors — and that was frequent — he'd try and shut his ears. But some books said one thing was best and some another, and he couldn't rightly decide.

"Well," he said to himself, when he'd read and read till his head felt as stuffed with book learning as a sausage with meat, "it's interesting, but it isn't exactly contemporaneous. So I think I'll go down to Washington and ask the wise men there. For it must take a lot of wisdom to run a country like the United States, and if there's people who can answer my questions, it's there they ought to be found."

So he packed his bag and off to Washington he went. He was modest for a youngster, and he didn't intend to try and see the President right away. He thought probably a congressman was about his size. So he saw a congressman, and the congressman told him the thing to be was an upstanding young American and vote the Republican ticket — which sounded all right to Johnny Pye, but not exactly what he was after.

Then he went to a senator, and the senator told him to be an upstanding young American and vote the Democratic ticket — which sounded all right, too, but not what he was after, either. And, somehow, though both men had been impressive and affable, right in the middle of their speeches he'd seemed to hear steps — you know.

But a man has to eat, whatever else he does, and Johnny found he'd better buckle down and get himself a job. It happened to be with the first congressman he struck, for that one came from Martinsville, which is why Johnny went to him in the first place. And, in a little while, he forgot his search entirely and the Fool-Killer, too, for the congressman's niece came East to visit him, and she was the Susie Marsh that Johnny had sat next in school. She'd been pretty then, but she was prettier now, and as soon as Johnny Pye saw her, his heart gave a jump and a thump.

"And don't think we don't remember you in Martinsville, Johnny Pye," she said, when her uncle had explained who his new clerk was. "Why, the whole town'll be excited when I write home. We've heard all about your killing Indians and inventing perpetual motion and traveling around the country with a famous doctor and making a fortune in dry goods and — oh, it's a wonderful story!"

"Well," said Johnny, and coughed, "some of that's just a little bit exaggerated. But it's nice of you to be interested. So they don't think I'm a fool any more, in Martinsville?"

"I never thought you were a fool," said Susie with a little smile, and Johnny felt his heart give another bump.

"And I always knew you were pretty, but never how pretty till now," said Johnny, and coughed again. "But, speaking of old times, how's the miller and his wife? For I did leave them right sudden, and while there were faults on both sides, I must have been a trial to them too."

"They've gone the way of all flesh," said Susie Marsh, "and there's a new miller now. But he isn't very well-liked, to tell the truth, and he's letting the mill run down."

"That's a pity," said Johnny, "for it was a likely mill." Then he began to ask her more questions and she began to remember things too. Well, you know how the time can go when two youngsters get talking like that.

Johnny Pye never worked so hard in his life as he did that winter. And it wasn't the Fool-Killer he thought about — it was Susie Marsh. First he thought she loved him and then he was sure she didn't, and then he was betwixt and between, and all perplexed and confused. But, finally, it turned out all right and he had her promise, and Johnny Pye knew he was the happiest man in the world. And that night, he waked up in the night and heard the Fool-Killer coming after him — step, step, step.

He didn't sleep much after that, and he came down to breakfast hollow-eyed. But his uncle-to-be didn't notice that — he was rubbing his hands and smiling.

"Put on your best necktie, Johnny!" he said, very cheerful, "for I've got an appointment with the President today, and, just to show I approve of my niece's fiancé, I'm taking you along."

"The President!" said Johnny, all dumfounded.

"Yes," said Congressman Marsh, "you see, there's a little bill — well, we needn't go into that. But slick down your back hair, Johnny — we'll make Martinsville proud of us this day!"

Then a weight seemed to go from Johnny's shoulders and a load from his heart. He wrung Mr. Marsh's hand.

"Thank you, Uncle Eben!" he said. "I can't thank you enough." For, at last, he knew he was going to look upon a man that was bound to be safe from the Fool-Killer — and it seemed to him if he could just once do that, all his troubles and searchings would be ended.

Well, it doesn't signify which President it was — you can take it from me that he was President and a fine-looking man. He'd just been elected, too, so he was lively as a trout, and the saddle galls he'd get from Congress hadn't even begun to show. Anyhow, there he was, and Johnny feasted his eyes on him. For if there was anybody in the country the Fool-Killer couldn't bother, it must be a man like this.

The President and the congressman talked politics for a while, and then it was Johnny's turn.

"Well, young man," said the President, affably, "and what can I do for you — for you look to me like a fine, upstanding young American."

The congressman cut in quick before Johnny could open his mouth.

"Just a word of advice, Mr. President," he said. "Just a word in season. For my young friend's led an adventurous life, but now he's going to marry my niece and settle down. And what he needs most of all is a word of ripe wisdom from you."

"Well," said the President, looking at Johnny rather keenly, "if that's all he needs, a short horse is soon curried. I wish most of my callers wanted as little."

But, all the same, he drew Johnny out, as such men can, and before Johnny knew it, he was telling his life story.

"Well," said the President, at the end, "you certainly have been a rolling stone, young man. But there's nothing wrong in that. And, for one of your varied experience there's one obvious career. Politics!" he said, and slapped his fist in his hand.

"Well," said Johnny, scratching his head, "of course, since I've been in Washington, I've thought of that. But I don't know that I'm rightly fitted."

"You can write a speech," said Congressman Marsh,

quite thoughtful, "for you've helped me with mine. You're a likeable fellow too. And you were born poor and worked up — and you've even got a war record — why, hell! Excuse me, Mr. President! — he's worth five hundred votes just as he stands!"

"I — I'm more than honored by you two gentlemen," said Johnny, abashed and flattered, "but supposing I did go into politics — where would I end up?"

The President looked sort of modest.

"The Presidency of the United States," said he, "is within the legitimate ambition of every American citizen. Provided he can get elected, of course."

"Oh," said Johnny, feeling dazzled, "I never thought of that. Well, that's a great thing. But it must be a great responsibility too."

"It is," said the President, looking just like his pictures on the campaign buttons.

"Why, it must be an awful responsibility!" said Johnny. "I can't hardly see how a mortal man can bear it. Tell me, Mr. President," he said, "may I ask you a question?"

"Certainly," said the President, looking prouder and more responsible and more and more like his picture on the campaign buttons every minute.

"Well," said Johnny, "it sounds like a fool question, but it's this: This is a great big country of ours, Mr. President, and it's got the most amazing lot of different people in it. How can any President satisfy all those people at one time? Can you yourself, Mr. President?"

The President looked a bit taken aback for a minute. But then he gave Johnny Pye a statesman's glance.

"With the help of God," he said, solemnly, "and in accordance with the principles of our great party, I intend . . ."

But Johnny didn't even hear the end of the sentence. For, even as the President was speaking, he heard a step outside in the corridor and he knew, somehow, it wasn't the step of a secretary or a guard. He was glad the President had said "with the help of God" for that sort of softened the step. And when the President finished, Johnny bowed.

"Thank you, Mr. President," he said; "that's what I wanted to know. And now I'll go back to Martinsville, I guess."

"Go back to Martinsville?" said the President, surprised.

"Yes, sir," said Johnny. "For I don't think I'm cut out for politics."

"And is that all you have to say to the President of the United States?" said his uncle-to-be, in a fume.

But the President had been thinking, meanwhile, and he was a bigger man than the congressman.

"Wait a minute, Congressman," he said. "This young man's honest, at least, and I like his looks. Moreover, of all the people who've come to see me in the last six months, he's the only one who hasn't wanted something — except the White House cat, and I guess she wanted something, too, because she meowed. You don't want to be President, young man — and, confidentially, I don't blame you. But how would you like to be postmaster at Martinsville?"

"Postmaster at Martinsville?" said Johnny. "But —"

"Oh, it's only a tenth-class post office," said the President, "but, for once in my life, I'll do something because I want to, and let Congress yell its head off. Come — is it yes or no?"

Johnny thought of all the places he'd been and all the trades he'd worked at. He thought, queerly enough, of the old drunk fiddler dead in the ditch, but he knew he couldn't be that. Mostly, though, he thought of Martinsville and Susie Marsh. And, though he'd just heard the Fool-Killer's step, he defied the Fool-Killer.

"Why, it's yes, of course, Mr. President," he said, "for then I can marry Susie."

"That's as good a reason as you'll find," said the President. "And now, I'll just write a note."

Well, he was as good as his word, and Johnny and his Susie were married and went back to live in Martinsville. And, as soon as Johnny learned the ways of postmastering, he found it as good a trade as most. There wasn't much mail in Martinsville, but, in between whiles, he ran the mill, and that was a good trade too. And all the time, he knew, at the back of his mind, that he hadn't quite settled accounts with the Fool-Killer. But he didn't much care about that, for he and Susie were happy. And after a while they had a child, and that was the most remarkable experience that had ever happened to any young couple, though the doctor said it was a perfectly normal baby.

One evening, when his son was about a year old, Johnny Pye took the river road, going home. It was a mite longer than the hill road, but it was the cool of the evening, and there's times when a man likes to walk by himself, fond as he may be of his wife and family.

He was thinking of the way things had turned out for him, and they seemed to him pretty astonishing and singular, as they do to most folks, when you think them over. In fact, he was thinking so hard that, before he knew it, he'd almost stumbled over an old scissors grinder who'd set up his grindstone and tools by the side of the road. The scissors grinder had his cart with him, but he'd turned the horse out to graze — and a lank, old, white horse it was, with every rib showing. And he was very busy, putting an edge on a scythe.

"Oh, sorry," said Johnny Pye. "I didn't know anybody was camping here. But you might come around to my house tomorrow — my wife's got some knives that need sharpening."

Then he stopped, for the old man gave him a long, keen look.

"Why, it's you, Johnny Pye," said the old man. "And how do you do, Johnny Pye! You've been a long time coming — in fact, now and then, I thought I'd have to fetch you. But you're here at last."

Johnny Pye was a grown man now, but he began to tremble.

"But it isn't you!" he said, wildly. "I mean you're not him! Why, I've known how he looks all my life! He's a big man, with a checked shirt, and he carries a hickory stick with a lump of lead in one end."

"Oh, no," said the scissors grinder, quite quiet. "You may have thought of me that way, but that's not the way I am." And Johnny Pye heard the scythe go whet-whet-whet on the stone. The old man ran some water on it and looked at the edge. Then he shook his head as if the edge didn't quite satisfy him. "Well, Johnny, are you ready?" he said, after a while.

"Ready?" said Johnny, in a hoarse voice. "Of course I'm not ready."

"That's what they all say," said the old man, nodding his head, and the scythe went whet-whet on the stone.

Johnny wiped his brow and started to argue it out.

"You see, if you'd found me earlier," he said, "or later. I don't want to be unreasonable, but I've got a wife and a child."

"Most has wives and many has children," said the old man, grimly, and the scythe went whet-whet on the stone as he pushed the treadle. And a shower of sparks flew, very clear and bright, for the night had begun to fall.

"Oh, stop that damn racket and let a man think for a minute!" said Johnny, desperate. "I can't go, I tell you. I won't. It isn't time. It's — "

The old man stopped the grindstone and pointed with the scythe at Johnny Pye.

"Tell me one good reason," he said. "There's men would be missed in the world, but are you one of them? A clever man might be missed, but are you a clever man?"

"No," said Johnny, thinking of the herb doctor. "I had a chance to be clever, but I gave it up."

"One," said the old man, ticking off on his fingers. "Well, a rich man might be missed — by some. But you aren't rich, I take it."

"No," said Johnny, thinking of the merchant, "nor wanted to be."

"Two," said the old man. "Cleverness — riches — they're done. But there's still martial bravery and being a hero. There might be an argument to make, if you were one of those."

Johnny Pye shuddered a little, remembering the way that battlefield had looked, out West, when the Indians were dead and the fight over.

"No," he said, "I've fought, but I'm not a hero."

"Well, then, there's religion," said the old man, sort of patient, "and science, and — but what's the use? We know what you did with those. I might feel a trifle of compunction if I had to deal with a President of the United States. But — "

"Oh, you know well enough I ain't President," said Johnny, with a groan. "Can't you get it over with and be done?"

"You're not putting up a very good case," said the old man, shaking his head. "I'm surprised at you, Johnny. Here you spend your youth running away from being a fool. And yet, what's the first thing you do, when you're man grown? Why, you marry a girl, settle down in your home town, and start raising children when you don't know how they'll turn out. You might have known I'd catch up with you, then — you just put yourself in my way."

"Fool I may be," said Johnny Pye in his agony, "and if you take it like that, I guess we're all fools. But Susie's my wife, and my child's my child. And, as for work in the world — well, somebody has to be post-master, or folks wouldn't get the mail."

"Would it matter much if they didn't?" said the old man, pointing his scythe.

"Well, no, I don't suppose it would, considering what's on the post cards," said Johnny Pye. "But while it's my business to sort it, I'll sort it as well as I can."

The old man whetted his scythe so hard that a long shower of sparks flew out on the grass.

"Well," he said, "I've got my job, too, and I do it likewise. But I'll tell you what I'll do. You're coming my way, no doubt of it, but, looking you over, you don't look quite ripe yet. So I'll let you off for a while. For that matter," said he, "if you'll answer one question of mine — how a man can be a human being and not be a fool — I'll let you off permanent. It'll be the first time in history," he said, "but you've got to do some-thing on your own hook, once in a while. And now you can walk along, Johnny Pye."

With that he grounded the scythe till the sparks flew out like the tail of a comet and Johnny Pye walked along. The air of the meadow had never seemed so sweet to him before.

All the same, even with his relief, he didn't quite forget, and sometimes Susie had to tell the children not to disturb father because he was thinking. But time went ahead, as it does, and pretty soon Johnny Pye found he was forty. He'd never expected to be forty, when he was young, and it kind of surprised him. But there it was, though he couldn't say he felt much dif-ferent, except now and then when he stooped over. And he was a solid citizen of the town, well-liked and well-respected, with a growing family and a stake in the community, and when he thought those things over, they kind of surprised him too. But, pretty soon, it was as if things had always been that way.

It was after his eldest son had been drowned out fishing that Johnny Pye met the scissors grinder again. But this time he was bitter and distracted, and, if he could have got to the old man, he'd have done him a mortal harm. But, somehow or other, when he tried to come to grips with him, it was like reaching for air and mist. He could see the sparks fly from the ground scythe, but he couldn't even touch the wheel.

"You coward!" said Johnny Pye. "Stand up and fight like a man!" But the old man just nodded his head and the wheel kept grinding and grinding.

"Why couldn't you have taken me?" said Johnny Pye, as if those words had never been said before. "What's the sense in all this? Why can't you take me now?"

Then he tried to wrench the scythe from the old man's hands, but he couldn't touch it. And then he fell down and lay on the grass for a while.

"Time passes," said the old man, nodding his head. "Time passes."

"It will never cure the grief I have for my son," said Johnny Pye.

"It will not," said the old man, nodding his head "But time passes. Would you leave your wife a widow and your other children fatherless for the sake of your grief?"

"No, God help me!" said Johnny Pye. "That wouldn't be right for a man."

"Then go home to your house, Johnny Pye," said the old man. And Johnny Pye went, but there were lines in his face that hadn't been there before.

And time passed, like the flow of the river, and Johnny Pye's children married and had houses and children of their own. And Susie's hair grew white, and her back grew bent, and when Johnny Pye and his children followed her to her grave, folks said she'd died in the fullness of years, but that was hard for Johnny Pye to believe. Only folks didn't talk as plain as they used to, and the sun didn't heat as much, and sometimes, before dinner, he'd go to sleep in his chair.

And once, after Susie had died, the President of those days came through Martinsville and Johnny Pye shook hands with him and there was a piece in the paper about his shaking hands with two Presidents, fifty years apart. Johnny Pye cut out the clipping and kept it in his pocketbook. He liked this President all right, but, as he told people, he wasn't a patch on the other one fifty years ago. Well, you couldn't expect it — you didn't have Presidents these days, not to call them Presidents. All the same, he took a lot of satisfaction in the clipping.

He didn't get down to the river road much any more — it wasn't too long a walk, of course, but he just didn't often feel like it. But, one day, he slipped away from the granddaughter that was taking care of him, and went. It was kind of a steep road, really — he didn't remember its being so steep.

"Well," said the scissors grinder, "and good afternoon to you, Johnny Pye."

"You'll have to talk a little louder," said Johnny Pye. "My hearing's perfect, but folks don't speak as plain as they used to. Stranger in town?"

"Oh, so that's the way it is," said the scissors grinder.

"Yes, that's the way it is," said Johnny Pye. He knew he ought to be afraid of this fellow, now he'd put on his spectacles and got a good look at him, but for the life of him, he couldn't remember why.

"I know just who you are," he said, a little fretfully. "Never forgot a face in my life, and your name's right on the tip of my tongue — "

"Oh, don't bother about names," said the scissors grinder. "We're old acquaintances. And I asked you a question, years ago — do you remember that?"

"Yes," said Johnny Pye, "I remember." Then he began to laugh — a high, old man's laugh. "And of all the fool questions I ever was asked," he said, "that certainly took the cake."

"Oh?" said the scissors grinder.

"Uh-huh," said Johnny Pye. "For you asked me how a man could be a human being and yet not be a fool. And the answer is — when he's dead and gone and buried. Any fool would know that."

"That so?" said the scissors grinder.

"Of course," said Johnny Pye. "I ought to know. I'll be ninety-two next November, and I've shook hands with two Presidents. The first President I shook — "

"I'll be interested to hear about that," said the scissors grinder, "but we've got a little business, first. For, if all human beings are fools, how does the world get ahead?"

"Oh, there's lots of other things," said Johnny Pye, kind of impatient. "There's the brave and the wise and the clever — and they're apt to roll it ahead as much as an inch. But it's all mixed in together. For, Lord, it's only some fool kind of creature that would have crawled out of the sea to dry land in the first place — or got dropped from the Garden of Eden, if you like it better that way. You can't depend on the kind of folks people think they are — you've got to go by what they do. And I wouldn't give much for a man that some folks hadn't thought was a fool, in his time."

"Well," said the scissors grinder, "you've answered my question — at least as well as you could, which is all you can expect of a man. So I'll keep my part of the bargain."

"And what was that?" said Johnny. "For, while it's all straight in my head, I don't quite recollect the details."

"Why," said the scissors grinder, rather testy, "I'm to let you go, you old fool! You'll never see me again till the Last Judgment. There'll be trouble in the office about it," said he, "but you've got to do what you like, once in a while."

"Phew!" said Johnny Pye. "That needs thinking over!" And he scratched his head.

"Why?" said the scissors grinder, a bit affronted. "It ain't often I offer a man eternal life."

"Well," said Johnny Pye, "I take it very kind, but, you see, it's this way." He thought for a moment. "No," he said, "you wouldn't understand. You can't have touched seventy yet, by your looks, and no young man would."

"Try me," said the scissors grinder.

"Well," said Johnny Pye, "it's this way," and he scratched his head again. I'm not saying — if you'd made the offer forty years ago, or even twenty. But, well, now, let's just take one detail. Let's say 'teeth.' "

"Well, of course," said the scissors grinder, "naturally — I mean you could hardly expect me to do anything about that."

"I thought so," said Johnny Pye. "Well, you see, these are good, bought teeth, but I'm sort of tired of hearing them click. And spectacles, I suppose, the same?"

"I'm afraid so," said the scissors grinder. "I can't interfere with time, you know — that's not my department. And, frankly, you couldn't expect, at a hundred and eighty, let's say, to be quite the man you was at ninety. But still, you'd be a wonder!"

"Maybe so," said Johnny Pye, "but, you see — well, the truth is, I'm an old man now. You wouldn't think it to look at me, but it's so. And my friends — well, they're gone — and Susie and the boy — and somehow you don't get as close to the younger people, except the children. And to keep on just going and going till Judgment Day, with nobody around to talk to that had real horse sense — well, no, sir, it's a handsome offer but I just don't feel up to accepting it. It may not be patriotic of me, and I feel sorry for Martinsville. It'd do wonders for the climate and the chamber of commerce to have a leading citizen live till Judgment Day. But a man's got to do as he likes, at least once in his life." He stopped and looked at the scissors grinder. "I'll admit, I'd kind of like to beat out Ike Leavis," he said. "To hear him talk, you'd think nobody had ever pushed ninety before. But I suppose — "

"I'm afraid we can't issue a limited policy," said the scissors grinder.

"Well," said Johnny Pye, "I just thought of it. And Ike's all right." He waited a moment. "Tell me," he said, in a low voice. "Well, you know what I mean. Afterwards. I mean, if you're likely to see" — he coughed —"your friends again. I mean, if it's so — like some folks believe."

"I can't tell you that," said the scissors grinder. "I only go so far."

"Well, there's no harm in asking," said Johnny Pye, rather humbly. He peered into the darkness; a last shower of sparks flew from the scythe, then the whir of the wheel stopped.

"H'm," said Johnny Pye, testing the edge. "That's a well-ground scythe. But they used to grind 'em better in the old days." He listened and looked, for a moment, anxiously. "Oh, Lordy!" he said, "there's Helen coming to look for me. She'll take me back to the house."

"Not this time," said the scissors grinder. "Yes, there isn't bad steel in that scythe. Well, let's go, Johnny Pye."

O'HALLORAN'S LUCK

THEY were strong men built the Big Road, in the early days of America, and it was the Irish did it. My grandfather, Tim O'Halloran, was a young man then, and wild. He could swing a pick all day and dance all night, if there was a fiddler handy; and if there was a girl to be pleased he pleased her, for he had the tongue and the eye. Likewise, if there was a man to be stretched, he could stretch him with the one blow.

I saw him later on in years when he was thin and white-headed, but in his youth he was not so. A thin, white-headed man would have had little chance, and they driving the Road to the West. It was two-fisted men cleared the plains and bored through the mountains. They came in the thousands to do it from every county in Ireland; and now the names are not known. But it's over their graves you pass, when you ride in the Pullmans. And Tim O'Halloran was one of them, six feet high and solid as the Rock of Cashel when he stripped to the skin.

He needed to be all of that, for it was not easy labor. 'Twas a time of great booms and expansions in the railroad line, and they drove the tracks north and south, east and west, as if the devil was driving behind. For this they must have the boys with shovel and pick, and every immigrant ship from Ireland was crowded with bold young men. They left famine and England's rule behind them — and it was the thought of many they'd pick up gold for the asking in the free States of America, though it's little gold that most of them ever saw. They found themselves up to their necks in the water of the canals, and burnt black by the suns of the prairie — and that was a great surprise to them. They saw their sisters and their mothers made servants that had not been servants in Ireland, and that was a strange change too. Eh, the death and the broken hopes it takes to make a country! But those with the heart and the tongue kept the tongue and the heart.

Tim O'Halloran came from Clonmelly, and he was the fool of the family and the one who listened to tales. His brother Ignatius went for a priest and his brother James for a sailor, but they knew he could not do those things. He was strong and biddable and he had the O'Halloran tongue; but there came a time of famine, when the younger mouths cried for bread and there was little room in the nest. He was not entirely wishful to emigrate, and yet, when he thought of it, he was wishful. 'Tis often enough that way, with a younger son. Perhaps he was the more wishful because of Kitty Malone.

'Tis a quiet place, Clonmelly, and she'd been the light of it to him. But now the Malones had gone to the States of America — and it was well known that Kitty had a position there the like of which was not to be found in all Dublin Castle. They called her a hired girl, to be sure, but did not she eat from gold plates, like all the citizens of America? And when she stirred her tea, was not the spoon made of gold? Tim O'Halloran thought of this, and of the chances and adventures that a bold young man might find, and at last he went to the boat. There were many from Clonmelly on that boat, but he kept himself to himself and dreamed his own dreams.

The more disillusion it was to him, when the boat landed him in Boston and he found Kitty Malone there, scrubbing the stairs of an American house with a pail and brush by her side. But that did not matter, after the first, for her cheeks still had the rose in them and she looked at him in the same way. 'Tis true there was an Orangeman courting her — conductor he was on the horsecars, and Tim did not like that. But after Tim had seen her, he felt himself the equal of giants; and when the call came for strong men to work in the wilds of the West, he was one of the first to offer. They broke a sixpence between them before he left — it was an English sixpence, but that did not matter greatly to them. And Tim O'Halloran was going to make his fortune, and Kitty Malone to wait for him, though her family liked the Orangeman best.

Still and all, it was cruel work in the West, as such work must be, and Tim O'Halloran was young. He liked the strength and the wildness of it — he'd drink with the thirstiest and fight with the wildest — and that he knew how to do. It was all meat and drink to him — the bare tracks pushing ahead across the bare prairie and the fussy cough of the wood-burning locomotives and the cold blind eyes of a murdered man, looking up at the prairie stars. And then there was the cholera and the malaria — and the strong man you'd worked on the grade beside, all of a sudden gripping his belly with the fear of death on his face and his shovel falling to the ground.

Next day he would not be there and they'd scratch a name from the pay roll. Tim O'Halloran saw it all.

He saw it all and it changed his boyhood and hardened it. But, for all that, there were times when the black fit came upon him, as it does to the Irish, and he knew he was alone in a strange land. Well, that's a hard hour to get through, and he was young. There were times when he'd have given all the gold of the Americas for a smell of Clonmelly air or a glimpse of Clonmelly sky. Then he'd drink or dance or fight or put a black word on the foreman, just to take the aching out of his mind. It did not help him with his work and it wasted his pay; but it was stronger than he, and not even the thought of Kitty Malone could stop it. 'Tis like that, sometimes.

Well, it happened one night he was coming back from the place where they sold the potheen, and perhaps he'd had a trifle more of it than was advisable. Yet he had not drunk it for that, but to keep the queer thoughts from his mind. And yet, the more that he drank, the queerer were the thoughts in his head. For he kept thinking of the Luck of the O'Hallorans and the tales his granda had told about it in the old country — the tales about pookas and banshees and leprechauns with long white beards.

"And that's a queer thing to be thinking and myself

at labor with a shovel on the open prairies of America," he said to himself. "Sure, creatures like that might live and thrive in the old country — and I'd be the last to deny it — but 'tis obvious they could not live here. The first sight of Western America would scare them into conniptions. And as for the Luck of the O'Hallorans, 'tis little good I've had of it, and me not even able to rise to foreman and marry Kitty Malone. They called me the fool of the family in Clonmelly, and I misdoubt but they were right. Tim O'Halloran, you're a worthless man, for all your strong back and arms." It was with such black, bitter thoughts as these that he went striding over the prairie. And it was just then that he heard the cry in the grass.

'Twas a strange little piping cry, and only the half of it human. But Tim O'Halloran ran to it, for in truth he was spoiling for a fight. "Now this will be a beautiful young lady," he said to himself as he ran, "and I will save her from robbers; and her father, the rich man, will ask me — but, wirra, 'tis not her I wish to marry, 'tis Kitty Malone. Well, he'll set me up in business, out of friendship and gratitude, and then I will send for Kitty — "

But by then he was out of breath, and by the time he had reached the place where the cry came from he could see that it was not so. It was only a pair of young wolf cubs, and they chasing something small and helpless and playing with it as a cat plays with a mouse. Where the wolf cub is the old wolves are not far, but Tim O'Halloran felt as bold as a lion. "Be off with you!" he cried and he threw a stick and a stone. They

ran away into the night, and he could hear them howling — a lonesome sound. But he knew the camp was
near, so he paid small attention to that but looked for
the thing they'd been chasing.

It scuttled in the grass but he could not see it. Then
he stooped down and picked something up, and when
he had it in his hand he stared at it unbelieving. For
it was a tiny shoe, no bigger than a child's. And more
than that, it was not the kind of shoe that is made in
America. Tim O'Halloran stared and stared at it — and
at the silver buckle upon it — and still he could not
believe.

"If I'd found this in the old country," he said to
himself, half aloud, "I'd have sworn that it was a leprechaun's and looked for the pot of gold. But here, there's
no chance of that — "

"I'll trouble you for the shoe," said a small voice
close by his feet.

Tim O'Halloran stared round him wildly. "By the
piper that played before Moses!" he said. "Am I drunk
beyond comprehension? Or am I mad? For I thought
that I heard a voice."

"So you did, silly man," said the voice again, but
irritated, "and I'll trouble you for my shoe, for it's cold
in the dewy grass."

"Honey," said Tim O'Halloran, beginning to believe his ears, "honey dear, if you'll but show yourself — "

"I'll do that and gladly," said the voice; and with
that the grasses parted, and a little old man with a long
white beard stepped out. He was perhaps the size of a

well-grown child, as O'Halloran could see clearly by
the moonlight on the prairie; moreover, he was dressed
in the clothes of antiquity, and he carried cobbler's
tools in the belt at his side.

"By faith and belief, but it *is* a leprechaun!" cried
O'Halloran, and with that he made a grab for the ap-
parition. For you must know, in case you've been ill
brought up, that a leprechaun is a sort of cobbler fairy
and each one knows the whereabouts of a pot of gold.
Or it's so they say in the old country. For they say you
can tell a leprechaun by his long white beard and his
cobbler's tools; and once you have the possession of
him, he must tell you where his gold is hid.

The little old man skipped out of reach as nimbly
as a cricket. "Is this Clonmelly courtesy?" he said with
a shake in his voice, and Tim O'Halloran felt ashamed.

"Sure, I didn't mean to hurt your worship at all,"
he said, "but if you're what you seem to be, well, then,
there's the little matter of a pot of gold — "

"Pot of gold!" said the leprechaun, and his voice
was hollow and full of scorn. "And would I be here
today if I had that same? Sure, it all went to pay my
sea passage, as you might expect."

"Well," said Tim O'Halloran, scratching his head,
for that sounded reasonable enough, "that may be so
or again it may not be so. But — "

"Oh, 'tis bitter hard," said the leprechaun, and his
voice was weeping, "to come to the waste, wild prairies
all alone, just for the love of Clonmelly folk — and then
to be disbelieved by the first that speaks to me! If it had

been an Ulsterman now, I might have expected it. But the O'Hallorans wear the green."

"So they do," said Tim O'Halloran, "and it shall not be said of an O'Halloran that he denied succor to the friendless. I'll not touch you."

"Do you swear it?" said the leprechaun.

"I swear it," said Tim O'Halloran.

"Then I'll just creep under your coat," said the leprechaun, "for I'm near destroyed by the chills and damps of the prairie. Oh, this weary emigrating!" he said, with a sigh like a furnace. " 'Tis not what it's cracked up to be."

Tim O'Halloran took off his own coat and wrapped it around him. Then he could see him closer — and it could not be denied that the leprechaun was a pathetic sight. He'd a queer little boyish face, under the long white beard, but his clothes were all torn and ragged and his cheeks looked hollow with hunger.

"Cheer up!" said Tim O'Halloran and patted him on the back. "It's a bad day that beats the Irish. But tell me first how you came here — for that still sticks in my throat."

"And would I be staying behind with half Clonmelly on the water?" said the leprechaun stoutly. "By the bones of Finn, what sort of a man do you think I am?"

"That's well said," said Tim O'Halloran. "And yet I never heard of the Good People emigrating before."

"True for you," said the leprechaun. "The climate here's not good for most of us and that's a fact. There's a boggart or so that came over with the English, but then the Puritan ministers got after them and they had to take to the woods. And I had a word or two, on my way West, with a banshee that lives by Lake Superior — a decent woman she was, but you could see she'd come down in the world. For even the bits of children wouldn't believe in her; and when she let out a screech, sure they thought it was a steamboat. I misdoubt she's died since then — she was not in good health when I left her.

"And as for the native spirits — well, you can say what you like, but they're not very comfortable people. I was captive to some of them a week and they treated me well enough, but they whooped and danced too much for a quiet man, and I did not like the long, sharp knives on them. Oh, I've had the adventures on my way here," he said, "but they're over now, praises be, for I've found a protector at last," and he snuggled closer under O'Halloran's coat.

"Well," said O'Halloran, somewhat taken aback, "I did not think this would be the way of it when I found O'Halloran's Luck that I'd dreamed of so long. For, first I save your life from the wolves; and now, it seems, I must be protecting you further. But in the tales it's always the other way round."

"And is the company and conversation of an ancient and experienced creature like myself nothing to you?" said the leprechaun fiercely. "Me that had my own castle at Clonmelly and saw O'Sheen in his pride? Then St. Patrick came — wirra, wirra! — and there was an end to it all. For some of us — the Old Folk of Ireland — he baptized, and some of us he chained with the demons of hell. But I was Lazy Brian, betwixt and between, and all I wanted was peace and a quiet life. So he changed me to what you see — me that had six tall harpers to harp me awake in the morning — and laid a doom upon me for being betwixt and between. I'm to serve Clonmelly folk and follow them wherever they go till I serve the servants of servants in a land at the world's end. And then, perhaps, I'll be given a Christian soul and can follow my own inclinations."

"Serve the servants of servants?" said O'Halloran. "Well, that's a hard riddle to read."

"It is that," said the leprechaun, "for I never once met the servant of a servant in Clonmelly, all the time I've been looking. I doubt but that was in St. Patrick's mind."

"If it's criticizing the good saint you are, I'll leave you here on the prairie," said Tim O'Halloran.

"I'm not criticizing him," said the leprechaun with a sigh, "but I could wish he'd been less hasty. Or more specific. And now, what do we do?"

"Well," said O'Halloran, and he sighed, too, " 'tis a great responsibility, and one I never thought to shoulder. But since you've asked for help, you must have it. Only there's just this to be said. There's little money in my pocket."

"Sure, 'tis not for your money I've come to you," said the leprechaun joyously. "And I'll stick closer than a brother."

"I've no doubt of that," said O'Halloran with a wry laugh. "Well, clothes and food I can get for you — but if you stick with me, you must work as well. And per-

haps the best way would be for you to be my young
nephew, Rory, run away from home to work on the
railroad."

"And how would I be your young nephew, Rory,
and me with a long white beard?"

"Well," said Tim O'Halloran with a grin, "as it
happens, I've got a razor in my pocket."

And with that you should have heard the leprechaun. He stamped and he swore and he pled — but it
was no use at all. If he was to follow Tim O'Halloran,
he must do it on Tim O'Halloran's terms and no two
ways about it. So O'Halloran shaved him at last, by the
light of the moon, to the leprechaun's great horror,
and when he got him back to the construction camp and
fitted him out in some old duds of his own — well, it
wasn't exactly a boy he looked, but it was more like a
boy than anything else. Tim took him up to the foreman the next day and got him signed on for a water
boy, and it was a beautiful tale he told the foreman.
As well, too, that he had the O'Halloran tongue to tell
it with, for when the foreman first looked at young
Rory you could see him gulp like a man that's seen a
ghost.

"And now what do we do?" said the leprechaun to
Tim when the interview was over.

"Why, you work," said Tim with a great laugh,
"and Sundays you wash your shirt."

"Thank you for nothing," said the leprechaun with
an angry gleam in his eye. "It was not for that I came
here from Clonmelly."

"Oh, we've all come here for great fortune," said

Tim, "but it's hard to find that same. Would you rathe
be with the wolves?"

"Oh, no," said the leprechaun.

"Then drill, ye tarrier, drill!" said Tim O'Hallorar
and shouldered his shovel, while the leprechaun trailec
behind.

At the end of the day the leprechaun came to him

"I've never done mortal work before," he said, "anc
there's no bone in my body that's not a pain and ar
anguish to me."

"You'll feel better after supper," said O'Halloran
"And the night's made for sleep."

"But where will I sleep?" said the leprechaun.

"In the half of my blanket," said Tim, "for are you
not young Rory, my nephew?"

It was not what he could have wished, but he saw
he could do no otherwise. Once you start a tale, you
must play up to the tale.

But that was only the beginning, as Tim O'Hallorar
soon found out. For Tim O'Halloran had tasted many
things before, but not responsibility, and now responsi
bility was like a bit in his mouth. It was not so bad the
first week, while the leprechaun was still ailing. Bu
when, what with the food and the exercise, he begar
to recover his strength, 'twas a wonder Tim O'Hallor
an's hair did not turn gray overnight. He was not a
bad creature, the leprechaun, but he had all the natura
mischief of a boy of twelve and, added to that, the craft
and knowledge of generations.

There was the three pipes and the pound of shag
the leprechaun stole from McGinnis — and the dear

frog he slipped in the foreman's tea — and the bottle of potheen he got hold of one night when Tim had to hold his head in a bucket of water to sober him up. A fortunate thing it was that St. Patrick had left him no great powers, but at that he had enough to put the jumping rheumatism on Shaun Kelly for two days — and it wasn't till Tim threatened to deny him the use of his razor entirely that he took off the spell.

That brought Rory to terms, for by now he'd come to take a queer pleasure in playing the part of a boy and he did not wish to have it altered.

Well, things went on like this for some time, and Tim O'Halloran's savings grew; for whenever the drink was running he took no part in it, for fear of mislaying his wits when it came to deal with young Rory. And as it was with the drink, so was it with other things — till Tim O'Halloran began to be known as a steady man. And then, as it happened one morning, Tim O'Halloran woke up early. The leprechaun had finished his shaving and was sitting cross-legged, chuckling to himself.

"And what's your source of amusement so early in the day?" said Tim sleepily.

"Oh," said the leprechaun, "I'm just thinking of the rare hard work we'll have when the line's ten miles farther on."

"And why should it be harder there than it is here?" said Tim.

"Oh, nothing," said the leprechaun, "but those fools of surveyors have laid out the line where there's hidden

springs of water. And when we start digging, there'll
be the devil to pay."

"Do you know that for a fact?" said Tim.

"And why wouldn't I know it?" said the leprechaun.
"Me that can hear the waters run underground."

"Then what should we do?" said Tim.

"Shift the line half a mile to the west and you'd
have a firm roadbed," said the leprechaun.

Tim O'Halloran said no more at the time. But for
all that, he managed to get to the assistant engineer in
charge of construction at the noon hour. He could not
have done it before, but now he was known as a steady
man. Nor did he tell where he got the information — he
put it on having seen a similar thing in Clonmelly.

Well, the engineer listened to him and had a test
made — and sure enough, they struck the hidden spring.
"That's clever work, O'Halloran," said the engineer.
"You've saved us time and money. And now how would
you like to be foreman of a gang?"

"I'd like it well," said Tim O'Halloran.

"Then you boss Gang Five from this day forward,"
said the engineer. "And I'll keep my eye on you. I like
a man that uses his head."

"Can my nephew come with me," said Tim, "for
'troth, he's my responsibility?"

"He can," said the engineer, who had children of
his own.

So Tim got promoted and the leprechaun along with
him. And the first day on the new work, young Rory
stole the gold watch from the engineer's pocket, because

he liked the tick of it, and Tim had to threaten him with fire and sword before he'd put it back.

Well, things went on like this for another while, till finally Tim woke up early on another morning and heard the leprechaun laughing.

"And what are you laughing at?" he said.

"Oh, the more I see of mortal work, the less reason there is to it," said the leprechaun. "For I've been watching the way they get the rails up to us on the line. And they do it thus and so. But if they did it so and thus, they could do it in half the time with half the work."

"Is that so indeed?" said Tim O'Halloran, and he made him explain it clearly. Then, after he'd swallowed his breakfast, he was off to his friend the engineer.

"That's a clever idea, O'Halloran," said the engineer. "We'll try it." And a week after that, Tim O'Halloran found himself with a hundred men under him and more responsibility than he'd ever had in his life. But it seemed little to him beside the responsibility of the leprechaun, and now the engineer began to lend him books to study and he studied them at nights while the leprechaun snored in its blanket.

A man could rise rapidly in those days — and it was then Tim O'Halloran got the start that was to carry him far. But he did not know he was getting it, for his heart was near broken at the time over Kitty Malone. She'd written him a letter or two when he first came West, but now there were no more of them and at last he got a word from her family telling him he should not be disturbing Kitty with letters from a laboring man.

That was bitter for Tim O'Halloran, and he'd think
about Kitty and the Orangeman in the watches of the
night and groan. And then, one morning, he woke up
after such a night and heard the leprechaun laughing.

"And what are you laughing at now?" he said sourly,
"For my heart's near burst with its pain."

"I'm laughing at a man that would let a cold letter
keep him from his love, and him with pay in his pocket
and the contract ending the first," said the leprechaun.

Tim O'Halloran struck one hand in the palm of the
other.

"By the piper, but you've the right of it, you queer
little creature!" he said. " 'Tis back to Boston we go
when this job's over."

It was laborer Tim O'Halloran that had come to
the West, but it was Railroadman Tim O'Halloran that
rode back East in the cars like a gentleman, with a free
pass in his pocket and the promise of a job on the railroad that was fitting a married man. The leprechaun,
may say, gave some trouble in the cars, more particularly when he bit a fat woman that called him a dear
little boy; but what with giving him peanuts all the
way, Tim O'Halloran managed to keep him fairly
quieted.

When they got to Boston he fitted them both out in
new clothes from top to toe. Then he gave the leprechaun some money and told him to amuse himself for
an hour or so while he went to see Kitty Malone.

He walked into the Malones' flat as bold as brass,
and there sure enough, in the front room, were Kitty
Malone and the Orangeman. He was trying to squeeze

her hand, and she refusing, and it made Tim O'Halloran's blood boil to see that. But when Kitty saw Tim O'Halloran she let out a scream.

"Oh, Tim!" she said. "Tim! And they told me you were dead in the plains of the West!"

"And a great pity that he was not," said the Orangeman, blowing out his chest with the brass buttons on it, "but a bad penny always turns up."

"Bad penny is it, you brass-buttoned son of iniquity," said Tim O'Halloran. "I have but the one question to put you. Will you stand or will you run?"

"I'll stand as we stood at Boyne Water," said the Orangeman, grinning ugly. "And whose backs did we see that day?"

"Oh, is that the tune?" said Tim O'Halloran. "Well, I'll give you a tune to match it. Who fears to speak of Ninety-Eight?"

With that he was through the Orangeman's guard and stretched him at the one blow, to the great consternation of the Malones. The old woman started to screech and Pat Malone to talk of policemen, but Tim O'Halloran silenced the both of them.

"Would you be giving your daughter to an Orangeman that works on the horsecars, when she might be marrying a future railroad president?" he said. And with that he pulled his savings out of his pocket and the letter that promised the job for a married man. That quieted the Malones a little and, once they got a good look at Tim O'Halloran, they began to change their tune. So, after they'd got the Orangeman out of the house — and he did not go willing, but he went as a whipped man must — Tim O'Halloran recounted all of his adventures.

The tale did not lose in the telling, though he did not speak of the leprechaun, for he thought that had better be left to a later day; and at the end Pat Malone was offering him a cigar. "But I find I have none upon me," said he with a wink at Tim, "so I'll just run down to the corner."

"And I'll go with you," said Kitty's mother, "for if Mr. O'Halloran stays to supper — and he's welcome — there's a bit of shopping to be done."

So the old folks left Tim O'Halloran and his Kitty alone. But just as they were in the middle of their planning and contriving for the future, there came a knock on the door.

"What's that?" said Kitty, but Tim O'Halloran knew well enough and his heart sank within him. He opened the door — and sure enough, it was the leprechaun.

"Well, Uncle Tim," said the creature, grinning, "I'm here."

Tim O'Halloran took a look at him as if he saw him for the first time. He was dressed in new clothes, to be sure, but there was soot on his face and his collar had thumbmarks on it already. But that wasn't what made the difference. New clothes or old, if you looked at him for the first time, you could see he was an unchancy thing, and not like Christian souls.

"Kitty," he said, "Kitty darlint, I had not told you. But this is my young nephew, Rory, that lives with me."

Well, Kitty welcomed the boy with her prettiest

manners, though Tim O'Halloran could see her giving him a side look now and then. All the same, she gave him a slice of cake, and he tore it apart with his fingers; but in the middle of it he pointed to Kitty Malone.

"Have you made up your mind to marry my Uncle Tim?" he said. "Faith, you'd better, for he's a grand catch."

"Hold your tongue, young Rory," said Tim O'Halloran angrily, and Kitty blushed red. But then she took the next words out of his mouth.

"Let the gossoon be, Tim O'Halloran," she said bravely. "Why shouldn't he speak his mind? Yes, Rory-een — it's I that will be your aunt in the days to come — and a proud woman too."

"Well, that's good," said the leprechaun, cramming the last of the cake in his mouth, "for I'm thinking you'll make a good home for us, once you're used to my ways."

"Is that to be the way of it, Tim?" said Kitty Malone very quietly, but Tim O'Halloran looked at her and knew what was in her mind. And he had the greatest impulse in the world to deny the leprechaun and send him about his business. And yet, when he thought of it, he knew that he could not do it, not even if it meant the losing of Kitty Malone.

"I'm afraid that must be the way of it, Kitty," he said with a groan.

"Then I honor you for it," said Kitty, with her eyes like stars. She went up to the leprechaun and took his hard little hand. "Will you live with us, young Rory?" she said. "For we'd be glad to have you."

"Thank you kindly, Kitty Malone — O'Halloran to be," said the leprechaun. "And you're lucky, Tim O'Halloran — lucky yourself and lucky in your wife. For if you had denied me then, your luck would have left you — and if she had denied me then, 'twould be but half luck for you both. But now the luck will stick to you the rest of your lives. And I'm wanting another piece of cake," said he.

"Well, it's a queer lad you are," said Kitty Malone, but she went for the cake. The leprechaun swung his legs and looked at Tim O'Halloran. "I wonder what keeps my hands off you," said the latter with a groan.

"Fie!" said the leprechaun, grinning, "and would you be lifting the hand to your one nephew? But tell me one thing, Tim O'Halloran, was this wife you're to take ever in domestic service?"

"And what if she was?" said Tim O'Halloran, firing up. "Who thinks the worse of her for that?"

"Not I," said the leprechaun, "for I've learned about mortal labor since I came to this country — and it's an honest thing. But tell me one thing more. Do you mean to serve this wife of yours and honor her through the days of your wedded life?"

"Such is my intention," said Tim, "though what business it is of — "

"Never mind," said the leprechaun. "Your shoelace is undone, bold man. Command me to tie it up."

"Tie up my shoe, you black-hearted, villainous little anatomy!" thundered Tim O'Halloran, and the leprechaun did so. Then he jumped to his feet and skipped about the room.

"Free! Free!" he piped. "Free at last! For I've served the servants of servants and the doom has no power on me longer. Free, Tim O'Halloran! O'Halloran's Luck is free!"

Tim O'Halloran stared at him, dumb; and even as he stared, the creature seemed to change. He was small, to be sure, and boyish — but you could see the unchancy look leave him and the Christian soul come into his eyes. That was a queer thing to be seen, and a great one too.

"Well," said Tim O'Halloran in a sober voice, "I'm glad for you, Rory. For now you'll be going back to Clonmelly, no doubt — and faith, you've earned the right."

The leprechaun shook his head.

"Clonmelly's a fine, quiet place," said he, "but this country's bolder. I misdoubt it's something in the air — you will not have noticed it, but I've grown two inches and a half since first I met you, and I feel myself growing still. No, it's off to the mines of the West I am, to follow my natural vocation — for they say there are mines out there you could mislay all Dublin Castle in — and wouldn't I like to try! But speaking of that, Tim O'Halloran," he said, "I was not quite honest with you about the pot of gold. You'll find your share behind the door when I've gone. And now good day and long life to you!"

"But, man dear," said Tim O'Halloran, " 'tis not good-by!" For it was then he realized the affection that was in him for the queer little creature.

"No, 'tis not good-by," said the leprechaun. "When

you christen your first son, I'll be at his cradle, though you may not see me — and so with your sons' sons and their sons, for O'Halloran's luck's just begun. But we'll part for the present now. For now I'm a Christian soul, I've work to do in the world."

"Wait a minute," said Tim O'Halloran. "For you would not know, no doubt, and you such a new soul. And no doubt you'll be seeing the priest — but a layman can do it in an emergency and I think this is one. I dare not have you leave me — and you not even baptized."

And with that he made the sign of the cross and baptized the leprechaun. He named him Rory Patrick.

" 'Tis not done with all the formalities," he said at the end, "but I'll defend the intention."

"I'm grateful to you," said the leprechaun. "And if there was a debt to be paid, you've paid it back and more."

And with that he was gone somehow, and Tim O'Halloran was alone in the room. He rubbed his eyes. But there was a little sack behind the door, where the leprechaun had left it — and Kitty was coming in with a slice of cake on a plate.

"Well, Tim," she said, "and where's that young nephew of yours?"

So he took her into his arms and told her the whole story. And how much of it she believed, I do not know. But there's one remarkable circumstance. Ever since then, there's always been one Rory O'Halloran in the family, and that one luckier than the lave. And when Tim O'Halloran got to be a railroad president, why, didn't he call his private car "The Leprechaun"? For that matter, they said, when he took his business trips there'd be a small boyish-looking fellow would be with him now and again. He'd turn up from nowhere, at some odd stop or other, and he'd be let in at once, while the great of the railroad world were kept waiting in the vestibule. And after a while, there'd be singing from inside the car.

JACOB AND THE INDIANS

IT goes back to the early days — may God profit all who lived then — and the ancestors.

Well, America, you understand, in those days was different. It was a nice place, but you wouldn't believe it if you saw it today. Without busses, without trains, without states, without Presidents, nothing!

With nothing but colonists and Indians and wild woods all over the country and wild animals to live in the wild woods. Imagine such a place! In these days, you children don't even think about it; you read about it in the schoolbooks, but what is that? And I put in a call to my daughter, in California, and in three minutes I am saying "Hello, Rosie," and there it is Rosie and she is telling me about the weather, as if I wanted to know! But things were not always that way. I remember my own days, and they were different. And in the times of my grandfather's grandfather, they were different still. Listen to the story.

My grandfather's grandfather was Jacob Stein, and he came from Rettelsheim, in Germany. To Philadelphia he came, an orphan in a sailing ship, but not a common man. He had learning — he had been to the *chedar* — he could have been a scholar among the scholars. Well, that is the way things happen in this bad world. There was a plague and a new grand duke — things are always

74

so. He would say little of it afterward — they had left his teeth in his mouth, but he would say little of it. He did not have to say — we are children of the Dispersion — we know a black day when it comes.

Yet imagine — a young man with fine dreams and learning, a scholar with a pale face and narrow shoulders, set down in those early days in such a new country. Well, he must work, and he did. It was very fine, his learning, but it did not fill his mouth. He must carry a pack on his back and go from door to door with it. That was no disgrace; it was so that many began. But it was not expounding the Law, and at first he was very homesick. He would sit in his room at night, with the one candle, and read the preacher Koheleth, till the bitterness of the preacher rose in his mouth. Myself, I am sure that Koheleth was a great preacher, but if he had had a good wife he would have been a more cheerful man. They had too many wives in those old days — it confused them. But Jacob was young.

As for the new country where he had come, it was to him a place of exile, large and frightening. He was glad to be out of the ship, but, at first, that was all. And when he saw his first real Indian in the street — well, that was a day! But the Indian, a tame one, bought a ribbon from him by signs, and after that he felt better. Nevertheless, it seemed to him at times that the straps of the pack cut into his very soul, and he longed for the smell of the *chedar* and the quiet streets of Rettelsheim and the good smoked goose-breast pious housewives keep for the scholar. But there is no going back — there is never any going back.

All the same, he was a polite young man, and a hardworking. And soon he had a stroke of luck — or at first it seemed so. It was from Simon Ettelsohn that he got the trinkets for his pack, and one day he found Simon Ettelsohn arguing a point of the Law with a friend, for Simon was a pious man and well thought of in the Congregation Mikveh Israel. Our grandfather's grandfather stood by very modestly at first — he had come to replenish his pack and Simon was his employer. But finally his heart moved within him, for both men were wrong, and he spoke and told them where they erred. For half an hour he spoke, with his pack still upon his shoulders, and never has a text been expounded with more complexity, not even by the great Reb Samuel. Till, in the end, Simon Ettelsohn threw up his hands and called him a young David and a candle of learning. Also, he allowed him a more profitable route of trade. But, best of all, he invited young Jacob to his house, and there Jacob ate well for the first time since he had come to Philadelphia. Also he laid eyes upon Miriam Ettelsohn for the first time, and she was Simon's youngest daughter and a rose of Sharon.

After that, things went better for Jacob, for the protection of the strong is like a rock and a well. But yet things did not go altogether as he wished. For, at first, Simon Ettelsohn made much of him, and there was stuffed fish and raisin wine for the young scholar, though he was a peddler. But there is a look in a man's eyes that says "H'm? Son-in-law?" and that look Jacob did not see. He was modest — he did not expect to win the maiden overnight, though he longed for her. But

gradually it was borne in upon him what he was in the
Ettelsohn house — a young scholar to be shown before
Simon's friends, but a scholar whose learning did not
fill his mouth. He did not blame Simon for it, but it
was not what he had intended. He began to wonder if
he would ever get on in the world at all, and that is
not good for any man.

Nevertheless, he could have borne it, and the aches
and pains of his love, had it not been for Meyer Kappelhuist. Now, there was a pushing man! I speak no ill of
anyone, not even of your Aunt Cora, and she can keep
the De Groot silver if she finds it in her heart to do so;
who lies down in the straw with a dog, gets up with
fleas. But this Meyer Kappelhuist! A big, red-faced
fellow from Holland with shoulders the size of a barn
door and red hair on the backs of his hands. A big
mouth for eating and drinking and telling schnorrer
stories — and he talked about the Kappelhuists, in
Holland, till you'd think they were made of gold. The
crane says, "I am really a peacock — at least on my
mother's side." And yet, a thriving man — that could
not be denied. He had started with a pack, like our
grandfather's grandfather. and now he was trading with
the Indians and making money hand over fist. It seemed
to Jacob that he could never go to the Ettelsohn house
without meeting Meyer and hearing about those
Indians. And it dried the words in Jacob's mouth and
made his heart burn.

For, no sooner would our grandfather's grandfather
begin to expound a text or a proverb, than he would
see Meyer Kappelhuist looking at the maiden. And

when Jacob had finished his expounding, and there
should have been a silence, Meyer Kappelhuist would
take it upon himself to thank him, but always in a tone
that said: "The Law is the Law and the Prophets are
the Prophets, but prime beaver is also prime beaver,
my little scholar!" It took the pleasure from Jacob's
learning and the joy of the maiden from his heart.
Then he would sit silent and burning, while Meyer
told a great tale of Indians, slapping his hands on his
knees. And in the end he was always careful to ask
Jacob how many needles and pins he had sold that day;
and when Jacob told him, he would smile and say very
smoothly that all things had small beginnings, till the
maiden herself could not keep from a little smile.
Then, desperately, Jacob would rack his brains for
more interesting matter. He would tell of the wars of
the Maccabees and the glory of the Temple. But even
as he told them, he felt they were far away. Whereas
Meyer and his accursed Indians were there, and the
maiden's eyes shone at his words.

Finally he took his courage in both hands and went
to Simon Ettelsohn. It took much for him to do it, for
he had not been brought up to strive with men, but
with words. But it seemed to him now that everywhere
he went he heard of nothing but Meyer Kappelhuist
and his trading with the Indians, till he thought it
would drive him mad. So he went to Simon Ettelsohn
in his shop.

"I am weary of this narrow trading in pins and
needles," he said, without more words.

Simon Ettelsohn looked at him keenly; for while he was an ambitious man, he was kindly as well.

"*Nu,*" he said. "A nice little trade you have and the people like you. I myself started in with less. What would you have more?"

"I would have much more," said our grandfather's grandfather stiffly. "I would have a wife and a home in this new country. But how shall I keep a wife? On needles and pins?"

"*Nu,* it has been done," said Simon Ettelsohn, smiling a little. "You are a good boy, Jacob, and we take an interest in you. Now, if it is a question of marriage, there are many worthy maidens. Asher Levy, the baker, has a daughter. It is true that she squints a little, but her heart is of gold." He folded his hands and smiled.

"It is not of Asher Levy's daughter I am thinking," said Jacob, taken aback. Simon Ettelsohn nodded his head and his face grew grave.

"*Nu,* Jacob," he said. "I see what is in your heart. Well, you are a good boy, Jacob, and a fine scholar. And if it were in the old country, I am not saying. But here, I have one daughter married to a Seixas and one to a Da Silva. You must see that makes a difference." And he smiled the smile of a man well pleased with his world.

"And if I were such a one as Meyer Kappelhuist?" said Jacob bitterly.

"Now — well, that is a little different," said Simon Ettelsohn sensibly. "For Meyer trades with the Indians. It is true, he is a little rough. But he will die a rich man."

"I will trade with the Indians too," said Jacob, and trembled.

Simon Ettelsohn looked at him as if he had gone out of his mind. He looked at his narrow shoulders and his scholar's hands.

"Now, Jacob," he said soothingly, "do not be foolish. A scholar you are, and learned, not an Indian trader. Perhaps in a store you would do better. I can speak to Aaron Copras. And sooner or later we will find you a nice maiden. But to trade with Indians — well, that takes a different sort of man. Leave that to Meyer Kappelhuist."

"And your daughter, that rose of Sharon? Shall I leave her, too, to Meyer Kappelhuist?" cried Jacob.

Simon Ettelsohn looked uncomfortable.

"*Nu*, Jacob," he said. "Well, it is not settled, of course. But — "

"I will go forth against him as David went against Goliath," said our grandfather's grandfather wildly. "I will go forth into the wilderness. And God should judge the better man!"

Then he flung his pack on the floor and strode from the shop. Simon Ettelsohn called out after him, but he did not stop for that. Nor was it in his heart to go and seek the maiden. Instead, when he was in the street, he counted the money he had. It was not much. He had meant to buy his trading goods on credit from Simon Ettelsohn, but now he could not do that. He stood in the sunlit street of Philadelphia, like a man bereft of hope.

Nevertheless, he was stubborn — though how stubborn he did not yet know. And though he was bereft of hope, he found his feet taking him to the house of Raphael Sanchez.

Now, Raphael Sanchez could have bought and sold Simon Ettelsohn twice over. An arrogant old man he was, with fierce black eyes and a beard that was whiter than snow. He lived apart, in his big house with his granddaughter, and men said he was very learned, but also very disdainful, and that to him a Jew was not a Jew who did not come of the pure sephardic strain.

Jacob had seen him, in the Congregation Mikveh Israel, and to Jacob he had looked like an eagle, and fierce as an eagle. Yet now, in his need, he found himself knocking at that man's door.

It was Raphael Sanchez himself who opened. "And what is for sale today, peddler?" he said, looking scornfully at Jacob's jacket where the pack straps had worn it.

"A scholar of the Law is for sale," said Jacob in his bitterness, and he did not speak in the tongue he had learned in this country, but in Hebrew.

The old man stared at him a moment.

"Now am I rebuked," he said. "For you have the tongue. Enter, my guest," and Jacob touched the scroll by the doorpost and went in.

They shared the noon meal at Raphael Sanchez's table. It was made of dark, glowing mahogany, and the light sank into it as sunlight sinks into a pool. There were many precious things in that room, but Jacob had no eyes for them. When the meal was over and the blessing said, he opened his heart and spoke, and

Raphael Sanchez listened, stroking his beard with one hand. When the young man had finished, he spoke.

"So, Scholar," he said, though mildly, "you have crossed an ocean that you might live and not die, and yet all you see is a girl's face."

"Did not Jacob serve seven years for Rachel?" said our grandfather's grandfather.

"Twice seven, Scholar," said Raphael Sanchez dryly, "but that was in the blessed days." He stroked his beard again. "Do you know why I came to this country?" he said.

"No," said Jacob Stein.

"It was not for the trading," said Raphael Sanchez. "My house has lent money to kings. A little fish, a few furs — what are they to my house? No, it was for the promise — the promise of Penn — that this land should be an habitation and a refuge, not only for the Gentiles. Well, we know Christian promises. But so far, it has been kept. Are you spat upon in the street here, Scholar of the Law?"

"No," said Jacob. "They call me Jew, now and then. But the Friends, though Gentile, are kind."

"It is not so in all countries," said Raphael Sanchez, with a terrible smile.

"No," said Jacob quietly, "it is not."

The old man nodded. "Yes, one does not forget that," he said. "The spittle wipes off the cloth, but one does not forget. One does not forget the persecutor or the persecuted. That is why they think me mad, in the Congregation Mikveh Israel, when I speak what is in my mind. For, look you" — and he pulled a map from a drawer — "here is what we know of these colonies, and here and here our people make a new beginning, in another air. But here is New France — see it? — and down the great river come the French traders and their Indians."

"Well?" said Jacob in puzzlement.

"Well?" said Raphael Sanchez. "Are you blind? I do not trust the King of France — the king before him drove out the Huguenots, and who knows what he may do? And if they hold the great rivers against us, we shall never go westward."

"We?" said Jacob in bewilderment.

"We," said Raphael Sanchez. He struck his hand on the map. "Oh, they cannot see it in Europe — not even their lords in parliament and their ministers of state," he said. "They think this is a mine, to be worked as the Spaniards worked Potosi, but it is not a mine. It is something beginning to live, and it is faceless and nameless yet. But it is our lot to be part of it — remember that in the wilderness, my young scholar of the Law. You think you are going there for a girl's face, and that is well enough. But you may find something there you did not expect to find."

He paused and his eyes had a different look.

"You see, it is the trader first," he said. "Always the trader, before the settled man. The Gentiles will forget that, and some of our own folk too. But one pays for the land of Canaan; one pays in blood and sweat."

Then he told Jacob what he would do for him and dismissed him, and Jacob went home to his room with his head buzzing strangely. For at times it seemed to him that the Congregation Mikveh Israel was right in thinking Raphael Sanchez half mad. And at other times it seemed to him that the old man's words were a veil, and behind them moved and stirred some huge and unguessed shape. But chiefly he thought of the rosy cheeks of Miriam Ettelsohn.

It was with the Scotchman, McCampbell, that Jacob made his first trading journey. A strange man was McCampbell, with grim features and cold blue eyes, but strong and kindly, though silent, except when he talked of the Ten Lost Tribes of Israel. For it was his contention that they were the Indians beyond the Western Mountains, and on this subject he would talk endlessly.

Indeed, they had much profitable conversation, McCampbell quoting the doctrines of a rabbi called John Calvin, and our grandfather's grandfather replying with Talmud and Torah till McCampbell would almost weep that such a honey-mouthed scholar should be destined to eternal damnation. Yet he did not treat our grandfather's grandfather as one destined to eternal damnation, but as a man, and he, too, spoke of cities of refuge as a man speaks of realities, for his people had also been persecuted.

First they left the city behind them, and then the outlying towns and, soon enough, they were in the wilderness. It was very strange to Jacob Stein. At first he would wake at night and lie awake listening, while his heart pounded, and each rustle in the forest was the step of a wild Indian, and each screech of an owl in the forest the whoop before the attack. But gradually this passed. He began to notice how silently the big man, McCampbell, moved in the woods; he began to imitate him. He began to learn many things that even a scholar of the Law, for all his wisdom, does not know — the girthing of a packsaddle and the making of fires, the look of dawn in the forest and the look of evening. It was all very new to him, and sometimes he thought he would die of it, for his flesh weakened. Yet always he kept on.

When he saw his first Indians — in the woods, not in the town — his knees knocked together. They were there as he had dreamt of them in dreams, and he thought of the spirit, Iggereth-beth-Mathlan, and her seventy-eight dancing demons, for they were painted and in skins. But he could not let his knees knock together, before heathens and a Gentile, and the first fear passed. Then he found they were grave men, very ceremonious and silent at first, and then when the silence had been broken, full of curiosity. They knew McCampbell, but him they did not know, and they discussed him and his garments with the frankness of children, till Jacob felt naked before them, and yet not afraid. One of them pointed to the bag that hung at Jacob's neck — the bag in which, for safety's sake, he carried his phylactery — then McCampbell said something and the brown hand dropped quickly, but there was a buzz of talk.

Later on, McCampbell explained to him that they, too, wore little bags of deerskin and inside them sacred objects — and they thought, seeing his, that he must be a person of some note. It made him wonder. It made him wonder more to eat deer meat with them, by a fire.

It was a green world and a dark one that he had fallen in — dark with the shadow of the forest, green with its green. Through it ran trails and paths that were not yet roads or highways — that did not have the dust and smell of the cities of men, but another scent, another look. These paths Jacob noted carefully, making a map, for that was one of the instructions of Raphael Sanchez. It seemed a great labor and difficult and for no purpose; yet, as he had promised, so he did. And as they sank deeper and deeper into the depths of the forest, and he saw pleasant streams and wide glades, untenanted but by the deer, strange thoughts came over him. It seemed to him that the Germany he had left was very small and crowded together; it seemed to him that he had not known there was so much width to the world.

Now and then he would dream back — dream back to the quiet fields around Rettelsheim and the red-brick houses of Philadelphia, to the stuffed fish and the raisin wine, the chanting in the *chedar* and the white twisted loaves of calm Sabbath, under the white cloth. They would seem very close for the moment, then they would seem very far away. He was eating deer's meat in a forest and sleeping beside embers in the open night. It was so that Israel must have slept in the wilderness. He had not thought of it as so, but it was so.

Now and then he would look at his hands — they seemed tougher and very brown, as if they did not belong to him any more. Now and then he would catch a glimpse of his own face, as he drank at a stream. He had a beard, but it was not the beard of a scholar – it was wild and black. Moreover, he was dressed in skins, now; it seemed strange to be dressed in skins at first, and then not strange.

Now all this time, when he went to sleep at night, he would think of Miriam Ettelsohn. But, queerly enough, the harder he tried to summon up her face in his thoughts, the vaguer it became.

He lost track of time — there was only his map and the trading and the journey. Now it seemed to him that they should surely turn back, for their packs were full. He spoke of it to McCampbell, but McCampbell shook his head. There was a light in the Scotchman's eyes now – a light that seemed strange to our grandfather's grandfather — and he would pray long at night, sometimes too loudly. So they came to the banks of the great river, brown and great, and saw it, and the country beyond it, like a view across Jordan. There was no end to that country — it stretched to the limits of the sky and Jacob saw it with his eyes. He was almost afraid at first, and then he was not afraid.

It was there that the strong man, McCampbell, fell sick, and there that he died and was buried. Jacob buried him on a bluff overlooking the river and faced the grave to the west. In his death sickness, McCampbell raved of the Ten Lost Tribes again and swore they were just across the river and he would go to them. It took all Jacob's strength to hold him — if it had been the beginning of the journey, he would not have had the strength. Then he turned back, for he, too.

had seen a Promised Land, not for his seed only, but for nations yet to come.

Nevertheless, he was taken by the Shawnees, in a season of bitter cold, with his last horse dead. At first, when misfortune began to fall upon him, he had wept for the loss of the horses and the good beaver. But, when the Shawnees took him, he no longer wept; for it seemed to him that he was no longer himself, but a man he did not know.

He was not concerned when they tied him to the stake and piled the wood around him, for it seemed to him still that it must be happening to another man. Nevertheless he prayed, as was fitting, chanting loudly; for Zion in the wilderness he prayed. He could smell the smell of the *chedar* and hear the voices that he knew — Reb Moses and Reb Nathan, and through them the curious voice of Raphael Sanchez, speaking in riddles. Then the smoke took him and he coughed. His throat was hot. He called for drink, and though they could not understand his words, all men know the sign of thirst, and they brought him a bowl filled. He put it to his lips eagerly and drank, but the stuff in the bowl was scorching hot and burned his mouth. Very angry then was our grandfather's grandfather, and without so much as a cry he took the bowl in both hands and flung it straight in the face of the man who had brought it, scalding him. Then there was a cry and a murmur from the Shawnees and, after some moments, he felt himself unbound and knew that he lived.

It was flinging the bowl at the man while yet he stood at the stake that saved him, for there is an eti-

quette about such matters. One does not burn a madman, among the Indians; and to the Shawnees, Jacob's
flinging the bowl proved that he was mad, for a sane
man would not have done so. Or so it was explained
to him later, though he was never quite sure that they
had not been playing cat-and-mouse with him, to test
him. Also they were much concerned by his chanting
his death song in an unknown tongue and by the
phylactery that he had taken from its bag and bound
upon brow and arm for his death hour, for these they
thought strong medicine and uncertain. But in any
case they released him, though they would not give
him back his beaver, and that winter he passed in the
lodges of the Shawnees, treated sometimes like a servant
and sometimes like a guest, but always on the edge of
peril. For he was strange to them, and they could not
quite make up their minds about him, though the man
with the scalded face had his own opinion, as Jacob
could see.

Yet when the winter was milder and the hunting
better than it had been in some seasons, it was he who
got the credit of it, and the holy phylactery also; and by
the end of the winter he was talking to them of trade,
though diffidently at first. Ah, our grandfather's grandfather, *selig*, what woes he had! And yet it was not all
woe, for he learned much woodcraft from the Shawnees
and began to speak in their tongue.

Yet he did not trust them entirely; and when spring
came and he could travel, he escaped. He was no longer
a scholar then, but a hunter. He tried to think what
day it was by the calendar, but he could only remember

the Bee Moon and the Berry Moon. Yet when he
thought of a feast he tried to keep it, and always he
prayed for Zion. But when he thought of Zion, it was
not as he had thought of it before — a white city set on
a hill — but a great and open landscape, ready for
nations. He could not have said why his thought had
changed, but it had.

I shall not tell all, for who knows all? I shall not tell
of the trading post he found deserted and the hundred
and forty French louis in the dead man's money belt.
I shall not tell of the half-grown boy, McGillvray, that
he found on the fringes of settlement — the boy who
was to be his partner in the days to come — and how
they traded again with the Shawnees and got much
beaver. Only this remains to be told, for this is true.

It was a long time since he had even thought of
Meyer Kappelhuist — the big pushing man with red
hairs on the backs of his hands. But now they were
turning back toward Philadelphia, he and McGillvray,
their packhorses and their beaver; and as the paths
began to grow familiar, old thoughts came into his
mind. Moreover, he would hear now and then, in the
outposts of the wilderness, of a red-haired trader. So
when he met the man himself, not thirty miles from
Lancaster, he was not surprised.

Now, Meyer Kappelhuist had always seemed a big
man to our grandfather's grandfather. But he did not
seem such a big man, met in the wilderness by chance,
and at that Jacob was amazed. Yet the greater surprise
was Meyer Kappelhuist's, for he stared at our grandfather's grandfather long and puzzledly before he cried

out, "But it's the little scholar!" and clapped his hand on his knee. Then they greeted each other civilly and Meyer Kappelhuist drank liquor because of the meeting, but Jacob drank nothing. For, all the time, they were talking, he could see Meyer Kappelhuist's eyes fixed greedily upon his packs of beaver, and he did not like that. Nor did he like the looks of the three tame Indians who traveled with Meyer Kappelhuist and, though he was a man of peace, he kept his hand on his arms, and the boy, McGillvray, did the same.

Meyer Kappelhuist was anxious that they should travel on together, but Jacob refused, for, as I say, he did not like the look in the red-haired man's eyes. So he said he was taking another road and left it at that.

"And the news you have of Simon Ettelsohn and his family — it is good, no doubt, for I know you are close to them," said Jacob, before they parted.

"Close to them?" said Meyer Kappelhuist, and he looked black as thunder. Then he laughed a forced laugh. "Oh, I see them no more," he said. "The old rascal has promised his daughter to a cousin of the Seixas, a greeny, just come over, but rich, they say. But to tell you the truth, I think we are well out of it, Scholar — she was always a little too skinny for my taste," and he laughed coarsely.

"She was a rose of Sharon and a lily of the valley," said Jacob respectfully, and yet not with the pang he would have expected at such news, though it made him more determined than ever not to travel with Meyer Kappelhuist. And with that they parted and Meyer Kappelhuist went his way. Then Jacob took a fork in the trail that McGillvray knew of and that was as well for him. For when he got to Lancaster, there was news of the killing of a trader by the Indians who traveled with him; and when Jacob asked for details, they showed him something dried on a willow hoop. Jacob looked at the thing and saw the hairs upon it were red.

"Sculped all right, but we got it back," said the frontiersman, with satisfaction. "The red devil had it on him when we caught him. Should have buried it, too, I guess, but we'd buried him already and it didn't seem feasible. Thought I might take it to Philadelphy, sometime — might make an impression on the governor. Say, if you're going there, you might — after all, that's where he come from. Be a sort of memento to his folks."

"And it might have been mine, if I had traveled with him," said Jacob. He stared at the thing again, and his heart rose against touching it. Yet it was well the city people should know what happened to men in the wilderness, and the price of blood. "Yes, I will take it," he said.

Jacob stood before the door of Raphael Sanchez, in Philadelphia. He knocked at the door with his knuckles and the old man himself peered out at him.

"And what is your business with me, Frontiersman?" said the old man, peering.

"The price of blood for a country," said Jacob Stein. He did not raise his voice, but there was a note in it that had not been there when he first knocked at Raphael Sanchez's door.

The old man stared at him soberly. "Enter, my son,"

ᵉe said at last, and Jacob touched the scroll by the
doorpost and went in.

He walked through the halls as a man walks in a
dream. At last he was sitting by the dark mahogany
able. There was nothing changed in the room — he
wondered greatly that nothing in it had changed.

"And what have you seen, my son?" said Raphael
anchez.

"I have seen the land of Canaan, flowing with milk
and honey," said Jacob, Scholar of the Law. "I have
brought back grapes from Eshcol, and other things that
are terrible to behold," he cried, and even as he cried
he felt the sob rise in his throat. He choked it down.
"Also there are eighteen packs of prime beaver at the
warehouse and a boy named McGillvray, a Gentile, but
very trusty," he said. "The beaver is very good and
the boy under my protection. And McCampbell died
by the great river, but he had seen the land and I
think he rests well. The map is not made as I would
have it, but is shows new things. And we must trade
with the Shawnees. There are three posts to be established — I have marked them on the map — and later,
more. And beyond the great river there is country that
stretches to the end of the world. That is where my
friend McCampbell lies, with his face turned west. But
what is the use of talking? You would not understand."

He put his head on his arms, for the room was too
quiet and peaceful, and he was very tired. Raphael
Sanchez moved around the table and touched him on
the shoulder.

"Did I not say, my son, that there was more than a girl's face to be found in the wilderness?" he said.

"A girl's face?" said Jacob. "Why, she is to be married and, I hope, will be happy, for she was a rose of Sharon. But what are girls' faces beside this?" and he flung something on the table. It rattled dryly on the table, like a cast snakeskin, but the hairs upon it were red.

"It was Meyer Kappelhuist," said Jacob childishly, "and he was a strong man. And I am not strong, but a scholar. But I have seen what I have seen. And we must say Kaddish for him."

"Yes, yes," said Raphael Sanchez. "It will be done. I will see to it."

"But you do not understand," said Jacob. "I have eaten deer's meat in the wilderness and forgotten the month and the year. I have been a servant to the heathen and held the scalp of my enemy in my hand. I will never be the same man."

"Oh, you will be the same," said Sanchez. "And no worse a scholar, perhaps. But this is a new country."

"It must be for all," said Jacob. "For my friend McCampbell died also, and he was a Gentile."

"Let us hope," said Raphael Sanchez and touched him again upon the shoulder. Then Jacob lifted his head and he saw that the light had declined and the evening was upon him. And even as he looked, Raphael Sanchez's granddaughter came in to light the candles for Sabbath. And Jacob looked upon her, and she was a dove, with dove's eyes.

THE DIE-HARD

THERE was a town called Shady, Georgia, and a time that's gone, and a boy named Jimmy Williams who was curious about things. Just a few years before the turn of the century it was, and that seems far away now. But Jimmy Williams was living in it, and it didn't seem far away to him.

It was a small town, Shady, and sleepy, though it had two trains a day and they were putting through a new spur to Vickery Junction.

They'd dedicated the War Memorial in the Square, but, on market days, you'd still see oxcarts on Main Street. And once, when Jimmy Williams was five, there'd been a light fall of snow and the whole town had dropped its business and gone out to see it. He could still remember the feel of the snow in his hands, for it was the only snow he'd ever touched or seen.

He was a bright boy — maybe a little too bright for his age. He'd think about a thing till it seemed real to him — and that's a dangerous gift. His father was the town doctor, and his father would try to show him the difference, but Doctor Williams was a right busy man. And the other Williams children were a good deal younger and his mother was busy with them. So Jimmy had more time to himself than most boys — and youth's a dreamy time.

95

I reckon it was that got him interested in Old Man Cappalow, in the first place. Every town has its legends and characters, and Old Man Cappalow was one of Shady's. He lived out of town, on the old Vincey place, all alone except for a light-colored Negro named Sam that he'd brought from Virginia with him; and the local Negroes wouldn't pass along that road at night. That was partly because of Sam, who was supposed to be a conjur, but mostly on account of Old Man Cappalow. He'd come in the troubled times, right after the end of the war, and ever since then he'd kept himself to himself. Except that once a month he went down to the bank and drew money that came in a letter from Virginia. But how he spent it, nobody knew. Except that he had a treasure — every boy in Shady knew that.

Now and then, a gang of them would get bold and they'd rattle sticks along the sides of his fence and yell, "Old Man Cappalow! Where's your money?" But then the light-colored Negro, Sam, would come out on the porch and look at them, and they'd run away. They didn't want to be conjured, and you couldn't be sure. But on the way home, they'd speculate and wonder about the treasure, and each time they speculated and wondered, it got bigger to them.

Some said it was the last treasure of the Confederacy, saved right up to the end to build a new *Alabama*, and that Old Man Cappalow had sneaked it out of Richmond when the city fell and kept it for himself; only now he didn't dare spend it, for the mark of Cain was on every piece. And some said it came from the sea islands, where the pirates had left it, protected by h'ants and devils, and Old Man Cappalow had had to fight devils for it six days and six nights before he could take it away. And if you looked inside his shirt, you could see the long white marks where the devils had clawed him. Well, sir, some said one thing and some said another. But they all agreed it was there, and it got to be a byword among the boys of the town.

It used to bother Jimmy Williams tremendously. Because he knew his father worked hard, and yet sometimes he'd only get fifty cents a visit, and often enough he'd get nothing. And he knew his mother worked hard, and that most folks in Shady weren't rich. And yet, all the time, there was that treasure, sitting out at Old Man Cappalow's. He didn't mean to steal it exactly. I don't know just what he did intend to do about it. But the idea of it bothered him and stayed at the back of his mind. Till, finally, one summer when he was turned thirteen, he started making expeditions to the Cappalow place.

He'd go in the cool of the morning or the cool of the afternoon, and sometimes he'd be fighting Indians and Yankees on the way, because he was still a boy, and sometimes he was thinking what he'd be when he grew up, for he was starting to be a man. But he never told the other boys what he was doing — and that was the mixture of both. He'd slip from the road, out of sight of the house, and go along by the fence. Then he'd lie down in the grass and the weeds, and look at the house.

It had been quite a fine place once, but now the porch was sagging and there were mended places in the roof and paper pasted over broken windowpanes. But that didn't mean much to Jimmy Williams; he was used to houses looking like that. There was a garden patch at the side, neat and well-kept, and sometimes he'd see the Negro, Sam, there, working. But what he looked at mostly was the side porch. For Old Man Cappalow would be sitting there.

He sat there, cool and icy-looking, in his white linen suit, on his cane chair, and now and then he'd have a leather-bound book in his hand, though he didn't often read it. He didn't move much, but he sat straight, his hands on his knees and his black eyes alive. There was something about his eyes that reminded Jimmy Williams of the windows of the house. They weren't blind, indeed they were bright, but there was something living behind them that wasn't usual. You didn't expect them to be so black, with his white hair. Jimmy Williams had seen a governor once, on Memorial Day, but the governor didn't look half as fine. This man was like a man made of ice — ice in the heat of the South. You could see he was old, but you couldn't tell how old, or whether he'd ever die.

Once in a great while he'd come out and shoot at a mark. The mark was a kind of metal shield, nailed up on a post, and it had been painted once, but the paint had worn away. He'd hold the pistol very steady, and the bullets would go "whang, whang" on the metal, very loud in the stillness. Jimmy Williams would watch him and wonder if that was the way he'd fought with his devils, and speculate about all kinds of things.

All the same, he was only a boy, and though it was fun and scary, to get so near Old Man Cappalow with·

out being seen, and he'd have a grand tale to tell the others, if he ever decided to tell it, he didn't see any devils or any treasure. And probably he'd have given the whole business up in the end, boylike, if something hadn't happened.

He was lying in the weeds by the fence, one warm afternoon, and, boylike, he fell asleep. And he was just in the middle of a dream where Old Man Cappalow was promising him a million dollars if he'd go to the devil to get it, when he was wakened by a rustle in the weeds and a voice that said, "White boy."

Jimmy Williams rolled over and froze. For there, just half a dozen steps away from him, was the light-colored Negro, Sam, in his blue jeans, the way he worked in the garden patch, but looking like the butler at the club for all that.

I reckon if Jimmy Williams had been on his feet, he'd have run. But he wasn't on his feet. And he told himself he didn't mean to run, though his heart began to pound.

"White boy," said the light-colored Negro, "Marse John see you from up at the house. He send you his obleegances and say will you step that way." He spoke in a light, sweet voice, and there wasn't a thing in his manners you could have objected to. But just for a minute, Jimmy Williams wondered if he was being conjured. And then he didn't care. Because he was going to do what no boy in Shady had ever done. He was going to walk into Old Man Cappalow's house and not be scared. He wasn't going to be scared, though his heart kept pounding.

He scrambled to his feet and followed the line of the fence till he got to the driveway, the light-colored Negro just a little behind him. And when they got near the porch, Jimmy Williams stopped and took a leaf and wiped off his shoes, though he couldn't have told you why. The Negro stood watching while he did it, perfectly at ease. Jimmy Williams could see that the Negro thought better of him for wiping off his shoes, but not much. And that made him mad, and he wanted to say, "I'm no white trash. My father's a doctor," but he knew better than to say it. He just wiped his shoes and the Negro stood and waited. Then the Negro took him around to the side porch, and there was Old Man Cappalow, sitting in his cane chair.

"White boy here, Marse John," said the Negro in his low, sweet voice.

The old man lifted his head, and his black eyes looked at Jimmy Williams. It was a long stare and it went to Jimmy Williams' backbone.

"Sit down, boy," he said, at last, and his voice was friendly enough, but Jimmy Williams obeyed it. "You can go along, Sam," he said, and Jimmy Williams sat on the edge of a cane chair and tried to feel comfortable. He didn't do very well at it, but he tried.

"What's your name, boy?" said the old man, after a while.

"Jimmy Williams, sir," said Jimmy Williams. "I mean James Williams, Junior, sir."

"Williams," said the old man, and his black eyes glowed. "There was a Colonel Williams with the Sixty-fifth Virginia — or was it the Sixty-third? He came from

Fairfax County and was quite of my opinion that we should have kept to primogeniture, in spite of Thomas Jefferson. But I doubt if you are kin."

"No, sir," said Jimmy Williams. "I mean, Father was with the Ninth Georgia. And he was a private. They were aiming to make him a corporal, he says, but they never got around to it. But he fit — he fought lots of Yankees. He fit tons of 'em. And I've seen his uniform. But now he's a doctor instead."

The old man seemed to look a little queer at that. "A doctor?" he said. "Well, some very reputable gentlemen have practiced medicine. There need be no loss of standing."

"Yes, sir," said Jimmy Williams. Then he couldn't keep it back any longer: "Please, sir, were you ever clawed by the devil?" he said.

"Ha-hrrm!" said the old man, looking startled. "You're a queer boy. And suppose I told you I had been?"

"I'd believe you," said Jimmy Williams, and the old man laughed. He did it as if he wasn't used to it, but he did it.

"Clawed by the devil!" he said. "Ha-hrrm! You're a bold boy. I didn't know they grew them nowadays. I'm surprised." But he didn't look angry, as Jimmy Williams had expected him to.

"Well," said Jimmy Williams, "if you had been, I thought maybe you'd tell me about it. I'd be right interested. Or maybe let me see the clawmarks. I mean, if they're there."

"I can't show you those," said the old man, "though

they're deep and wide." And he stared fiercely at Jimmy Williams. "But you weren't afraid to come here and you wiped your shoes when you came. So I'll show you something else." He rose and was tall. "Come into the house," he said.

So Jimmy Williams got up and went into the house with him. It was a big, cool, dim room they went into, and Jimmy Williams didn't see much at first. But then his eyes began to get used to the dimness.

Well, there were plenty of houses in Shady where the rooms were cool and dim and the sword hung over the mantelpiece and the furniture was worn and old. It wasn't that made the difference. But stepping into this house was somehow like stepping back into the past, though Jimmy Williams couldn't have put it that way. He just knew it was full of beautiful things and grand things that didn't quite fit it, and yet all belonged together. And they knew they were grand and stately, and yet there was dust in the air and a shadow on the wall. It was peaceful enough and handsome enough, yet it didn't make Jimmy Williams feel comfortable, though he couldn't have told you why.

"Well," said the old man, moving about among shadows, "how do you like it, Mr. Williams?"

"It's — I never saw anything like it," said Jimmy Williams.

The old man seemed pleased. "Touch the things, boy," he said. "Touch the things. They don't mind being touched."

So Jimmy Williams went around the room, staring at the miniatures and the pictures, and picking up one thing or another and putting it down. He was very careful and he didn't break anything. And there were some wonderful things. There was a game of chess on a table — carved-ivory pieces — a game that people had started, but hadn't finished. He didn't touch those, though he wanted to, because he felt the people might not like it when they came back to finish their game. And yet, at the same time, he felt that if they ever did come back, they'd be dead, and that made him feel queerer. There were silver-mounted pistols, long-barreled, on a desk by a big silver inkwell; there was a quill pen made of a heron's feather, and a silver sand-box beside it — there were all sorts of curious and interesting things. Finally Jimmy Williams stopped in front of a big, tall clock.

"I'm sorry, sir," he said, "but I don't think that's the right time."

"Oh, yes, it is." said the old man. "It's always the right time."

"Yes, sir," said Jimmy Williams, "but it isn't running."

"Of course not," said the old man. "They say you can't put the clock back, but you can. I've put it back and I mean to keep it back. The others can do as they please. I warned them — I warned them in 1850, when they accepted the Compromise. I warned them there could be no compromise. Well, they would not be warned."

"Was that bad of them, sir?" asked Jimmy Williams.

"It was misguided of them," said the old man. "Misguided of them all." He seemed to be talking more to himself than to Jimmy, but Jimmy Williams couldn't help listening. "There can be no compromise with one's class or one's breeding or one's sentiments," the old man said. "Afterwards — well, there were gentlemen I knew who went to Guatemala or elsewhere. I do not blame them for it. But mine is another course." He paused and glanced at the clock. Then he spoke in a different voice. "I beg your pardon," he said. "I fear I was growing heated. You will excuse me. I generally take some refreshment around this time in the afternoon. Perhaps you will join me, Mr. Williams?"

It didn't seem to Jimmy Williams as if the silver hand bell in the old man's hand had even stopped ringing before the Negro, Sam, came in with a tray. He had a queer kind of old-fashioned long coat on now, and a queer old-fashioned cravat, but his pants were the pants of his blue jeans. Jimmy Williams noticed that, but Old Man Cappalow didn't seem to notice.

"Yes," he said, "there are many traitors. Men I held in the greatest esteem have betrayed their class and their system. They have accepted ruin and domination in the name of advancement. But we will not speak of them now." He took the frosted silver cup from the tray and motioned to Jimmy Williams that the small fluted glass was for him. "I shall ask you to rise, Mr. Williams," he said. "We shall drink a toast." He paused for a moment, standing straight. "To the Confederate States of America and damnation to all her enemies!" he said.

Jimmy Williams drank. He'd never drunk any wine before, except blackberry cordial, and this wine seemed

to him powerfully thin and sour. But he felt grown up
as he drank it, and that was a fine feeling.

"Every night of my life," said the old man, "I drink
that toast. And usually I drink it alone. But I am glad
of your company, Mr. Williams."

"Yes, sir," said Jimmy Williams, but all the same,
he felt queer. For drinking the toast, somehow, had
been very solemn, almost like being in church. But in
church you didn't exactly pray for other people's damnation, though the preacher might get right excited
over sin.

Well, then the two of them sat down again, and Old
Man Cappalow began to talk of the great plantation
days and the world as it used to be. Of course, Jimmy
Williams had heard plenty of talk of that sort. But this
was different. For the old man talked of those days as
if they were still going on, not as if they were past. And
as he talked, the whole room seemed to join in, with
a thousand, sighing, small voices, stately and clear, till
Jimmy Williams didn't know whether he was on his
head or his heels and it seemed quite natural to him
to look at the fresh, crisp Richmond newspaper on the
desk and see it was dated "June 14, 1859" instead of
"June 14, 1897." Well, maybe it was the wine, though
he'd only had a thimbleful. But when Jimmy Williams
went out into the sun again, he felt changed, and excited too. For he knew about Old Man Cappalow now,
and he was just about the grandest person in the world.

The Negro went a little behind him, all the way to
the gate, on soft feet. When they got there, the Negro
opened the gate and spoke.

"Young marster," he said, "I don't know why Marse John took in his head to ask you up to the house. But we lives private, me and Marse John. We lives very private." There was a curious pleading in his voice.

"I don't tell tales," said Jimmy Williams, and kicked at the fence.

"Yes, sir," said the Negro, and he seemed relieved. "I knew you one of the right ones. I knew that. But we'se living very private till the big folks come back. We don't want no tales spread before. And then we'se going back to Otranto, the way we should."

"I know about Otranto. He told me," said Jimmy Williams, catching his breath.

"Otranto Marse John's plantation in Verginny," said the Negro, as if he hadn't heard. "He owns the river and the valley, the streams and the hills. We got four hundred field hands at Otranto and stables for sixty horses. But we can't go back there till the big folks come back. Marse John say so, and he always speak the truth. But they's goin' to come back, a-shootin' and pirootin', they pistols at they sides. And every day I irons his Richmond paper for him and he reads about the old times. We got boxes and boxes of papers down in the cellar." He paused. "And if he say the old days come back, it bound to be so," he said. Again his voice held that curious pleading. "You remember, young marster," he said. "You remember, white boy."

"I told you I didn't tell tales," said Jimmy Williams. But after that, things were different for him. Because there's one thing about a boy that age that most grown people forget. A boy that age can keep a secret in a way that's perfectly astonishing. And he can go through queer hells and heavens you'll never hear a word about, not even if you got him or bore him.

It was that way with Jimmy Williams; it mightn't have been for another boy. It began like a game, and then it stopped being a game. For, of course, he went back to Old Man Cappalow's. And the Negro, Sam, would show him up to the house and he'd sit in the dim room with the old man and drink the toast in the wine. And it wasn't Old Man Cappalow any more; it was Col. John Leonidas Cappalow, who'd raised and equipped his own regiment and never surrendered. Only, when the time was ripe, he was going back to Otranto, and the old days would bloom again, and Jimmy Williams would be part of them.

When he shut his eyes at night, he could see Otranto and its porches, above the rolling river, great and stately; he could hear the sixty horses stamping in their stalls. He could see the pretty girls, in their wide skirts, coming down the glassy, proud staircases; he could see the fine, handsome gentlemen who ruled the earth and the richness of it without a thought of care. It was all like a storybook to Jimmy Williams — a storybook come true. And more than anything he'd ever wanted in his life, he wanted to be part of it.

The only thing was, it was hard to fit the people he really knew into the story. Now and then Colonel Cappalow would ask him gravely if he knew anyone else in Shady who was worthy of being trusted with the secret. Well, there were plenty of boys like Bob Miller and Tommy Vine, but somehow you couldn't see them in the dim room. They'd fit in, all right, when the great days came back — they'd have to — but meanwhile — well, they might just take it for a tale. And then there was Carrie, the cook. She'd have to be a slave again, of course, and though Jimmy Williams didn't imagine that she'd mind, now and then he had just a suspicion that she might. He didn't ask her about it, but he had the suspicion.

It was even hard to fit Jimmy's father in, with his little black bag and his rumpled clothes and his laugh. Jimmy couldn't quite see his father going up the front steps of Otranto — not because he wasn't a gentleman or grand enough, but because it just didn't happen to be his kind of place. And then, his father didn't really hate anybody, as far as Jimmy knew. But you had to hate people a good deal, if you wanted to follow Colonel Cappalow. You had to shoot at the mark and feel you were really shooting the enemy's colors down. You had to believe that even people like General Lee had been wrong, because they hadn't held out in the mountains and fought till everybody died. Well, it was hard to believe a wrong thing of General Lee, and Jimmy Williams didn't quite manage it. He was willing to hate the Yankees and the Republicans — hate them hot and hard — but there weren't any of them in Shady. Well, come to think of it, there was Mr. Rosen, at the dry-goods store, and Mr. Ailey, at the mill. They didn't look very terrible and he was used to them, but he tried to hate them all he could. He got hold of the Rosen boy one day and rocked him home, but the Rosen boy cried, and Jimmy felt mean about it. But if he'd ever seen a real live Republican, with horns and a tail, he'd have done him a mortal injury — he felt sure he would.

And so the summer passed, and by the end of the summer Jimmy didn't feel quite sure which was real — the times now or the times Colonel Cappalow talked about. For he'd dream about Otranto at night and think of it during the day. He'd ride back there on a black horse, at Colonel Cappalow's left, and his saber would be long and shining. But if there was a change in him, there was a change in Colonel Cappalow too. He was a lot more excitable than he used to be, and when he talked to Jimmy sometimes, he'd call him by other names, and when he shot at the mark with the enemy's colors on it, his eyes would blaze. So by that, and by the news he read out of the old papers, Jimmy suddenly got to know that the time was near at hand. They had the treasure all waiting, and soon they'd be ready to rise. And Colonel Cappalow filled out Jimmy Williams' commission as captain in the army of the New Confederate States of America and presented it to him, with a speech. Jimmy Williams felt very proud of that commission, and hid it under a loose brick in his fireplace chimney, where it would be safe.

Well, then it came to the plans, and when Jimmy Williams first heard about them, he felt a little surprised. There were maps spread all over the big desk in the dim room now, and Colonel Cappalow moved pins and showed Jimmy strategy. And that was very exciting, and like a game. But first of all, they'd have to give a signal and strike a blow. You had to do that first, and then the country would rise. Well, Jimmy Williams could see the reason in that.

They were going into Shady and capture the post office first, and then the railroad station and, after that, they'd dynamite the railroad bridge to stop the trains, and Colonel Cappalow would read a proclamation from the steps of the courthouse. The only part Jimmy Williams didn't like about it was killing the postmaster and the station agent, in case they resisted. Jimmy Williams felt pretty sure they would resist, particularly the station agent, who was a mean customer. And, somehow, killing people you knew wasn't quite like killing Yankees and Republicans. The thought of it shook something in Jimmy's mind and made it waver. But after that they'd march on Washington, and everything would be all right.

All the same, he'd sworn his oath and he was a commissioned officer in the army of the New Confederate States. So, when Colonel Cappalow gave him the pistol that morning, with the bullets and the powder, and explained how he was to keep watch at the door of the post office and shoot to kill if he had to, Jimmy said, "I shall execute the order, sir," the way he'd been taught. After that, they'd go for the station agent and he'd have a chance for a lot more shooting. And it was all going to be for noon the next day.

Somehow, Jimmy Williams couldn't quite believe it was going to be for noon the next day, even when he was loading the pistol in the woodshed of the Williams house, late that afternoon. And yet he saw, with a kind of horrible distinctness, that it was going to be. It might sound crazy to some, but not to him — Colonel Cappalow was a sure shot; he'd seen him shoot at the mark. He could see him shooting, now, and he wondered if a bullet went "whang" when it hit a man. And, just as he was fumbling with the bullets, the woodshed door opened suddenly and there was his father.

Well, naturally, Jimmy dropped the pistol and jumped. The pistol didn't explode, for he'd forgotten it needed a cap. But with that moment something seemed to break inside Jimmy Williams. For it was the first time he'd really been afraid and ashamed in front of his father, and now he was ashamed and afraid. And then it was like waking up out of an illness, for his father saw his white face and said, "What's the matter, son?" and the words began to come out of his mouth.

"Take it easy, son," said his father, but Jimmy couldn't take it easy. He told all about Otranto and Old Man Cappalow and hating the Yankees and killing the postmaster, all jumbled up and higgledy-piggledy. But Doctor Williams made sense of it. At first he smiled a little as he listened, but after a while he stopped smiling, and there was anger in his face. And when Jimmy was quite through, "Well, son," he said, "I reckon we've let you run wild. But I never thought . . ." He asked Jimmy a few quick questions, mostly about the dynamite, and he seemed relieved when Jimmy told him they were going to get it from the men who were blasting for the new spur track.

"And now, son," he said, "when did you say this massacre was going to start?"

"Twelve o'clock at the post office." said Jimmy.

"But we weren't going to massacre. It was just the folks that resisted — "

Doctor Williams made a sound in his throat. "Well," he said, "you and I are going to take a ride in the country, Jimmy. No, we won't tell your mother, I think."

It was the last time Jimmy Williams went out to Old Man Cappalow's, and he remembered that. His father didn't say a word all the way, but once he felt in his back pocket for something he'd taken out of the drawer of his desk, and Jimmy remembered that too.

When they drove up in front of the house, his father gave the reins to Jimmy. "Stay in the buggy, Jimmy," he said. "I'll settle this."

Then he got out of the buggy, a little awkwardly, for he was a heavy man, and Jimmy heard his feet scrunch on the gravel. Jimmy knew again, as he saw him go up the steps, that he wouldn't have fitted in Otranto, and somehow he was glad.

The Negro, Sam, opened the door.

"Tell Colonel Cappalow Doctor Williams wishes to speak with him," said Jimmy's father, and Jimmy could see that his father's neck was red.

"Colonel Cappalow not receivin'," said Sam, in his light sweet voice, but Jimmy's father spoke again.

"Tell Colonel Cappalow," he said. He didn't raise his voice, but there was something in it that Jimmy had never heard in that voice before. Sam looked for a moment and went inside the house.

Then Colonel Cappalow came to the door himself. There was red from the evening sun on his white suit and his white hair, and he looked tall and proud. He looked first at Jimmy's father and then at Jimmy. And his voice said, quite coldly, and reasonably and clearly, "Traitor! All traitors!"

"You'll oblige me by leaving the boy out of it," said Jimmy's father heavily. "This is 1897, sir, not 1860," and for a moment there was something light and heady and dangerous in the air between them. Jimmy knew what his father had in his pocket then, and he sat stiff in the buggy and prayed for time to change and things to go away.

Then Colonel Cappalow put his hand to his forehead. "I beg your pardon, sir," he said, in an altered voice. "You mentioned a date?"

"I said it was 1897," said Doctor Williams, standing square and stocky, "I said Marse Robert's dead — God bless him! — and Jefferson Davis too. And before he died, Marse Robert said we ought to be at peace. The ladies can keep up the war as long as they see fit — that's their privilege. But men ought to act like men."

He stared for a moment at the high-chinned, sculptural face.

"Why, damn your soul!" he said, and it was less an oath than a prayer. "I was with the Ninth Georgia; I went through three campaigns. We fought till the day of Appomattox and it was we-uns' fight." Something rough and from the past had slipped back into his speech — something, too, that Jimmy Williams had never heard in it before. "We didn't own niggers or plantations — the men I fought with. But when it was over, we reckoned it was over and we'd build up the land. Well, we've had a hard time to do it, but we're hoeing corn. We've got something better to do than fill up a boy with a lot of magnolious notions and aim to shoot up a postmaster because there's a Republican President. My God," he said, and again it was less an oath than a prayer, "it was bad enough getting licked when you thought you couldn't be — but when I look at you — well, hate stinks when it's kept too long in the barrel, no matter how you dress it up and talk fine about it. I'm warning you. You keep your hands off my boy. Now, that's enough."

"Traitors," said the old man vaguely, "all traitors." Then a change came over his face and he stumbled forward as if he had stumbled over a stone. The Negro and the white man both sprang to him, but it was the Negro who caught him and lowered him to the ground. Then Jimmy Williams heard his father calling for his black bag, and his limbs were able to move again.

Doctor Williams came out of the bedroom, drying his hands on a towel. His eyes fell upon Jimmy Williams, crouched in front of the chessboard.

"He's all right, son," he said. "At least — he's not all right. But he wasn't in pain."

Jimmy Williams shivered a little. "I heard him talking," he said difficultly. "I heard him calling people things."

"Yes," said his father. "Well, you mustn't think too much of that. You see, a man — " He stopped and began again, "Well, I've no doubt he was considerable of a man once. Only — well, there's a Frenchman calls it a fixed idea. You let it get a hold of you . . . and the

way he was brought up. He got it in his head, you see
— he couldn't stand it that he might have been wrong
about anything. And the hate — well, it's not for a man.
Not when it's like that. Now, where's that Nigra?"

Jimmy Williams shivered again; he did not want
Sam back in the room. But when Sam came, he heard
the Negro answer, politely.

"H'm," said Doctor Williams. "Twice before. He
should have had medical attention."

"Marse John don't believe in doctors," said the low,
sweet voice.

"He wouldn't," said Doctor Williams briefly. "Well,
I'll take the boy home now. But I'll have to come back.
I'm coroner for this county. You understand about
that?"

"Yes, sir," said the low, sweet voice, "I understand
about that." Then the Negro looked at the doctor.
"Marse Williams," he said, "I wouldn't have let him do
it. He thought he was bound to. But I wouldn't have
let him do it."

"Well," said the doctor. He thought, and again said,
"Well." Then he said, "Are there any relatives?"

"I take him back to Otranto," said the Negro. "It
belongs to another gentleman now, but Marse John got
a right to lie there. That's Verginny law, he told me."

"So it is," said the doctor. "I'd forgotten that."

"He don't want no relatives," said the Negro. "He
got nephews and nieces and all sorts of kin. But they
went against him and he cut them right out of his
mind. He don't want no relatives." He paused. "He cut
everything out of his mind but the old days," he said.

"He start doing it right after the war. That's why we come here. He don't want no part nor portion of the present days. And they send him money from Verginny, but he only spend it the one way — except when we buy this place." He smiled as if at a secret.

"But how?" said the doctor, staring at furniture and pictures.

"Jus' one muleload from Otranto," said the Negro, softly. "And I'd like to see anybody cross Marse John in the old days." He coughed. "They's just one thing, Marse Williams," he said, in his suave voice. "I ain't skeered of sittin' up with Marse John. I always been with him. But it's the money."

"What money?" said Doctor Williams. "Well, that will go through the courts — "

"No, sir," said the Negro patiently. "I mean Marse John's special money that he spend the other money for. He got close to a millyum dollars in that blind closet under the stairs. And nobody dare come for it, as long as he's strong and spry. But now I don't know. I don't know."

"Well," said Doctor Williams, receiving the incredible fact, "I suppose we'd better see."

It was as the Negro had said — a blind closet under the stairs, opened by an elementary sliding catch.

"There's the millyum dollars," said the Negro as the door swung back. He held the cheap glass lamp high — the wide roomy closet was piled from floor to ceiling with stacks of printed paper.

"H'm," said Doctor Williams. "Yes, I thought so . . . . Have you ever seen a million dollars, son?"

"No, sir," said Jimmy Williams.

"Well, take a look," said his father. He slipped a note from a packet, and held it under the lamp.

"It says 'One Thousand Dollars,'" said Jimmy Williams. "Oh!"

"Yes," said his father gently. "And it also says 'Confederate States of America'. . . . You don't need to worry, Sam. The money's perfectly safe. Nobody will come for it. Except, maybe, museums."

"Yes, Marse Williams," said Sam unquestioningly, accepting the white man's word, now he had seen and judged the white man. He shut the closet.

On his way out, the doctor paused for a moment and looked at the Negro. He might have been thinking aloud — it seemed that way to Jimmy Williams.

"And why did you do it?" he said. "Well, that's something we'll never know. And what are you going to do, once you've taken him back to Otranto?"

"I got my arrangements, thank you, sir," said the Negro.

"I haven't a doubt of it," said Jimmy Williams' father. "But I wish I knew what they were."

"I got my arrangements, gentlemen," the Negro repeated, in his low, sweet voice. Then they left him, holding the lamp, with his tall shadow behind him.

"Maybe I oughtn't to have left him," said Jimmy Williams' father, after a while, as the buggy jogged along. "He's perfectly capable of setting fire to the place and burning it up as a sort of a funeral pyre. And maybe that wouldn't be a bad thing," he added, after

a pause. Then he said, "Did you notice the chessmen?
I wonder who played that game. It was stopped in the
middle." Then, after a while, he said, "I remember the
smell of the burning woods in the Wilderness. And I
remember Reconstruction. But Marse Robert was right,
all the same. You can't go back to the past. And hate's
the most expensive commodity in the world. It's never
been anything else, and I've seen a lot of it. We've got
to realize that — got too much of it, still, as a nation."

But Jimmy Williams was hardly listening. He was
thinking it was good to be alone with his father in a
buggy at night and good they didn't have to live in
Otranto after all.

DOC MELLHORN AND THE PEARLY GATES

DOC MELLHORN had never expected to go any-where at all when he died. So, when he found himself on the road again, it surprised him. But per-haps I'd better explain a little about Doc Mellhorn first. He was seventy-odd when he left our town; but when he came, he was as young as Bates or Filsinger or any of the boys at the hospital. Only there wasn't any hospital when he came. He came with a young man's beard and a brand-new bag and a lot of newfangled ideas about medicine that we didn't take to much. And he left, forty-odd years later, with a first-class county health record and a lot of people alive that wouldn't have been alive if he hadn't been there. Yes, a country doctor. And nobody ever called him a man in white or a death grappler that I know of, though they did think of giving him a degree at Pewauket College once. But then the board met again and decided they needed a new gymnasium, so they gave the degree to J. Prentiss Parmalee instead.

They say he was a thin young man when he first came, a thin young man with an Eastern accent who'd wanted to study in Vienna. But most of us remember him chunky and solid, with white hair and a little bald spot that always got burned bright red in the first hot

weather. He had about four card tricks that he'd do for
you, if you were a youngster — they were always the
same ones — and now and then, if he felt like it, he'd
take a silver half dollar out of the back of your neck.
And that worked as well with the youngsters who were
going to build rocket ships as it had with the youngsters
who were going to be railway engineers. It always
worked. I guess it was Doc Mellhorn more than the
trick.

But there wasn't anything unusual about him, except maybe the card tricks. Or, anyway, he didn't think
so. He was just a good doctor and he knew us inside
out. I've heard people call him a pigheaded, obstinate
old mule — that was in the fight about the water supply.
And I've heard a weepy old lady call him a saint. I took
the tale to him once, and he looked at me over his
glasses and said, "Well, I've always respected a mule.
Got ten times the sense of a — horse." Then he took a
silver half dollar out of my ear.

Well, how do you describe a man like that? You
don't — you call him up at three in the morning. And
when he sends in his bill, you think it's a little steep.

All the same, when it came to it, there were people
who drove a hundred and fifty miles to the funeral.
And the Masons came down from Bluff City, and the
Poles came from across the tracks, with a wreath the
size of a house, and you saw cars in town that you didn't
often see there. But it was after the funeral that the
queer things began for Doc Mellhorn.

The last thing he remembered, he'd been lying in
bed, feeling pretty sick, on the whole, but glad for the

rest. And now he was driving his Model T down a long straight road between rolling, misty prairies that seemed to go from nowhere to nowhere.

It didn't seem funny to him to be driving the Model T again. That was the car he'd learned on, and he kept to it till his family made him change. And it didn't seem funny to him not to be sick any more. He hadn't had much time to be sick in his life — the patients usually attended to that. He looked around for his bag, first thing, but it was there on the seat beside him. It was the old bag, not the presentation one they'd given him at the hospital, but that was all right too. It meant he was out on a call and, if he couldn't quite recollect at the moment just where the call was, it was certain to come to him. He'd wakened up often enough in his buggy, in the old days, and found the horse was taking him home, without his doing much about it. A doctor gets used to things like that.

All the same, when he'd driven and driven for some time without raising so much as a traffic light, just the same rolling prairies on either hand, he began to get a little suspicious. He thought, for a while, of stopping the car and getting out, just to take a look around, but he'd always hated to lose time on a call. Then he noticed something else. He was driving without his glasses. And yet he hadn't driven without his glasses in fifteen years.

"H'm," said Doc Mellhorn. "I'm crazy as a June bug. Or else — Well, it might be so, I suppose."

But this time he did stop the car. He opened his bag and looked inside it, but everything seemed to be in order. He opened his wallet and looked at that, but there were his own initials, half rubbed away, and he recognized them. He took his pulse, but it felt perfectly steady.

"H'm," said Doc Mellhorn. "Well."

Then, just to prove that everything was perfectly normal, he took a silver half dollar out of the steering wheel of the car.

"Never did it smoother," said Doc Mellhorn. "Well, all the same, if this is the new highway, it's longer than I remember it."

But just then a motorcycle came roaring down the road and stopped with a flourish, the way motor cops do.

"Any trouble?" said the motor cop. Doc Mellhorn couldn't see his face for his goggles, but the goggles looked normal.

"I am a physician," said Doc Mellhorn, as he'd said a thousand times before to all sorts of people, "on my way to an urgent case." He passed his hand across his forehead. "Is this the right road?" he said.

"Straight ahead to the traffic light," said the cop. "They're expecting you, Doctor Mellhorn. Shall I give you an escort?"

"No; thanks all the same," said Doc Mellhorn, and the motor cop roared away. The Model T ground as Doc Mellhorn gassed her. "Well, they've got a new breed of traffic cop," said Doc Mellhorn, "or else — "

But when he got to the light, it was just like any light at a crossroads. He waited till it changed and the officer waved him on. There seemed to be a good deal of traffic going the other way, but he didn't get a chance to notice it much, because Lizzie bucked a little, as she usually did when you kept her waiting. Still, the sight of traffic relieved him, though he hadn't passed anybody on his own road yet.

Pretty soon he noticed the look of the country had changed. It was parkway now and very nicely land-scaped. There was dogwood in bloom on the little hills, white and pink against the green; though, as Doc Mell-horn remembered it, it had been August when he left his house. And every now and then there'd be a nice little white-painted sign that said TO THE GATES.

"H'm," said Doc Mellhorn. "New State Parkway, I guess. Well, they've fixed it up pretty. But I wonder where they got the dogwood. Haven't seen it bloom like that since I was East."

Then he drove along in a sort of dream for a while, for the dogwood reminded him of the days when he was a young man in an Eastern college. He remembered the look of that college and the girls who'd come to dances, the girls who wore white gloves and had rolls of hair. They were pretty girls, too, and he wondered what had become of them. "Had babies, I guess," thought Doc Mellhorn. "Or some of them, anyway." But he liked to think of them as the way they had been when they were just pretty, and excited at being at a dance.

He remembered other things too — the hacked desks in the lecture rooms, and the trees on the campus, and the first pipe he'd ever broken in, and a fellow called Paisley Grew that he hadn't thought of in years — a rawboned fellow with a gift for tall stories and playing the jew's-harp.

"Ought to have looked up Paisley," he said. "Yes, ought. Didn't amount to a hill of beans, I guess, but always liked him. I wonder if he still plays the jew's harp. Pshaw, I know he's been dead twenty years."

He was passing other cars now and other cars were passing him, but he didn't pay much attention, except when he happened to notice a license you didn't often see in the state, like Rhode Island or Mississippi. He was too full of his own thoughts. There were foot passengers, too, plenty of them — and once he passed a man driving a load of hay. He wondered what the man would do with the hay when he got to the Gates. But probably there were arrangements for that.

"Not that I believe a word of it," he said, "but it'll surprise Father Kelly. Or maybe it won't. I used to have some handsome arguments with that man, but I always knew I could count on him, in spite of me being a heretic."

Then he saw the Wall and the Gates, right across the valley. He saw them, and they reached to the top of the sky. He rubbed his eyes for a while, but they kept on being there.

"Quite a sight," said Doc Mellhorn.

No one told him just where to go or how to act, but it seemed to him that he knew. If he'd thought about it, he'd have said that you waited in line, but there wasn't any waiting in line. He just went where he was expected to go and the reception clerk knew his name right away.

"Yes, Doctor Mellhorn," he said. "And now, what would you like to do first?"

"I think I'd like to sit down," said Doc Mellhorn. So he sat, and it was a comfortable chair. He even bounced the springs of it once or twice, till he caught the reception clerk's eye on him.

"Is there anything I can get you?" said the reception clerk. He was young and brisk and neat as a pin, and you could see he aimed to give service and studied about it. Doc Mellhorn thought, "He's the kind that wipes off your windshield no matter how clean it is."

"No," said Doc Mellhorn. "You see, I don't believe this. I don't believe any of it. I'm sorry if that sounds cranky, but I don't."

"That's quite all right, sir," said the reception clerk. "It often takes a while." And he smiled as if Doc Mellhorn had done him a favor.

"Young man, I'm a physician," said Doc Mellhorn, "and do you mean to tell me — "

Then he stopped, for he suddenly saw there was no use arguing. He was either there or he wasn't. And it felt as if he were there.

"Well," said Doc Mellhorn, with a sigh, "how do I begin?"

"That's entirely at your own volition, sir," said the reception clerk briskly. "Any meetings with relatives, of course. Or if you would prefer to get yourself settled first. Or take a tour, alone or conducted. Perhaps these will offer suggestions," and he started to hand over a handful of leaflets. But Doc Mellhorn put them aside.

"Wait a minute," he said. "I want to think. Well,

naturally, there's Mother and Dad. But I couldn't se
them just yet. I wouldn't believe it. And Grandma -
well, now, if I saw Grandma — and me older than sh
is — was — used to be — well, I don't know what i
would do to me. You've got to let me get my breath
Well, of course, there's Uncle Frank — he'd be easier.'
He paused. "Is he here?" he said.

The reception clerk looked in a file. "I am happy t
say that Mr. Francis V. Mellhorn arrived July 12, 1907,'
he said. He smiled winningly.

"Well!" said Doc Mellhorn. "Uncle Frank! Well
I'll be — well! But it must have been a great consolation
to Mother. We heard — well, never mind what we hear
— I guess it wasn't so. . . . No, don't reach for that phon
just yet, or whatever it is. I'm still thinking."

"We sometimes find," said the reception clerk
eagerly, "that a person not a relative may be the best in
troduction. Even a stranger sometimes — a distinguishec
stranger connected with one's own profession — "

"Well, now, that's an idea," said Doc Mellhorr
heartily, trying to keep his mind off how much he dis
liked the reception clerk. He couldn't just say why he
disliked him, but he knew he did.

It reminded him of the time he'd had to have his
gall bladder out in the city hospital and the young.
brisk interns had come to see him and called him "Doctor" every other word.

"Yes, that's an idea," he said. He reflected. "Well,
of course, I'd like to see Koch," he said. "And Semmel-
weiss. Not to speak of Walter Reed. But, shucks, they'd

e busy men. But there is one fellow — only he lived
retty far back — "

"Hippocrates, please," said the reception clerk into
he telephone or whatever it was. "*H* for horse — "

"No!" said Doc Mellhorn quite violently. "Excuse
ne, but you just wait a minute. I mean if you can wait.
mean, if Hippocrates wants to come, I've no objection.
But I never took much of a fancy to him, in spite of his
ath. It's Aesculapius I'm thinking about. George W.
Oh, glory!" he said. "But he won't talk English. I
orgot."

"I shall be happy to act as interpreter," said the
eception clerk, smiling brilliantly.

"I haven't a doubt," said Doc Mellhorn. "But just
vait a shake." In a minute, by the way the clerk was
cting, he was going to be talking to Aesculapius. "And
vhat in time am I going to say to the man?" he thought.
It's too much." He gazed wildly around the neat re-
eption room — distempered, as he noticed, in a warm
hade of golden tan. Then his eyes fell on the worn
black bag at his feet and a sudden warm wave of relief
looded over him.

"Wait a minute," he said, and his voice gathered
orce and authority. "Where's my patient?"

"Patient?" said the reception clerk, looking puzzled
or the first time.

"Patient," said Doc Mellhorn. "*P* for phlebitis." He
apped his bag.

"I'm afraid you don't quite understand, sir," said
he reception clerk.

"I understand this," said Doc Mellhorn. "I was

called here. And if I wasn't called professionally, wh
have I got my bag?"

"But, my dear Doctor Mellhorn — " said the recep
tion clerk.

"I'm not your dear doctor," said Doc Mellhorn. "
was called here, I tell you. I'm sorry not to give you th
patient's name, but the call must have come in m
absence and the girl doesn't spell very well. But in an
well-regulated hospital — "

"But I tell you," said the reception clerk, and hi
hair wasn't slick any more, "nobody's ill here. Nobod
can be ill. If they could, it wouldn't be He — "

"Humph," said Doc Mellhorn. He thought it over
and felt worse. "Then what does a fellow like Koc
do?" he said. "Or Pasteur?" He raised a hand. "Oh
don't tell me," he said. "I can see they'd be busy. Yes
I guess it'd be all right for a research man. But I neve
was . . . Oh, well, shucks, I've published a few papers
And there's that clamp of mine — always meant to d
something about it. But they've got better ones now
Mean to say there isn't so much as a case of mumps i
the whole place?"

"I assure you," said the reception clerk, in a wear
voice. "And now, once you see Doctor Aesculapius — "

"Funny," said Doc Mellhorn. "Lord knows there'
plenty of times you'd be glad to be quit of the whol
thing. And don't talk to me about the healer's art o
grateful patients. Well, I've known a few . . . a few. Bu
I've known others. All the same, it's different, bein;
told there isn't any need for what you can do."

"*A* for Ararát," said the reception clerk into his ınstrument. "*E* for Eden."

"Should think you'd have a dial," said Doc Mell-ıorn desperately. "We've got 'em down below." He hought hard and frantically. "Wait a shake. It's com-ng back to me," he said. "Got anybody named Grew ıere? Paisley Grew?"

"*S* for serpent . . ." said the reception clerk. "What vas that?"

"Fellow that called me," said Doc Mellhorn. "G-r-:-w. First name, Paisley."

"I will consult the index," said the reception clerk.

He did so, and Doc Mellhorn waited, hoping against ıope.

"We have 94,183 Grews, including 83 Prescotts and ɔne Penobscot," the reception clerk said at last. "But I ail to find Paisley Grew. Are you quite sure of the ıame?"

"Of course," said Doc Mellhorn briskly. "Paisley Ɔrew. Chronic indigestion. Might be appendix — can't ;ay — have to see. But anyhow, he's called." He picked ıp his bag. "Well, thanks for the information," he said, iking the reception clerk better than he had yet. "Not ʝour fault, anyway."

"But — but where are you going?" said the reception :lerk.

"Well, there's another establishment, isn't there?" ;aid Doc Mellhorn. "Always heard there was. Call prob-ıbly came from there. Crossed wires, I expect."

"But you can't go there!" said the reception clerk. 'I mean — "

"Can't go?" said Doc Mellhorn. "I'm a physician. A patient's called me."

"But if you'll only wait and see Aesculapius!" said the reception clerk, running his hands wildly through his hair. "He'll be here almost any moment."

"Please give him my apologies," said Doc Mellhorn. "He's a doctor. He'll understand. And if any messages come for me, just stick them on the spike. Do I need a road map? Noticed the road I came was all one way."

"There is, I believe, a back road in rather bad repair," said the reception clerk icily. "I can call Information if you wish."

"Oh, don't bother," said Doc Mellhorn. "I'll find it. And I never saw a road beat Lizzie yet." He took a silver half dollar from the doorknob of the door. "See that?" he said. "Slick as a whistle. Well, good-by, young man."

But it wasn't till he'd cranked up Lizzie and was on his way that Doc Mellhorn really felt safe. He found the back road and it was all the reception clerk had said it was and more. But he didn't mind — in fact, after one particularly bad rut, he grinned.

"I suppose I ought to have seen the folks," he said. "Yes, I know I ought. But — not so much as a case of mumps in the whole abiding dominion! Well, it's lucky I took a chance on Paisley Grew."

After another mile or so, he grinned again.

"And I'd like to see old Aesculapius' face. Probably rang him in the middle of dinner — they always do. But shucks, it's happened to all of us."

Well, the road got worse and worse and the sky

above it darker and darker, and what with one thing and another, Doc Mellhorn was glad enough when he got to the other gates. They were pretty impressive gates, too, though of course in a different way, and reminded Doc Mellhorn a little of the furnaces outside Steeltown, where he'd practiced for a year when he was young.

This time Doc Mellhorn wasn't going to take any advice from reception clerks and he had his story all ready. All the same, he wasn't either registered or expected, so there was a little fuss. Finally they tried to scare him by saying he came at his own risk and that there were some pretty tough characters about. But Doc Mellhorn remarked that he'd practiced in Steeltown. So, after he'd told them what seemed to him a million times that he was a physician on a case, they finally let him in and directed him to Paisley Grew. Paisley was on Level 346 in Pit 68,953, and Doc Mellhorn recognized him the minute he saw him. He even had the jew's-harp, stuck in the back of his overalls.

"Well, Doc," said Paisley finally, when the first greetings were over, "you certainly are a sight for sore eyes! Though, of course, I'm sorry to see you here," and he grinned.

"Well, I can't see that it's so different from a lot of places," said Doc Mellhorn, wiping his forehead. "Warmish, though."

"It's the humidity, really," said Paisley Grew. "That's what it really is."

"Yes, I know," said Doc Mellhorn. "And now tell me, Paisley; how's that indigestion of yours?"

"Well, I'll tell you, Doc," said Paisley. "When I first came here, I thought the climate was doing it good. I did for a fact. But now I'm not so sure. I've tried all sorts of things for it — I've even tried being transferred to the boiling asphalt lakes. But it just seems to hang on, and every now and then, when I least expect it, it catches me. Take last night. I didn't have a thing to eat that I don't generally eat — well, maybe I did have one little snort of hot sulphur, but it wasn't the sulphur that did it. All the same, I woke up at four, and it was just like a knife. Now . . ."

He went on from there and it took him some time. And Doc Mellhorn listened, happy as a clam. He never thought he'd be glad to listen to a hypochondriac, but he was. And when Paisley was all through, he examined him and prescribed for him. It was just a little soda bicarb and pepsin, but Paisley said it took hold something wonderful. And they had a fine time that evening, talking over the old days.

Finally, of course, the talk got around to how Paisley liked it where he was. And Paisley was honest enough about that.

"Well, Doc," he said, "of course this isn't the place for you, and I can see you're just visiting. But I haven't many real complaints. It's hot, to be sure, and they work you, and some of the boys here are rough. But they've had some pretty interesting experiences, too, when you get them talking — yes, sir. And anyhow, it isn't Peabodyville, New Jersey," he said with vehemence. "I spent five years in Peabodyville, trying to work up in the leather business. After that I bust out, and I guess that's what landed me here. But it's an improvement on Peabodyville." He looked at Doc Mellhorn sidewise. "Say, Doc," he said, "I know this is a vacation for you, but all the same there's a couple of the boys — nothing really wrong with them of course — but — well, if you could just look them over — "

"I was thinking the office hours would be nine to one," said Doc Mellhorn.

So Paisley took him around and they found a nice little place for an office in one of the abandoned mine galleries, and Doc Mellhorn hung out his shingle. And right away patients started coming around. They didn't get many doctors there, in the first place, and the ones they did get weren't exactly the cream of the profession, so Doc Mellhorn had it all to himself. It was mostly sprains, fractures, bruises and dislocations, of course, with occasional burns and scalds — and, on the whole, it reminded Doc Mellhorn a good deal of his practice in Steeltown, especially when it came to foreign bodies in the eye. Now and then Doc Mellhorn ran into a more unusual case — for instance, there was one of the guards that got part of himself pretty badly damaged in a rock slide. Well, Doc Mellhorn had never set a tail before, but he managed it all right, and got a beautiful primary union, too, in spite of the fact that he had no X-ray facilities. He thought of writing up the case for the State Medical Journal, but then he couldn't figure out any way to send it to them, so he had to let it slide. And then there was an advanced carcinoma of the liver -- a Greek named Papadoupolous or Prometheus or something. Doc Mellhorn couldn't do much for him, considering the circumstances, but he did what he could, and he and the Greek used to have long conversations. The rest was just everyday practice — run of the mine — but he enjoyed it.

Now and then it would cross his mind that he ought to get out Lizzie and run back to the other place for a visit with the folks. But that was just like going back East had been on earth — he'd think he had everything pretty well cleared up, and then a new flock of patients would come in. And it wasn't that he didn't miss his wife and children and grandchildren — he did. But there wasn't any way to get back to them, and he knew it. And there was the work in front of him and the office crowded every day. So he just went along, hardly noticing the time.

Now and then, to be sure, he'd get a suspicion that he wasn't too popular with the authorities of the place. But he was used to not being popular with authorities and he didn't pay much attention. But finally they sent an inspector around. The minute Doc Mellhorn saw him, he knew there was going to be trouble.

Not that the inspector was uncivil. In fact, he was a pretty high-up official — you could tell by his antlers. And Doc Mellhorn was just as polite, showing him around. He showed him the free dispensary and the clinic and the nurse — Scotch girl named Smith, she was — and the dental chair he'd rigged up with the help of a fellow named Ferguson, who used to be an engineer before he was sentenced. And the inspector looked them all over, and finally he came back to Doc Mellhorn's office. The girl named Smith had put up curtains in the office, and with that and a couple of potted gas plants it looked more homelike than it had. The inspector looked around it and sighed.

"I'm sorry, Doctor Mellhorn," he said at last, "but you can see for yourself, it won't do."

"What won't do?" said Doc Mellhorn, stoutly. But, all the same, he felt afraid.

"Any of it," said the inspector. "We could overlook the alleviation of minor suffering — I'd be inclined to do so myself — though these people are here to suffer, and there's no changing that. But you're playing merry Hades with the whole system."

"I'm a physician in practice," said Doc Mellhorn.

"Yes," said the inspector. "That's just the trouble. Now, take these reports you've been sending," and he took out a sheaf of papers. "What have you to say about that?"

"Well, seeing as there's no county health officer, or at least I couldn't find one — " said Doc Mellhorn.

"Precisely," said the inspector. "And what have you done? You've condemned fourteen levels of this pit as unsanitary nuisances. You've recommended 2136 lost souls for special diet, remedial exercise, hospitalization — Well — I won't go through the list."

"I'll stand back of every one of those recommendations," said Doc Mellhorn. "And now we've got the chair working, we can handle most of the dental work on the spot. Only Ferguson needs more amalgam."

"I know," said the inspector patiently, "but the money has to come from somewhere — you must realize that. We're not a rich community, in spite of what

people think. And these unauthorized requests — oh,
we fill them, of course, but — "

"Ferguson needs more amalgam," said Doc Mellhorn. "And that last batch wasn't standard. I wouldn't
use it on a dog."

"He's always needing more amalgam!" said the inspector bitterly, making a note. "Is he going to fill every
tooth in Hades? By the way, my wife tells me I need
a little work done myself — but we won't go into that.
We'll take just one thing — your entirely unauthorized
employment of Miss Smith. Miss Smith has no business
working for you. She's supposed to be gnawed by a
never-dying worm every Monday, Wednesday and
Friday."

"Sounds silly to me," said Doc Mellhorn.

"I don't care how silly it sounds," said the inspector.
"It's regulations. And, besides, she isn't even a registered nurse."

"She's a practical one," said Doc Mellhorn. "Of
course, back on earth a lot of her patients died. But
that was because when she didn't like a patient, she
poisoned him. Well, she can't poison anybody here and
I've kind of got her out of the notion of it anyway.
She's been doing A-1 work for me and I'd like to
recommend her for — "

"Please!" said the inspector. "Please! And as if that
wasn't enough, you've even been meddling with the
staff. I've a note here on young Asmodeus — Asmodeus
XIV — "

"Oh, you mean Mickey!" said Doc Mellhorn, with a

chuckle. "Short for Mickey Mouse. We call him that in the clinic. And he's a young imp if I ever saw one."

"The original Asmodeus is one of our most prominent citizens," said the inspector severely. "How do you suppose he felt when we got your report that his fourteenth great-grandson had rickets?"

"Well," said Doc Mellhorn, "I know rickets. And he had 'em. And you're going to have rickets in these youngsters as long as you keep feeding 'em low-grade coke. I put Mickey on the best Pennsylvania anthracite, and look at him now!"

"I admit the success of your treatment," said the inspector, "but, naturally — well, since then we've been deluged with demands for anthracite from as far south as Sheol. We'll have to float a new bond issue. And what will the taxpayers say?"

"He was just cutting his first horns when he came to us," said Doc Mellhorn reminiscently, "and they were coming in crooked. Now, I ask you, did you ever see a straighter pair? Of course, if I'd had cod liver oil — My gracious, you ought to have somebody here that can fill a prescription; I can't do it all."

The inspector shut his papers together with a snap. "I'm sorry, Doctor Mellhorn," he said, "but this is final. You have no right here, in the first place; no local license to practice in the second — "

"Yes, that's a little irregular," said Doc Mellhorn, "but I'm a registered member of four different medical associations — you might take that into account. And I'll take any examination that's required."

"No," said the inspector violently. "No, no, no!

You can't stay here! You've got to go away! It isn't possible!"

Doc Mellhorn drew a long breath. "Well," he said, "there wasn't any work for me at the other place. And here you won't let me practice. So what's a man to do?"

The inspector was silent.

"Tell me," said Doc Mellhorn presently. "Suppose you do throw me out? What happens to Miss Smith and Paisley and the rest of them?"

"Oh, what's done is done," said the inspector impatiently, "here as well as anywhere else. We'll have to keep on with the anthracite and the rest of it. And Hades only knows what'll happen in the future. If it's any satisfaction to you, you've started something."

"Well, I guess Smith and Ferguson between them can handle the practice," said Doc Mellhorn. "But that's got to be a promise."

"It's a promise," said the inspector.

"Then there's Mickey — I mean Asmodeus," said Doc Mellhorn. "He's a smart youngster — smart as a whip — if he is a hellion. Well, you know how a youngster gets. Well, it seems he wants to be a doctor. But I don't know what sort of training he'd get — "

"He'll get it," said the inspector feverishly. "We'll found the finest medical college you ever saw, right here in West Baal. We'll build a hospital that'll knock your eye out. You'll be satisfied. But now, if you don't mind — "

"All right," said Doc Mellhorn, and rose.

The inspector looked surprised. "But don't you want to — " he said. "I mean my instructions are we're to give you a banquet, if necessary — after all, the community appreciates — "

"Thanks," said Doc Mellhorn, with a shudder, "but if I've got to go, I'd rather get out of town. You hang around and announce your retirement, and pretty soon folks start thinking they ought to give you a testimonial. And I never did like testimonials."

All the same, before he left he took a silver half dollar out of Mickey Asmodeus' chin.

When he was back on the road again and the lights of the gates had faded into a low ruddy glow behind him, Doc Mellhorn felt alone for the first time. He'd been lonely at times during his life, but he'd never felt alone like this before. Because, as far as he could see, there was only him and Lizzie now.

"Now, maybe if I'd talked to Aesculapius — " he said. "But pshaw, I always was pigheaded."

He didn't pay much attention to the way he was driving and it seemed to him that the road wasn't quite the same. But he felt tired for a wonder — bone-tired and beaten — and he didn't much care about the road. He hadn't felt tired since he left earth, but now the loneliness tired him.

"Active — always been active," he said to himself. "I can't just lay down on the job. But what's a man to do?"

"What's a man to do?" he said. "I'm a doctor. I can't work miracles."

Then the black fit came over him and he remembered all the times he'd been wrong and all the people he couldn't do anything for. "Never was much of a doctor, I guess," he said. "Maybe, if I'd gone to Vienna. Well, the right kind of man would have gone. And about that Bigelow kid," he said. "How was I to know he'd hemorrhage? But I should have known.

"I've diagnosed walking typhoid as appendicitis. Just the once, but that's enough. And I still don't know what held me back when I was all ready to operate. I used to wake up in a sweat, six months afterward, thinking I had.

"I could have saved those premature twins, if I'd known as much then as I do now. I guess that guy Dafoe would have done it anyway — look at what he had to work with. But I didn't. And that finished the Gorhams' having children. That's a dandy doctor, isn't it? Makes you feel fine.

"I could have pulled Old Man Halsey through. And Edna Biggs. And the little Lauriat girl. No, I couldn't have done it with her. That was before insulin. I couldn't have cured Ted Allen. No, I'm clear on that. But I've never been satisfied about the Collins woman. Bates is all right — good as they come. But I knew her, inside and out — ought to, too — she was the biggest nuisance that ever came into the office. And if I hadn't been down with the flu . . .

"Then there's the flu epidemic. I didn't take my clothes off, four days and nights. But what's the good of that, when you lose them? Oh, sure, the statistics looked good. You can have the statistics.

"Should have started raising hell about the water supply two years before I did.

"Oh, yes, it makes you feel fine, pulling babies into

the world. Makes you feel you're doing something. And just fine when you see a few of them, twenty-thirty years later, not worth two toots on a cow's horn. Can't say I ever delivered a Dillinger. But there's one or two in state's prison. And more that ought to be. Don't mind even that so much as a few of the fools. Makes you wonder.

"And then, there's incurable cancer. That's a daisy. What can you do about it, Doctor? Well, Doctor, we can alleviate the pain in the last stages. Some. Ever been in a cancer ward, Doctor? Yes, Doctor, I have.

"What do you do for the common cold, Doctor? Two dozen clean linen handkerchiefs. Yes, it's a good joke — I'll laugh. And what do you do for a boy when you know he's dying, Doctor? Take a silver half dollar out of his ear. But it kept the Lane kid quiet and his fever went down that night. I took the credit, but I don't know why it went down.

"I've only got one brain. And one pair of hands.

"I could have saved. I could have done. I could have.

"Guess it's just as well you can't live forever. You make fewer mistakes. And sometimes I'd see Bates looking at me as if he wondered why I ever thought I could practice.

"Pigheaded, opinionated, ineffective old imbecile! And yet, Lord, Lord, I'd do it all over again."

He lifted his eyes from the pattern of the road in front of him. There were white markers on it now and Lizzie seemed to be bouncing down a residential street. There were trees in the street and it reminded him of town. He rubbed his eyes for a second and Lizzie rolled on by herself — she often did. It didn't seem strange to him to stop at the right house.

"Well, Mother," he said rather gruffly to the group on the lawn. "Well, Dad. . . . Well, Uncle Frank." He beheld a small, stern figure advancing, hands out-stretched. "Well, Grandma," he said meekly.

Later on he was walking up and down in the grape arbor with Uncle Frank. Now and then he picked a grape and ate it. They'd always been good grapes, those Catawbas, as he remembered them.

"What beats me," he said, not for the first time, "is why I didn't notice the Gates. The second time, I mean."

"Oh, that Gate," said Uncle Frank, with the easy, unctuous roll in his voice that Doc Mellhorn so well remembered. He smoothed his handle-bar mustaches. "That Gate, my dear Edward — well, of course it has to be there in the first place. Literature, you know. And then, it's a choice," he said richly.

"I'll draw cards," said Doc Mellhorn. He ate another grape.

"Fact is," said Uncle Frank, "that Gate's for one kind of person. You pass it and then you can rest for all eternity. Just fold your hands. It suits some."

"I can see that it would," said Doc Mellhorn.

"Yes," said Uncle Frank, "but it wouldn't suit a Mellhorn. I'm happy to say that very few of our family remain permanently on that side. I spent some time there myself." He said, rather self-consciously, "Well, my last years had been somewhat stormy. So few people

cared for refined impersonations of our feathered song-
sters, including lightning sketches. I felt that I'd earned
a rest. But after a while — well, I got tired of being at
liberty."

"And what happens when you get tired?" said Doc
Mellhorn.

"You find out what you want to do," said Uncle
Frank.

"My kind of work?" said Doc Mellhorn.

"Your kind of work," said his uncle. "Been busy,
haven't you?"

"Well," said Doc Mellhorn. "But here. If there isn't
so much as a case of mumps in — "

"Would it have to be mumps?" said his uncle. "Of
course, if you're aching for mumps, I guess it could be
arranged. But how many new souls do you suppose we
get here a day?"

"Sizable lot, I expect."

"And how many of them get here in first-class condition?" said Uncle Frank triumphantly. "Why, I've
seen Doctor Rush — Benjamin Rush — come back so
tired from a day's round he could hardly flap one pinion
against the other. Oh, if it's work you want — And
then, of course, there's the earth."

"Hold on," said Doc Mellhorn. "I'm not going to
appear to any young intern in wings and a harp. Not at
my time of life. And anyway, he'd laugh himself sick."

" 'Tain't that," said Uncle Frank. "Look here.
You've left children and grandchildren behind you,
haven't you? And they're going on?"

"Yes," said Doc Mellhorn.

"Same with what you did," said Uncle Frank. "I mean the inside part of it — that stays. I don't mean any funny business — voices in your ear and all that. But haven't you ever got clean tuckered out, and been able to draw on something you didn't know was there?"

"Pshaw, any man's done that," said Doc Mellhorn. "But you take the adrenal — "

"Take anything you like," said Uncle Frank placidly. "I'm not going to argue with you. Not my department. But you'll find it isn't all adrenalin. Like it here?" he said abruptly. "Feel satisfied?"

"Why, yes," said Doc Mellhorn surprisedly, "I do." He looked around the grape arbor and suddenly realized that he felt happy.

"No, they wouldn't all arrive in first-class shape," he said to himself. "So there'd be a place." He turned to Uncle Frank. "By the way," he said diffidently, "I mean, I got back so quick — there wouldn't be a chance of my visiting the other establishment now and then? Where I just came from? Smith and Ferguson are all right, but I'd like to keep in touch."

"Well," said Uncle Frank, "you can take that up with the delegation." He arranged the handkerchief in his breast pocket. "They ought to be along any minute now," he said. "Sister's been in a stew about it all day. She says there won't be enough chairs, but she always says that."

"Delegation?" said Doc Mellhorn. "But — "

"You don't realize," said Uncle Frank, with his rich chuckle. "You're a famous man. You've broken pretty near every regulation except the fire laws, and refused the Gate first crack. They've got to do something about it."

"But — " said Doc Mellhorn, looking wildly around for a place of escape.

"Sh-h!" hissed Uncle Frank. "Hold up your head and look as though money were bid for you. It won't take long — just a welcome." He shaded his eyes with his hand. "My," he said with frank admiration, "you've certainly brought them out. There's Rush, by the way."

"Where?" said Doc Mellhorn.

"Second from the left, third row, in a wig," said Uncle Frank. "And there's — "

Then he stopped, and stepped aside. A tall grave figure was advancing down the grape arbor — a bearded man with a wise, majestic face who wore robes as if they belonged to him, not as Doc Mellhorn had seen them worn in college commencements. There was a small fillet of gold about his head and in his left hand, Doc Mellhorn noticed without astonishment, was a winged staff entwined with two fangless serpents. Behind him were many others. Doc Mellhorn stood straighter.

The bearded figure stopped in front of Doc Mellhorn. "Welcome, Brother," said Aesculapius.

"It's an honor to meet you, Doctor," said Doc Mellhorn. He shook the outstretched hand. Then he took a silver half dollar from the mouth of the left-hand snake.

III

THE STORY ABOUT THE ANTEATER

THE younger child sat bolt upright, her bedclothes wrapped around her.

"If you're going down to look at them," she whispered accusingly, "I'm coming, too! And Alice'll catch you."

"She won't catch me." Her elder sister's voice was scornful. "She's out in the pantry, helping. With the man from Gray's."

"All the same, I'm coming. I want to see if it's ice cream in little molds or just the smashed kind with strawberries. And, if Alice won't catch you, she won't catch me."

"It'll be molds," said the other, from the depths of experience, "Mother always has molds for the Whitehouses. And Mr. Whitehouse sort of clicks in his throat and talks about sweets to the sweet. You'd think he'd know that's dopey but he doesn't. And, anyhow, it isn't your turn."

"It never is my turn," mourned her junior, tugging at the bedclothes.

"All right," said the elder. "If you *want* to go! And make a noise. And then they hear us and somebody comes up — "

"Sometimes they bring you things, when they come

149

up," said the younger dreamily. "The man with the pink face did. And he said I was a little angel."

"Was he dopey!" said her elder, blightingly, "and anyhow, you were sick afterwards and you know what Mother said about it."

The younger child sighed, a long sigh of defeat and resignation.

"All right," she said. "But next time it *is* my turn. And you tell me if it's in molds." Her elder nodded as she stole out of the door.

At the first turn of the stairs, a small landing offered an excellent observation post, provided one could get there unperceived. Jennifer Sharp reached it soundlessly and, curling herself up into the smallest possible space, stared eagerly down and across into the dining room.

She couldn't see the whole table. But she saw at once that Mrs. Whitehouse had a thing like a silver beetle in her hair, that Colonel Crandall looked more like a police dog than ever, and that there were little silver baskets of pink and white mints. That meant that it was really a grand dinner. She made a special note of the ice cream for Joan.

Talk and laughter drifted up to her — strange phrases and incomprehensible jests from another world, to be remembered, puzzled over, and analyzed for meaning or the lack of it, when she and Joan were alone. She hugged her knees, she was having a good time. Pretty soon, Father would light the little blue flame under the mysterious glass machine that made the coffee. She liked to see him do that.

She looked at him now, appraisingly. Colonel Crandall had fought Germans in trenches and Mr. Whitehouse had a bank to keep his money in. But Father, on the whole, was nicer than either of them. She remembered, as if looking back across a vast plain, when Father and Mother had merely been Father and Mother — huge, natural phenomena, beloved but inexplicable as the weather — unique of their kind. Now she was older — she knew that other people's fathers and mothers were different. Even Joan knew that, though Joan was still a great deal of a baby. Jennifer felt very old and rather benevolent as she considered herself and her parents and the babyishness of Joan.

Mr. Whitehouse was talking, but Father wanted to talk, too — she knew that from the quick little gesture he made with his left hand. Now they all laughed and Father leaned forward.

"That reminds me," he was saying, "of one of our favorite stories — " How young and amused his face looked, suddenly!

His eldest daughter settled back in the shadow, a bored but tolerant smile on her lips. She knew what was coming.

When Terry Farrell and Roger Sharp fell in love, the war to end war was just over, bobbed hair was still an issue, the movies did not talk and women's clothes couldn't be crazier. It was also generally admitted that the younger generation was wild but probably sound at heart and that, as soon as we got a businessman in the White House, things were going to be all right.

As for Terry and Roger, they were both wild and sophisticated. They would have told you so. Terry had been kissed by several men at several dances and Roger could remember the curious, grimy incident of the girl at Fort Worth. So that showed you. They were entirely emancipated and free. But they fell in love very simply and unexpectedly — and their marriage was going to be like no other marriage, because they knew all the right answers to all the questions, and had no intention of submitting to the commonplaces of life. At first, in fact, they were going to form a free union — they had read of that, in popular books of the period. But, somehow or other, as soon as Roger started to call, both families began to get interested. They had no idea of paying the slightest attention to their families. But, when your family happens to comment favorably on the man or girl that you are in love with, that is a hard thing to fight. Before they knew it, they were formally engaged, and liking it on the whole, though both of them agreed that a formal engagement was an outworn and ridiculous social custom.

They quarreled often enough, for they were young, and a trifle ferocious in the vehemence with which they expressed the views they knew to be right. These views had to do, in general, with freedom and personality, and were often supported by quotations from *The Golden Bough*. Neither of them had read *The Golden Bough* all the way through, but both agreed that it was a great book. But the quarrels were about generalities and had no sting. And always, before and after, was the sense of discovering in each other previously unsuspected but delightful potentialities and likenesses and beliefs.

As a matter of fact, they were quite a well-suited couple — "made for each other," as the saying used to go; though they would have hooted at the idea. They had read the minor works of Havelock Ellis and knew the name of Freud. They didn't believe in people being "made for each other" — they were too advanced.

It was ten days before the date set for their marriage that their first real quarrel occurred. And then, unfortunately, it didn't stop at generalities.

They had got away for the day from the presents and their families, to take a long walk in the country, with a picnic lunch. Both, in spite of themselves, were a little solemn, a little nervous. The atmosphere of Approaching Wedding weighed on them both — when their hands touched, the current ran, but, when they looked at each other, they felt strange. Terry had been shopping the day before — she was tired, she began to wish that Roger would not walk so fast. Roger was wondering if the sixth usher — the one who had been in the marines — would really turn up. His mind also held dark suspicions as to the probable behavior of the best man, when it came to such outworn customs as rice and shoes. They were sure that they were in love, sure now, that they wanted to be married. But their conversation was curiously polite.

The lunch did something for them, so did the peace of being alone. But they had forgotten the salt and Terry had rubbed her heel. When Roger got out his pipe, there was only tobacco left for half a smoke. Still, the wind was cool and the earth pleasant and, as they sat with their backs against a gray boulder in the middle of a green field, they began to think more naturally. The current between their linked hands ran stronger — in a moment or two, they would be the selves they had always known.

It was, perhaps, unfortunate that Roger should have selected that particular moment in which to tell the anteater story.

He knocked out his pipe and smiled, suddenly, at something in his mind. Terry felt a knock at her heart, a sudden sweetness on her tongue — how young and amused he always looked when he smiled! She smiled back at him, her whole face changing.

"What is it, darling?" she said.

He laughed. "Oh nothing," he said. "I just happened to remember. Did you ever hear the story about the anteater?"

She shook her head.

"Well," he began. "Oh, you must have heard it — sure you haven't? Well, anyway, there was a little town down South . . .

"And the coon said, 'Why, lady, that ain't no anteater — that's Edward!'" he finished, triumphantly, a few moments later. He couldn't help laughing when he had finished — the silly tale always amused him, old as it was. Then he looked at Terry and saw that she was not laughing.

"Why, what's the matter?" he said, mechanically. "Are you cold, dear, or — "

Her·hand, which had been slowly stiffening in his clasp, now withdrew itself entirely from his.

"No" she said, staring ahead of her, "I'm all right. Thanks."

He looked at her. There was somebody there he had never seen before.

"Well," he said, confusedly, "well." Then his mouth set, his jaw stuck out, he also regarded the landscape.

Terry stole a glance at him. It was terrible and appalling to see him sitting there, looking bleak and estranged. She wanted to speak, to throw herself at him, to say: "Oh, it's all my fault — it's all my fault!" and know the luxury of saying it. Then she remembered the anteater and her heart hardened.

It was not even, she told herself sternly, as if it were a dirty story. It wasn't — and, if it had been, weren't they always going to be frank and emancipated with each other about things like that? But it was just the kind of story she'd always hated — cruel and — yes — vulgar. Not even healthily vulgar — vulgar with no redeeming adjective. He ought to have known she hated that kind of story. He ought to have known!

If love meant anything, according to the books, it meant understanding the other person, didn't it? And, if you didn't understand them, in such a little thing, why, what was life going to be afterwards? Love was like a new silver dollar — bright, untarnished and whole. There could be no possible compromises with love.

All these confused but vehement thoughts flashed through her mind. She also knew that she was tired and wind-blown and jumpy and that the rub on her heel was a little red spot of pain. And then Roger was speaking.

"I'm sorry you found my story so unamusing," he said in stiff tones of injury and accusation. "If I'd known about the way you felt, I'd have tried to tell a funnier one — even if we did say —"

He stopped, his frozen face turned toward her. She could feel the muscles of her own face tighten and freeze in answer.

"I wasn't in the *least* shocked, I assure you," she said in the same, stilted voice. "I just didn't think it was very funny. That's all."

"I get you. Well, pardon my glove," he said, and turned to the landscape.

A little pulse of anger began to beat in her wrist. Something was being hurt, something was being broken. If he'd only been Roger and kissed her instead of saying — well, it was his fault, now.

"No, I didn't think it was funny at all," she said, in a voice whose sharpness surprised her, "if you want to know. Just sort of cruel and common and — well, the poor Negro — "

"That's right!" he said, in a voice of bitter irritation, "pity the coon! Pity everybody but the person who's trying to amuse you! I think it's a damn funny story — always have — and — "

They were both on their feet and stabbing at each other, now.

"And it's vulgar," she was saying, hotly, "plain vulgar — not even dirty enough to be funny. Anteater indeed! Why, Roger Sharp, it's — "

"Where's that sense of humor you were always talking about?" he was shouting. "My God, what's happened to you, Terry? I always thought you were — and here you — "

"Well, we both of us certainly seem to have been mistaken about each other," she could hear her strange voice, saying. Then, even more dreadfully, came his unfamiliar accents, "Well, if that's the way you feel about it, we certainly have."

They looked at each other, aghast. "Here!" she was saying, "here! Oh, Lord, why won't it come off my finger?"

"You keep that on — do you hear, you damn little fool?" he roared at her, so unexpectedly that she started, tripped, caught her shoe in a cleft of rock, fell awkwardly, and, in spite of all her resolves, burst undignifiedly and conventionally into a passion of tears.

Then there was the reconciliation. It took place, no doubt, on entirely conventional lines, and was studded with "No, it was my fault! Say it was!" but, to them it was an event unique in history.

Terry thought it over remorsefully, that evening, waiting for Roger. Roger was right. She had been a little fool. She knew the inexplicable solace of feeling that she had been a little fool.

And yet, they had said those things to each other, and meant them. He had hurt her, she had actually meant to hurt him. She stared at these facts, solemnly.

Love, the bright silver dollar. Not like the commonplace coins in other people's pockets. But something special, different — already a little, ever-so-faintly tarnished, as a pane is tarnished by breath?

She had been a little fool. But she couldn't quite forget the anteater.

Then she was in Roger's arms — and knew, with utter confidence, that she and Roger were different. They were always going to be different. Their marriage wouldn't ever be like any other marriage in the world.

The Sharps had been married for exactly six years and five hours and Terry, looking across the table at the clever, intelligent face of her affectionate and satisfactory husband, suddenly found herself most desolately alone.

It had been a mistake in the first place — going to the Lattimores for dinner on their own anniversary. Mr. Lattimore was the head of Roger's company — Mrs. Lattimore's invitation had almost the force of a royal command. They had talked it over, Roger and she, and decided, sensibly, that they couldn't get out of it. But, all the same, it had been a mistake.

They were rational, modern human beings, she assured herself ferociously. They weren't like the horrible married couples in the cartoons — the little woman asking her baffled mate if he remembered what date it was, and the rest of it. They thought better of life and love than to tie either of them to an artificial scheme of days. They were different. Nevertheless, there had been a time when they had said to each other, with foolish smiles, "We've been married a week — or a month — or a year! Just think of it!" This time now seemed to her, as she looked back on it coldly, a geologic age away.

She considered Roger with odd dispassionateness. Yes, there he was — an intelligent, rising young man in his first thirties. Not particularly handsome but indubitably attractive — charming, when he chose — a loyal friend, a good father, a husband one could take pride in. And it seemed to her that if he made that nervous little gesture with his left hand again — or told the anteater story — she would scream.

It was funny that the knowledge that you had lost everything that you had most counted upon should come to you at a formal dinner party, while you talked over the war days with a dark-haired officer whose voice had the honey of the South in it. Then she remembered that she and Roger had first discovered their love for each other, not upon a moon-swept lawn, but in the fly-specked waiting room of a minor railroad station — and the present event began to seem less funny. Life was like that. It gave, unexpectedly, abruptly, with no regard for stage setting or the properties of romance. And, as unexpectedly and abruptly, it took away.

While her mouth went on talking, a part of her mind searched numbly and painfully for the reasons which had brought this calamity about. They had loved each other in the beginning — even now, she was sure of that. They had tried to be wise, they had not broken faith, they had been frank and gay. No deep division of nature sundered them — no innate fault in either, spreading under pressure, to break the walls of their house apart. She looked for a guilty party but she could find none. There was only a progression of days; a succession of tiny events that followed in each others' footsteps without haste or rest. That was all, but that seemed to have been enough. And Roger was looking over at her — with that same odd, exploring glance she had used a moment ago.

What remained? A house with a little boy asleep in it, a custom of life, certain habits, certain memories, certain hardships lived through together. Enough for most people, perhaps? They had wanted more than that.

Something said to her, "Well and if — after all — the real thing hasn't even come?" She turned to her dinner partner, for the first time really seeing him. When you did see him, he was quite a charming person. His voice was delightful. There was nothing in him in the least like Roger Sharp.

She laughed and saw, at the laugh, something wake in his eyes. He, too, had not been really conscious of her, before. But he was, now. She was not thirty, yet — she had kept her looks. She felt old powers, old states of mind flow back to her; things she had thought forgotten, the glamor of first youth. Somewhere, on the curve of a dark lake, a boat was drifting — a man was talking to her — she could not see his face but she knew it was not Roger's —

She was roused from her waking dream by Mrs. Lattimore's voice.

"Why, I'd never have dreamt!" Mrs. Lattimore was saying "I had no idea!" She called down the table,

"George! Do you know it's these people's anniversary — so sweet of them to come — and I positively had to worm it out of Mr. Sharp!"

Terry went hot and cold all over. She was sensible, she was brokenhearted, love was a myth, but she had particularly depended on Roger not to tell anybody that this was their anniversary. And Roger had told.

She lived through the congratulations and the customary jokes about "Well, this is your seventh year beginning — and you know what they say about the seventh year!" She even lived through Mrs. Lattimore's pensive "Six years! Why, my dear, I never would have believed it! You're children — positive children!"

She could have bitten Mrs. Lattimore. "Children!" she thought, indignantly, "When I — when we — when everything's in ruins!" She tried to freeze Roger, at long distance, but he was not looking her way. And then she caught her breath, for a worse fate was in store for her.

Someone, most unhappily, had brought up the subject of pet animals. She saw a light break slowly on Roger's face — she saw him lean forward. She prayed for the roof to fall, for time to stop, for Mrs. Lattimore to explode like a Roman candle into green and purple stars. But, even as she prayed, she knew that it was no use. Roger was going to tell the anteater story.

The story no longer seemed shocking to her, or even cruel. But it epitomized all the years of her life with Roger. In the course of those years, she calculated desperately, she had heard that story at least a hundred times.

Somehow — she never knew how — she managed to

survive the hundred-and-first recital, from the hideously familiar, "Well, there was a little town down South . . ." to the jubilant "That's Edward!" at the end. She even summoned up a fixed smile to meet the tempest of laughter that followed. And then, mercifully, Mrs. Lattimore was giving the signal to rise.

The men hung behind — the anteater story had been capped by another. Terry found herself, unexpectedly, tête-à-tête with Mrs. Lattimore.

"My dear," the great lady was saying, "I'd rather have asked you another night, of course, if I'd known. But I am very glad you could come tonight. George particularly wished Mr. Colden to meet your brilliant husband. They are going into that Western project together, you know, and Tom Colden leaves tomorrow. So we both appreciate your kindness in coming."

Terry found a sudden queer pulse of warmth through the cold fog that seemed to envelop her. "Oh," she stammered, "but Roger and I have been married for years — and we were delighted to come — " She looked at the older woman. "Tell me, though," she said, with an irrepressible burst of confidence, "doesn't it ever seem to you as if you couldn't bear to hear a certain story again — not if you *died?*"

A gleam of mirth appeared in Mrs. Lattimore's eyes.

"My dear," she said "has George ever told you about his trip to Peru?"

"No."

"Well, don't let him." She reflected, "or, no — d· let him," she said. "Poor George — he does get such fu·

out of it. And you would be a new audience. But it happened fifteen years ago, my dear, and I think I could repeat every word after him verbatim, once he's started. Even so — I often feel as if he'd never stop."

"And then what do you do?" said Terry, breathlessly — far too interested now to remember tact.

The older woman smiled. "I think of the story I am going to tell about the guide in the Uffizi gallery," she said. "George must have heard that story ten thousand times. But he's still alive."

She put her hand on the younger woman's arm.

"We're all of us alike, my dear," she said. "When I'm an old lady in a wheel chair, George will still be telling me about Peru. But then, if he didn't, I wouldn't know he was George."

She turned away, leaving Terry to ponder over the words. Her anger was not appeased — her life still lay about her in ruins. But, when the dark young officer came into the room, she noticed that his face seemed rather commonplace and his voice was merely a pleasant voice.

Mr. Colden's car dropped the Sharps at their house. The two men stayed at the gate for a moment, talking — Terry ran in to see after the boy. He was sleeping peacefully with his fists tight shut; he looked like Roger in his sleep. Suddenly, all around her were the familiar sights and sounds of home. She felt tired and as if she had come back from a long journey.

She went downstairs. Roger was just coming in. He looked tired, too, she noticed, but exultant as well.

"Colden had to run," he said at once. "Left good-by

for you — hoped you wouldn't mind — said awfully nice things. He's really a great old boy, Terry. And, as for this new Western business — "

He noticed the grave look on her face and his own grew grave.

"I *am* sorry, darling," he said. "Did you mind it a lot? Well, I did — but it couldn't be helped. You bet your life that next time — "

"Oh, next time — " she said, and kissed him. "Of course I didn't mind. We're different, aren't we?"

That intelligent matron, Mrs. Roger Sharp, now seated at the foot of her own dinner table, from time to time made the appropriate interjections — the "Really?"'s and "Yes indeed"'s and "That's what I always tell Roger"'s — which comprised the whole duty of a hostess in Colonel Crandall's case. Colonel Crandall was singularly restful — give him these few crumbs and he could be depended upon to talk indefinitely and yet without creating a conversational desert around him. Mrs. Sharp was very grateful to him at the moment. She wanted to retire to a secret place in her mind and observe her own dinner party, for an instant, as a spectator — and Colonel Crandall was giving her the chance.

It was going very well indeed. She had hoped for it from the first, but now she was sure of it and she gave a tiny, inaudible sigh of relief. Roger was at his best — the young Durwards had recovered from their initial shyness — Mr. Whitehouse had not yet started talking politics — the soufflé had been a success. She relaxed a little and let her mind drift off upon other things.

Tomorrow, Roger must remember about the light gray suit, she must make a dental appointment for Jennifer, Mrs. Quaritch must be dealt with tactfully in the matter of the committee. It was too early to decide about camp for the girls but Roger Junior must know they were proud of his marks, and if Mother intended to give up her trip just because of poor old Miss Tompkins — well, something would have to be done. There were also the questions of the new oil furnace, the School board and the Brewster wedding. But none of these really bothered her — her life was always busy — and, at the moment, she felt an unwonted desire to look back into Time.

Over twenty years since the Armistice. Twenty years. And Roger Junior was seventeen — and she and Roger had been married since nineteen-twenty. Pretty soon they would be celebrating their twentieth anniversary. It seemed incredible but it was true.

She looked back through those years, seeing an ever-younger creature with her own face, a creature that laughed or wept for forgotten reasons, ran wildly here, sat solemn as a young judge there. She felt a pang of sympathy for that young heedlessness, a pang of humor as well. She was not old but she had been so very young.

Roger and she — the beginning — the first years — Roger Junior's birth. The house on Edgehill Road, the one with the plate rail in the dining room, and crying when they left because they'd never be so happy again, but they had, and it was an inconvenient house. Being jealous of Milly Baldwin — and how foolish! — and the awful country-club dance where Roger got drunk; and it wasn't awful any more. The queer, piled years of the boom — the crash — the bad time — Roger coming home after Tom Colden's suicide and the look on his face. Jennifer. Joan. Houses. People. Events. And always the headlines in the papers, the voices on the radio, dinning, dinning "No security — trouble — disaster — no security." And yet, out of insecurity, they had loved and made children. Out of insecurity, for the space of breath, for an hour, they had built, and now and then found peace.

No, there's no guarantee, she thought. There's no guarantee. When you're young, you think there is, but there isn't. And yet I'd do it over. Pretty soon we'll have been married twenty years.

"Yes, that's what I always tell Roger," she said, automatically. Colonel Crandall smiled and proceeded. He was still quite handsome, she thought, in his dark way, but he was getting very bald. Roger's hair had a few gray threads in it but it was still thick and unruly. She liked men to keep their hair. She remembered, a long while ago, thinking something or other about Colonel Crandall's voice, but she could not remember what she had thought.

She noticed a small white speck on the curve of the stairway but said nothing. The wrapper was warm and, if Jennifer wasn't noticed, she would creep back to bed soon enough. It was different with Joan.

Suddenly, she was alert. Mrs. Durward, at Roger's end of the table, had mentioned the Zoo. She knew what that meant — Zoo — the new buildings — the new Housing Commissioner — and Mr. Whitehouse let loose on his favorite political grievance all through the end of dinner. She caught Roger's eye for a miraculous instant. Mr. Whitehouse was already clearing his throat. But Roger had the signal. Roger would save them. She saw his left hand tapping in its little gesture — felt him suddenly draw the party together. How young and amused his face looked, under the candlelight!

"That reminds me of one of our favorite stories," he was saying. She sank back in her chair. A deep content pervaded her. He was going to tell the anteater story — and, even if some of the people had heard it, they would have to laugh, he always told it so well. She smiled in anticipation of the triumphant "That's Edward!" And, after that, if Mr. Whitehouse still threatened, she herself would tell the story about Joan and the watering pot.

Jennifer crept back into the darkened room.

"Well?" said an eager whisper from the other bed.

Jennifer drew a long breath. The memory of the lighted dinner table rose before her, varicolored, glittering, portentous — a stately omen — a thing of splendor and mystery, to be pondered upon for days. How could she ever make Joan see it as she had seen it? And Joan was such a baby, anyway.

"Oh — nobody saw me," she said, in a bored voice. "But it was in molds, that's all — oh yes — and Father told the anteater story again."

A LIFE AT ANGELO'S

I DON'T know why everybody keeps on going to Angelo's. The drinks aren't any better — in fact, they're a little worse, if anything — and the dinner never was much. I'm getting so I can hardly look a sardine in the eye any more.

Of course it's a quiet place, and they don't let in many college boys. It's generally just the old crowd from five o'clock on. Oh, people come and go naturally — the way they do in New York. If they didn't, I don't suppose Angelo could keep on running. But what I mean is, you can drop in almost any time after curfew and find somebody you know to have a quick one or a couple of quick ones with. And then, if that's your weakness, you can stay and get dinner; though I wish they'd try another brand of sardines.

Suppose everyone stopped coming, all at once? Or suppose the place closed? I don't like to think about that. I suppose it's bound to happen, sooner or later, when Angelo's made his pile — they always go back to Italy. Then there'll be all the trouble and bother of finding another place; and the crowd won't be the same. You can't keep a crowd together, once you move the place, in New York. It seems pretty safe, though, at the moment, I'm glad to say. There's never been any real trouble, you see; no one ever gets shot at Angelo's, and

168

when the visiting firemen get too noisy, Rocco just eases them out. Rocco's the little one with the grin, and he doesn't look strong, but how he can ease a fellow out when it's necessary! He did it to me only once, and I've never held it against him. That was just after Evie and I had broken up.

No, I don't think there's any need to worry for a while yet. And when there is, I'm sure Angelo will tell me about it far enough ahead so I can make my arrangements. After all, I'm one of his oldest customers. I don't go back to the Twelfth Street place, the way Mr. Forman does, but seven years is a long time in this man's town. They're easing Mr. Forman out at 11:30 these days. It used to be all hours when I first knew him, but a man can't expect to drink like that at his age and not show it in the whites of the eyes. That's another thing I have against all this changing around. You get started going from one place to another and buying taxis and going in for general snake dancing; and before you know where you are you're on a party, and the whole next day is bad. Well, now, if you work at all, you can't afford to have the week days go bad on you. I'm not talking of Saturday night — there's a law about that. And of course those impromptu harvest homes are a lot of fun when you're young and new to the town. But when you've had a little sense knocked into you you're a fool if you don't run on schedule. Isn't that so?

Now, at Angelo's, you always know where you are. A couple of quick ones or so before dinner, and the red at dinner — or the white, if you're dining with a girl. Then a little touch after the coffee and a couple of long ones and a nightcap, and home at twelve by the old college clock. And all the time you're talking with somebody you know — about their wives, or their husbands, or religion, or the market, or what's new in the crowd — just rational conversation and maybe a little quiet singing, like "Work is the Curse of the Drinking Classes." Sometimes Mr. Forman sits down and tells one of his long stories, but generally he'd rather stand at the bar. And sometimes the whole crowd clicks, and sometimes it doesn't, and sometimes that Page girl gets started on her imitations.

But anyway, it's something you're used to, and you're doing it again, and it's warm, and you know the people, and you don't have to go home. And Angelo's there, getting a little fatter and sleeker every year, and with a little bigger white edge around his waistcoat. Now and then he'll set up some *strega* for you, if he's feeling right. I don't like *strega* myself, but it would hurt his feelings to refuse. And then, in summer, there's the little back garden, and the fat cat that always has kittens, and the pink shades on the lamps. Rocco will be telling you the fish is ver' fine — and you know it isn't, but who cares? — and you can sit and watch the lights in the skyscrapers and hear the roar of the town, going by outside. You don't have to think at all. It's restful that way.

I can remember when I used to think a lot. And wonder about the people who came to places like Angelo's, and who they were, and why they came, and what they did with the rest of their time. I used to make up stories about them, going back to the apartment with Evie, and we'd both get excited over them; and forget to turn off at our own corner, we were talking so hard. That was when everybody we met was brand-new and bound to be interesting, and it was fun going to shows together in the gallery and having pancakes afterward at Childs'. I was always going to write some of those stories down, and she helped me make notes of them. I found the start of the one about Mr. Forman the other day. Well, what was the percentage in keeping it? I've seen a good deal of this writing racket since; and I ought to know what will sell and what won't. And anyhow, I'd just made him an old soak, and he's really a pretty interesting man.

Besides, that's something you get over. Wondering, I mean. Once you're on a normal schedule, you don't have time. I used to think it was funny — meeting people the way you do and having them tell you all sorts of inside things, the way it happens, and yet not really knowing them or tying them up with anything outside. But that's stopped bothering me. You just have to let them come and go, or it breaks the charm.

Going home to dinner with Jim Hewitt was what cured me, finally. I never met a fellow I liked better at Angelo's, and we told our real names. So, when he suggested breaking the family bread one evening, I took him up. Good Lord, he lived at Scarsdale and they had three children! The baby was sounding off like a police siren as we came in, and we had one round of weak orange blossoms before the fodder. Mrs. Hewitt liked orange blossoms. Then, afterward, we sat around and played three-handed bridge and Mrs. Hewitt and Jim discussed the squeak in the car. I couldn't have stayed all night; I'd have had the mimies. Jim was sort of ritzy for a while after that, but he got all right again, finally. I guess they must have hitched up the sled dogs and moved north to White Plains or something, for I haven't seen him in I don't now how long.

Of course, now and then something comes along that you have to take notice of. People get married or divorced, and Angelo will always open a bottle of champagne, no matter which it is, if they're really old customers. I remember the party the crowd of us gave to cheer up Helen Ashland when she heard about Jake's remarriage. She certainly took it like a sport — we were thinking up funny telegrams to send the bridal couple all evening. I don't believe she really had hysterics either. That was just Bing Otis' idea. And she couldn't have meant it when she said she hated us — she'd always been the life of the crowd. Anyhow, I think she got married again last year — somebody was broadcasting about it. If she ever comes back to Angelo's, I'll have to get the low-down.

That's another thing about the crowd — the way they stick together when anything happens. I'll never forget the night Ted Harrison went out. Of course, he'd been going into reverse for quite a while, and whenever he got particularly sunk, he'd talk about doing a one-way jump through a window; but we knew Ted and just kidded him along. So when he did do it, after all, it was mean. Anyhow, he had the sense not to stage his act at Angelo's.

We went to the service afterward — those of us that could. That's what I mean by all of us sticking together. It was one of those gray winter days, and cold. There was a little boy, and he was crying. I don't see why they brought him there. I didn't know Ted had a boy. I know the rest of Ted's family sort of upstaged us. But we felt we ought to be there; though it was funny how little you could remember about Ted except parties. Well, there isn't much to those services, the way I look at it. But then we went back to Angelo's and he was fine.

Evie never took to Angelo's somehow, even at first. She felt she had to like the dinner, because it was cheap, but the atmosphere of the place never really appealed to her. She liked going to places where there was music or where somebody famous might be sitting at the next table. Of course, it was generally an out-of-town buyer or a cloak model, really, but she got just as big a kick out of pretending. We used to have dinner home a lot, too, that first year. It's wonderful how much food you can get for the money, living like that. Though, of course, it's really cheaper for me to eat at Angelo's, now I'm alone.

I've thought sometimes of getting a regular maid or one of those Japs who just come in and get dinner and clear away. There'd be money enough, for Evie never would take alimony, and now she's married again she doesn't need it anyway. But then, what would you do after dinner? You can't go to the movies every night in the week, and a man who works all day needs some relaxation.

When Evie and I were married, we used to go to all sorts of places — we even went to museums on Sundays and to those concerts they have way uptown. But there's not much point in doing that sort of thing by yourself. And if you start trotting a girl around, why, anybody knows how that finishes. You may not mean to get hooked up together at all, but some little thing happens and you're in for it, one way or the other. And if it's one way, you're bound to feel like a bum sooner or later, while if it's the other — well, I've been married to Evie, and once is enough. I'm not going to repeat at my age. This child is too wise.

Now, you can see as much of a girl as you like at Angelo's, and that's all right because you're both part of the crowd. You've got protection, if you see what I mean. And even if you should stop playing for matches, it wouldn't mean much to either of you. We're all pretty modern in the crowd and we understand about things like that. Of course, we've had some fairly wild birds at one time or another, and I don't say I agree with all the talk I hear. But there's no use being Victorian, like people were in 1910. You just have to be wise.

It's queer, though — you certainly couldn't call Evie Victorian. And yet she never genuinely fitted in with the crowd. She wasn't a gloom either, or a bluenose; she was really awfully pretty and the kind of girl that everybody likes right off. Why, Mr. Forman took a great shine to her and used to come over and sit at our table and tell her how he wished he had a daughter her age. But she just couldn't stand him. She said it was

the look of his hands. Now, when anybody's been drinking for thirty semesters or so, like Mr. Forman, I think
they're lucky if they have any hands at all. And if they
do remind you of an alligator-skin bag, you ought to
overlook it and be broad-minded. But Evie simply
couldn't see it that way.

She was always wanting us to make friends with
other young married people, even when they lived up
by Grant's Tomb, where the climate's different. Well,
that's all right, but once you go in for that sort of
thing, you might as well stay in Waynesburg. That's
what I kept telling her: "This is New York," I said,
"this is New York." Let the Weather Bureau worry
about the wide-open spaces. But all the same, after she
was gone, I found a whole envelope full of real-estate
ads — you know those mortgage manors with the built-
in kiddie coops that all the Westchester cowboys come
home to on the 5:49. Now, can you imagine that in a
sensible girl?

So there it was, you see, and we didn't make a go
of it. Well, it's no use crying over spilt giggle water,
as they say, and a man has to take things like that in
his stride. If he doesn't, he's lost in the shuffle in this
man's hamlet. I can see it wasn't anybody's fault; I'm
modern. Maybe if Evie had really liked the crowd —
but there, I won't blame her. She's happy the way she
is, I guess; and you can see the way I am. The only
thing that ever hurts this little head is to think of
Angelo's closing down, sardines or no sardines. But
I'm sure he'll give me the eye, long enough ahead, if
it does. He's always shot square with me.

Of course, occasionally you get sort of philosophic about this time in the evening, and wonder how things would have turned out if they'd been different. But I've almost quit doing that. There's no percentage in it.

I remember Mr. Forman, one of the first times Evie and I were here. She hadn't noticed his hands then, and when he got talking to us, we both thought he was a pretty quaint old character. I guess he took to us so because we both of us must have looked young and green. Anyhow, he started philosophizing. "Youth," he says. "Youth against the city; coming in every day —" Oh, he ought to have had it syndicated! "I've watched 'em come," says he, "and I've seen 'em go. And some it makes, and some it breaks, and some just dry up gradually till the whitewing sweeps 'em away. Go back to your cornfields, young people," says he — as if Waynesburg didn't have car tracks! — "Go back and raise a family of nice little mortgages, because I'm a bad old man and you're breaking my heart" — and pretty soon he's crying into his glass.

We didn't pay any attention to him. We knew we were going to lick the world. But all the same, there's something in what he said. This town is a tough spot till you get wise to it — and it's too bad to see a fine man like Mr. Forman going to pieces the way he has these last two years. But then he's got what I call too much system in his drinking. You have to have just enough so it doesn't worry you.

Take me. If I'm stepping out a little more than usual tonight, it's just because of seeing Evie again. Of course it was bound to happen sometime, the way people come to New York; but a thing like that is apt to make you a little nervous just the same. It's easier, being modern the way we are. All the same, when I stepped out of the elevator and saw her waiting where she generally used to wait . . .

She hadn't come upstairs to the office, and that was decent of her. That girl at the front desk never could see me, and it's a laugh, your ex-wife ringing you up to pass the time of day or waiting out in the reception room. Though it wouldn't have been exactly a laugh to me.

I'd thought of all sorts of things to say to her when we did meet, but I didn't say any of them. I even forgot to take off my hat. I just said, "Hello, Evie. I didn't know you were in town," and she said, "Hello, Dick. I'm just here between trains" — and then we stared at each other.

I knew her right away, and yet I didn't know her, if you can get that. She was just as pretty as ever, but we weren't married any more. And then, her face was different. It didn't have that sort of quiet look on it when we were married. Of course, she'd let her hair grow too. She always had pretty hair. It had been five years. Well, there we were.

I must have looked. like something, for, when we were out on the street she touched me on the arm.

"Don't worry, Dick," she said. "Everything's all right. I just thought, as long as I was in New York, it was silly not to see each other. Do you mind?"

"Not a bit," I said. . . . Well, you have to be polite, haven't you?

"How's Mr. Barris?" I said. . . . That's Evie's husband. It's a funny name.

"Oh, he's fine . . ." she said, "just fine."

"And the children?" I said. . . . I couldn't imagine them. "I suppose they're fine too?"

"Oh, they're fine," she said.

"Well, I'm glad to hear that, Evie," I said.

I don't know why it was so hard to talk; we ought to have been used to talking to each other.

She looked at me and laughed, quite the way she used to. "We can't stand here and gape at each other, Dick," she said.

"That's right," I said, so I flagged a taxi and told him Angelo's. Then I remembered she didn't like Angelo's. But she was decent and said that it was all right.

I'll hand it to Rocco. He knew who she was, all right, but he didn't even bat an eye — just took the order. We were the only people in the little room. She said she wanted some sherry; so that was that, with a double old-fashioned for me.

When he was gone, "Was that Rocco?" she said. "He didn't remember me."

"Well," said I, "you've been away a long time."

Then we looked at each other and knew we had nothing to say. She made rings with the bottom of the sherry glass.

"Oh, Dick," she said, "it's all so different from the way I thought it would be. Tell me about yourself."

"Oh, I'm still at the old stand," I said. "Same desk, as a matter of fact. Same salary, just about."

"How about the novel?"

"Oh," I said, "I'm working at it."

But she saw through me. "It's been five years," she said.

"A good idea's worth putting time on," said I, so she gave that up. Well, I wasn't going to cry on her.

"How about yourself?" said I. "Still living in Des Moines?"

"You know Mr. Barris lives in Cleveland," she said.

"I never can keep those two towns straight," I said. I felt better now, with that old-fashioned inside me, especially as Rocco was bringing another.

"Who came from Waynesburg?" she said, trying to kid me out of it.

"Me," I said. "But you'll have to admit I've come a long way."

I don't know why that made her look as if she wanted to cry. She hardly ever did cry — that was one thing about her.

"Oh, show me the snapshots!" I said. "I know you've got them." So she did. There was the house and the children and everything, including Mr. Barris in golf pants, and the family sedan. The little girl looks like Evie. That's a break for her. I don't know what our kids would have looked like. Terrible, I suppose.

I passed the pictures back. "They're nice," I said. "It's quite a house. I suppose you've even got a garbage incinerator."

"Of course," she said. "Why?"

"It looks like a house that would have a garbage incinerator," I said. "But you'd think Barris could afford a better car now he's a family man."

"Don't talk about George," she said.

"I'm through," I said. "So you're happy, Evie?"

She looked straight at me. "I am happy," she said — and that's the hell of it; I could see she was.

"Well," I said, "skoal!" — and that was the end of that old-fashioned. I was certainly coming back to normal in grand style. I could feel it creeping all over me. Then I heard her sort of talking to herself.

"It was a mistake," she was saying. "I ought to have known, but I couldn't help it. I thought —"

"Why say that?" I said. "It's always nice to revive old times. . . . Rocco! . . . Ah, there you are, sir. And in a minute some of the crowd may blow in."

She started putting on her gloves. "I suppose they're the same too," she said.

"Who?"

"Oh, the Parsons, and that man you called the Poached Egg, and — what was her name? — Ruth something . . . and —"

"Wait a minute," I said. "You're moving too fast for me. The Parsons broke up, and they say she's up at Saranac for her lungs. I don't know whatever did happen to the Poached Egg. As for that Ruth girl — well, after Ted Harrison popped himself —"

"Ted Harrison?" she said. "Who was Ted Harrison?"

Well, there we were. We just didn't have any point of contact at all. Of course, it wasn't her fault; she'd been away, and you do get quick action in this town. But she didn't even know who Ted Harrison had been.

"Oh, well," I said, "it doesn't signify. Just wait

around a little. Some people I want you to meet will be coming in pretty soon. You'll like them; they're really awfully nice people."

"I don't think I can wait, Dick," she said. "I've got to get back to the hotel. I'm taking the night train."

"Back to Cleveland?" I said.

"Back to Cleveland," she said.

"Well," I said, "if you must, you must. And I won't tell Barris on you." I felt pretty cheery by now. She looked at me. "I'm sorry," I said.

"Oh, Dick, Dick!" she said. "Whatever are you going to do with your life? You had such a lot. I can't stand it."

"If you mean my hair," I said, "it's the barber's fault, not mine."

But she didn't pay any attention. "I didn't come back to show off," she said. "Really I didn't. I hoped — I really did — I'd come back and find you —"

"Clean and sober?" said I. "Well, I'm all of that."

"I — oh, what's the use? — I even thought you might be married."

"To some nice girl?" I said. "No, thanks. I've been."

"I held on as long as I could," she said.

"I'm not denying it," said I. "Let's leave it at that. No hard feelings."

She looked as if she wanted to say a whole lot more. Then she looked around the room and at Rocco coming in with the fresh supply. I don't know what she saw to make her look like that.

"No, it wouldn't have been," she said, sort of low

to herself. "It couldn't have been. Good-by, Dick, and thank you."

"The pleasure is all mine," said I. "Only sorry you won't have another. Just a second and I'll get you a taxi."

But when I'd settled the bill and got my hat and coat, she was gone.

I went back to the little room and sat down again. I didn't feel like thinking, but I couldn't help it. For one thing, Evie's asking about all those people who had been in the crowd — why, they'd just disappeared. And I hadn't even realized it. Come to think of it, the only two left of that particular crowd who still came to Angelo's were Mr. Forman and myself. And what was that novel about that I'd been going to write?

"Rocco!" I called.

"Right with you, mister."

"You have the right idea," I said, but when he came in, I made him stay.

"Rocco," I said, "tell me something. How do I look today?"

"Oh, mister look ver' fine; seem ver' well."

That's the trouble with Rocco. He's always so darn pleasant.

"Don't two-time me, Rocco," I said. "Do you remember when I first started coming here?"

"Oh, yes: remember ver' well. Mister ver' good customer; ver' steady customer. Wish we had all like mister."

"Leave that outside," I said. "Just tell me one thing: Do I look a lot different?"

He spread out his hands. "Sure, mister look little different. Why not? Time pass. Rocco look different too."

"You're a liar," I said. "You haven't changed that Dago grin in twenty years. . . . All right, I look different, but how old do I look?"

He spread out his hands again. "Rocco don't know. Mister maybe forty, forty-one — mister in his prime."

"You low snake," I said. "I'm thirty-two." This was serious.

"Thirty-two? That's right. That's what Rocco mean" — and he grinned. But I didn't feel so funny.

"Tell me, Rocco," I said. "You've always been a friend of mine. Now be a friend. Tell me honestly. Do you think I drink too much?"

Gosh, you couldn't get anywhere with him! He just kept on grinning.

"Mister ver' good customer," he said; "ver' old, ver' steady customer. Mister carry what he drink ver' well."

"I know that!" I said. I was getting mad by now. "But is it too much? Be sensible, Rocco. I don't put away half what Mr. Forman does."

"Nobody drink so much as Mr. Forman. Some day Mr. Forman go pop. Rocco ver' sorry then, for Mr. Forman old customer."

"Well, that's a swell way of encouraging me. How about yourself, Rocco? How's your health?"

"Fine; thanks, mister. We have new bambino only other day."

"Well, I'm certainly glad to hear that. But look here, Rocco; you take a snifter —"

"Sure. Rocco drink wine — *strega* — ver' good. But Rocco have to work. Can't drink alla time."

"I get that. But I work too."

"Sure, mister work. But Rocco work alla time. Rocco have wife, tree bambini; have to work. Work to go back to Italy, buy *trattoria,* buy farm, have more bambini, be big man in town. That work for a man. Mister have another old-fashioned?"

He wouldn't talk any more. And the next one didn't go so well, because I'd started looking at myself in the mirror.

Oh, it just shows what a state I was in. And it shows you never ought to go back on your tracks. You know, for a while there I didn't like my face a bit.

That's why I say, modern or not, things like seeing Evie again don't do you any good. Because, when Mr. Forman came in and touched me on the shoulder, I jumped a mile. And just before I jumped I caught his face in the glass right over mine. I've apologized to him since, and I guess he's forgotten it. But they all must have thought I was crazy, running out like that and leaving the money on the table. And all that week I just got crazier and crazier, getting up and taking a cold shower in the mornings, and eating at tearooms and coming right back after dinner and hunting around to see if I could find whatever became of that novel. One good thing, I did get the room pretty well cleaned up. That woman who comes in never really cleans.

But what's the use of all that when you keep getting the fidgets? And getting the fidgets makes you think too much. Anyway, one evening it was nice and warm, and

I thought, "I'll just take a walk. I can't sit here any more."

Well, I didn't have any particular direction in mind, but after a while, sure enough, there I was in front of Angelo's. Man, you should have seen the welcome they gave me. Angelo set up the drinks himself, and Rocco was grinning all over.

"Angelo think we lose our mos' steady customer," he said, "but mister come back. I know he come back."

And Mr. Forman never said a word about how I'd acted.

He wasn't a bit standoffish; in fact, Rocco had to ease him out at eleven that night.

Now, the only worry I've got is Angelo's retiring, as I say. But even if he does, maybe Rocco will keep the place on. Of course, even that would be a change, but I'd hardly mind. We've known each other a long while, and he knows I'm a good customer.

TOO EARLY SPRING

I'M writing this down because I don't ever want to forget the way it was. It doesn't seem as if I could, now, but they all tell you things change. And I guess they're right. Older people must have forgotten or they couldn't be the way they are. And that goes for even the best ones, like Dad and Mr. Grant. They try to understand but they don't seem to know how. And the others make you feel dirty or else they make you feel like a goof. Till, pretty soon, you begin to forget yourself — you begin to think, "Well, maybe they're right and it was that way." And that's the end of everything. So I've got to write this down. Because they smashed it forever — but it wasn't the way they said.

Mr. Grant always says in comp. class: "Begin at the beginning." Only I don't know quite where the beginning was. We had a good summer at Big Lake but it was just the same summer. I worked pretty hard at the practice basket I rigged up in the barn, and I learned how to do the back jackknife. I'll never dive like Kerry but you want to be as all-around as you can. And, when I took my measurements, at the end of the summer, I was 5 ft. 9¾ and I'd gained 12 lbs. 6 oz. That isn't bad for going on sixteen and the old chest expansion was O. K. You don't want to get too heavy, because basketball's a fast game, but the year before was the

186

year when I got my height, and I was so skinny, I got tired. But this year, Kerry helped me practice, a couple of times, and he seemed to think I had a good chance for the team. So I felt pretty set up — they'd never had a Sophomore on it before. And Kerry's a natural athlete, so that means a lot from him. He's a pretty good brother too. Most Juniors at State wouldn't bother with a fellow in High.

It sounds as if I were trying to run away from what I have to write down, but I'm not. I want to remember that summer, too, because it's the last happy one I'll ever have. Oh, when I'm an old man — thirty or forty — things may be all right again. But that's a long time to wait and it won't be the same.

And yet, that summer was different, too, in a way. So it must have started then, though I didn't know it. I went around with the gang as usual and we had a good time. But, every now and then, it would strike me we were acting like awful kids. They thought I was getting the big head, but I wasn't. It just wasn't much fun — even going to the cave. It was like going on shooting marbles when you're in High.

I had sense enough not to try to tag after Kerry and his crowd. You can't do that. But when they all got out on the lake in canoes, warm evenings, and somebody brought a phonograph along, I used to go down to the Point, all by myself, and listen and listen. Maybe they'd be talking or maybe they'd be singing, but it all sounded mysterious across the water. I wasn't trying to hear what they said, you know. That's the kind of thing Tot Pickens does. I'd just listen, with my arms around

my knees — and somehow it would hurt me to listen —
and yet I'd rather do that than be with the gang.

I was sitting under the four pines, one night, right
down by the edge of the water. There was a big moon
and they were singing. It's funny how you can be unhappy and nobody know it but yourself.

I was thinking about Sheila Coe. She's Kerry's girl.
They fight but they get along. She's awfully pretty and
she can swim like a fool. Once Kerry sent me over with
her tennis racket and we had quite a conversation. She
was fine. And she didn't pull any of this big sister stuff,
either, the way some girls will with a fellow's kid
brother.

And when the canoe came along, by the edge of
the lake, I thought for a moment it was her. I thought
maybe she was looking for Kerry and maybe she'd stop
and maybe she'd feel like talking to me again. I don't
know why I thought that — I didn't have any reason.
Then I saw it was just the Sharon kid, with a new kind
of bob that made her look grown-up, and I felt sore.
She didn't have any business out on the lake at her age.
She was just a Sophomore in High, the same as me.

I chunked a stone in the water and it splashed right
by the canoe, but she didn't squeal. She just said,
"Fish," and chuckled. It struck me it was a kid's trick,
trying to scare a kid.

"Hello, Helen," I said. "Where did you swipe the
gunboat?"

"They don't know I've got it," she said. "Oh, hello,
Chuck Peters. How's Big Lake?"

"All right," I said. "How was camp?"

"It was peachy," she said. "We had a peachy counselor, Miss Morgan. She was on the Wellesley field-hockey team."

"Well," I said, "we missed your society." Of course we hadn't, because they're across the lake and don't swim at our raft. But you ought to be polite.

"Thanks," she said. "Did you do the special reading for English? I thought it was dumb."

"It's always dumb," I said. "What canoe is that?"

"It's the old one," she said. "I'm not supposed to have it out at night. But you won't tell anybody, will you?"

"Be your age," I said. I felt generous. "I'll paddle a while, if you want," I said.

"All right," she said, so she brought it in and I got aboard. She went back in the bow and I took the paddle. I'm not strong on carting kids around, as a rule. But it was better than sitting there by myself.

"Where do you want to go?" I said.

"Oh, back towards the house," she said in a shy kind of voice. "I ought to, really. I just wanted to hear the singing."

"K. O.," I said. I didn't paddle fast, just let her slip. There was a lot of moon on the water. We kept around the edge so they wouldn't notice us. The singing sounded as if it came from a different country, a long way off.

She was a sensible kid, she didn't ask fool questions or giggle about nothing at all. Even when we went by Petters' Cove. That's where the lads from the bungalow colony go and it's pretty well populated on a warm

night. You can hear them talking in low voices and
now and then a laugh. Once Tot Pickens and a gang
went over there with a flashlight, and a big Bohunk
chased them for half a mile.

I felt funny, going by there with her. But I said,
"Well, it's certainly Old Home Week" — in an offhand
tone, because, after all, you've got to be sophisticated.
And she said, "People are funny," in just the right sort
of way. I took quite a shine to her after that and we
talked. The Sharons have only been in town three years
and somehow I'd never really noticed her before. Mrs.
Sharon's awfully good-looking but she and Mr. Sharon
fight. That's hard on a kid. And she was a quiet kid.
She had a small kind of face and her eyes were sort of
like a kitten's. You could see she got a great kick out
of pretending to be grown-up — and yet it wasn't all
pretending. A couple of times, I felt just as if I were
talking to Sheila Coe. Only more comfortable, because,
after all, we were the same age.

Do you know, after we put the canoe up, I walked
all the way back home, around the lake? And most of
the way, I ran. I felt swell too. I felt as if I could run
forever and not stop. It was like finding something. I
hadn't imagined anybody could ever feel the way I did
about some things. And here was another person, even
if it was a girl.

Kerry's door was open when I went by and he stuck
his head out, and grinned.

"Well, kid," he said. "Stepping out?"

"Sure. With Greta Garbo," I said, and grinned back

to show I didn't mean it. I felt sort of lightheaded, with the run and everything.

"Look here, kid —" he said, as if he was going to say something. Then he stopped. But there was a funny look on his face.

And yet I didn't see her again till we were both back in High. Mr. Sharon's uncle died, back East, and they closed the cottage suddenly. But all the rest of the time at Big Lake, I kept remembering that night and her little face. If I'd seen her in daylight, first, it might have been different. No, it wouldn't have been.

All the same, I wasn't even thinking of her when we bumped into each other, the first day of school. It was raining and she had on a green slicker and her hair was curly under her hat. We grinned and said hello and had to run. But something happened to us, I guess.

I'll say this now — it wasn't like Tot Pickens and Mabel Palmer. It wasn't like Junior David and Betty Page — though they've been going together ever since kindergarten. It wasn't like any of those things. We didn't get sticky and sloppy. It wasn't like going with a girl.

Gosh, there'd be days and days when we'd hardly see each other, except in class. I had basketball practice almost every afternoon and sometimes evenings and she was taking music lessons four times a week. But you don't have to be always twos-ing with a person, if you feel that way about them. You seem to know the way they're thinking and feeling, the way you know yourself.

Now let me describe her. She had that little face and the eyes like a kitten's. When it rained, her hair curled all over the back of her neck. Her hair was yellow. She wasn't a tall girl but she wasn't chunky — just light and well made and quick. She was awfully alive without being nervous — she never bit her fingernails or chewed the end of her pencil, but she'd answer quicker than anyone in the class. Nearly everybody liked her, but she wasn't best friends with any particular girl, the mushy way they get. The teachers all thought a lot of her, even Miss Eagles. Well, I had to spoil that.

If we'd been like Tot and Mabel, we could have had a lot more time together, I guess. But Helen isn't a liar and I'm not a snake. It wasn't easy, going over to her house, because Mr. and Mrs. Sharon would be polite to each other in front of you and yet there'd be something wrong. And she'd have to be fair to both of them and they were always pulling at her. But we'd look at each other across the table and then it would be all right.

I don't know when it was that we knew we'd get married to each other, some time. We just started talking about it, one day, as if we always had. We were sensible, we knew it couldn't happen right off. We thought maybe when we were eighteen. That was two years but we knew we had to be educated. You don't get as good a job, if you aren't. Or that's what people say.

We weren't mushy either, like some people. We got to kissing each other good-by, sometimes, because that's what you do when you're in love. It was cool, the way she kissed you, it was like leaves. But lots of the time we wouldn't even talk about getting married, we'd just play checkers or go over the old Latin, or once in a while go to the movies with the gang. It was really a wonderful winter. I played every game after the first one and she'd sit in the gallery and watch and I'd know she was there. You could see her little green hat or her yellow hair. Those are the class colors, green and gold.

And it's a queer thing, but everybody seemed to be pleased. That's what I can't get over. They liked to see us together. The grown people, I mean. Oh, of course, we got kidded too. And old Mrs. Withers would ask me about "my little sweetheart," in that awful damp voice of hers. But, mostly, they were all right. Even Mother was all right, though she didn't like Mrs. Sharon. I did hear her say to Father, once, "Really, George, how long is this going to last? Sometimes I feel as if I just couldn't stand it."

Then Father chuckled and said to her, "Now, Mary, last year you were worried about him because he didn't take any interest in girls at all."

"Well," she said, "he still doesn't. Oh, Helen's a nice child — no credit to Eva Sharon — and thank heaven she doesn't giggle. Well, Charles is mature for *his* age too. But he acts so solemn about her. It isn't natural."

"Oh, let Charlie alone," said Father. "The boy's all right. He's just got a one-track mind."

But it wasn't so nice for us after the spring came. In our part of the state, it comes pretty late, as a rule. But it was early this year. The little kids were out with scooters when usually they'd still be having snowfights and, all of a sudden, the radiators in the classrooms smelt dry. You'd got used to that smell for months — and then, there was a day when you hated it again and everybody kept asking to open the windows. The monitors had a tough time, that first week — they always do when spring starts — but this year it was worse than ever because it came when you didn't expect it.

Usually, basketball's over by the time spring really breaks, but this year it hit us while we still had three games to play. And it certainly played hell with us as a team. After Bladesburg nearly licked us, Mr. Grant called off all practice till the day before the St. Matthew's game. He knew we were stale — and they've been state champions two years They'd have walked all over us, the way we were going.

The first thing I did was telephone Helen. Because that meant there were six extra afternoons we could have, if she could get rid of her music lessons any way. Well, she said, wasn't it wonderful, her music teacher had a cold? And that seemed just like Fate.

Well, that was a great week and we were so happy. We went to the movies five times and once Mrs. Sharon let us take her little car. She knew I didn't have a driving license but of course I've driven ever since I was thirteen and she said it was all right. She was funny — sometimes she'd be awfully kind and friendly to you and sometimes she'd be like a piece of dry ice. She was that way with Mr. Sharon too. But it was a wonderful

ride. We got stuff out of the kitchen — the cook's awfully sold on Helen — and drove way out in the country. And we found an old house, with the windows
gone, on top of a hill, and parked the car and took
the stuff up to the house and ate it there. There weren't
any chairs or tables but we pretended there were.

We pretended it was our house, after we were married. I'll never forget that. She'd even brought paper
napkins and paper plates and she set two places on the
floor.

"Well, Charles," she said, sitting opposite me, with
her feet tucked under, "I don't suppose you remember
the days we were both in school."

"Sure," I said — she was always much quicker pretending things than I was — "I remember them all
right. That was before Tot Pickens got to be President." And we both laughed.

"It seems very distant in the past to me — we've
been married so long," she said, as if she really believed
it. She looked at me.

"Would you mind turning off the radio, dear?" she
said. "This modern music always gets on my nerves."

"Have we got a radio?" I said.

"Of course, Chuck."

"With television?"

"Of course, Chuck."

"Gee, I'm glad," I said. I went and turned it off.

"Of course, if you *want* to listen to the late market
reports —" she said just like Mrs. Sharon.

"Nope," I said. "The market — uh — closed firm today. Up twenty-six points."

"That's quite a long way up, isn't it?"

"Well, the country's perfectly sound at heart, in spite of this damfool Congress," I said, like Father.

She lowered her eyes a minute, just like her mother, and pushed away her plate.

"I'm not very hungry tonight," she said. "You won't mind if I go upstairs?"

"Aw, don't be like that," I said. It was too much like her mother.

"I was just seeing if I could," she said. "But I never will, Chuck."

"I'll never tell you you're nervous, either," I said. "I — oh, gosh!"

She grinned and it was all right. "Mr. Ashland and I have never had a serious dispute in our wedded lives," she said — and everybody knows who runs *that* family. "We just talk things over calmly and reach a satisfactory conclusion, usually mine."

"Say, what kind of house have we got?"

"It's a lovely house," she said. "We've got radios in every room and lots of servants. We've got a regular movie projector and a library full of good classics and there's always something in the icebox. I've got a shoe closet."

"A what?"

"A shoe closet. All my shoes are on tipped shelves, like Mother's. And all my dresses are on those padded hangers. And I say to the maid, 'Elise, Madam will wear the new French model today.'"

"What are my clothes on?" I said. "Christmas trees?"

"Well," she said. "You've got lots of clothes and

dogs. You smell of pipes and the open and something called Harrisburg tweed."

"I do not," I said. "I wish I had a dog. It's a long time since Jack."

"Oh, Chuck, I'm sorry," she said.

"Oh, that's all right," I said. "He was getting old and his ear was always bothering him. But he was a good pooch. Go ahead."

"Well," she said, "of course we give parties —"

"Cut the parties," I said.

"Chuck! They're grand ones!"

"I'm a homebody," I said. "Give me — er — my wife and my little family and — say, how many kids have we got, anyway?"

She counted on her fingers. "Seven."

"Good Lord," I said.

"Well, I always wanted seven. You can make it three, if you like."

"Oh, seven's all right, I suppose," I said. "But don't they get awfully in the way?"

"No," she said. "We have governesses and tutors and send them to boarding school."

"O. K.," I said. "But it's a strain on the old man's pocketbook, just the same."

"Chuck, will you ever talk like that? Chuck, this is when we're rich." Then suddenly, she looked sad. "Oh, Chuck, do you suppose we ever will?" she said.

"Why, sure," I said.

"I wouldn't mind if it was only a dump," she said. "I could cook for you. I keep asking Hilda how she makes things."

I felt awfully funny. I felt as if I were going to cry.
"We'll do it," I said. "Don't you worry."

"Oh, Chuck, you're a comfort," she said.

I held her for a while. It was like holding something awfully precious. It wasn't mushy or that way.
I know what that's like too.

"It takes so long to get old," she said. "I wish I
could grow up tomorrow. I wish we both could."

"Don't you worry," I said. "It's going to be all
right."

We didn't say much, going back in the car, but we
were happy enough. I thought we passed Miss Eagles
at the turn. That worried me a little because of the
driving license. But, after all, Mrs. Sharon had said
we could take the car.

We wanted to go back again, after that, but it was
too far to walk and that was the only time we had the
car. Mrs. Sharon was awfully nice about it but she said,
thinking it over, maybe we'd better wait till I got a
license. Well, Father didn't want me to get one till I
was seventeen but I thought he might come around.
I didn't want to do anything that would get Helen in
a jam with her family. That shows how careful I was
of her. Or thought I was.

All the same, we decided we'd do something to cele-
brate if the team won the St. Matthew's game. We
thought it would be fun if we could get a steak and
cook supper out somewhere — something like that. Of
course we could have done it easily enough with a gang,
but we didn't want a gang. We wanted to be alone
together, the way we'd been at the house. That was

all we wanted. I don't see what's wrong about that. We even took home the paper plates, so as not to litter things up.

Boy, that was a game! We beat them 36-34 and it took an extra period and I thought it would never end. That two-goal lead they had looked as big as the Rocky Mountains all the first half. And they gave me the full school cheer with nine Peters when we tied them up. You don't forget things like that.

Afterwards, Mr. Grant had a kind of spread for the team at his house and a lot of people came in. Kerry had driven down from State to see the game and that made me feel pretty swell. And what made me feel better yet was his taking me aside and saying, "Listen, kid, I don't want you to get the swelled head, but you did a good job. Well, just remember this. Don't let anybody kid you out of going to State. You'll like it up there." And Mr. Grant heard him and laughed and said, "Well, Peters, I'm not proselytizing. But your brother might think about some of the Eastern colleges." It was all like the kind of dream you have when you can do anything. It was wonderful.

Only Helen wasn't there because the only girls were older girls. I'd seen her for a minute, right after the game, and she was fine, but it was only a minute. I wanted to tell her about that big St. Matthew's forward and — oh, everything. Well, you like to talk things over with your girl.

Father and Mother were swell but they had to go on to some big shindy at the country club. And Kerry was going there with Sheila Coe. But Mr. Grant said he'd run me back to the house in his car and he did. He's a great guy. He made jokes about my being the infant phenomenon of basketball, and they were good jokes too. I didn't mind them. But, all the same, when I'd said good night to him and gone into the house, I felt sort of let down.

I knew I'd be tired the next day but I didn't feel sleepy yet. I was too excited. I wanted to talk to somebody. I wandered around downstairs and wondered if Ida was still up. Well, she wasn't, but she'd left half a chocolate cake, covered over, on the kitchen table, and a note on top of it, "Congratulations to Mister Charles Peters." Well, that was awfully nice of her and I ate some. Then I turned the radio on and got the time signal — eleven — and some snappy music. But still I didn't fell like hitting the hay.

So I thought I'd call up Helen and then I thought — probably she's asleep and Hilda or Mrs. Sharon will answer the phone and be sore. And then I thought — well, anyhow, I could go over and walk around the block and look at her house. I'd get some fresh air out of it, anyway, and it would be a little like seeing her.

So I did — and it was a swell night — cool and a lot of stars — and I felt like a king, walking over. All the lower part of the Sharon house was dark but a window upstairs was lit. I knew it was her window. I went around back of the driveway and whistled once — the whistle we made up. I never expected her to hear.

But she did, and there she was at the window, smiling. She made motions that she'd come down to the side door.

Honestly, it took my breath away when I saw her. She had on a kind of yellow thing over her night clothes and she looked so pretty. Her feet were so pretty in those slippers. You almost expected her to be carrying one of those animals kids like — she looked young enough. I know I oughtn't to have gone into the house. But we didn't think anything about it — we were just glad to see each other. We hadn't had any sort of chance to talk over the game.

We sat in front of the fire in the living room and she went out to the kitchen and got us cookies and milk. I wasn't really hungry, but it was like that time at the house, eating with her. Mr. and Mrs. Sharon were at the country club, too, so we weren't disturbing them or anything. We turned off the lights because there was plenty of light from the fire and Mr. Sharon's one of those people who can't stand having extra lights burning. Dad's that way about saving string.

It was quiet and lovely and the firelight made shadows on the ceiling. We talked a lot and then we just sat, each of us knowing the other was there. And the room got quieter and quieter and I'd told her about the game and I didn't feel excited or jumpy any more — just rested and happy. And then I knew by her breathing that she was asleep and I put my arm around her for just a minute. Because it was wonderful to hear that quiet breathing and know it was hers. I was going to wake her in a minute. I didn't realize how tired I was myself.

And then we were back in that house in the country and it was our home and we ought to have been happy. But something was wrong because there still wasn't any glass in the windows and a wind kept blowing through them and we tried to shut the doors but they wouldn't shut. It drove Helen distracted and we were both running through the house, trying to shut the doors, and we were cold and afraid. Then the sun rose outside the windows, burning and yellow and so big it covered the sky. And with the sun was a horrible, weeping voice. It was Mrs. Sharon's saying, "Oh, my God, oh my God."

I didn't know what had happened, for a minute, when I woke. And then I did and it was awful. Mrs. Sharon was saying "Oh, Helen — I trusted you . . ." and looking as if she were going to faint. And Mr. Sharon looked at her for a minute and his face was horrible and he said, "Bred in the bone," and she looked as if he'd hit her. Then he said to Helen —

I don't want to think of what they said. I don't want to think of any of the things they said. Mr. Sharon is a bad man. And she is a bad woman, even if she is Helen's mother. All the same, I could stand the things he said better than hers.

I don't want to think of any of it. And it is all spoiled now. Everything is spoiled. Miss Eagles saw us going to that house in the country and she said horrible things. They made Helen sick and she hasn't been back at school. There isn't any way I can see her. And if I could, it would be spoiled. We'd be thinking about the things they said.

I don't know how many of the people know, at school. But Tot Pickens passed me a note. And, that afternoon. I caught him behind his house. I'd have broken his nose if they hadn't pulled me off. I meant to. Mother cried when she heard about it and Dad took me into his room and talked to me. He said you can't lick the whole town. But I will anybody like Tot Pickens. Dad and Mother have been all right. But they say things about Helen and that's almost worse. They're for me because I'm their son. But they don't understand.

I thought I could talk to Kerry but I can't. He was nice but he looked at me such a funny way. I don't know — sort of impressed. It wasn't the way I wanted him to look. But he's been decent. He comes down almost every weekend and we play catch in the yard.

You see, I just go to school and back now. They want me to go with the gang, the way I did, but I can't do that. Not after Tot. Of course my marks are a lot better because I've got more time to study now. But it's lucky I haven't got Miss Eagles though Dad made her apologize. I couldn't recite to her.

I think Mr. Grant knows because he asked me to his house once and we had a conversation. Not about that, though I was terribly afraid he would. He showed me a lot of his old college things and the gold football he wears on his watch chain. He's got a lot of interesting things.

Then we got talking, somehow, about history and things like that and how times had changed. Why, there were kings and queens who got married younger than Helen and me. Only now we lived longer and had a lot more to learn. So it couldn't happen now. "It's civilization," he said. "And all civilization's against nature. But I suppose we've got to have it. Only sometimes it isn't easy." Well somehow or other, that made me feel less lonely. Before that I'd been feeling that I was the only person on earth who'd ever felt that way.

I'm going to Colorado, this summer, to a ranch, and next year, I'll go East to school. Mr. Grant says he thinks I can make the basketball team, if I work hard enough, though it isn't as big a game in the East as it is with us. Well, I'd like to show them something. It would be some satisfaction. He says not to be too fresh at first, but I won't be that.

It's a boy's school and there aren't even women teachers. And, maybe, afterwards, I could be a professional basketball player or something, where you don't have to see women at all. Kerry says I'll get over that; but I won't. They all sound like Mrs. Sharon to me now, when they laugh.

They're going to send Helen to a convent — I found out that. Maybe they'll let me see her before she goes. But, if we do, it will be all wrong and in front of people and everybody pretending. I sort of wish they don't — though I want to, terribly. When her mother took her upstairs that night — she wasn't the same Helen. She looked at me as if she was afraid of me. And no matter what they do for us now, they can't fix that.

SCHOONER FAIRCHILD'S CLASS

WHEN he said good night to his son and Tom Drury and the rest of them, Lane Parrington walked down the steps of the Leaf Club and stood, for a moment, breathing in the night air. He had made the speech they'd asked him to make, and taken pains with it, too — but now he was wondering whether it wasn't the same old graduate's speech after all. He hadn't meant it to be so, but you ran into a lingo, once you started putting thoughts on paper — you began to view with alarm and talk about imperiled bulwarks and the American way of life.

And yet he'd been genuinely pleased when the invitation came — and they'd asked him three months ahead. That meant something, even to the Lane Parrington of United Investments — it was curious how old bonds held. He had been decorated by two foreign governments and had declined a ministry — there was the place in Virginia, the place on Long Island, the farm in Vermont and the big apartment on the river. There were the statements issued when sailing for Europe and the photographs and articles in news weeklies and magazines. And yet he had been pleased when they asked him to speak at the annual dinner of an undergraduate club in his own college. Of course, the Leaf was a little different, as all Leaf members knew.

When he had been a new member, as his son was now, the speech had been made by a Secretary of State.

Well, he'd done well enough, he supposed — at least Ted had come up, afterward, a little shyly, and said, "Well, Dad, you're quite an orator." But, once or twice, in the course of the speech, he had caught Ted fiddling with his coffee spoon. They were almost always too long — those speeches by graduates — he had tried to remember that. But he couldn't help running a little overtime — not after he'd got up and seen them waiting there. They were only boys, of course, but boys who would soon be men with men's responsibilities — he had even made a point of that.

One of the things about the Leaf — you got a chance of hearing what — well, what really important men thought of the state of the world and the state of the nation. They could get a lot from professors but hardly that. So, when a sensible fellow got up to explain what sensible men really thought about this business at Washington — why, damn it, nobody was going to ring a gong on him! And they'd clapped him well, at the end, and Ted's face had looked relieved. They always clapped well, at the end.

Afterward, he had rather hoped to meet Ted's friends and get in a little closer touch with them than he did at the place in Virginia or the place on Long Island or the apartment in New York. He saw them there, of course — they got in cars and out of cars, they dressed and went to dances, they played on the tennis courts and swam in the pool. They were a good crowd — a typical Leaf crowd, well-exercised and well-mannered. They were polite to Cora and polite to him. He offered them cigars now and then; during the last two years he offered them whisky and soda. They listened to what he had to say and, if he told a good story, they usually laughed at it. They played tennis with him, occasionally, and said, "Good shot, sir!" — afterward, they played harder tennis. One of them was Ted, his son, well-mannered, well-exercised, a member of the Leaf. He could talk to Ted about college athletics, the college curriculum, his allowance, the weather, the virtues of capitalism and whether to get a new beach wagon this summer. Now, to these subjects was added the Leaf and the virtues of the Leaf. He could talk to Ted about any number of things.

Nevertheless, sometimes when the annual dinner was over, there would be a little group at the Leaf around this graduate or that. He remembered one such group his senior year, around a sharp-tongued old man with hooded eyes. The ex-senator was old and broken, but they'd stayed up till two while his caustic voice made hay of accepted catchwords. Well, he had met Ted's friends and remembered most of their names. They had congratulated him on his speech and he had drunk a highball with them. It had all been in accord with the best traditions of the Leaf but it hadn't lasted very long.

For a moment, indeed, he had almost gotten into an argument with one of them — the pink-faced, incredibly youthful one with the glasses who was head of the Student Union — they hadn't had student unions in his time. He had been answering a couple of questions quite informally, using slang, and the pink-faced youth had broken in with, "But, look here, sir — I mean, that was a good speech you made from the conservative point of view and all that — but when you talk about labor's being made responsible, just what do you mean and how far do you go? Do you mean you want to scrap the Wagner Act or amend it or what?"

But then the rest of them had said, "Oh, don't mind Stu — he's our communist. Skip it, Stu — how's dialectic materialism today?" and it had passed off in kidding. Lane Parrington felt a little sorry about that — he would have enjoyed a good argument with an intelligent youngster — he was certainly broad-minded enough for that. But, instead, he'd declined another highball and said, well, he supposed he ought to be getting back to the inn. It had all been very well-mannered and in accord with the best traditions of the Leaf. He wondered how the old ex-senator had got them to talk.

Ted had offered to walk along with him, of course, and, equally, of course, he had declined. Now he stood for a moment on the sidewalk, wondering whether he ought to look in at class headquarters before going back to the inn. He ought to, he supposed — after all, it was his thirtieth reunion. It would be full of cigar smoke and voices and there would be a drunk from another class — there was always, somehow or other, a drunk from another class who insisted on leading cheers. And Schooner Fairchild, the class funny man, would be telling stories — the one about the Kickapoo chief, the one about President Dodge and the telephone. As it was in the beginning, is now and ever shall be. He didn't dislike Schooner Fairchild any more — you couldn't dislike a man who had wasted his life. But Schooner, somehow, had never seemed conscious of that.

Yes, he'd go to class headquarters — he'd go, if for no other reason than to prove that he did not dislike Schooner Fairchild. He started walking down Club Row. There were twelve of the clubhouses now — there had been only eight in his time. They all looked very much alike, even the new ones — it took an initiated eye to detect the slight enormous differences — to know that Wampum, in spite of its pretentious lanterns, was second-rate and would always be second-rate, while Abbey, small and dingy, ranked with Momus and the Leaf. Parrington stood still, reliving the moment of more than thirty years ago when he'd gotten the bid from Wampum and thought he would have to accept it. It hadn't been necessary — the Leaf messenger had knocked on his door at just three minutes to nine. But whenever he passed the Wampum house he remembered. For, for almost an hour, it had seemed as if the destined career of Lane Parrington wasn't going to turn out right after all.

The small agonies of youth — they were unimportant, of course, but they left a mark. And he'd had to succeed — he'd had to have the Leaf, just as later on, he'd had to have money — he wasn't a Schooner Fairchild, to take things as they came. You were geared like that or you weren't — if you weren't, you might as well stay in Emmetsburg and end up as a harried high school principal with sick headaches and a fine Spencerian handwriting, as his father had. But he had wanted to get out of Emmetsburg the moment he had realized there were other places to go.

He remembered a look through a microscope and a lashing, tailed thing that swam. There were only two classes of people, the wigglers and the ones who stood still — he should have made his speech on that — it would have been a better speech. And the ones who stood still didn't like the wigglers — that, too, he knew, from experience. If they saw a wiggler coming, they closed ranks and opposed their large, well-mannered inertia to the brusque, ill-mannered life. Later on, of course, they gave in gracefully, but without real liking. He had made the Leaf on his record — and a very good record it had had to be. He had even spent three painful seasons with the track squad, just to demonstrate that desirable all-aroundness that was one of the talking points. And even so, they had smelled it — they had known, instinctively, that he wasn't quite their kind. Tom Drury, for instance, had always been pleasant enough — but Tom Drury had always made him feel that he was talking a little too much and a little too loud. Tom Drury, who, even then, had looked like a magnificent sheep. But he had also been class president, and the heir to Drury and Son. And yet, they all liked Schooner Fairchild — they liked him still.

And here was the end of Club Row, and the Momus House. He stopped and took out a cigar. It was silly to fight old battles, especially when they were won. If they asked the Drurys to dinner now, the Drurys came – he'd been offered and declined a partnership in Drury and Son. But he had helped Tom out with some of their affiliates and Tom had needed help — Tom would always be impressive, of course, but it took more than impressiveness to handle certain things. And now Ted was coming along — and Ted was sound as a bell. So sound he might marry one of the Drury daughters, if he wanted — though that was Ted's business. He wondered if he wanted Ted to marry young. He had done so himself — on the whole, it had been a mistake.

Funny, how things mixed in your mind. As always, when he remembered Dorothy, there was the sharp, sweet smell of her perfume; then the stubborn, competent look of her hands on the wheel of a car. They had been too much alike to have married — lucky they'd found it out in time. She had let him keep the child — of course he would have fought for it anyway — but it was considered very modern in those days. Then the war had washed over and obliterated a great deal — afterward, he had married Cora. And that had worked out as it should — Ted was fond of her and she treated him with just the right shade of companionableness. Most things worked out in the end. He wondered if Dorothy had gotten what she wanted at last — he supposed she had, with her Texan. But she'd died in a hospital at Galveston, ten years ago, trying to have the Texan's child, so he couldn't ask her now. They had warned her about having more children — but, as soon as you warned Dorothy about anything, that was what she wanted to do. He could have told them. But the Texan was one of those handsome, chivalrous men.

Strange, that out of their two warring ambitions should have come the sound, reliable, healthy Ted. But, no, it wasn't strange — he had planned it as carefully as one could, and Cora had helped a great deal. Cora never got out of her depth and she had a fine social sense. And the very best nurses and schools from the very first — and there you were! You did it as you ran a business — picked the right people and gave them authority. He had hardly ever had to interfere himself.

There would be a great deal of money — but that could be taken care of — there were ways. There were trust funds and foundations and clever secretaries. And Ted need never realize it. There was no reason he should — no reason in the least. Ted could think he was doing it all.

He pulled hard on his cigar and started to walk away. For the door of the Momus Club had suddenly swung open, emitting a gush of light and a small, chubby, gray-haired figure with a turned-up nose and a jack-o'-lantern grin. It stood on the steps for a moment, saying good night a dozen times and laughing. Lane Parrington walked fast — but it was no use. He heard pattering footsteps behind him — a voice cried, "Ought-Eight!" with conviction, then, "Lane Parrington, b'gosh!" He stopped and turned.

"Oh, hello, Schooner," he said, unenthusiastically. "Your dinner over, too?"

"Oh, the boys'll keep it up till three," said Schooner Fairchild, mopping his pink brow. "But, after an hour and a half, I told them it was time they got some other poor devil at the piano. I'm not as young as I was." He panted, comically, and linked arms with Lane Parring-

ton. "Class headquarters?" he said. "I shouldn't go —
Minnie will scalp me. But I will."

"Well," said Lane Parrington uncomfortably — he
hated having his arm held, "I suppose we ought to
look in."

"Duty, Mr. Easy, always duty," said Schooner Fairchild and chuckled. "Hey, don't walk so fast — an old
man can't keep up with you." He stopped and mopped
his brow again. "By the way," he said, "that's a fine
boy of yours, Lane."

"Oh," said Lane Parrington awkwardly. "Thanks.
But I didn't know — "

"Saw something of him last summer," said Schooner
Fairchild cheerfully. "Sylvia brought him around to
the house. He could have a rather nice baritone, if he
wanted."

"Baritone?" said Lane Parrington. "Sylvia?"

"Eldest daughter and pride of the Fairchild
château," said Schooner Fairchild, slurring his words
by a tiny fraction. "She collects 'em — not always —
always with Father's approval. But your boy's a nice
boy. Serious, of course." He chuckled again, it seemed
to Lane Parrington maddeningly. "Oh, the sailor said
to the admiral, and the admiral said he — " he chanted.
"Remember that one, Lane?"

"No," said Lane Parrington.

"That's right," said Schooner Fairchild, amiably.
"Stupid of me. I thought for a minute, you'd been in
the quartet. But that was dear old Pozzy Banks. Poor
Pozzy — he never could sing 'The Last Rose of Summer'
properly till he was as drunk as an owl. A man of

great talents. I hoped he'd be here this time but he couldn't make it. He wanted to come," he hummed, "but he didn't have the fare . . ."

"That's too bad," said Lane Parrington, seriously. "And yet, with business picking up . . ."

Schooner Fairchild looked at him queerly, for an instant. "Oh, bless you!" he said. "Pozzy never had a nickel. But he was fun." He tugged at Lane Parrington's arm, as they turned a corner and saw an electric sign — 1908 — above the door. "Well, here we go!" he said.

An hour later, Lane Parrington decided that it was just as he had expected. True, the drunk from the unidentified class had gone home. But others, from other classes, had arrived. And Schooner Fairchild was sitting at the piano.

He himself was wedged uncomfortably at the back of the room between Ed Runner and a man whose name, he thought, was either Ferguson or Whitelaw, but who, in any case, addressed him as "Lane, old boy." This made conversation difficult, for it was hard to call his neighbor either "Fergy" or "Whitey" without being sure of his name. On the other hand, conversation with Ed Runner was equally difficult, for that gentleman had embarked upon an interminable reminiscence whose point turned upon the exact location of Bill Webley's room Sophomore year. As Lane Parrington had never been in any of Bill Webley's rooms, he had very little to add to the discussion. He was also drinking beer, which never agreed with him, and the cigar smoke stung his eyes. And around the singer and the piano boiled and seethed a motley crew of graduates of all classes — the Roman togas of 1913, the convict stripes of 1935, the shorts and explorers' helmets of 1928. For the news had somehow gone around, through the various class headquarters, that Schooner Fairchild was doing his stuff — and, here and there, among the crowd, were undergraduates, who had heard from brothers and uncles about Schooner Fairchild, but had never seen him before in the flesh.

He had told the story of the Kickapoo chief, he had given the imitation of President Dodge and the telephone. Both these and other efforts, Lane Parrington noted wonderingly, had been received with tumultuous cheers. Now he played a few chords and swung around on the piano stool.

"I shall now," he said, with his cherubic face very solemn, "emit my positively last and final number — an imitation of dear old Pozzy Banks, attempting to sing 'The Last Rose of Summer' while under the influence of wine. Not all of you have been privileged to know dear old Pozzy — a man of the most varied and diverse talents — it is our great regret that he is not with us tonight. But for those of you who were not privileged to know Pozzy, may I state as an introduction that dear old Pozzy is built something on the lines of a truck, and that, when under the influence of wine, it was his custom to sing directly into his hat, which he held out before him like a card tray. We will now begin." He whirled round, struck a few lugubrious notes and began to sing.

It was, as even Lane Parrington had to admit, extremely funny. He heard himself joining in the wild, deep roar of laughter that greeted the end of the first verse — he was annoyed at himself but he could not help it. By some magic, by some trick of gesture and voice, the chubby, bald-headed figure had suddenly become a large and lugubrious young man — a young man slightly under the influence of wine but still with the very best intentions, singing sentimentally and lugubriously into his hat. It was a trick and an act and a sleight of hand not worth learning — but it did not fail in its effect. Lane Parrington found himself laughing till he ached — beside him, the man named either Ferguson or Whitelaw was whooping and gasping for breath.

"And now," said Schooner Fairchild, while they were still laughing, "let somebody play who *can* play!" And, magically crooking his finger, he summoned a dark-haired undergraduate from the crowd, pushed him down on the piano stool, and, somehow or other, slipped through the press and vanished, while they were still calling his name.

Lane Parrington, a little later, found himself strolling up and down the dejected back yard of class headquarters. They had put up a tent, some iron tables and a number of paper lanterns, but, at this hour, the effect was not particularly gay. It must be very late and he ought to go to bed. But he did not look at his watch. He was trying to think about certain things in his life and get them into a proportion. It should be a simple thing to do, as simple as making money, but it was not.

Ted — Dorothy — the Leaf — Emmetsburg — Schooner Fairchild — Tom Drury — the place in Vir-

ginia and the mean house at Emmetsburg — United
Investments and a sleight-of-hand trick at a tiny piano.
He shuffled the factors of the equation about; they
should add up to a whole. And, if they did, he would
be willing to admit it; he told himself that. Yes, even
if the final sum proved him wrong for years — that had
always been one of the factors of his own success, his
knowing just when to cut a loss.

A shaky voice hummed behind him:

> "Oh, the ship's cat said to the cabin boy,
> To the cabin boy said she . . ."

He turned — it was Schooner Fairchild and, he
thought at first, Schooner Fairchild was very drunk.
Then he saw the man's lips were gray, caught him and
helped him into one of the iron chairs.

"Sorry," wheezed Schooner Fairchild. "Must have
run too fast, getting away from the gang. Damn' silly —
left my medicine at the inn."

"Here — wait — " said Lane Parrington, remembering the flask of brandy in his pocket. He uncorked it
and held it to the other man's lips. "Can you swallow?"
he said solicitously.

An elfish, undefeated smile lit Schooner Fairchild's
face. "Always could, from a child," he gasped. "Never
ask a Fairchild twice." He drank and said, incredibly,
it seemed to Lane Parrington, "Napoleon . . . isn't it?
Sir, you spoil me." His color began to come back.
"Better," he said.

"Just stay there," said Lane Parrington. He dashed
back into club headquarters — deserted now, he noticed,

except for the gloomy caretaker and the man called Ferguson or Whitelaw, who was ungracefully asleep on a leather couch. Efficiently, he found glasses, ice, soda, plain water and ginger ale, and returned, his hands full of these trophies, to find Schooner Fairchild sitting up in his chair and attempting to get a cigarette from the pocket of his coat.

His eyes twinkled as he saw Lane Parrington's collection of glassware. "My!" he said. "We *are* going to make a night of it. Great shock to me — never thought it of you, Lane."

"Hadn't I better get a doctor?" said Lane Parrington. "There's a telephone — "

"Not a chance," said Schooner Fairchild. "It would worry Minnie sick. She made me promise before I came up to take care. It's just the old pump — misses a little sometimes. But I'll be all right, now — right as a trivet, whatever a trivet is. Just give me another shot of Napoleon."

"Of course," said Lane Parrington, "but — "

"Brandy on beer, never fear," said Schooner Fairchild. "Fairchild's Medical Maxims, Number One. And a cigarette . . . thanks." He breathed deeply. "And there we are," he said, with a smile. "Just catches you in the short ribs, now and then. But, when it's over, it's over. You ought to try a little yourself, Lane — damn' silly performance of mine and you look tired."

"Thanks," said Lane Parrington, "I will." He made himself, neatly, an efficient brandy and soda and raised the glass to his lips. "Well — er — here's luck," he said, a little stiffly.

"Luck!" nodded Schooner Fairchild. They both drank. Lane Parrington looked at the pleasant, undefeated face.

"Listen, Schooner," said Lane Parrington, suddenly and harshly, "if you had the whole works to shoot over again — " He stopped.

"That's the hell of a question to ask a man at three o'clock in the morning," said Schooner equably. "Why?"

"Oh, I don't know," said Lane Parrington. "But that stuff at the piano you did — well, how did you do it?" His voice was oddly ingenious, for Lane Parrington.

"Genius, my boy, sheer, untrammeled genius," said Schooner Fairchild. He chuckled and sobered. "Well, somebody has to," he said reasonably. "And you wouldn't expect Tom Drury to do it, would you? — poor old Tom!"

"No," said Lane Parrington, breathing. "I wouldn't expect Tom Drury to do it."

"Oh, Tom's all right," said Schooner Fairchild. "He was just born with an ingrowing Drury and never had it operated on. But he's a fine guy, all the same. Lord," he said, "it must be a curse — to have to be a Drury, whether you like it or not. I never could have stood it — I never could have played the game. Of course," he added hastily, "I suppose it's different, if you do it all yourself, the way you have. That must be a lot of fun."

"I wouldn't exactly call it fun," said Lane Parrington earnestly. "You see, after all, Schooner, there are quite a good many things that enter into . . ." He paused, and laughed hopelessly. "Was I always a stuffed shirt?" he said. "I suppose I was."

"Oh, I wouldn't call you a stuffed shirt," said Schooner, a little quickly. "You just had to succeed -- and you've done it. Gosh, we all knew you were going to, right from the first — there couldn't be any mistake about that. It must be a swell feeling." He looked at Lane Parrington and his voice trailed off. He began again. "You see, it was different with me," he said. "I couldn't help it. Why, just take a look at me — I've even got a comedy face. Well, I never wanted anything very much except — oh, to have a good time and know other people were having a good time. Oh, I tried taking the other things seriously — I tried when I was a broker, but I couldn't, it was just no go. I made money enough — everybody was making money — but every now and then, in the middle of a million-share day, I'd just think how damn silly it was for everybody to be watching the board and getting all excited over things called ATT and UGI. And that's no way for a broker to act — you've got to believe those silly initials mean something, if you want to be a broker.

"Well, I've tried a good many things since. And now and then I've been lucky, and we've gotten along. And I've spent most of Minnie's money, but she says it was worth it — and we've got the five girls and they're wonders — and I'll probably die playing the piano at some fool party, for you can't keep it up forever, but I only hope it happens before somebody says, 'There goes poor old Schooner. He used to be pretty amusing, in his time!' But, you see, I couldn't help it," he ended diffidently. "And, you know, I've tried. I've tried hard. But then I'd start laughing, and it always got in the way."

Lane Parrington looked at the man who had spent his wife's money and his own for a sleight-of-hand trick, five daughters, and the sound of friendly laughter. He looked at him without understanding, and yet with a curious longing.

"But, Schooner — " he said, "with all you can do — you ought to — "

"Oh," said Schooner, a trifle wearily, "one has one's dreams. Sure, I'd like to be Victor Boucher — he's a beautiful comedian. Or Bill Fields, for instance. Who wouldn't? But I don't kid myself. It's a parlor talent — it doesn't go over the footlights. But, Lord, what fun I've had with it! And the funny things people keep doing, forever and ever, amen. And the decent — the very decent things they keep doing, too. Well, I always thought it would be a good life, while you had it." He paused, and Lane Parrington saw the fatigue on his face. "Well, it's been a good party," he said. "I wish old Pozzy could have been here. But I guess we ought to go to bed."

"I'll phone for a cab," said Lane Parrington. "Nope — you're riding."

Lane Parrington shut the door of Schooner Fairchild's room behind him and stood, for a moment, with his hand on the knob. He had seen Schooner safely to bed — he had even insisted on the latter's taking his medicine, though Schooner had been a little petulant about it. Now, however, he still wondered about calling a doctor — if Schooner should be worse in the morning, he would have Anstey come up by plane. It was nothing to do, though not everybody could do it, and Anstey was much the best man. In any case, he would insist on Schooner's seeing Anstey this week. Then he wondered just how he was going to insist.

The old elevator just across the corridor came to a wheezing stop. Its door opened and a dark-haired girl in evening dress came out. Lane Parrington dropped his hand from the doorknob and turned away. But the girl took three quick steps after him.

"I'm sorry," she said, a little breathlessly, "but I'm Sylvia Fairchild. Is Father ill? The elevator boy said something — and I saw you coming out of his room."

"He's all right," said Lane Parrington. "It was just the slightest sort of —"

"Oh!" said the girl, "do you mind coming back for a minute? You're Ted's father, aren't you? My room's next door, but I've got a key for his, too — Mother told me to be sure —" She seemed very self-possessed. Lane Parrington waited uncomfortably in the corridor for what seemed to him a long time, while she went into her father's room. When she came out again, she seemed relieved.

"It's all right," she said, in a low voice. "He's asleep, and his color's good. And he's . . ." She paused. "Oh, damn!" she said. "We can't talk out here. Come into my room for a minute — we can leave the door open — after all, you *are* Ted's father. I'll have to tell Mother, you see — and Father will just say it wasn't anything."

She opened the door and led the way into the room.

"Here," she said. "Just throw those stockings off the chair — I'll sit on the bed. Well?"

"Well, I asked him if he wanted a doctor . . ." said Lane Parrington humbly.

When he had finished a concise, efficient report, the girl nodded, and he saw for the first time that she was pretty, with her dark, neat head and her clever, stubborn chin.

"Thank you," she said. "I mean, really. Father's a perfect lamb — but he doesn't like to worry Mother, and it worries her a lot more not to know. And sometimes it's rather difficult, getting the truth out of Father's friends. Not you," she was pleased to add. "You've been perfectly truthful. And the brandy was quite all right."

"I'm glad," said Lane Parrington. "I wish your father would see Anstey," he added, a trifle awkwardly. "I could — er — make arrangements."

"He has," said the girl. Her mouth twitched. "Oh," she said. "I shouldn't have gone to the dance. I couldn't help the Momus Club, but he might have come back afterward, if I'd been here. Only, I don't know."

"I wouldn't reproach myself," said Lane Parrington. "After all — "

"Oh, I know," said the girl. "After all! If you don't all manage to kill him, between you! Friends!" she sniffed. Then, suddenly, her face broke into lines of amusement. "I sound just like Aunt Emma," she said. "And that's pretty silly of me. Aunt Emma's almost pure poison. Of course it isn't your fault and I really do thank you. Very much. Do you know, I never expected you'd be a friend of Father's."

"After all," said Lane Parrington stiffly, "we were in the same class."

"Oh, I know," said the girl. "Father's talked about you, of course." Her mouth twitched again, but this time, it seemed to Lane Parrington, with a secret merriment. "And so has Ted, naturally," she added politely.

"I'm glad he happened to mention me," said Lane Parrington, and she grinned, frankly.

"I deserved that," she said, while Lane Parrington averted his eyes from what seemed to be a remarkably flimsy garment hung over the bottom of the bed. "But Ted has, really. He admires you quite a lot, you know, though, of course, you're different generations."

"Tell me —" said Lane Parrington. "No, I won't ask you."

"Oh, you know Ted," said the girl, rather impatiently. "It's awfully hard to get him to say things — and he will spend such a lot of time thinking he ought to be noble, poor lamb. But he's losing just a little of that, thank goodness — when he first came to Widgeon Point, he was trying so hard to be exactly like that terrible Drury boy. You see —" she said, suddenly and gravely, "he could lose quite a lot of it and still have more than most people."

Lane Parrington cleared his throat. There seemed nothing for him to say. Then he thought of something.

"His mother was — er — a remarkable person," he said. "We were not at all happy together. But she had remarkable qualities."

"Yes," said the girl. "Ted's told me. He remembers her." They looked at each other for a moment — he noted the stubborn chin, the swift and admirable hands. Then a clock on the mantel struck and the girl jumped.

"Good heavens!" she said. "It's four o'clock! Well — good night. And I do thank you, Mr Parrington."

"It wasn't anything," said Lane Parrington. "But remember me to your father. But I'll see you in the morning, of course."

The following afternoon, Lane Parrington found himself waiting for his car in the lobby of the inn. There had been a little trouble with the garage and it was late. But he did not care, particularly, though he felt glad to be going back to New York. He had said good-by to Ted an hour before — Ted was going on to a house party at the Chiltons' — they'd eventually meet on Long Island, he supposed. Meanwhile, he had had a pleasant morning, attended the commencement exercises, and had lunch with Ted and the Fairchilds at the inn. Schooner had been a little subdued and both Ted and the girl frankly sleepy, but he had enjoyed the occasion nevertheless. And somehow the fact that the president's baccalaureate address had also viewed with alarm and talked about imperiled bulwarks and the American way of life — had, in fact, repeated with solemn precision a good many of the points in his own speech — did not irk Lane Parrington as it might have the day before. After all, the boys were young and could stand it. They had stood a good deal of nonsense, even in his own time.

Now he thought once more of the equation he had

tried too earnestly to solve, in the back yard of commencement headquarters — and, for a moment, almost
grinned. It was, of course, insoluble — life was not as
neat as that. You did what you could, as it was given
you to do — very often you did the wrong things. And
if you did the wrong things, you could hardly remedy
them by a sudden repentance — or, at least, he could
not. There were still the wigglers and the ones who
stood still — and each had his own virtues. And because
he was a wiggler, he had thoughtfully and zealously
done his best to make his son into the image of one of
the magnificent sheep — the image of Tom Drury, who
was neither hungry nor gay. He could not remedy that,
but he thought he knew somebody who could remedy
it, remembering the Fairchild girl's stubborn chin. And,
in that case at least, the grandchildren ought to be
worth watching.

"Your car, Mr. Parrington," said a bellboy. He
moved toward the door. It was hard to keep from being
a stuffed shirt, if you had the instinct in you, but one
could try. A good deal might be done, with trying.

As he stepped out upon the steps of the inn, he
noticed a figure, saluting — old Negro Mose, the campus
character who remembered everybody's name.

"Hello, Mose!" said Lane Parrington. "Remember
me?"

"Remember you — sho', Mr. Parrington," said Mose.
He regarded Lane Parrington with beady eyes. "Let's
see — you was 1906."

"Nineteen hundred and eight," said Lane Parrington, but without rancor.

Mose gave a professional chuckle. "Sho'!" he said. "I was forgettin'! Let's see — you hasn't been back fo' years, Mister Parrington — but you was in Tom Drury's class — an' Schooner Fairchild's class — "

"No," said Lane Parrington and gave the expected dollar, "not Tom Drury's class, Schooner Fairchild's class."

AMONG THOSE PRESENT

MY dear, I'm exhausted. They just wouldn't leave El Morocco, and then we went on to hear that girl sing those songs. Irish ballads, you know, and she's really a Brazilian — it gives them a quality you simply wouldn't believe. And the wonderful thing it, she learned them from a phonograph record. She can't speak a word of English otherwise. So she just sings them over and over, and everybody cheers. But everybody. Ted said he'd always been against inventing the phonograph, and now he was sure of it — but that's just the way he talks.

Well, if I do say it myself, it was rather an amusing crowd. Larry Dunn, you know — the Dunns are stuffy rich, but Larry's a darling — he does candid-camera studies that are just as good as Werbe's and you'd never know he was rich at all, except, as Ted says, when it comes to not reaching for the check. And the Necropuloffs — Russians, my dear, and so brave! Their father was actually eaten by wolves or something and they know the most ghastly stories about Stalin. And Mike Glatto — he's movies — All-American Productions — and rather unbrushed, in a way, but quite fascinating — and the Jenkinses, of course — and Jane Pierce, who does the cocktail column for *Sport and Society*. Oh, yes, and the little Lindsay girl that Ted knows — but she didn't come on to the other place. She couldn't — she works or something — so Ted dropped her and met us afterward.

Just as well, in a way. She didn't really quite fit in and she lives in some unheard-of place like Riverside Drive — Ted was hours finding us. But the rest of it — well, they're just the sort of people you can only find in New York.

I suppose it was my fault, staying quite so late. Ted growled a bit, coming home — said, wouldn't it be cheaper in the end, if we rented the house and lived in the checkroom at the Stork Club. But I think that was the guinea hen we had for dinner — guinea hen always disagrees with him, but there's a new way of basting it with brandy that Jane Pierce taught me and I couldn't resist it. And, to be utterly frank, my dear, I needed something. A little revelry. You see, I'd been to the Coles' that afternoon. And that was grim.

Oh, just a rather grim party. Hordes of people and warm Martinis. They usually give such good parties too. No, it wasn't seeing Bob and the bride — Lucille Cole phoned me they'd probably be there. And we're utterly friendly, of course — I always ask him how his work's going. I think you have to be civilized about these things. You don't scream and faint any more when you meet your ex-husband. And I'm hardly Alice Ben Bolt. But I did feel a little hurt that he hadn't told me. After all, it's still a surprise to pick up the paper and see that your former helpmeet has married somebody you've never even heard of. And in Florida, of all places! Of course, he's been painting down there. But I did send him a telegram when I married Ted.

Funny, too, I always imagined he'd pick somebody rather maternal. A nice widow or one of those hearty, earthy girls with rather flat feet. Painters are so apt. But this. . . .

Oh, that fresh, untouched type, my dear, if you happen to like it. A brave little profile, you know — a gallant little figure in sports clothes. And, I'm afraid, dancing curls. Just another Joan of Arc. They seem to produce them, nowadays. Only, I fail to see why they call her "little." She'd be quite as tall as I am if she wore heels.

No, but really an infant. Really. Twenty-one. And — oh, yes — they're going to live in the country. They were rapt about it. In fact, they've got their eye on a farmhouse. I suppose she'll raise chickens. Or doves. She's the type for doves. And Bob will turn the old stable into a studio, and they'll do it all themselves and take photographs too. It's too grim to think about, really. And she'll greet him with a flushed, happy face, when he comes home from his work, and cook little meals. Only they say she has money — so it'll probably be two very good maids. Till the children come, of course, and they have to build on the wing. . . . No, not yet, but they certainly will. Dozens of them — all Joans of Arc.

I think I'll have another cocktail, my dear, I'm a little tired. . . .

Ted? No, he was spared, though I'm sure the bride would have liked him. . . . Oh, he's very well. He liked you, my dear, by the way. . . . No, really — no, I could see. And next time it must just be ourselves and we'll have a good long talk about the old days. Ted's so funny. He's always insisted that there never could be such a place as Little Prairie. So I was delighted when you phoned. I said, "It's little Kitty Harris — the child with the bang that used to have a crush on me in school. And she's here in New York with her husband — and, my dear, they'll be babes in the wood and we must rescue them." So, you see.

Now, tell me again just what your husband does. . . . Oh, research. That's always so intelligent. And that rather lean-jawed look — very attractive, my dear. Oh, you'll have no difficulty at all. But you must begin as you mean to go on — that's the important thing. And anything I can do — well, just treat me as a mother confessor. After all, I was a mouse myself when I first came to New York — but a mouse!

The one thing is, it's so easy to get tangled up with a lot of stodgy, unimportant people. And no husband is a help about that. Why, if Ted had his way, we'd do nothing but give dinners for his partners and his Harvard classmates — not to speak of the family. And Bob was just the same about painters. He thought putting on a dress shirt meant prostituting your art. While, as a matter of fact, it's just as easy to meet the amusing people as the dull ones. All you need is the tiniest start, and perhaps a wee bit of guidance. After that, as I've often said, it just rolls like a snowball. Ted says they'll come anywhere for free liquor. Isn't it wicked of him? Well, of course, you can hardly give a party on Aunt

Emma's dandelion wine. But that's only a part of it; it needs a certain sense. Take our little party last night — well, perhaps I am supposed to have a gift for that sort of thing, but it was so simple, really. And Paul Necropuloff said it reminded him of his Great-Uncle Feodor's *dacha* in the Caucasus and nearly cried. . . .

Oh, you'll have a wonderful time. You don't really live till you're here, my dear — I assure you. I sound positively dewy-eyed, don't I? But there you are. I always knew it was going to be my town, and you'll feel the same way. Little Kitty Harris! And you'd sit reading "The Five Little Peppers" while we big girls played jacks on the porch — I can see it all so plainly. I must get some jacks; I believe they still have them in stores. We'll have a party and play them; it'll be a furor. We introduced parcheesi, you know, while I was still married to Bob, and people played it for months. . . .

Well, of course, my dear, you've kept up so much more. I do think it's so brave of you. It sometimes seems to me as if I could never have lived there at all. And Mother will send me long clippings about Hick's Garage being torn down and Willy Snamm being made head teller at the Drovers' National — as if I remembered people named Willy Snamm! . . . Oh, my dear, I'm so sorry. I didn't realize that he married your cousin. But it is a quaint name. And four children — darling, how forthright of them! That's wonderful. I suppose if I'd stayed in Little Prairie, I'd have four children myself. . . . No, we haven't. . . . Somehow, one keeps putting it off.

But when I think of what we've both escaped — at

least now you're here, too, my dear — it seems absolutely providential. I so well remember our first winter — Bob's and mine. And how discouraged he got. His work wasn't going well, though he was quite sweet about it, and he kept saying he'd like to feel the earth under his feet again. They will say the weirdest things. And I must say that, now and then, I felt pretty discouraged myself. Sometimes, when Bob was out, I'd take a bus uptown and then walk past the old Waldorf-Astoria and wonder if I'd ever know the people who went there. The Waldorf! Imagine! And I had to look up the Ritz in the telephone book to find out where it was. Why, we didn't even know a speak-easy, except the Italian place on Charlton Street, with the dollar dinner and the menu in purple ink. And then, that spring, I got my job on *Modes and Manners*. And we met the Halleys and things really began.

Though, as a matter of fact, it was Ben Christian who first took us to the Charlton Street place. . . . Oh, yes, my dear, very well. He used to sleep on our couch when they'd evict him. He was writing *Bitter Harvest* then, and I must say he'd read it aloud at the drop of a hat. Well, I did make a few suggestions — the women were simply impossible, and he knew it. Rather sensitive and sweet in those days, with untamed hair and a thin face — well, his face is still thin. He used to call me "The Kid from Little Prairie" and say we made him believe in marriage or something. And we'd sit around in the Charlton Street place and he and Bob would talk for hours. I still remember that awful wine.

There were moth balls in it, I'm sure. But we thought it was wonderful.

Well, of course, that sort of thing is all very nice when you're new. Very picturesque and all that, when you're looking back — though the ravioli always tasted of thumbs. And Ben used the place in *Bitter Harvest,* so that was all right. In fact, it got to be quite celebrated and people would come from uptown. Ben was rather rude about that — he'd call them "slummers" and say they came to watch the quaint animals perform. Of course, I'd know now that it was just an inferiority complex, because he was born on Hester Street himself — but I was a child in those days. I hadn't even read Jung.

He wasn't rude to the Halleys, exactly, but he was — well, suspicious. And the worst of it was, he made Bob suspicious too. I had quite a time getting him over that. And, really, I can't imagine why. Because, after all — and in spite of everything that's happened — the Halleys were our kind. But he used to say that the worst thing about the arts was the people who thought you could collect them like Pekingese. I'm sure I don't know what he meant by it. It must have been just a psychosis. Like washing your hands too much.

Now, I must say, I have an instinct about those things. I don't claim any credit for it; it's just in you or it's not. And I knew, when we first saw the Halleys, they were people we ought to know. It was weird, my dear — just like a premonition. Though I don't suppose I'd think that Miriam was quite so distinguished now.

She's gone off terribly, recently. And one does get tired of Halstead's imitations. He's been doing them so long. Well, I suppose you'd have to do something if you were married to Miriam.

But they were the first real New Yorkers we really knew. I don't mean people like Ben Christian, who happened to be born here, but people that counted. They took us to our first first-night, and I'll never forget it. And Miriam wore her long gold earrings and they knew the star. But, my dear, the struggle I had to get Bob into a dinner coat! I finally just had to show him that it was an investment, as, of course, it is. And even then, he would call it a tuxedo. But the Halleys just laughed and thought it was quaint and American.

They'd have asked Ben Christian, too, if they'd thought he'd come. They were always very nice about Ben, and Miriam bought dozens of copies of *Bitter Harvest* after the reviews came out. But he simply couldn't understand them — it was a blind spot. He kept on saying they were slummers and that he'd respect Halstead a lot more if he spent his money on a racing stable instead of backing bad plays and collecting worse pictures, just to please Miriam. Because, he said, there are certain people who are born to own racing stables. And there's one thing about being a horse — now and then you get a chance to kick somebody like Halstead square in the slats.

Which I think was very unfair, when Halstead had got Bob three game rooms to decorate and Miriam had started him on book jackets. Of course, it wasn't Bob's real work, but it meant he was beginning to be known.

And they'd have done just as much for Ben, if he'd let
them. I used to tell him so. But he'd just grin at me
and say, "Don't be fooled, kid. I know those helping
hands. Remember Little Prairie!" Well, it didn't
mean much, in the first place, and finally, he got to
saying it all the time. And I do think that's boring.

I'm certainly the last person in the world to come
between a husband and his friends. I've always been
very careful about that, with both Bob and Ted. But
there does come a point — you'll see. And the first big
party we gave in the old studio. . . . Oh, Christian came,
my dear, if you can call it coming. We were blessed with
his physical presence. But he wouldn't even drink —
just sat in a corner and glared. As if he wanted to get
away, but didn't quite know how. And for no reason.

Of course, I didn't know as much about parties as
I do now, but still it was fun. And Bob almost sold a
water color because of it. I'm sure the woman would
have bought it if she'd ever seen it again.

Well, we patched things up afterward, but they
never were quite the same. I think it really hurt Bob —
and I certainly tried to make it up to him. I even
thought we might have a baby, just to take his mind off
things; though where we'd have put it, I don't know.
But then, thank heaven, Ben fell in love with a girl and
moved to Brooklyn — and, my dear, the relief! She was
years older than either of us and wore embroidered
smocks — and even Bob saw there was simply no use
going on.

And by that time the Charlton Street place had put
in a garden and waiters, so it wasn't fun any more.

There were too many people who went there, and you'd be bothered. So we took our courage in both hands and moved uptown. Beekman Place — it hadn't really begun then. Bob never liked the light quite as well, but it looked much more like a studio when I'd fixed it up, and, after all, when you're doing game rooms, you have to do them on the spot.

And then the rush began. There's nothing like it — we simply went everywhere. Of course, I'd be a little more selective now. But I remember Halstead saying to me, "Well, little one, you two have certainly taken the town," and Halstead never exaggerates. And Bob's first show went over with a bang — they even ran a photograph of him in *Vanity Fair*. I don't know why he wasn't more pleased with it; he may have thought the pastel sketches were hasty, but everybody else thought they were divine.

Well, of course, if one critic calls your work "superficial," that's the one review you read. You ought to be glad that your husband's a scientist.

Naturally, it was prohibition then — it sounds quite prehistoric, doesn't it? But New York's always the same. We went to 42 long before it was 42. And the most amusing people were around — it's really sad to think back. That's the one sad thing about the city — the people who drop out. Of course, there are always new ones, but it isn't quite the same. Well, the Reeces, for instance — they were darlings, and had a perfect doll's house of a place. But then they started having children and now they're living in Jersey, of all places, and one never sees them any more. And Allan Lark is per-

manently in Hollywood and they say he drinks terribly.
And Ethel Shand — my dear, you wouldn't remember
her, but she made a great hit in "Welcome, Folks",
and then she just dropped out of sight. The last I heard,
she was doing some ghastly sort of work for a Middle
Western radio station and she'd lost her looks completely. Oh, it's a casualty list. I think of it every time
I go into Tony's.

One must just keep the chin up, that's all. And I've
always tried. Even when Bob began drinking — and I've
never quite understood that. My dear, I'm not a prude,
but I can take it or leave it alone. And, as a matter of
fact, it has very little effect on me. It never has. You
wouldn't know I'd had a cocktail before I came here,
would you? While Bob has always had a weak head. I
suppose it's his shyness, partly. He needs just about two
drinks to get over it and be amusing and affable. But
after that you have to call in the marines.

And I certainly never tried to stop him or play the
injured wife. I don't believe in that. But I did think it
was a pity he should spoil things when we were having
such a nice time and meeting all the right people — and
I suppose he saw it. Men are so sensitive. And if I could
take a cocktail or two without making a spectacle of
myself, I don't see why he should feel he had to do the
same. As I said, once or twice, we could just admit we
were different and let it go at that. But that only seemed
to make him worse. Ted says it would, but then Ted
hardly knows Bob at all. And when I asked Ted what
the real reason was — because men stick together so —

he only said, "Well, perhaps he felt it deadened the pain." Which doesn't make sense, my dear.

Anyhow, I noticed he was just drinking milk at the Coles'. The bride, I suppose. But it's just as artificial, I always think.

I remember one enormous party at the Nesbitts' — well, I saw how things were going and I felt simply desperate — the Nesbitts are so important. And I just couldn't get to Bob. So I was perfectly frantic — and then I looked across the room, and there was Ben Christian! In a white tie and tails, my dear — imagine! Well, he'd had his second big success. Well, any port in a storm, so I went over. And he was really quite friendly. He grinned and said, "Hello, kid! Remember Little Prairie!" And I said, "Well, how do you like it?" looking at his tie. And he grinned again and said, "It's the biggest, shiniest merry-go-round in the world. That's all right. But, gosh, what funny people they get on the horses!"

Then he asked after Bob, and I said, "He's over there," and he looked, and the queerest expression came over his face. "Why, he's tight!" he said.

"Are you telling me?" I said.

"I wouldn't have believed it," he said. "But why? Oh, well. We'd better take him home."

"If you only would," I said. "He's got his keys and the light turns on by the door. And, of course, I want to pay for the taxi."

He looked at me again, with that funny expression. "No, thanks," he said. "I can manage. Well, so long, Little Prairie!"

That's the way he is, you know — abrupt. And he
did take Bob home, and everything was all right when
I came in. I've always been very grateful. Of course, I
meant to thank Ben when he came back to the party
himself, but he didn't come back. And when I tried to
phone, next day, they said at his publisher's that he'd
left for the Coast.

Well, of course, that was just one time, but there
were others. Really, dear, I don't know how I stood it.
I couldn't have, except for my friends. They were wonderful. And most of them understood so perfectly —
though I must say, I always said, "You mustn't take
sides. And just treat Bob as you always have. We can't
all of us succeed." I've always been like that; I try to
see both sides. Though I must say it did hurt me a
little, about the Halleys.

It may be very provincial of me, but I don't quite
see what business it was of theirs. Though, of course,
I appreciated their loyalty to Bob. I suppose that was
why they did it. But, really, to hear them talk, you'd
have thought I'd Led Him to the Bottle. Well, dear,
you can see for yourself. And about children making a
difference — why, it was pre-Victorian! When I'd told
Bob in the beginning that I didn't mean to tie him
down, like so many wives.

Then, finally, Halstead started on the Perils of the
Big City and What New York Does to People, and it
was a little too dreary. And as far as Ted was concerned
— why, I'd barely met him then — though, of course,
I knew who he was. But I never dreamt. Oh, well, I
suppose they meant it for the best. But it rather hurt

me. They didn't even offer me a cocktail — I had to stop by at Tony's afterward. And there was Bob, with the Russian friend. So that was that.

All the same, I really hated breaking up the apartment. Those things are a trifle grim. Especially when they look at you in that blond, rather appealing way. You just have to be quite sensible and talk about the furniture. Remember that, my dear. Not that I wouldn't have been glad to let Bob have it. But he meant to go South anyway — he told me so. . . .

Reno? Well, dear, it isn't New York, but it isn't bad. I met some very interesting people and let my hair grow out. That was really for Ted, and I hope he appreciated it. Of course, I never thought, at the time, we'd be anything more than very good friends. Why, he'd been a bachelor for years! But it must have been -- well, predestined, for he's often said it was quite as much of a surprise to him. Don't you think that's rather sweet?

I remember how dazed he was when we drove down to City Hall for the license. . . . Oh, after I'd got back, of course — almost six months. And he hadn't even brought a ring, poor lamb; we had to stop at a jewelry store on the way. Men are such babies, aren't they, about practical things? Well, it seemed to me there was absolutely no use in putting it off, when he was supposed to go to California for the firm. He might have been out there for months, and that would have been trying for both of us. Especially as people were beginning to talk a little. You know how they are. Well, someone has to make the decisions. And, as it turned out, the business wasn't so important after all and we had a whole heavenly month at Santa Barbara. But we were glad to get back. After all, there's no place like New York.

It was quite a change, of course, but, if there's one thing I do know, it's how to make adjustments. Of course, it's rather a distinguished family, really. My dear, I should be honored, I hope you know. And a divorced woman too. Why, the family halls on the Hudson rocked to their foundations. At least, I suppose they did. But there's only Brother Eugene in New York, thank goodness. Not to speak of Sister Claudia — that's his wife. And there, my dear, is a woman. . . . Oh, you know. On the boards of schools and things, and takes an intelligent interest in politics — too tiring. And just a simple string of real pearls — the kind that look false. I asked her once if she knew the Stork Club — just to make conversation — and she said, "Was it anything like the Metropolitan?" Well, at least I've rescued Ted from people like that.

But I do what I can, and we have them at least twice a winter. I think that's only fair. When I go to see Ted's mother, I always wear my hair over my ears and knot it in the back. And we always spend two weeks with her in the summer. And that works out quite nicely — I've a definite plan for it. I just consider it a rest cure — shorts and lying around in the sun. The food's good, too — that's one comfort — and Madeira, if if you like Madeira. I'm afraid Grimes — he's the butler and positively antediluvian — was rather shocked by my shorts, at first. But he's got over that.

And Ted really has a wonderful sense of humor about it all. Because I remember asking him — oh, just amusingly — if I wasn't a little of a surprise. Though, heaven knows, I do everything I can. And he looked at me in that quizzical way he has, and said, "Well, Great-Uncle Marshall married a lady called Toots Latour, and the family stood that for fourteen years. So I guess they can stand you, darling." Wasn't it quaint of him? I simply screamed. So, now and then, I call myself the Skeleton in the Closet and he always laughs.

I asked him what happened to Toots Latour — well, the poor thing finally died and Great-Uncle Marshall married again — oh, very respectably, this time! Of course, they didn't have divorces in those days. But such interesting things happen in old families. Ted's got quite interested in the family history recently — he even found a miniature of Great-Uncle Marshall, and he's got it in his study, over his desk. He says he feels it ought to be there. Touching of him, isn't it? I asked him if he couldn't find one of Toots Latour, too, but he said he really didn't think it was necessary. . . .

Yes, I think we've adjusted very well. Of course, there's always a certain amount of weeding out to do — you'll start with a clean slate and that's such a comfort. But when Ted's partners come to dinner, I just jolly them along and pretend they're gay and amusing, even when they aren't. I feel it's the least I can do. And Judge Willoughby — he's the senior partner — and, my dear, a real old buck, with a darling little beard. I always have a wonderful time with him. Well, his wife's one of those iron-gray women with nutcracker faces, so you can hardly blame him. I do think there's so much a woman can do for her husband, if she tries. And that's the real criticism I make of women like Mrs. Willoughby. You can see that she's never tried at all. Ted says that's because she's never had to, but I can hardly agree. And, as for distinction — my dear, I don't care if she does know that stodgy set in London. We're Americans over here, I should hope, not title hunters. Why, Paul Necropuloff hardly uses his title at all — and he's really a prince!

Of course, it's meant giving up my own work. But I was willing to make the sacrifice — I told Ted so. Though I've been wondering about it just a little bit, of late. After all, we've been married almost six years — quite an age. But then, the magazines have changed so. And people are quite different, somehow, when you ask them about real jobs. I wouldn't want a full-time one, of course, with my responsibilities. But take somebody like Dorothy Thompson. She doesn't run a column every day. And after all, what did she do but live in Germany? I'm sure I've done more interesting things than that.

Naturally, I know what Ted's family would expect. But I think rather definitely not. After all, there are plenty of grandchildren, with Claudia and Eugene. It isn't that I'm afraid in the least. But one has to look at it from a sensible point of view. Even if some people do, at all ages. And as a matter of fact, Ted hasn't even brought up the subject in a long time.

And then — well, you're lucky, my dear. After all, you are quite an infant. . . . Well, that's sweet of you, but I know. There seem to be so many of them about, nowadays. Not that it really makes any difference what age you are. But I noticed the other day how gray Miriam Halley is getting. Of course, she's years older than I am, but it gave me a turn.

Then, they're so exclusive, too, the young. One just has to grab, I suppose, and I do hate grabbing. I leave that to people like the Ingram woman. But that's what I mean. She's supposed to write, I believe, and it does make things easier. And really, one should do something. It gets to be three o'clock in the afternoon so soon.

My dear, I'll tell you a secret. I've been thinking about a novel. Or even reminiscences — they're doing them earlier now. And I haven't told a soul about it — well, of course, I mentioned it to Ted — and then, Ben Christian. I thought he'd be interested and I hadn't seen him in ages. . . .

Well, he's rather hard to get nowadays, my dear — especially since they talked about him for the Nobel prize. But we got him. Just a quiet little party.

I kept it down to twelve for dinner; though, of course, people swarmed in afterward.

Well, he's improved in some ways. His dress collars fit him, for one thing. But of course one never gets a chance to really talk at a dinner party. And then he had to leave early. Just when Marcus Leigh was doing his divinely naughty songs.

So, I just called him up the next day — and, my dear, the to-do! You'd think the man was royalty. But he finally said he was free from four to five, if I cared to run in. My dear, it's the dreariest hotel and the dingiest little cocktail bar. I can't imagine why he stays there.

He's abrupt, you know — very abrupt. The same old Ben. The first thing he said was, "I like that husband of yours. Nice guy." Well, that was pleasant of him, of course. But when I started asking his advice about writing, he hardly seemed to be listening.

Finally he said to me, "Well, Myra, you know how it is. The people who are going to write novels, write them. And the ones who want to be writers just talk about it. But I'll give you a note to my agent — he's got good nerves. By the way, have you written any of it yet?"

"Well, not exactly," I said. I'm always honest.

"I thought so," he said. "And what's it going to be about, if I may ask?"

"Why, New York, of course," I said, and he just looked at me. He has the queerest way of looking at you sometimes.

"New York?" he said. "Why not Little Prairie? You knew something, then."

"Oh, Ben — do we have to be tiresome?" I said — for, really, that old joke!

"I'm not tiresome," he said. "Just surprised. After all, I was born here. And I don't pretend to know all of it. But you — "

"What do they know of England that only England know?" I said.

"Well," he said. "you do know one thing if you're

born on Hester Street. You know it's more than forty restaurants, five night clubs and a hospital."

And then he went on and talked the queerest stuff. All about little people living in the Bronx and butchers in the market, and Wall Street and corporation lawyers and the men who dig the new subways. And how it was fifty cities and you never got to the end of them, and how a man could spend his whole life looking, and still not know it all. I suppose it'll all be in his next book — it sounded like that.

"But you know it!" he said. "You know it!" and he sounded quite angry. "Forty restaurants, five night clubs and a hospital! You know it all! Well, I only hope you write the book! Can I lend you a map of the city? No, it wouldn't do any good."

Well, of course, there's no use arguing with a man in his condition, so I just thanked him for his interest, and let it go at that. He looked at me again.

"Look here, Myra. I'm going to talk to you," he said. And then he said, "No. What's the use? It's got into the bloodstream."

"I don't know what you mean," I said.

"Oh, nothing," he said. "I was just thinking aloud. Because they come every year, I suppose — ten thousand of them — the kids with a little talent and a lot of youth. And they end up thinking it's wonderful to hear a Class B heel sing dirty little songs. Or some of them. Oh, well."

"I'm glad you're so appreciative of my friends," I said.

"Oh, forget it," he said. "I was just remembering

things — it's a bad practice. But remember what I said about that husband of yours. He's a nice guy, but he looks as if he might have brains. And sometimes, you know, you can make the dose too strong."

Well, that was cryptic, I suppose — poor dear Ben, he always loved to make those mysterious remarks. But, all the same, he gave me the note to his agent. So, if I burst into print, my dear, you musn't be surprised. The only thing is, I haven't quite decided just what publisher to have. I was going to start in yesterday and rough out an outline. But, of course, one must find the time. And then, seeing Bob and the bride — well, it does give one something of a shock.

So it was such a relief — just sitting and visiting with little Kitty Harris, and hearing all about your plans. You can't imagine. . . . Well, my dear, just the barest touch and then I must fly. Your husband will think me very naughty, but I did want you to see the place. It's rather a favorite *boîte* of ours, and everybody comes here, but everybody! Bob might even bring the bride here — though, really, she might as well go to the Grand Central. They have milk bars there.

And we'll see each other very soon, shan't we? I've so enjoyed chatting about the old days. And the least little thing you want advice on — I'm right on the end of the phone. We're having a party tomorrow night, but you wouldn't be interested. Just dullish people — Harvard classmates and such — but I thought this would be a good time to work some of them off. I rather wish I'd thought of you before, though — you might have helped me out with the little Lindsay. She's rather a firm-faced child. She'll fit in all right with Ted's friends — after all, they like them young. And I needed an extra woman. But I can't think how Ted happened to think of her — he doesn't often make suggestions. And we'd just had her too. But he happened to be looking at the miniature of Great-Uncle Marshall, and out it came.

IV

VI

THE LAST OF THE LEGIONS

THE governor wanted to have everything go off as quietly as possible, but he couldn't keep the people from the windows or off the streets. After all, the legion had been at Deva ever since there was a town to speak of, and now we were going away. I don't want to say anything against the Sixth or the Second — there are good men under all the eagles. But we're not called the Valeria Victrix for nothing, and we've had the name some few centuries. It takes a legion with men in it to hold the northwest.

I think, at first, they intended to keep the news secret, but how could you do that, in a town? There's always someone who tells his girl in strict confidence, and then there are all the peddlers and astrologers and riffraff, and the sharp-faced boys with tips on the races or the games. I tell you, they knew about it as soon as the general or the governor — not to speak of the rumors before. As a matter of fact, there had been so many rumors that, when the orders came at last, it was rather a relief. You get tired of telling women that nothing will happen to them even if the legion does go, and being stopped five times in ten minutes whenever you go into town.

All the same, I had to sit up half the night with one recruit of ours. He had a girl in the town he was mad about, and a crazy notion of deserting. I had to point out to the young imbecile that even if the legion goes, Rome stays, and describe the two men I'd happened to see flogged to death, before he changed his mind. The girl was a pretty little weak-mouthed thing — she was crying in the crowd when we marched by, and he bit his lips to keep steady. But I couldn't have him deserting out of our cohort — we haven't had a thing like that happen in twenty years.

It was queer, their not making more noise. They tried to cheer — governor's orders — when we turned the camp over to the native auxiliaries in the morning, but it wasn't much of a success. And yet, the auxiliaries looked well enough, for auxiliaries. I wouldn't give two cohorts of Egyptians for them myself, but they had their breastplates shined and kept a fairly straight front. I imagined they'd dirty up our quarters — auxiliaries always do — and that wasn't pleasant to think of. But the next legion that came to Deva — us or another — would put things straight again. And it couldn't be long.

Then we had our own march past — through the town — and, as I say, it was queer. I'm a child of the camp — I was brought up in the legion. The tale is that the first of us came with Caesar — I don't put much stock in that — and of course we've married British ever since. Still, I know what I know, and I know what a crowd sounds like, on most occasions. There's the mutter of a hostile one, and the shouts when they throw flowers, and the sharp, fierce cheering when they know you're going out to fight for them. But this was different. There wasn't any heart or pith in it — just a queer sort of sobbing wail that went with us all the way to the gates. Oh, here and there, people shouted, "Come back with their heads!" or, "Bring us a Goth for a pet!" the way they do, but not as if they believed what they were saying. Too many of them were silent, and that queer sort of sobbing wail went with us all the way.

I march with the first cohort; it wasn't so bad for me. Though here and there, I saw faces in the crowd — old Elfrida, who kept the wine shop, with the tears running down her fat cheeks, shouting like a good one, and Parmesius, the usurer, biting his nails and not saying anything at all. He might have given us a cheer; he'd had enough of our money. But he stood there, looking scared. I expect he was thinking of his money bags and wondering if somebody would slip a knife in his ribs at night. We'd kept good order in the town.

It took a long time, at the gates, for the governor had to make a speech — like all that old British stock, he tries to be more Roman than the Romans. Our general listened to him, sitting his horse like a bear. He's a new general, one of Stilicho's men, and a good one in spite of his hairiness and his Vandal accent. I don't think he cared very much for the governor's speech — it was the usual one. The glorious Twentieth, you know, and our gallant deeds, and how glad they'd be to have us back again. Well, we knew that without his telling — we could read it in the white faces along the walls. They were very still, but you could feel them, looking. The whole town must have been at the walls. Then the speech ended, and our general nodded his bear head and we marched. I don't know how long they stayed at the walls — I couldn't look back.

But my recruit got away, after all, at the second halt, and that bothered me. He was a likely looking young fellow, though I'd always thought his neck was too long. Still, he was one of the children of the camp — you wouldn't have picked him to desert. After that, half a dozen others tried it — those things are like a disease — but our general caught two and made an example, and that stopped the rest. I don't care for torture, myself — it leaves a bad taste in your mouth — but there are times when you have to use a firm hand. They were talking too much about Deva and remembering too many things. Well, I could see, myself, that if we had to be marched half across Britain to take ship at Anderida, that meant the Northmen were strong again. And I wouldn't like to hold the northwest against Northmen and Scots with nothing but auxiliaries. But that was the empire's business — it wasn't mine.

After it was over, I was having a cup of wine and chatting with Agathocles — he's a small man, but clever with the legion accounts and very proud that his father was a Greek. He has special privileges, and that's apt to get a man disliked, but I always got along well with him. If you're senior centurion, you have your own rights, and he didn't often try the nasty side of his tongue on me.

"Well, Death's-Head," I said — we call him that because of his bony face — "were you present at the ceremonies?"

"Oh, I was present," he said. He shivered a little.

"I suppose you liked hearing them squeal," he said, with his black eyes full of malice.

"Can't say that I did," I said, "but it'll keep the recruits in order."

"For a while," he said, and laughed softly. But I wasn't really thinking of the men who had been caught — I was thinking of my own recruit who'd gotten away. I could see him, you know, quite plainly, with his long neck and his bright blue Northern eyes — a tiny, running figure, hiding in ditches and traveling by night. He'd started in full marching order, too, like an idiot. Pretty soon, he'd be throwing pieces of equipment away. And what would he do when he did get back to Deva — hide on one of the outlying farms? Our farmers were a rough lot — they'd turn him over to the governor, if they didn't cut his throat for the price of his armor. It's a bad feeling, being hunted — I've had it myself. You begin to hear noises in the bracken and feel the joints in your armor where an arrow could go through. He'd scream, too, if he were caught — scream like a hare. And all for a weak-faced girl and because he felt homesick! I couldn't understand it.

"Worried about your recruit?" said Agathocles, though I hadn't said a word.

"The young fool!" I said. "He should have known better."

"Perhaps he was wiser than you think," said Agathocles. "Perhaps he's a soothsayer and reads omens."

"Soothsayer!" I said. "He'll make a pretty-looking soothsayer if the governor catches him! Though I suppose he has friends in the town."

"Why, doubtless," said Agathocles. "And, after all, why should they waste a trained man? He might even change his name and join the auxiliaries. He might have a good story, you know."

I thought, for a moment. Of course they'd be slack, now we'd left, but I couldn't believe they'd be as slack as that.

"I should hope not, I'm sure," I said, rather stiffly. "After all, the man's a deserter."

"Old Faithful," said Agathocles, laughing softly. "Always Old Faithful. You like the boy, but you'd rather see him cut to ribbons like our friends today. Now, I'm a Greek and a philosopher — I look for causes and effects."

"All Greeks are eaters of wind," I said, not insultingly, you know, but just to show him where he stood. But he didn't seem to hear me.

"Yes," he said, "I look for causes and effects. You think the man a deserter, I think him a soothsayer — that is the difference between us. Would a child of the camp have deserted the legion a century ago, or two centuries ago, Old Faithful?"

"How can I tell what anyone would do a century ago?" I said, for it was a foolish question.

"Exactly," he said. "And a century ago they would not have withdrawn the Twentieth — not from that border — not unless Rome fell." He clapped me on the back with an odious familiarity. "Do not worry about your recruit, Old Faithful," he said. "Perhaps he will even go over to the other side, and, indeed, that might be wise of him."

"Talk treason to your accounts, Greek," I growled, "and take your hand off my shoulder. I am a Roman."

He looked at me with sad eyes.

"After three hundred years in Britain," he said. "And yet he says he is a Roman. Yes, it is a very strong law. And yet we had a law and states once, too, we Greeks. Be comforted, my British Roman. I am not talking treason. After all, I, too, have spent my life with the eagles. But I look for causes and effects."

He sighed in his wine cup and, in spite of his nonsense, I could not help but feel sorry for him. He was not a healthy man and his chest troubled him at night.

"Forget them," I said, "and attend to your accounts. You'll feel better when we're really on the march."

He sighed again. "Unfortunately, I am a philosopher," he said. "It takes more than exercise to cure that. I can even hear a world cracking, when it is under my nose. But you are not a philosopher, Old Faithful — do not let it give you bad dreams."

I manage to get my sleep without dreams, as a rule, so I told him that and left him. But, all the same, some of his nonsense must have stuck in my head. For, all the way down to Anderida, I kept noticing little things. Usually, on a long march, once you get into the swing of it, you live in that swing. There's the back of the neck of the man in front of you, and the weather, fine or wet, and the hairy general, riding his horse like a bear, and the dust kicked up by the column and the business of billets for the night. The town life drops away from you like the cloak you left behind in the pawnshop and, pretty soon, you've never led any other kind of life. You have to take care of your men and see the cooks are up to their work and tell from the look on a man's face whether he's the sort of fool who rubs his feet raw before he complains. And all that's pleasant enough and so is the change in the country, and the villages you go through, likely never to see again, but there was good wine in one, and a landlord's daughter in another, and perhaps you washed your feet in a third and joked with the old girl who came down by the stream and told you you were a fine-looking soldier. It's all there, and nothing to remember, but pleasant while it lasts. And, toward the end, there's the little tightness at the back of the mind that makes you know you're coming near the fighting. But, before that, you hardly think at all.

This wasn't any different and yet I kept looking at the country. I'd been south before, as far as Londinium, but not for years, and there's no denying that it's a pleasant land. A little soft, as the people are, but very green, very smiling, between the forests. You could see they took care of their fields; you could see it was a rich place, compared to the north. There were sheep in the pastures, whole flocks of them, fat and baaing, and the baths in the towns we passed through got better all the way. And yet I kept looking for places where a cohort or two could make a stand without being cut off completely — now, why should I do that? You can say it was my business, but Mid-Britain has been safe for years. You have only to look at the villas — we've got nothing like them in the northwest. I couldn't help wondering what a crew of wild Scots or long-haired

Northmen would do to some of them. We'd have blocked up half those windows where I come from — once they start shooting fire arrows, big windows are a nuisance, even in a fortified town.

And yet, in spite of the way Agathocles rode along like a death's-head, it was reassuring too. For it showed you how solid the empire was, a big solid block of empire, green and smiling, with its magistrates and fine special ladies and theaters and country houses, all the way from Mid-Britain to Rome, and getting richer all the way. I didn't feel jealous about it or particularly proud, but there it was, and it meant civilized things. That's the difference between us and the barbarians — you may not think of it often, but, when you see it, you know. I remember a young boy, oh, eight or nine. He'd been sent down from the big house on his fat pony with his tutor, to look at the soldiers, and there he sat, perfectly safe, while his pony cropped the grass and the old man had a hand in the pony's mane. He was clean out of bowshot of the big house, and the hedges could have held a hundred men, but you could see he'd never been afraid in his life, or lived in disputed ground. Not even the old tutor was afraid — he must have been a slave, but he grinned at us like anything. Well, that shows you. I thought the worse of Agathocles, after that.

And yet, there were other things — oh, normal enough. But, naturally, you can't move a legion without people asking questions, and civilians are like hens when they start to panic. Well, we knew there was trouble in Gaul — that was all we could say. Still, they'd follow you out of the town, and that would be unpleasant. But that didn't impress me nearly as much as the one old man.

We'd halted for half an hour and he came down from his fields, a countryman and a farmer. He had a speckled straw hat on, but it takes more than a dozen years' farming to get the look out of a man's back.

"The Twentieth," he said slowly, when he saw our badge of the boar, "the Valeria Victrix. Welcome, comrade!" so I knew at once that he'd served. I gave him the regulation salute and asked him a question, and his eyes glowed.

"Marcus Hostus," he said. "Centurion of the Third Cohort of the Second, twenty years ago." He pulled his tunic aside to show me the seamed scar.

"That was fighting the Welsh tribesmen," he said. "They were good fighters. After that, they gave me my land. But I still remember the taste of black beans in a helmet," and he laughed a high old man's laugh.

"Well," I said, "I wouldn't regret them. You've got a nice little place here." For he had.

He looked around at his fields. The woman had come to the door of the hut by then, with a half-grown girl beside her, and a couple of recruits were asking her for water.

"Yes," he said, "it's a nice little place and my sons are strong. There are two of them in the upper field. Are you halting for long, Centurion? I should like them to see the eagles before I die."

"Not for long," I said. "As a matter of fact, we're

on our way to the seacoast. They seem to need us in Gaul."

"Oh," he said, "they need you in Gaul. But you'll be coming back."

"As Caesar wills it," I said. "You know what orders are, Centurion."

He looked at the eagles again.

"Yes," he said. "I know what orders are. The Valeria Victrix, the bulwark of the northwest. And you are marching to the ships — Oh, do not look at me, Centurion — I have been a centurion too. It must be a very great war that calls the Valeria Victrix from Britain."

"We have heard of such a war," I said, for he, too, had served with the eagles.

He nodded his old head once or twice. "Yes," he said, "a very great war. Even greater than the wars of Theodosius, for he did not take the Twentieth. Well, I can still use a sword."

I wanted to tell him that he would not have to use one, for there was the hut and the fields and the half-grown girl. But, looking at him, the words stuck in my throat. He nodded again.

"When the eagles go, Britain falls," he said, very quietly. "If I were twenty years younger, I would go back to the Second — that would be good fighting. Or, perhaps, to the Sixth, at Eboracum — they will not withdraw the Sixth till the last of all. As it is, I die here, with my sons." He straightened himself. "Hail, Centurion of the Valeria Victrix — and farewell," he said.

"Hail, Marcus Hostus, Centurion," I said, and they raised the eagles. I know that he watched us out of sight; though, again, I could not look back. It is true that he was an old man, and old men dream, but I was as glad that Agathocles had not heard his words.

For it seemed to me that Agathocles was always at my elbow and I grew very weary indeed of his company and his cough and what he called his philosophy. The march had done him no good — he was bonier than ever and his cheeks burned — but that did not stop his talkativeness. He was always pointing out to me little things I would hardly have noticed by myself — where a plowland had been left fallow or where a house or a barn still showed the scars of old burnings. By Hercules! As if a man couldn't plant wheat for a year without the empire's falling — but he'd point and nod his head. And then he'd keep talking — oh, about the states and the law they'd had in Greece, long before the city was founded. Well, I never argue with a man about the deeds of his ancestors — it only makes bad feeling. But I told him once, to shut him up, that I knew about Athens. A friend of mine had been stationed there once and said they had quite decent games for a provincial capital. His eyes flashed at that and he muttered something in his own tongue.

"Yes," he said. "They have decent games there. And buildings that make the sacred Forum at Rome — which I have seen, by the way, and which you have not seen — look like a child's playing with mud and rubble. That was when we had states and a law. Then we fought with each other, and it went — yes, even before the man from Macedon. And then you came and now, at last, it is your turn. Am I sorry or glad? I do not know.

Sorry, I think, for the life is out of my people — they are clever and will always be clever, but the life is out of them. And I am not philosopher enough not to grieve when an end comes."

"Oh, talk as you like, Agathocles," I said, for I was resolved he shouldn't anger me again. "But you'd better not talk like that in front of the general."

"Thank you, Old Faithful," he said, and coughed till he nearly fell from his mule. "But I do not talk like that to the general — only to persons of rare intelligence, like yourself. The general does not like me very well, as it is, but I am still useful with the accounts. Perhaps, when we get to Gaul — if we go to Gaul — he will have me flayed or impaled. I believe those are Vandal customs. Yes, that is very probable, I think, if my cough does not kill me before. But, meanwhile, I must observe — we Greeks are so curious."

"Observe all you like," I said, "but the legion's shaking down very nicely, it seems to me."

"Yes, shaking down very nicely," he said. "Do you ever think of your deserter, who went back to Deva? No, I thought not. And yet he was the first effect of the cause I seek, and there have been others since." He chuckled quite cheerfully at that and went along reciting Greek poetry to himself till the cough took him again. The poetry was all about the fall of a city called Troy — he translated some of it to me, and it sounded quite well, if you care for that sort of thing, though, as I pointed out to him, our own Vergil had covered the same subjects, as I understand it.

We had turned toward the seacoast by then — we

weren't going through Londinium after all. That disappointed our recruits, but of course the general was right about it. We'd kept excellent discipline so far, but it's a very different thing, letting the men loose in a capital. I was sorry not to see it again myself. I told the men that when they complained. This was southern country we passed through, very soft and gentle; though, on the coasts, there is danger. But, when we halted for the night, there had been no danger for years — it was a wide pocket of peace.

I remember the look of the big painted rooms of the villa, when I was summoned there. A very fine villa it was — it belonged to a rich man. They'd had Roman names so long, they'd forgotten their own stock, though the master looked British enough when you looked him full in the face. They had winged cupids painted on the walls of the dining room — they were sharpening arrows and driving little cars with doves — very pretty and bright. It must have been imported work — no Briton could paint like that. And the courtyard had orange trees in it, growing in tubs — I know what an orange tree costs, for my cousin was a gardener. A swarm of servants, too, better trained than our northern ones and sneakingly insolent, as rich men's servants are apt to be. But they were all honey to me, and sticky speeches — they knew better than to mock an officer on duty.

Well, I went into the room, and there was my general and the master of the house, both with wreaths around their heads in the old-fashioned way, and Agathocles making notes on his tablets in a corner and hiding his cough with his hand. My general had his wreath on crooked and he looked like a baited bear, though they must have had a good feed, and he liked wine. There were other people in the room — some sons and sons-in-law — all very well dressed, but a little shrill in their conversation, as that sort is apt to be, but the master of the house and my general were the ones I noticed.

My general called me in and told them who I was, while I stood at attention and Agathocles coughed. Then he said: "This is my senior centurion. . . . And how many leagues does the legion cover in a day, Centurion?"

I told him, though he knew well enough.

"Good," he said, in his thick Vandal accent. "And how many leagues would we cover in a day — let me see — accompanied by civilians, with litters and baggage?"

I told him; though, of course, he knew. It was less, of course; it made a decided difference. A legion does not march like the wind — that is not its business — but civilians slow everything up. Especially when there are women.

"As I thought," he said to the master of the villa. "As you see, it is quite impossible," and, in spite of his crooked wreath, his eyes were bleak and shrewd. Then arose a babble of talk and expostulation from the sons and the sons-in-law. I have heard such talk before — it is always the same. As I say, rich men are apt to think that all government, including the army, exists for their personal convenience. I stood at attention, waiting to be dismissed.

The master of the villa waited till the others had had their say. He was a strong man with a beaky nose, much stronger than his sons. He waited till the babble had ceased, his eyes calm, regarding our general. Then he said, in the smooth, careless voice of such men:

"The general forgets, perhaps, that I am a cousin of the legate. I merely ask protection for myself and my household. And we would be ready to move — well, within twenty-four hours. Yes, I can promise you, within twenty-four hours." There was such perfect assurance in his voice that I could have admired the man.

"I am sorry not to oblige a cousin of the legate," said my general, with his bear's eyes gleaming dully. "Unfortunately, I have my orders."

"And yet," said the master of the villa, charmingly, "a certain laxity — a certain interpretation, let us say . . ."

He left his words in the air — you could see he had done this sort of thing before, and always successfully. You could see that, all his life, he had been accustomed to rules being broken for him because of his place and name. I have liked other generals better than this general — after all, the Vandals are different from us — but I liked the way he shook his head now.

"I have my orders," he said, and lay hunched like a bear on his couch.

"Let us hope you will never regret your strict interpretation of them, General," the master of the villa said without rancor, and a cool wind blew through the room. I felt the cool wind on my own cheek, though I am a senior centurion and my appeal is to Caesar. The man was strong enough for that.

"Let us hope not," said my general gruffly, and rose. "Your hospitality has been very enjoyable." I must say, for a Vandal, he made his manners well. On the way out, the master of the villa stopped me unobtrusively.

"And what would it be worth, Centurion," he said in a low voice, "to carry a single man on your rolls who was not on your rolls before? A single man — I do not ask for more."

"It would be worth my head," I said; for though my general did not seem to be looking at me, I knew that he was looking.

The master of the villa nodded, and a curious, dazed look came over his strong face. "I thought so," he said, as if to himself. "And, after all, what then? My nephew in Gaul writes me that Gaul is not safe; my bankers in Rome write me that Rome itself is not safe. Will you tell me what place is safe if Rome is not safe any more?" he said in a stronger voice, and caught at my arm. I did not know how to answer him, so I kept silent. He looked, suddenly, very much older than he had when I entered the room.

"A king's ransom out at loan and the interest of the interest," he muttered. "And yet, how is a man to be safe? And my cousin is the legate, too — I have first-hand information. They will not bring back the legions — blood does not flow back, once it is spilt. And yet, how can I leave my house here, with everything so uncertain?"

It seemed a fine house to me, though not very defensible; but, even as he spoke, I could see the rain beating through the walls. I could see the walls fallen, and the naked people, the barbarians, huddled around a dim fire. I had not believed that possible before, but now I believed it. There was ruin in the face of that man. I could feel Agathocles tugging at my elbow and I went away — out through the courtyard where the orange trees stood in their tubs, and the bright fish played in the pool.

When we were back in our billets, Agathocles spoke to me.

"The general is pleased with you," he said. "He saw that they tried to bribe you, but you were not bribed. If you had been bribed, he would have had your head."

"Do I care for that?" I said, a little wildly. "What matters one head or another? But if Rome falls, something ends."

He nodded soberly, without coughing. "It is true," he said. "You had nothing but an arch, a road, an army and a law. And yet a man might walk from the east to the west because of it — yes, and speak the same tongue all the way. I do not admire you, but you were a great people."

"But tell me," I said, "why does it end?"

He shook his head. "I do not know," he said. "Men build and they go on building. And then the dream is shaken — it is shaken to bits by the storm. Afterwards, there follow darkness and the howling peoples. I think that will be for a long time. I meant to be a historian, when I first joined the eagles. I meant to write of the later wars of Rome as Thucydides wrote of the Greek wars. But now my ink is dry and I have nothing to say."

"But," I said, "it is there — it is solid — it will last," for I thought of the country we had marched through, and the boy, unafraid, on his pony.

"Oh," said Agathocles, "it takes time for the night to fall — that is what people forget. Yes, even the master of your villa may die in peace. But there are still the two spirits in man — the spirit of building and the spirit of destruction. And when the second drives the faster horse, then the night comes on."

"You said you had a state and a law," I said. "Could you not have kept them?"

"Why, we could," said Agathocles, "but we did not. We had Pericles, but we shamed him. And now you and I — both Romans" — and he laughed and coughed — "we follow a hairy general to an unknown battle. And, beyond that, there is nothing."

"They say it is Alaric, the Goth," I said. "They say he marches on Rome," for, till then, except in jest, we had not spoken of these wars.

"Alaric, or another, what matters?" said Agathocles. "Who was that western chieftain — he called himself Niall of the Hundred Battles, did he not? And we put him down, in the end, but there were more behind him. Always more. It is time itself we fight, and no man wins against time. How long has the legion been in Britain, Centurion?"

"Three hundred and fifty years and eight," I said, for that is something that even children know.

"Yes," said Agathocles, "the Valeria Victrix. And who remembers the legions that were lost in Parthia and Germany? Who remembers their names?"

But by then I had come back to myself and did not wish to talk to him.

"All Greeks are eaters of wind," I said. "Caw like a crow, if you like; I do not listen."

"It does not matter to me," he said, with a shrug, and a cough. "I tell you, I shall be flayed before the ending, unless my cough ends it. No sensible general would let me live, after the notes I have taken tonight. But have it your own way."

I did not mean to let him see that he had shaken me, but he had. And when, six days later, we came to Anderida and the sea, I was shaken again. The ships should have been ready for us, but they were not, though our general raged like a bear, and we had to wait four days at Anderida. That was hard, for, in four days you get to know the look of a town. They had felt the strength of the sea pirates; they were not like Mid-Britain. I thought of my man at the villa and how he might die in peace, even as Agathocles had said. But all the time, the moss would be creeping on the stone and the rain beating at the door. Till, finally, the naked people gathered there, without knowledge — they would have forgotten the use of the furnace that kept the house warm in winter and the baths that made men clean. And the fields of my veteran centurion of the

Second, would go back to witch grass and cockleburs because they were too busy with killing to plant the wheat in the field. I even thought back to my deserter and saw him living, on one side or the other, but with memory of order and law and civilized things. Then that, too, would go, and his children would not remember it, except as a tale. I wanted to ask Agathocles what a race should leave to its kind, but I did not, for I knew he would talk of Greece, and I am a Roman.

Then we sailed, on a very clear day, with little wind, but enough to get us out of harbor. It came suddenly, as those things do, and we did not have time to think. I was very busy — it was only when we were ready to embark that I thought at all. I am a child of the camp and the legion is my hearth. But I knew, as we stood there, waiting, what we were leaving — the whole green, rainy, smoky, windy island, with its seas on either hand and its deep graves in the earth. We had been there three hundred and fifty and eight — we had been the Valeria Victrix. Now we followed a hairy general to an unknown battle, over the rim of the world, and we would win fights and lose them, but our time was over.

I heard the speech for the last time — the British Latin. After that, it would only be the legion, wherever we went. Our general stood like a bear — he would take care of us as long as he could. Agathocles looked seasick already — his face was pinched and thin, and he coughed behind his hand. Before us lay the wide channel and the great darkness. And the Sixth still held Eboracum — I wished, for a moment, that I had been with the Sixth.

"Get your packs on board, you sons!" I shouted to the men.

As the crowd began to cheer, a little, I wanted to say to somebody, "Remember the Valeria Victrix! Remember our name!" But I could not have said it to anyone, and there was no time for those things.